Articles of Faith

Articles of Faith

Ronald Harwood

Holt, Rinehart and Winston
New York   Chicago   San Francisco

Library of Congress Cataloging in Publication Data
Harwood, Ronald, 1934-
Articles of faith.
I. Title.
PZ4.H344Ar3   [PR6058.A73]   823'.9'14   73-12857
ISBN 0-03-007706-0

First published in the United States in 1974
Printed in the United States of America: 065

TO
CASPER WREDE

Articles of Faith

PROLOGUE

A Family Historian

THE HENNINGS   THE THOMPSONS

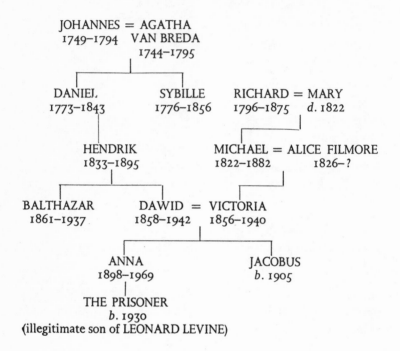

JOHANNES = AGATHA
1749–1794 VAN BREDA
1744–1795

DANIEL
1773–1843

SYBILLE
1776–1856

RICHARD = MARY
1796–1875 d. 1822

HENDRIK
1833–1895

MICHAEL = ALICE FILMORE
1822–1882 1826–?

BALTHAZAR
1861–1937

DAWID = VICTORIA
1858–1942 1856–1940

ANNA
1898–1969

JACOBUS
b. 1905

THE PRISONER
b. 1930
(illegitimate son of LEONARD LEVINE)

Prologue:
A family historian

The prisoner discovered the box on a blazing hot Christmas Day. It was a battered cardboard container with the words *Lipton's Tea* stencilled on four sides, and it was hidden under an advocate's silk gown. It contained a bundle of parchment, more than a ream, a report on the conduct of the Reverend Johannes Henning, Minister of the Reformed Church of the Netherlands, completed at the Cape of Good Hope on 10 February 1794, written in an elaborate but clear hand, in High Dutch.

The prisoner took the box that had once contained Lipton's Tea to the library, and with the aid of an old dictionary began to translate; formerly, he had been a schoolmaster and was fluent in Afrikaans, having taught it for seventeen years; he also knew enough German and Dutch to manage. The title page was headed 'Report on the events at Henningsdorp'. Although Henning was the prisoner's name, he had never known of a town named after his family; it was the first time he had ever heard of its existence.

After a day or two at the translation, he learned enough to realise that the town was named after this ancestor, this minister, Johannes Henning; a little later he discovered that the place had been burned to the ground. Puzzled, he took from the shelves a book long familiar to him written by his grandfather, Dawid Henning, entitled 'The Hennings: their history. A short account of an early Cape family', and turned to the first page: 'Little is known of our ancestor the Reverend Johannes Henning . . .'

Unaccountably, the prisoner felt he was no longer alone in the world. A strange but powerful bond was instantly forged between him and his ancestor so long dead, for both had been swept under the carpet to preserve the family's name: Johannes for two centuries; the prisoner for three months.

When you live amidst the great concourse of the world, coincidence and the unexpected are acknowledged as part of the pattern of everyday life. But in solitude there are no patterns, no events, apart from thoughts, and the prisoner, enduring solitude for so long, was forced to conclude that thoughts produce their own energy beyond the confines of the mind in which they were born. All thought, he decided, whether it was directed towards God or to denying Him, towards order or chaos, was a matter of faith, and he felt no more that he had ceased to exist, and no longer doubted his sanity.

The obsession began by what in ordinary circumstances would seem like chance. While clearing books from his desk, one fell to the floor; when he went to retrieve it, he found it open and read, almost casually, that in the religion of the Abantu there is a belief that the dead go on living underground just as they had done here on earth. The place which they inhabit is called *Kuzimu* in Swahili, and you may reach it by following a porcupine or a mole. In Uganda it happened to Mpobe, the hunter, and to the Zulu, Uncama, and also to one of the Wairamba. The phrase 'the dead go on living underground' stuck.

At first, he viewed the idea of a family history as a kind of revenge, but as he grew more absorbed even his bitterness dissolved and he worked for the work's sake, totally immersed and driven. The history served another purpose, too: time passed where before it stood still.

Privately, he called it a history of white sheep.

The prisoner: small and dark, flat strands of hair combed sideways but which no longer conceal his baldness; large ears, slender, delicate hands.

Like Mpobe, he follows the mole and the porcupine.

He is the only son of Anna Henning and a Jewish lawyer, Leonard Levine; he was given his mother's name because he was illegitimate. As a boy, any virtues he displayed at school or on the rugby field were attributed to his mother's family. His subsequent behaviour and disgrace was thought to be a direct inheritance from his father.

4

He was born in the Orange Free State in 1930, in a small, dusty town set in arid countryside where the land is a dull reddish brown, sprinkled with scrub of lifeless olive-green. It is a scorched and cracked landscape where drought is regarded as the one perpetual season of the year.

A month after his birth, his mother Anna took him south to the family home at Paarl, which means pearl, and lies among blue-grey mountains thirty-six miles north-east of Cape Town, straggling along the Berg river. Here there is a sense of growth; the earth has a richer look, and there are vineyards and orange groves and gardens.

It was made clear to the little boy that the name he had been allowed to use was an illustrious one of which he could be duly proud. The Hennings had come to the Cape in the last decade of the eighteenth century, had helped to repel the marauding Kaffir and to tame the wild, unfriendly land. Was not the little boy's own grandfather, Dawid, now a Judge of the Supreme Court, and his uncle Jacobus an up-and-coming politician? To hear them, you would have imagined it was a family without fault. Yet, what of Henningsdorp, and why was it burned to the ground?

Dawid, the Judge, it was who first took an interest in the family's history. As a young lawyer on circuit duties he had, by necessity, to travel much and in the course of his journeys collected anything and everything that related to his family name; journals, diaries, newspaper reports, family Bibles, letters, autographs. He too, the prisoner realised, became obsessed.

About the year 1886, he heard of a journal that had belonged to one of the members of the early Cape family, Agatha Henning, until then nothing more than a name in the family Bible. The diary was in the possession of an English family called Thompson, living near Grahamstown. Accordingly, Dawid made the journey north to the Thompson farm, and there met and fell in love with Victoria Thompson. The following year they were married; Anna and Jacobus Henning were their children.

Agatha's diary was a curious document: for the most part it was filled with personal confessions and later, after her death, the journal was continued by her daughter Sybille, a strange, demented creature who allowed it, so Dawid concluded, to degenerate into a rambling, incoherent account of a deranged mind. But one reference in the earlier part was of real interest to the amateur historian, in

5

Agatha's hand, the entry for 4 February 1794: 'Today we learned that Johannes was interned in the Castle. No one is allowed to see him'; and later: 'He has brought shame on us at last'; and: 'I have forbidden Daniel and Sybille ever to mention their Father's name in this house again'. Dawid was intrigued, for, like his grandson years later, this was the first he had ever heard of such an incident. He began to search for further clues, not passionately, not yet obsessively, but when he had time or the inclination he would delve into the Archives at Cape Town, wade through dusty files, or read the records of a hundred long-forgotten, easily forgettable lives. It became a hobby, like a collector who searches for one item to complete the set, but he was unable to unearth the reason for his ancestor's imprisonment.

He did not discover the answer, so the prisoner now knew from the contents of the battered cardboard box, until 1928; by then the Report had come into the possession of another family; this connection, too, plays a part in the Hennings' secret history.

When he had read it, Dawid wished he had never learned of its existence; it was as though he was suddenly and irrevocably cursed by what he read, and why he never destroyed the papers is not known. Instead, he hid them, ineptly, in the Lipton's Tea box, in the attic of his house, covered with his advocate's silk gown which he had recently discarded for the judge's scarlet and ermine. It was as if he meant the box to be discovered.

The family documents of which he was less ashamed, which included Agatha's diary, he had beautifully bound, and housed the collection in an alcove off the library. About that time he began to write his brief family history which began, 'Little is known of our ancestor Johannes Henning . . .'

The prisoner writes as if in a fever, as if time is short, yet time is his one luxury; time is his to squander or to hoard.

There he sits, Mpobe, in the library, day and night, eating when he is hungry, sleeping when he is too tired for sleep. Occasionally, a policeman pauses at the window to make sure the prisoner is still alive. In the beginning they used to talk to each other, but seldom now.

His arrest was sudden and unexpected, the usual procedure borrowed from other regimes who also lack imagination: early hours of the morning, four detectives—two to guard, two to search. They take papers from your desk, even from your waste paper basket; they examine your photograph albums and do not recognise you perched upon the knee of Jan Christian Smuts; they do not recognise Jan Christian Smuts. Now the books: Koestler, *Darkness at Noon*; Clarke, *The Nude*—'Hey, man, look at this!'—Hardy, *Return of the Native*; Basker, *John Knox as Revolutionary*; Conrad, *Black Narcissus*; Joyce, *Ulysses*—'Don't you know this one is *really* banned?'—and Paton, *J. H. Hofmeyr*. A curious bibliography when you consider they missed out Marx and Engels.

They show him a document; it is signed by his uncle Jacobus, Minister of Justice for the Republic; it informs him that he is banned and placed under house arrest.

No wife or children to kiss, thank God; no tears, no pain, just questions.

'But what am I supposed to have done?' The question of all guilty men.

'Listen, man, if it wasn't for your name, you'd be behind bars. Thank your lucky stars your name is Henning.'

As they hustle him towards a waiting car, one of the detectives swings open the door so that the handle catches the prisoner in the groin. 'Man,' says the detective, 'it's going to be difficult stirring black coffee with a bent spoon.' The prisoner asks where they are taking him, but receives no answers. One of the others says, 'And you a schoolmaster! Thank Christ I don't send my children to your school, that's all, just thank Christ for that!'

At dawn, he recognised the road they were taking, towards Paarl where he spent his childhood. Was it any less beautiful because he was a prisoner?

Soon, the car passed through the scrolled white archway that marked the entrance to the long winding drive leading to the house: brown and cream, turn-of-the-century elegance with the railings on the stoep decorated in fretwork *fleurs-de-lis*. An old man, whom the prisoner knows as Oom Erik, was on the verandah, the stoep, waiting. He has been the family lawyer for more than forty years, so naturally the prisoner assumed that he was there to help. But Oom Erik turned away, flustered and embarrassed. It seemed that all he had come for was to give the officer-in-charge the keys of the house; he hurried off at once, not having uttered a single word. Strange to think he used to tell the prisoner bed-time stories.

The house was shrouded in must and silence; no one had lived there since his mother's death; even her presence had detached itself; it was like a museum to which no visitors ever came.

Two plainclothes policemen took up positions back and front; the prisoner was told to stay in the empty house and he sat in the billiards room like a waxwork exhibit. God knows why the billiards room.

Then, at noon, a police car spraying dust drew up outside. A middle-aged, austere figure emerged who introduced himself as the personal representative of the Minister, Uncle Jacobus. In a dispassionate voice the minion recited the regulations: the prisoner is to be confined to the house and garden until further notice; he is not allowed newspapers, letters, or the radio; visitors, except a doctor in case of illness, are strictly forbidden, and this state of affairs is to continue at the Minister's pleasure. You will answer all questions asked by authorised officers and your co-operation will be taken into account. Your name cannot be mentioned in the press or on the radio. You are banned. You cease to exist.

'Even people who don't exist have to eat.'

Meals will be provided. A woman from the village will come in daily to cook and clean but you may not talk to her or even be in the same room with her. She is over seventy, but nevertheless, with your record . . .

And then, the prisoner, knowing that what he was about to ask would be as good as an admission of guilt, asked nevertheless, 'How did the police find out?'

The Minister's Personal Representative dusted imaginary crumbs from the official document and gave no sign of having heard the question. But after some thought, he looked up at the prisoner and with surprising passion cried, 'My God, man, but you're a bloody fool! Her husband reported it!'

'Her husband?'

'You didn't know she was married,' the official said, observing the blank disbelief on the prisoner's face. 'You fellows,' he added, shaking his head disapprovingly. 'Don't you think Coloured servant-girls have got husbands, or what? No, the trouble with you lot is you don't think at all, you just act like animals. And writing her letters! "If snow be white why then her breasts are dun!" Listen, if I didn't understand these things better I'd say they were love-letters! Calling her "thou"! Are you really mad, or do you just look stupid?'

'What's happened to her?' asked the prisoner.

8

'I cannot discuss any further details. Good day,' and he is gone; the prisoner is alone once more.

And so his days unfolded, consumed with stillness. A kind of perpetual mystery clouded every room and he had a feeling of unreality, as though he were observing another's experience. When thinking about himself 'I' became 'he'.

He watched himself walk in the garden, but the November heat was more oppressive than being alone. He preferred to haunt the house where it was cooler and where, because he kept the shutters closed, he could not only enjoy the tepid shadows, but also avoid seeing the policemen at his gates.

Fleetingly, he contemplated suicide. But since he believed that non-existence was preferable to extinction he had no choice but to sit out the countless, endless seconds, hoping to find an external means of passing immovable time.

He heard nothing, he knew nothing, he was nothing. They had hidden him in a dark and secret place for the sake of a name. He knew that 'they' was the pronoun of paranoiacs and decided that insanity would be a refuge. The only books he discovered he had any desire to read were *Jock of the Bushveld* and *King Solomon's Mines*.

One of the guards, the oldest, a man of about forty, persists in entering the house each day, and seeking out the prisoner for a chat; perhaps he is lonely too. No matter how determined the prisoner is to be rid of him, the guard ignores the hints, the innuendoes and even the direct requests. But after a few days, the prisoner becomes agitated if the guard does not appear at his regular time, and finds himself confessing all manner of things to this slow, insensitive man.

'Sometimes I can't control my thoughts. They jump here and there. For example, a senseless phrase keeps running through my head: "Descartes arrived today by 'plane from Johannesburg".'

'Is that a Huguenot name, Descartes? Sounds Huguenot.'

On another occasion, the policeman smuggles in a newspaper. 'I thought you might want to read about the cricket. Western Province won by three wickets.'

'I think I'm going mad.'

'Rubbish, you'll be all right. You want to hear a joke?'

'No.'

'Yes, 'course you do. Something to make you laugh.'

'What happens if I don't?'

'You'll laugh. I can tell a good story. This is a van der Merwe joke. Right? Van der Merwe is charged under the Immorality Act with a black woman. The magistrate's an old family friend and, man, he's really upset that van der Merwe's come up before him. "Van der Merwe," he says, "how can a man like you who comes from such a fine family behave in this disgusting fashion?" "Well," says van der Merwe, "I'm only following my father's advice: he told me to vote Nationalist and fuck the Kaffirs!" '

The prisoner laughed for almost an hour. The kind policeman promised to tell him another joke soon.

And so it was that finding the *Lipton's Tea* box on Christmas Day appeared to him an accident of salvation, and many times he relived the moment of discovery in the small, clean attic neatly piled with faded materials, old curtains, bed covers and an advocate's silk gown covering the cardboard box. And he loved to recall the moment of exultation which began so inauspiciously with the photograph of his father inscribed 'To Anna from Leonard, June 1929' lying on the top, and the letters, newspaper cuttings, pressed flowers, the copy of Ibsen's plays given, the fly-leaf informed, by Leonard to Anna with love concealing, at the bottom of the box, the parchment.

'I've never seen anyone write as much as you. What's it about, hey?'

'About white sheep.'

'You having me on?'

'Yes. Now, go away.'

'You want to hear another van der Merwe story?'

'No.'

'Okay, it'll keep.'

The prisoner has ceased to live in time present. Mpobe sits at his desk, and follows the porcupine and the mole to that place where the dead go on living underground, to that place called *Kuzimu*. He is gathering together the strands of which he himself is made.

BOOK ONE

I

Kuzimu

1

Johannes Henning first smudges the pages of history on the night of 3 February 1794. He lies on the rough wooden boards of a covered wagon with his hands and feet bound together behind his back, his face and body bruised and cut from the severe jolting he receives on the long journey to Cape Town. He has been travelling for fourteen days but soon the ordeal will be over. The soldier who is guarding him says, 'Not long now, dominee.'

Outside the wagon, front and rear, ride a troop of armed soldiers and, at their head, astride a clumsy grey horse, sits Abraham van der Goes, the district magistrate or landdrost of Blauwzand whose duty it is to deliver his prisoner to the authorities. The prisoner, the soldiers and the landdrost are all in the employ of the United East India Company of the Netherlands.

Van der Goes has sent a messenger ahead to prepare for his arrival. The mission is cloaked in secrecy and the landdrost has taken every precaution. He has asked for permission to intern his prisoner in the Castle, and not in the gaol known as the Tronk where run-of-the-mill criminals are housed. Furthermore, he has dispatched a summary of the case to Willem Berg, the Fiscal and chief legal officer of the Cape of Good Hope, and also requested an urgent interview at the earliest possible moment. Van der Goes, by the way, is a man of enormous bulk, with a large bulbous nose and purple cheeks which are traversed by an intricate network of tiny veins. He is a man who is aware of his own importance and sits proudly.

He has every reason to feel pleased with himself as he jogs along in the warm, still night. His prisoner is safe and, more or less, in good health; in his saddle-bag he carries thirty sworn statements from witnesses who can attest to Henning's crimes, and he has arranged things so perfectly that the prisoner will arrive at the Castle at dead of night. He has judged from the first that secrecy is essential: in his report to the Fiscal he has recommended that the prisoner be banished to Batavia without trial.

Shortly after midnight, the little procession makes its way along the dirt road that leads to the Castle, the very heart of the Cape, the seat of government, a forbidding pentagonal structure built of dark, brown stone. The wagon and its escort clatter into the unroofed courtyard, open to the luxurious black sky, the stars so bright and clear that you feel they are close enough to touch. The prisoner is carried out of the wagon and his bonds are cut.

'Stand up, stand up,' orders the sergeant-of-the-guard.

Henning struggles to his feet but the cramp in his legs is unbearable, and he staggers forward blindly, holding out his arms for anything or anyone who will give him support; by chance, he catches hold of the leather belt that girds the landdrost's enormous belly, but van der Goes pulls away and Henning topples over onto the stones.

'Come along, come along, get up, get up!' But even the sergeant, who is accustomed to the malingering of prisoners, sees that the man is really in pain and commands two of the soldiers to help him; they haul the prisoner to his feet and hold him under his armpits.

'I better give you a receipt,' says the sergeant to van der Goes.

'You better,' agrees van der Goes. 'This is an important bugger, this one.'

'Right,' says the sergeant. 'Take him away.'

The soldiers are compelled to drag their prisoner across the courtyard, for he cannot find the strength to move his legs. Below ground level they pull him, down worn stone steps into a dungeon five feet by six but with high walls and one narrow, barred window which is, in fact, at ground level, but through it the prisoner may breathe fresh air and see two stars, a corner of the Southern Cross.

The heavy wooden door closes, and the prisoner lies on the damp, uneven earth that is the floor of the cell. Water drips intermittently, difficult to say whether inside or out; it is a hot February night, prickly and oppressive; sleep would be difficult enough in more comfortable surroundings; here it is unthinkable.

He is a shadow, a name entered by the sergeant-of-the-guard into

14

his duty book; now he sits, hugging his legs, very like the position in which he was bound for so long and which he finds more comfortable than being able to stretch. His face is bathed in sweat, glistening even in the pale light of the two distant stars; leaning up against the cold, jagged wall, he tries to pray. Shutting his eyes, screwing them up tightly, he struggles with all his might to pronounce the name of God, to beseech Christ for help. After a little while, he says, 'Forgive me, I cannot, I cannot pray.' He remains perfectly still, like a child in terror. After some hours, he begins to moan: quietly at first, rocking to and fro, then swelling to a harsh, grating sound that echoes and reverberates in the enclosed space.

'Shut up in there!' comes a disembodied voice through a sliding panel in the door. But the prisoner does not hear. The soldier calls his companion.

'Look at him, man, he's going mad!'

Henning is writhing, screaming, a silhouette in torment. 'Alalalalala!' he seems to cry.

'Get some water, quickly!' says the soldier, opening the door as his companion fetches a wooden pail and spews the water over the man; at once, he is quiet.

'That's better. Now you shut up with that noise, hey? We're trying to sleep, so shut up!'

They leave him, lying at full stretch, his clothes and body wringing wet, his teeth chattering with cold. Then, at dawn, as if the lightening of the sky were a signal, Henning murmurs 'Amen, amen, amen,' over and over again.

Thus ended the first night in captivity of the Reverend Johannes Henning, Minister of the Reformed Church of the Netherlands.

2

The sun rises abruptly; no warning, no glimmer of light that will imperceptibly grow into day; the dawn is a sudden affair: the sky is red, the sun is there, it is day. The mountains, which a moment before had been dark blue in the night, now are tinged with the sun's rays and turn pearl-grey before your eyes. The Devil's Peak, The Table, Lion's Head, rivalled only by the tall spire of the Reformed Church, embrace the neat, compact town with its clean white houses and regular streets. Beyond lies the sea, wave upon wave gently washing the sands of Table Bay in unending succession. It is a place of majestic beauty that was once a green and flourishing wilderness, inhabited by a small and sallow people called the San, and the taller Khoikhoi. The first Dutch settlers, one hundred and fifty years before, called the San Bushmen, and the Khoikhoi Hottentots. Now the San no longer live there, and the Khoikhoi are mostly slaves.

The town is waking; here and there the slave bells ring and in the houses, in rooms apart, or in the Company's Lodge, the natives of Malabar and Malay, of Madagascar and Java, Hottentots and half-breeds answer the call and begin the first chores of the day. They will call each other by the names their masters have given them: Ajax, Achilles, Juno, Jupiter, Mars and Melpomene, for the whole heathen mythology has been ransacked, and the Old Testament, too: Samson, Delilah, Ahasuerus and Saul. Now, they wake their masters, draw their water, cook their food, nurse their children and clean their houses. They will watch those same masters fall on their knees and offer up prayers of thanks to God for a safe night and a good life.

The morning mist clears to reveal a dazzling, cloudless blue sky which, in turn, promises another day of summer heat, relieved by the gentlest of sea breezes that lightly ruffles the oaks and the hedges of myrtle in the Company Gardens. In Market Square, the traders are already displaying their vegetables and fruits, flowers and herbs, ostrich eggs and feathers. Towards the slope of Lion's Head, in Hottentot Square, covered wagons from the outlying country districts are disgorging their occupants who have spent the night there and now stretch and yawn and greet the day. All over town you may begin to hear a raucous chatter, a strident laughter which is the inexhaustible vitality of the slaves, calling to each other in a confusion of foreign tongues, defiant, haughty, insolent and irrepressible.

And in Table Bay more than a dozen ships bob on the water: tall East Indiamen, traders, men o' war, pausing at this peninsula on their way to the gaudier riches of the East or, already laden, returning home to Holland. For the Cape is a half-way house, a refreshment station that, against everyone's will and better judgement, mushroomed into a Colony. In days gone by they had called the place the *Cabo de Tormentosa*, the Cape of Storms, but John II of Portugal, sensitive to the superstitions of sailors, renamed it the *Cabo de Boa Esperanze*, the Cape of Good Hope. Like the beauty of the place, it is a sour, ironic joke.

The Fiscal, Willem Berg, was rather like the sunrise: quick, sudden, impulsive. He was always at work before anyone else and he liked things done yesterday. Not that he achieved much, but he did enjoy feeling that a great buzz of activity was going on around him; this way he mistook action for movement. Berg was a German, which was not unusual; more than half the Dutch East India Company's employees hailed from Hamburg, Bonn, Leipzig or thereabouts: no one objected; it had been a satisfactory work arrangement: the Germans organised and the Dutch grew rich. But times had changed: the Germans still organised but the Dutch no longer grew rich.

Berg was a newcomer to the Cape, though a Company man all his life. Thirty-three years he had served and seen the decline with his own eyes. When he joined, the Company had been a giant; now the body was rotting with gangrene, with bribery and corruption, with seething discontent. It was stretching out diseased limbs from the Straits of Magellan westward to the Cape of Good Hope, trying to hold on to Malacca, Lombok, Macassar, Banda, Ternate and the brightest jewel of all, Batavia. Batavia, a city built by slaves upon the ruins of their own ancient capital, Jakarta. A city built for a Company! And the ships, in their hundreds, laden with spices and jewels; and the men: officials, soldiers, seamen, merchants, yes, even ministers of God, all servants not as you may think of an Empire, but of a vast trading emporium; and now it was disintegrating with each year that passed. And what of the Cape, the Company's only colony? Best not to think about it, best to think about something else for a change, something you could come to grips with like a de-generate minister of the Reformed Church. When everything about you was falling apart at the seams, what could be more welcome than a cut-and-dried moral issue? At least, you could deal with that.

'I see you recommend banishment, landdrost.'

'Most fervently, Fiscal.'

They were an odd contrast these two men: the landdrost like a rogue elephant, ruddy, gross; the Fiscal nervous as a bird, pale and thin, but not out of place, as his visitor was, in the surroundings, for the office predictably reflected his personality: whitewashed walls, bare floors, a plain table for a desk and uncomfortable upright chairs; no frills, no fuss.

'Disgusting case,' said Berg, pushing the summary away from him, as though it might be infectious.

'Contrary to the laws of God,' thundered the landdrost, finger pointed upwards like a Greek orator.

'I wouldn't know about that. I'm a Lutheran.' It was meant to be a joke; the landdrost did not smile.

'The man's a reprobate, Fiscal: an adulterer, a bigamist and a blasphemer!'

'There you are, you'd know more about these things than I.'

'Banishment's the only course!' said van der Goes and thumped the table.

'My assistant will first compose a report for the Commissioner-General,' said Berg.

'What d'you mean, a report? Aren't you going to banish the antichrist?'

'First we must have a report,' repeated Berg impatiently.

'Why?' growled the landdrost who felt he was being cheated of victory.

Berg tried to explain. In the past fifty years, more than forty men had been summarily banished to India or Batavia, somewhere far, far away where they could do no harm. Each time, the action caused bitter resentment. Petitions were organised in protest, secret meetings held, a deputation even managed to reach Amsterdam with a list of complaints a mile long. And how does the Company respond? Sends out Commissioners to investigate, dismisses officials and replaces them with worse scoundrels. (There was, indeed, a Commissioner-General, Abraham Josias Sluysken, administering the government of the Cape at the moment: he had been appointed with special powers to stop the financial rot and had therefore much to occupy him.) Berg knew the Company too well. Quick, he might be, but he was also cautious. The whole art of making a decision was to let others make it for you. Berg had no intention of putting his head on the block. Banish the man, yes: but at least cover yourself with a report in case of complaints.

'But who'd complain about this fellow?'

'His wife, friends, other predikants,' snapped Berg. 'Who knows? Proceed with caution but with speed. Do we want the Company sending out yet more Commissioners? Do we want the Church complaining to the Company that we treated one of their ministers unfairly? No, landdrost, caution, caution!'

Van der Goes, used to the more ponderous ways of countrymen, was not at ease in the Fiscal's presence. He listened as carefully as he could while Berg seemed to want to justify his decision and talked rapidly as though he were sending urgent despatches from the field of battle. The landdrost, who liked to chew things over, could not take it all in. Why, he wondered, was Berg going on about declining standards of the clergy, the Church, moral excellence, discipline? He could not make the necessary connections of thought. At one moment he felt he had caught the gist of the Fiscal's speech, at the next he lost it. Why, for example, was he so concerned with Amsterdam? This was a local problem, nothing to do with the Council of Seventeen, or the *Classis* who ordained ministers and sent them out here. Why was he so preoccupied with men of better quality? What difference did it make *why* Henning was sent to the Cape? All that mattered was what he did after he arrived! There—he'd lost the thread again. Is the man mad? What's the American Revolution to do with us? (The landdrost, to be honest, did not even know that the Americans had had a revolution.) And what were these pamphlets the Fiscal was waving as though he were going to perform a conjuring trick? Grotius, Pufendorf, Locke? Who the hell were they? *Who* was reading these pamphlets and holding secret meetings and demanding a greater share in the government? Didn't Berg know that the landdrost had been riding all night, and that he hadn't had anything to eat or drink?

'We will not put up with any more second-raters, failures and discontents!'

'Couldn't agree more—'

'They must stop palming off agitators on us. How do they expect us to govern when even the ministers of the church are corrupt? Won't have it! You know my motto, landdrost? Strong church, strong colony!'

'I see!' The landdrost liked the slogan.

'Every intention of banishing this—this Henning. But I must have a report first. Essential.'

Berg was simply bumbling; to talk expansively, to analyse problems, that, too, gave him a feeling of action, as if, with enough power, he could put the whole Colony to rights; it was an impression he liked to give and it disguised, even from himself, his own pettiness and inadequacy. What really mattered to Berg were minutiae, viewed even then with a blinkered gaze. He also disliked more than anything to take responsibility.

'My assistant, Danie Reenan, will write the report. Had him do several for me—quite expert—only a couple of days, then we'll go to the Commissioner-General.'

'You'll banish Henning after the report,' van der Goes stated as bluntly as he could, making certain that he had understood the Fiscal.

'We mustn't anticipate the decision of the Commissioner-General,' said Berg with a funny little shake of his head. 'It's up to him.'

'But you said a moment ago—'

'Let's see what the report says, shall we?'

'But as the local magistrate *I* recommended banishment. You agreed with me!'

'Mustn't keep you, landdrost. We have a great deal to do. Good morning.'

4

A spider runs over Henning's face. 'Agatha! Agatha!' he cries.

In fits and starts he sleeps, waking suddenly as if kicked, then dozing off again.

He stands, his legs still painfully weak. Up and down he marches, round and round, stumbling as if drunk. He looks up at the barred window, high in the wall, cannot tell if it is night or day, and feels like an insect observed by a hidden eye, an insect at the bottom of a tall, narrow shaft. His teeth are still chattering; his clothes are still damp, and he is chilled to the bone.

For the first time since his incarceration, he thinks of his physical needs, for his throat is dry and he finds it agony to swallow. He tries to call out for water, but discovers that he has no voice, only a cracked whisper.

The sliding panel in the door opens, and a long stick, like a paddle, is pushed through; on it a plate and a mug. 'Food!' calls a voice. Henning reaches out for it, but misses his footing and falls. 'Food!' calls the voice again. Henning tries to cry out, 'Wait!' but he can hardly make any sound. Then, the paddle is rapidly withdrawn, the plate and mug falling to the floor, their contents soon to be devoured by the rats.

It is the second time since morning that the rats have been fed.
'Alala,' he says.

5

Van der Goes looked forward to relaxing, but the pleasure was to be denied him for a little time. On his way from Fiscal Berg's office, as he was crossing the courtyard, now drenched in sun, a voice called to him. The landdrost turned to see a pale man with gold-rimmed spectacles which glinted uncomfortably in the light.

'My name is Reenan,' the man said. 'I am the Assistant-Fiscal.' He was forty, and aggressively ordinary. His face, which was fast becoming the face of the Colonists, was square, slightly flabby in the cheeks, narrow-browed, with a little upturned nose that looked as if it had been made of putty and was slightly comic. His complexion, like his personality, was indeterminate: sallow and unhealthy. He belonged heart and soul to the Cape; he knew its ways, the ins and outs, the dos and don'ts. 'I wonder if I could have a word with you, landdrost.'

'Is it important?'

'About Henning.'

The two walked together, up a stone staircase that led to Reenan's office. 'I have been charged with writing the report. I wonder if you would mind answering some questions.'

They passed into shadow and then into Reenan's office, quite as plainly furnished as his superior's. But on the desk was the landdrost's summary and the pile of statements; the sight of them gave van der Goes confidence. He looked round hopefully. 'Are there no comfortable chairs in this Castle?'

'Not in here, I'm afraid,' said Reenan, with a modest little smile. 'We question people in here; we don't want them to be too comfortable, do we?' Was it a smile or a nervous twitch?

Van der Goes settled himself as best he could on a chair that looked in danger of collapsing under his bulk. He perched on the edge, his fleshy hands resting on his knees. 'Well, I hope *you* agree with my recommendation?' He was still smarting from his unsatisfactory meeting with the Fiscal.

Reenan disturbed the papers on his desk, trying to find the landdrost's report. 'Banishment?' he queried at last.

'Correct.'

'I don't think there's any other choice,' said Reenan.

'You've read my summary?'

'Not thoroughly. Just the main points. I haven't really had time—'

'No. Well. You read it thoroughly. It'll turn your stomach. Filthy, filthy, the whole thing!'

'There are one or two questions I have to ask you, landdrost, about the testimony of the witnesses.'

'Ask.'

'Were they taken under oath?'

Van der Goes looked incredulously at his questioner. 'What do you think I am, hey? Some kind of Kaffir? You think I'm a Hottentot?'

'I didn't mean to imply—'

'You impertinent little pisspot! God, man, I've been landdrost for over seven years. You think I don't know the form? You think I don't know that testimony has to be obtained under oath? What do you take me for? A Goddamned Hottentot from the bush?' His voice rose incongruously and he almost had to stand to keep pace with it.

Reenan, flustered, removed his glasses and polished them industriously. 'I wasn't meaning to criticise you, landdrost. It's simply that I've got to be able to put it all down in my report—'

'Fuck your report! I know how to behave! Don't try your smart Cape Town stuff on me! Listen, I'm up with the worm, don't you worry. I'm telling you then and there, I took the Holy Bible, God help me, from Henning's hand, then and there, I got the witnesses to swear in front of him. You take care, boy, I'm no Hottentot!'

'Landdrost, believe me, I'm not prying, or doubting your actions, but I must know how and when you took the evidence.'

Van der Goes's voice did not lose its whine. He continued to tell the story but as if he were still chastising the Assistant-Fiscal. 'Listen, boy, I nearly had a riot on my hands, you get that straight. You've got to remember how we welcomed the man. And how does he repay us? With debauchery! It's enough to make you sick!'

'As to the taking of the evidence, landdrost—'

'Hold your mouth and you'll hear.' The landdrost was enjoying himself, and saying what he had not been given a chance to say to Berg. 'Right, now, you imagine the scene, hey? They must have known we were coming, look-outs or some such. Right. So all of them make for the little church, if you can call it a church, just a pigsty really, and there they conduct a so-called service. That's an abomination to begin with. So me and my men—'

22

'How many of you were there?'

'Hey? Agh, about a dozen or so, all armed, mind you, we weren't taking any chances. So, me and my men we burst in on them, all right? And I want to tell you I've never seen anything like it in a holy place. Listen, I'm no angel, and I'm telling you I've never seen anything like it!' Van der Goes paused, cleared his throat and spat into a large brown handkerchief. Reenan, meanwhile, had replaced his spectacles and now sat, shielding his eyes as though to save himself embarrassment at what he was about to hear.

'They were singing *heathen* songs!' van der Goes continued, pointing his finger to give emphasis. 'Songs like you hear in the bush at night, Kaffir songs. And one of these black bitches, stark naked she was, going wild in the middle of the church, as close to the Lord's Table as I am to you. And do you know what they're doing? Henning and that fellow Muller? They're holding on to her, trying to keep her still. And I'm telling you, I saw it with my own eyes, their hands were slipping all over the place, on her tits, up between her legs, everywhere! And when they saw us they let go of her all right, but she, the Kaffir bitch, she goes screaming up to the Table and begins to dance round it like you see them dance round fires. Well, I tell you, my men wanted to hang the lot of them then and there. But I stopped them, oh yes, I said this has got to be done according to the book. After all, the man's a predikant and you can't start messing about with God's Elect.'

In the brief pause for breath, Reenan managed to murmur, 'Very true.'

'I arrested him then and there in the church. I want to tell you I've got a loud voice and I yelled at the top of my lungs and they went quiet. So we dragged them out, the whole lot of them, Henning, van Haarten, Muller, the lot. And the women. Dragged them out. My men started to set fire to the houses—'

'On your orders?' Reenan said, making a hasty note.

'What orders! I couldn't stop them if I tried. We're none of us angels, far from it, but we're only human after all. This was our land, we tamed the Hottentots, we got them working for us and then this bugger comes along and wants to undo all the good we've done for the last hundred and fifty years. I'm telling you I was glad to see the houses burn. Scenes of total degradation those houses. God's will they should be burnt.

'So, where was I? Oh, yes, well, as I say, we dragged them out.

My men had the ropes ready, slung over the trees, dangling there. That's when Henning spoke, shouted really, at the top of his voice.' Van der Goes looked from right to left as if he was scared of being overheard. 'By the way, you won't find any of this in the summary.'

'Why not?' asked Reenan, with his nervous little smile.

'Why not?' Van der Goes became angrier than ever. 'You expect me to write down every Goddamn thing that happened. I've only got two hands!'

'Do you remember what Henning said?' asked Reenan, pen poised.

'Are you going to write this down?' asked van der Goes, genuinely puzzled.

'If it's important—'

'If it was important *I* would have written it down!' the landdrost bellowed.

'Just—just tell me,' said Reenan trying to seem casual and unconcerned.

'Right. They're ready to hang him, you understand? So he says, "We've committed no crime!" ' He paused, his eyes fixed firmly on Reenan's pen.

'But—but why didn't you write that down, I—'

'What? A denial of guilt? You mad or something? No, sir. I've seen these buggers wriggle out of tighter corners. No chance. I'm not putting down any denial of guilt.' He stared hard at the Assistant-Fiscal, who felt obliged to lower his pen.

'What happened after that?'

' "No crime," I said? "Listen to me, you've broken every law in the book." My people cheered.'

'Did he answer that?'

' "I may have sinned," he said. "But I've committed no crime and nor have these men!" "*May* have sinned," I said? "Boy, you've just booked a passage to Hell!" '

Reenan laughed, but self-effacingly. 'I hope you don't think of banishment to Batavia as Hell, landdrost.'

'No, no. I was speaking theologically.'

Reenan let it pass. 'Did he say anything else?'

'No. From that moment on, until I saw the back of him last night, he never uttered again.'

'And what happened to the others?'

Van der Goes lowered his eyes, shifted uncomfortably, and said, 'They got away into the hills. You see, we didn't set off at once. We got a bit pissed, I have to admit. They escaped. But we'll get them, the buggers. My men went after them at first light while I took Henning into custody.'

'But what about the testimony?'

'The testimony? Oh yes. Well, that night, over a bottle, I asked Henning for his Bible and I took statements from the men. That was before we got drunk,' he added hastily. 'By the time I left for Cape Town I had sworn statements from a dozen others who'd seen the goings-on. So you can rely on what's there.' He tapped the pile of parchment that lay on Reenan's desk.

'No news about the others, then?'

'You mean the ones that got away? No. But we may hear any day now. If we'd have caught them, I would have brought them all here.'

'Well, thank you, landdrost,' said Reenan, nodding earnestly. 'That was all I wanted to know, about the testimony, that's all, really—'

'I can go now?'

'Thank you.'

With enormous difficulty, van der Goes rose. The two men shook hands. 'Write your report quickly,' said van der Goes. 'The sooner we get that antichrist out of here, the better. And take my advice, boy: don't write in any denials of guilt.' He marched towards the door. 'If you want me, you can find me at the Haarlem. I always stay there.'

'Then you'll have much to distract you.'

When the landdrost had gone, Reenan sank into a chair with relief, and then rang a small brass bell that stood on his desk. His clerk, Pierre Malan, entered; his first name was pronounced Pirry. A gangling youth with a long bony face, he had mournful, staring eyes, as though he'd been born with too little skin, and what there was had had to be stretched to go round. He was, as his name suggests, of French origin, a direct descendant of the Huguenots who had escaped persecution in Europe, and were given shelter at the Cape in 1688. By one of history's great conjuring tricks, the Huguenots vanished into thin air, only to reappear again as solid and as phlegmatic as any Dutchman. Nothing but their names lingered to remind them of their heritage. Malan had a habit of keeping his hands clasped on his chest, as though in prayer, but one could sense the tension, for his knuckles were forever twisted white.

'I do not want to be disturbed until I have read all this,' said Reenan, indicating the pile of statements. 'When I'm finished I'll want the prisoner brought up here for questioning. You'll take a record of everything that's said, so be prepared to stay late tonight. I won't get through this lot till after lunch.'

'I'm always free in the evenings, mynheer,' the boy answered keenly.

'I don't want to be disturbed by anyone, you understand, not even by Fiscal Berg?'

'I understand, mynheer. Just one thing—'

'What?'

'I've got the prisoner's file from records, mynheer. He's got a son working here in the Castle, clerk to the Court of Petty Cases.'

'Well you know the form, boy. Get the Fiscal to sign a suspension order. At once, man. Don't bother me with stuff like that. I've got enough work on my hands. Just look at all this I've got to read.'

It was the custom to suspend relatives of accused men. So many in the employ of the Company were brothers or uncles or cousins or nephews, that it had long been considered politic to remove the possibility of conspiracy among families. As most of the cases involving officials were concerned with financial fraud, the system worked well: more often than not, whole families had been found guilty of being involved in the same offence. And so Malan retired, scribbled out a suspension order and took it to Fiscal Berg for signature.

Alone, Reenan untied the bundle of parchment and began to read. 'I, Abraham van der Goes, do solemnly swear that the Reverend Johannes Henning is guilty of blasphemy, incitement to riot and other grievous offences against Almighty God and the United East India Company of the Netherlands . . .'

6

Strong church, strong colony. The Colony was never strong. Like an unwanted, weakling child it grew and grew, gaining not in strength but in disability. So far from head office in Amsterdam, it developed into an autonomous branch office with two sets of books.

A market garden, that was all they had meant it to be: grow fruit and vegetables and supply the passing ships. But a spirit of independence was born early; soon they were growing more than enough to feed the ships, more than enough to feed themselves. When the ships returned from the East, already laden with riches, the farmers of the Cape could find no space for their produce. Unless, of course, you knew the right people, or, indeed, if you were the right people; the right people were the Company's employees. To control the economy, the Company fixed prices. At a stroke, the employees undercut them, not for the well-being of the Colony, but in order to line their own pockets. The government functioned by graft, otherwise it would have ground to a halt. From the private, illegal farms, from smuggling, from a thousand ingenious rackets, the officials at the Cape drained the company and the burghers dry and hid behind the façade of reports. There were reports on everything: on the overproduction of farm produce, on uncollected taxes, on Hottentots who stole cattle, on slaves who escaped, on slaves who were freed—reluctantly. The administration stumbled over its own reports and could not find the energy to rise again. Slack, lazy, inefficient, resentful, the officials were hated by the burghers, and the burghers were hated by the officials. The Company and the century were drawing to their close.

And the church? Another subsidiary, its ministers the travelling salesmen, selling God, Divine will, and the harshness of life, commission collected in obedience and discipline. You, my brethren, are the chosen people, and this is the Promised Land. He is the God of Abraham, Isaac, Jacob and the Dutch East India Company. Jehovah comes first, but only on Sundays. Jesus *who*?

There are ten law books in the whole of the Cape. Ten. And no one has read them. Easier to make the ordinances up as you go along. Yes, there's your High Court of Justice and your Court of Petty Cases, so clogged with crime it would take two years to try the lot. They sit behind closed doors, these courts, the judges are the jury, and the jury are the judges, one and the same. The Fiscal prosecutes. Up country, in honour of the office, they call a bird of prey *fiskaal*. And, if the worst comes to the worst, you can always banish a man without trial—just so long as you have had the foresight to commission a report.

The Colony is a wild, uncontrolled, lawless free-for-all which fervently believes in Almighty God. The Colonists are not hypocrites but simply live their lives in self-contained worlds which never need to meet.

There is also a world of slaves, twenty-five thousand of them to serve twenty thousand Colonists. Not to mention the Khoikhoi who wander lost and unwanted; and a new race, created here and nowhere else, as yet unnamed, but their skins are neither dark nor fair, not black or white or yellow, but a mixture, the sad hue of a lost tribe.

The Colonists are already outnumbered; they are already frightened. If that were all.

2

Scandal

The landdrost, Abraham van der Goes, was drinking brandy. After leaving Reenan, he had marched down the Heeregeracht, a fashionable street which formed one side of the Grand Parade, towards the harbour in search of food and lodgings. He found both under the same roof of his favourite tavern, the Haarlem. Being a port, and a place where men broke their journey, the town teemed with hotels and bars, with gaming clubs and brothels; the harbour area was particularly rich in the latter. You could always be sure of getting a drink or a woman at any hour of the day or night. And, if you knew where to go, you could always buy French brandy at far below the price set by the Company, and nobody asked any questions, not even an official like van der Goes. Where would the questions stop? At the Governor? Everyone smuggled something or other. What harm did it do?

They knew van der Goes at the Haarlem. The landlord, a freed Hottentot called Piet-Piet, greeted him warmly and, at the sight of the familiar, heaving figure approaching along the quayside, immediately produced a bottle of cognac which he pronounced by sounding the 'g' gutturally. Van der Goes settled in a corner to the side of the door and in no time at all had claimed three bottles, without apparent effect. 'Something to do with my size,' he would explain when people marvelled at his capacity. Indeed, he had a mental picture of the liquid flowing straight down to his feet and being stored in his large, swollen toes which, in his mind, filled up one by one. If van der Goes said, 'I have had enough,' it was because he imagined the brandy to be rising above his ankles. Now on his fourth bottle, the brandy, he estimated, had reached no further than his heels.

'Well, Piet-Piet, how goes things?'

'Trouble, master, all the time trouble.' The Hottentot spoke the local slang, the *taal* it was called, a mixture of his own clicking tongue and Dutch, with a sprinkling of Portuguese, Malay and the French double-negative thrown in for good measure.

'What sort of trouble?'

'Girls, master.'

'A-ha,' muttered van der Goes, not paying much attention, watching the handful of other customers, sailors mostly, and the half-caste women who were neither free nor slaves.

'Master, last years we have eight girl working here,' Piet-Piet continued. 'Now all of them have baby. Master, I got to find other eight girl.'

'But you found 'em, I hope?'

'Oh, ja, master, we find, oh ja, lovely blossoms.'

'Is Tantira still here?'

'Here but not free, master, no.'

'Let me know when she's free.'

'On that second,' Piet-Piet promised, bowing politely before going off to answer the summons of another customer; the landdrost could hear him repeating the same complaint to the same question.

Van der Goes narrowed his eyes and surveyed the sprinkling of girls at the bar, every shape and size, every colour of the rainbow. He favoured the Malays most, but he would make do with a half-caste if necessary, at any rate, those of that indeterminate shade of yellow, well, not quite yellow, more an olive, an ochre, a kind of golden amber. God, that colour excited him! Just look at them there: eyes that slant, eyes that are round, high noses, flat noses, lips full and sensual, necks slender and tempting. And breasts the size of melons, that's what he liked, full, ripe breasts, and nipples, like staring eyes, so black the nipples on those sallow breasts. And what tricks these women knew, tricks of tongue and teeth, of infinitely subtle hands. Give him a Malay woman any day, far superior to women of full colour who were usually too damned modest and shy. Anyway, van der Goes had enough of full-coloured women up country. No, what he liked was a *whore*, a warm-blooded, abandoned whore. Well, if you were his size, you'd also want someone to do the work for you. Lovely things, these blossoms; you'd think that all the races of the earth had been present at their making.

'What brings you to Cape Town, landdrost?'

Van der Goes had not seen the man enter, but he now brought his eyes to bear upon a tall, thin fellow, with no chin, who twisted and twitched his head like a cockerel in a farmyard.

'Who are you?' asked van der Goes.

'Van Rensburg. You remember. We did some business over those slaves. Two females from Java, you remember? Big-titted things, four hundred rixdollars a piece, good teeth.' He tapped his own broken incisors, hoping to remind the landdrost.

'Good teeth?' repeated van der Goes, shaking his head. 'No, I don't remember any with good teeth.'

'Mother and daughter but they looked like sisters.' He poked his head forward nervously and lowered his voice to a whisper. 'The mother, man, you sent her back pregnant and asked me to get rid of her. I gave you a good price, two hundred and fifty. I would have given you more if you were buying another. As a matter of fact, I got rid of her to a French sea-captain. I told him she was just a little fat—well, he liked them fat. He paid five-fifty for her, so I did very well in the end. You must remember. Van Rensburg's the name.' The landdrost shrugged indifferently and poured himself another glass; the newcomer slipped into the seat opposite. 'Listen,' he said. 'I can fix you up with three females from Madagascar.'

'Too ugly,' said van der Goes, waving his glass in the other's face.

'You haven't seen them yet! These are really strong things, and no mistake. These females from Madagascar work all day and night if you require, good leg muscles, that's the secret. They can work literally for hours without rest. I can let you have the three for five hundred. You hear what I'm saying? Three females in first-class condition for only five hundred!'

'Not interested,' said van der Goes.

'Listen, landdrost, there's one other thing you should know about Madagascan females. They've got to have the flagpole up them every night. Listen, they expect it, it's what they like, not only like, they *got* to have it! It's like this: you and me, we've got to eat, right? Females from Madagascar, it's a well-known fact, they've got to have it every night of their lives, and if they don't, they can't work.' Van Rensburg helped himself to the landdrost's brandy.

'Every night?' repeated van der Goes, then shook his head doubtfully. 'No boy, I couldn't manage it every night. They're a slave for a young man by the sound of it.'

Van Rensburg did not pursue the matter: he had committed his usual mistake of overselling. 'So, what brings you to the big city, eh, landdrost?'

Van der Goes flapped his huge hands several times and again shook his head, but this time implying that his lips were sealed.

'You here to prosecute?' asked van Rensburg, but received no answer. 'What sort of case this time?'

'I am not allowed to discuss the matter,' van der Goes said with half-closed eyes that gave him the look of an all-knowing Buddha.

'Is it that serious?'

'All I'll tell you is this,' said van der Goes. 'The Commissioner-General is dealing with it personally.'

'You're lucky it's not Fiscal Berg. That's a slimy little rabbit if ever there was one. And that assistant of his, Reenan? God, those two together, enough to freeze the sea.'

'I was in conference with them all morning,' van der Goes said grandly.

'Yes, well, you look a bit chilly. I tell you something, that fellow Reenan? He's a spy, you take my word for it, he's a spy. They're after illegal payments to officials, and I'm telling you that fellow knows everything. Dangerous. If he had his way all those who work in the Castle would be in the Tronk! The only thing he doesn't know is what his cock's for. He thinks it's for pissing out of!'

'I've got my prisoner in the Castle,' admitted van der Goes with a certain pride.

'Not the Tronk? Well then, it can't be as bad as you think. All the worst are thrown in the Tronk.' They called for more brandy.

Van der Goes covered his mouth with a hand, to give himself a greater feeling of intimacy. 'This is semi-political what I'm involved in, concerning the Church.'

'Not a rebellion, by any chance?'

The landdrost, with his hands still to his eyes, looked carefully from side to side. 'You promise not to breathe a word?'

'Promise.'

'My prisoner's a predikant—'

'No!'

'True.'

'What's he done?'

'Everything.'

'How d'you mean?'

'Bestiality, blasphemy, buggery and fornication!'

'What's his name?'

'My lips are sealed.'

'Bestiality *and* fornication?'

'The lot. He defiled the Table of the Lord.'

'Where was this?'

'Henningsdorp. Named after him, too.'

'Sounds an active fellow!'

'All I'm telling you is this: first he baptises the little black bitches, then he fucks them!'

'What they going to do with him?'

'Banish him, of course!'

'The sooner the better, hey?'

'That's all I'm waiting for, see him on the ship, then I can go back home happy.'

At that moment, Piet-Piet approached and whispered in the landdrost's ear. Van der Goes nodded and winked and with the aid of his companion and Piet-Piet, rose to his feet.

The Malay girl Tantira, her body young but her face lined and tired, stood by a faded blue curtain behind the bar counter. At the approach of van der Goes, she smiled dutifully.

'Good teeth,' called van der Goes over his shoulder.

Van Rensburg answered, 'If you change your mind about the Madagascans . . .'

Heaving and puffing, van der Goes edged round the counter. Tantira took him by the arm and the couple disappeared through the curtain. As they went, van der Goes asked, 'Ever been baptised?' and gave a loud chuckle which turned into a wheeze.

Van Rensburg could barely contain himself. His mind was buzzing with what he had just heard, and in his confused state, wild, orgiastic images clouded his brain. Rising unsteadily, he spied two friends at the bar and lurched towards them.

'Listen,' he said, 'this is confidential, but you saw the big fellow? He's landdrost van der Goes from Blauwzand and did he have a tale to tell!' And to attendant gasps and whistles from his audience, van Rensburg launched forth. 'A predikant, Henning, what he's been up to! Listen, ssh, not a word, hey? He's been fucking black women on the Table of God in the church. Yes, man, I'm telling you, *in the*

33

church! You know what he does? First he baptises them, and then he fucks them. God, how the hell should I know what he baptises them for? But I'm telling you, he stands there naked, cannon and balls hanging there for everyone to see. First, he sprinkles the water you know where—I'm telling you, that's how he does it—then gets the woman to lie on the Table and then you know what he does? Climbs aboard, and that's the gospel truth!'

2

It is a small place, this Cape Peninsula which, like a drooping finger, hangs at the southern point of the African continent. Scandal, rumour, gossip are as much a part of the landscape as the trinity of mountains which embrace the town like an amphitheatre. It would seem that the place was expressly fashioned to transmit rumour quickly.

From the dockside taverns it is a short walk to Market Square and the Stadthouse, a clumsy building of red stone, ornamented with pilasters and a portico where the slaves gather to exchange the news of the day. The slaves are inveterate gossips. From the Stadthouse they cross the fashionable Heeregeracht, to the Parade where they draw the pure spring water that is brought in pipes from the foot of Table Mountain and feeds two square fountains in a perpetual stream; ceaseless, like their chatter. In a matter of hours, an old woman from Malabar claims that the Reverend Johannes Henning has visited her nightly, arriving out of a black sky, naked, astride a winged donkey. A Malay mother, who has twin daughters, both pregnant, attests that the predikant has a forked penis and has lain with the two girls, simultaneously.

You may find the slaves' masters seeking the shade in the Company Gardens, first planted in 1652 to provide fresh fruit and vegetables for the passing ships. Now the respectable inhabitants stroll the walks of oaks and hedges of myrtle, and you may listen to the babble of voices which will continue late into the night when the Gardens buzz with a greater multitude indulging in the favourite pastime, which the locals call 'street-walking'. Here, it is the men who discuss the affair at Henningsdorp, detaching themselves from the womenfolk to gather in tight little knots, adding a detail, correcting a fallacy. Van Rensburg's version has remained largely intact, except that, in the constant retelling, Henning has acquired a

34

sexual potency of satanic proportions which he expended only on virgins.

You may hear the gossip everywhere; in the taverns, in the shops, at the market stalls, echoing the sound of the solitary violin that is so much a part of the place, a haunting, busy melody that seems to follow you around wherever you go. Like calumny, you will hear it more than once.

3

The congregation
of saints

The walls of the Reformed Church and the front of the Company Slave Lodge form one side of Church Square which is a peaceful spot and cool, for the tall steeple of the Groote Kerk casts its shadow there, and people in need of quiet sit on the stout wooden benches under the plane trees escaping from the bustle of the town and the harshness of the noon sun.

But a running figure disturbed the quiet of that February day. Daniel Henning charged across the Square, frightening a circle of busy pigeons who exploded into the air as he passed. He was in panic, and ran as though pursued to the narrow, white house at the southern side, where on the ground floor, he, his mother Agatha, and sister Sybille, lived. The accommodation—five rooms in all— was meant to be temporary, for the family expected any day now that their father would send for them to join him up-country where he conducted his pastoral duties.

A garbled, incoherent account of the morning's events tumbled out of Daniel: he had been suspended, his father was in prison, everyone laughed and sniggered at him, he was not allowed even to tidy his desk, his father was being questioned by Reenan—

Agatha Henning grabbed hold of her son and shook him until he was still. Her strength was that of a man, and confined not only to her arms. Having silenced Daniel, she seated herself at the head of the polished dining-table, rested her hand on the Holy Bible, and ordered her son to pray before he next spoke. Sybille, who tried to intervene with questions, was silenced with a look. While Daniel covered his face with his hands and tried to pray, Agatha sat un-

36

moving, unmoved, and waited. The window was at her back, so that to her children she looked like a piece of dark, shadowy wood, matching the furniture which they had brought with them from Holland: tables, chairs, cupboards, beds, all too large for their present home that was, as a result, made to seem excessively cramped and pokey. There was an almost total absence of colour except for several strings of brightly, multi-coloured beads hanging on the walls, made by the Khoikhoi, and sent by Johannes as a gift from his parish up-country. In these close surroundings, the beads appeared limp and lifeless, like wilting flowers in the heat.

When you saw Daniel and Agatha together, the resemblance was striking: both were short and square, both had grim tight mouths set in determined chins and both had long, angular noses; and both were obstinate. There all similarity ended. Daniel was one of nature's bullies, cruel to the weak, grovelling to the strong. Agatha bowed her head to no one but her Maker. Her sin was the sin of pride, but shrouded and disguised in God's word, the confident knowledge of righteousness and in the Divine Will which had fashioned in her a soul of steel. Daniel, without the trappings of moral sensibility, was endowed with a soul of wax. Agatha ruled by terror, and her children obeyed accordingly. She was a few months short of her fiftieth birthday, but looked already aged, with deep lines dragging down her mouth.

Daniel prayed, snivelling into his hands; Agatha looked straight ahead as if she were unaware either of him or of her daughter who hovered anxiously beside her. Sybille was seventeen, three years younger than her brother. She had inherited her looks from neither parent: she was very fair and pale, with a serious, almost prim expression that could be thought enigmatic. The casual, superficial observer would put her down at once as plain.

'God has heard enough,' Agatha said to Daniel. 'Make your amen.'

'Amen,' said Daniel.

'Now tell me.'

He began again, this time with every effort to collect his thoughts and present them in a logical order.

'But what has father done?' asked Sybille.

'I don't know, that's just it, I don't know, no one would tell me—' He was once more in danger of incoherence; Agatha slapped the table sharply with her flat hand and the words stuck in his throat. The two children watched their mother, as if she alone could supply an explanation. Agatha said, 'He has brought shame on us at last.' The children did not dare respond. The stillness in the room was unrelieved and oppressive, like the noonday heat. Presently, Agatha spoke. 'He has preached against the slaves again. I am certain of it. Go to your rooms and pray. We are in need of help.' Grateful for the excuse to be out of her presence, Daniel and Sybille obeyed.

Agatha, too, was grateful to be alone and had ordered her children away for that reason. Her iron will had controlled her external reactions but she was powerless against the inner shock she had experienced. Repeatedly she said the word 'imprisoned' to herself, as if she could not fully appreciate the meaning. At intervals, she gave an odd little shake of her head which underlined her feeling of disbelief. A girlhood memory, inexplicably, flooded her mind, so vivid it was like being back in that time in Delft, on a misty November night, standing at the foot of her father's bed, watching him die. Then running—she could feel the slipperiness of the polished tile floor beneath her feet now—into the dining-room where the family Bible was kept—the same one on which her hand now rested. 'Will he live, O God, will he live?' she asked, opened the Book at random to St Luke and spun her finger to the verse, 'And he said unto them, Go ye, tell that fox, Behold, I cast out devils and I do cures today and tomorrow, and the third day I shall be perfected.' And on the third day her father's fever broke, and he lived.

Imprisoned. One memory prompted another: her father recovering and walking with her by the canal, and holding on to her arm; and another: the young minister who was sent to preach and conduct services while her father convalesced. Johannes Henning. Imprisoned. How else could it have ended? The Divine Will was perfect: in sin was the beginning. Imprisoned.

She was already twenty-six and resigned to solitude. Her mother had died giving birth to her and so she had known little companionship of any kind, and expected none. Her father, the Reverend Nikolas van Breda, was predikant in Delft, and she, by force of circumstance, had devoted her life to him. To look at, van Breda was the very model of a fierce patriarch: bearded against the fashion, long hooked nose and eyes of unbearable intensity. When he preached, the earth trembled. His daughter was his slave; he never reflected on her situation or saw any necessity for it to be different. God appoints us to our role in life and it is not for us to question or to change. Agatha accepted her servitude somewhat less meekly : she acknowledged the Divine Will in these matters, but could not help resenting God's decision in her case. This, in turn, produced in her a spiritual pride, a kind of defiance which made it seem that life was a contest between her and her Maker. With the passage of time, and the unchanging nature of her state, she grew to realise that God's will was more enduring than her own; after a violent inward struggle she submitted to the greater power, mistook it for a profound religious experience and thereafter accepted, without question, that life was preordained in every detail. There is no knowing what comfort this belief can bring.

In the winter of 1770, her father was struck down with fever—he was conducting a funeral service at the time—and for several weeks hovered between life and death. Prayers were said for his recovery, but not by his daughter; she saw no need; God's will be done. Yet, when the crisis was at its worst, she felt the uncontrollable need to determine for herself the course God had plotted. The revelation through Scripture, which was to her the only acceptable form of revelation, was so frighteningly accurate that Agatha was more confirmed in her beliefs than ever before. God's will be done.

Her father, although much better, was still not well enough to resume his duties. The Elders of the Delft Church arranged for a temporary replacement. In January, Johannes Henning arrived, twenty-one years old, and but recently ordained.

'What's he like?' asked her father.

'He has angel's wings for ears,' she replied.

Tall, gaunt, with eyes so deep-set you could barely see them. And those ears, exactly like wings, sticking out from the side of his head to make him look almost comic. And to add to the effect, his clothes seemed too small for him, the sleeves of his coat too short, so that one always saw his wrists. Yet, despite his odd appearance, Agatha had no positive impression of him whatsoever; she thought of him as somewhat colourless.

He lived in their house for four months and it was she who guided him in his duties, helped him prepare his sermons, chose the hymns for Sunday service and reminded him to visit the sick. Of all the invalids in Delft that winter, none demanded more attention than her father, the Reverend Nikolas van Breda. For hours on end, young Henning would be made to sit with him, and they would talk theology and scripture; or rather, van Breda talked, and Henning listened politely.

'And what do you think of him?' Agatha asked her father while making his bed.

'He is not the stuff predikants are made of,' the old man replied sternly. His illness had weakened him, and in his nightgown he looked like an elderly professor, rather distinguished and learned. 'He has a heavy Cross to bear.'

'Why do you say that?'

'He's too soft. He needs more iron.'

But the old man had misread the nature of the younger minister. It was not softness from which Henning suffered, but a kind of vacancy, as if he had not yet made up his mind as to what he would be. Agatha detected the confusion in him which expressed itself in diffidence. She was attracted by his gentleness, amused by his shyness, for she was very direct with him, and he was easily intimidated by her bullying manner. Almost from the first, she realised that she would be an ideal partner for him, providing strength where he was weakest. For, if he was bemused by the ways of the world, then Agatha was the perfect complement: fiercely practical and capable. She would be his anchor. And so, she began to discern the Divine pattern: if her father had not been ill, then Henning would not have been sent. Was he sent only to fill her father's place? Or was he there for a more important reason? Soon she convinced herself that God had sent Johannes Henning to be her husband.

She remembered a cold February night when a wind was howling round the house. She was woken by a terrible scream. At first, thinking it was her father, she ran to the old man's room but found him peacefully asleep. Realising that the cry must have come from Henning—he was the only other occupant of the house—she made her way to his room and knocked, but received no reply. When she put her ear to the door, she heard sobbing, like that of a child's, and taking her courage in her hands, entered.

Henning was lying face down on his bed, crying into the pillow, awful, painful sobs.

'Dominee, are you ill?'

He turned his head sharply towards her. 'Go away, please, go away,' he said, once more hiding his face.

'Stop crying,' she said, 'you'll wake my father.' But it was not a reprimand, simply an excuse to remain in the room.

He made an effort to control his sobs, but they only became more agonised and harsh. 'Christ Jesus have mercy,' he stammered. 'O Christ, have mercy.'

The invocation to his Saviour was sufficient reason for Agatha to set her candle on the chair by the door and to take up instead Henning's Bible which lay on a table near the bed. She turned to the sixth psalm of David, and read, 'O Lord, rebuke me not in thin anger, neither chasten me in thy hot displeasure. Have mercy upon me, O Lord; for I am weak: O Lord, heal me . . .' As she read his crying grew fainter, until at 'Let all mine enemies be ashamed and sore vexed: let them return and be ashamed suddenly,' he was quiet, but shuddering to regain his breath. She stood, the Bible open in her hands, watching him.

He said, 'But *I* am ashamed.'

She took a chair and sat beside the bed, like a nurse observing a patient. She remembered the screeching wind playing havoc with the candle flame, and one everlasting impression of the man on the bed: in agony, holding on to his head as though it were about to split open. How false was memory, she wondered? What tricks had it played? How did the conversation continue? Did she ask him why he was ashamed? Did he respond? Was there not something from him about emptiness and—yes—she remembered—'I cannot come to my God, I cannot find Him in my heart'—and then, how? Did he hold out his hand or did she move to comfort him? Was it not she who now held his head, pressing him tight against her breast, and was he not clutching her so fiercely that it hurt her to breathe? She, stroking him, and he, pulling her on to the bed. Which one of them cried, 'Return O Lord, deliver my soul'? And the penetration, like frozen pain—

Separation from God is worst for the servants of God, sin being the deliberate act of severance. He could not look at her, talk to her, be with her; the burden of guilt he could not bear, and he performed his duties like one pursued by an accusing spectre. But Agatha suffered no such torment. Even now she marvelled at her own strength, the ability to turn the situation on its head so that only the advantages showed uppermost. God's will be done. Even sin can be forgiven; especially sin. She found spiritual comfort in the knowledge that lust was without pleasure.

With her strident, practical nature, she cornered him and demanded marriage. He had been too dispirited by past events to resist. She asked him to pray with her so that God would cleanse their souls and bless their union. They were married by her disapproving father in the spring of 1771.

Her memory faltered, telescoped some events, by-passed others; looking back over twenty-three years of marriage was like gazing down an endless, uniform corridor, lit here and there by a dying torch. The cold of his body; his disgust at physical contact; even in marriage, he said, the act seemed to him infected, but he accepted her demands as a duty to God, he said, and she knew that he dreaded to touch her. Then she remembered the pain of Daniel's birth, and three years later, Sybille. After that she demanded no more and he thanked God.

She recalled their almost nomadic existence: the moves from parish to parish, like a wandering in the wilderness. The lack of passion in his ministry and in his life perpetuated itself from one place to the next. Distanced from people, the people neither feared nor respected him. Always the Elders demanded more severity; and so, another parish, and another.

Groningen. She remembered the canals and mist, November fog. The *trek schuits*, those covered barges, and the cry of the boatmen, like gliding into a netherworld of despair, he said. Such poverty of spirit he had never known; his life had slipped into a grey repetitive charade in which no one appeared and nothing happened.

Then she remembered him waking one night from a nightmare, soaked in sweat from head to foot. There, in the dark, the two lay, he telling her the awful content of his dream. He was a boy again, swimming in the River Lek near the family home; he could hear his mother calling him, but he paid no attention and swam further downstream. Then, as is the way with dreams, his mother was suddenly beside him in the river, both naked, swimming side by side. All at once he felt he could no longer swim, the water turned to clay and was suffocating him. His mother grabbed him by the foot, pulling him towards her until, like lovers, they were conjoined.

In the telling, it was Agatha who was roused; the revulsion she knew she should have felt did not materialise; instead, a blind longing for the man beside her; and with her intensity, she forced him to respond.

A child was born. A child: a misshapen little body, a deformity, but their child. A punishment, she said. Accusations spoken and unspoken, ever present. 'Search your soul,' she said, refusing to look at the baby. Suspicions, mutual distrust, decay, hatred. The passage of time, sour as her milk, and the solitude of shared emptiness. Why hast Thou forsaken me? Why hast thou forsaken Me?

But the birth wrought a change in Henning of a different kind. He loved the child. In all his life he had not known such compassion, not even for the torment of Christ Crucified. A helpless, passive child, crippled. No, not punishment, but reward. A curse, not rejected, but welcomed. He held the baby long hours, like caressing his own deformed spirit. No, not punishment but a benediction; the emptiness had been filled: a living proof of God, the Divine Will and the Redeemer in Christ.

After seven months the child died. He came to its cradle one morning and where there had been life, there was no life. Agatha remembered wrapping the body in a shawl and carrying it to the undertaker as though she were returning an unwanted article. But his was the desolation: God, do not snatch away that which I have loved. Our bodies are the lies, not the glorious innocence of a soul unmade, unmakeable. Inaction is the ideal of the spirit; provide me with those who are helpless and who are meek.

He could not preach without crying, he could not minister to others without intruding his own suffering. Yet again the Elders asked him to move on. Agatha it was who prayed for guidance, for her husband had taken to his bed and was unable to rise. She beseeched Christ to alter the course of their lives. And so casual the response: an Elder, mynheer Pretorius, had a brother important in the Dutch East India Company. Would not the Cape be the place to recover? They were in need of ministers there, any ministers. The Hennings set sail from Rotterdam on 26 December 1791. They left behind winter in Europe and arrived in the hateful glare of the Cape sun.

'I'm going out, I can't stand it here,' Daniel said, striding across the hall, out of the front door without giving her the chance to respond.

But Agatha's thoughts were too distant for her to care about her son. She cursed the heat. Imprisoned. Her memory kept returning to her sick father, before Johannes Henning had come into her life. She determined to anticipate God's will once more and, glancing up at the ceiling, commanded, 'Tell me what to do,' and opened the Bible —her father's Bible—and pointed. 'Praise ye the Lord. Sing unto the

Lord a new song, and his praise in the congregation of saints,' but she perceived no relevance and gained no comfort from those words. Angrily, she shut the book and turning her eyes upwards again said with dangerous intensity, 'Don't You desert me, don't You leave me now!'

2

Daniel wandered off down Strand Street, in the direction of a tavern where he was certain of finding friends. There was nothing quick or clever about Daniel Henning: he considered facts slowly, each in turn having to be carefully savoured and understood; it was a painful process for him because despite his stocky, muscular, and undeniably brutish appearance, he was an intensely emotional young man and his feelings, though often crude and wasteful, were fed by this slow, laboured insistence of thought. His first reaction to the morning's events had been instinctive and savage. The panic that consumed him was real and powerful; later, supported first by his mother's will, and then in the calm of his own room, the panic was channelled into seeking the path to salvation, not Agatha's heavenly variety, but his own, which was of a more earthy texture. Daniel Henning was concerned for no one but himself.

It was the prospect of disgrace that caused him, at first, most anxiety: the vilification, the eternal finger-pointing. Of all the Hennings, Daniel had fitted into the way of life at the Cape most easily, had made friends, found work irksome but not arduous, enjoyed the sun and the sea; and now it seemed that this comfort he had found was to be snatched from him. Now he was making his way towards a familiar haunt, to test, as it were, his friends. Would they taunt him. Or would they welcome him as if nothing had happened? He wanted to know.

The tavern was filled with clerks from the Castle who used the place over the lunch break. Unlike the Haarlem, it had no other purpose but to serve drink. It was a large, hollow room, with a long, straight counter, the floor covered in sawdust. Daniel knew, the moment he entered, that all was not well. His circle of friends did not open their ranks to him as was their custom; instead, they fell silent and he could feel hostile eyes watching him to the bar.

'Hey, Daniel!' called one. 'Has your sister ever been baptised?' Great guffaws of laughter. Although the particular reference passed him by, Daniel, with the instincts of a baiter, knew he was being

44

baited. He wanted to call out a reply, but could not think of one; he regretted having come to the place at all.

He ordered ale and carried the tankard across to a table in the furthest corner. 'Hey, Daniel! Is yours forked, too?' He tried not to look in their direction and concentrated on the patterns the sawdust made on the floor. But before long he was aware of someone approaching, and he stiffened, ready for anything.

'Can I drink with you?' The voice was unexpectedly friendly; it belonged to Mathias Janssens. There were more cat-calls. 'Didn't know you were religious, Mathias!' More laughter.

'You all right?' asked Mathias. Daniel shrugged. Mathias lived by smuggling, but he looked like an extremely respectable citizen with a white stock at his neck which gave him the appearance of a clerk in holy orders. He was five or six years older than Daniel, wiry and classically handsome, like a weathered Greek statue.

'You don't want to pay any attention to those buggers,' said Mathias.

Daniel did not reply, but gazed stubbornly at the floor, morose and suspicious.

'Listen, it's going to be tough for you.'

'I suppose the whole town knows, hey?'

'Rumours, man, you know, just talk.'

Daniel did not have the courage to ask the nature of the rumours, for that would have made him look even more ridiculous. He said, 'Get about quickly, I'll say that.'

'Why aren't you at work?' asked Mathias.

'I've got the day off.'

'You sure? They haven't thrown you out?'

'No.'

'They haven't found out about our little transaction, have they?'

'No.' (A minor matter: Daniel had lifted an incriminating file for Mathias in return for thirty rixdollars.) 'That father of mine!' he said and spat into the sawdust.

'Yes,' said Mathias. 'Man, the last thing you want is a predikant for a father.'

Daniel appeared to digest that remark for some time, during which he downed a further two tankards as if to assist the process. Then he said, 'I'll tell you this for free: he's the only man I've ever met who I've been frightened of,' which was a lie, but he intended it in a particular sense: he did not mean physically frightened.

'Used to knock you about, hey?'

'Him? No! Couldn't knock about a fly, that one. No, my mother did the knocking about. She could break an ass's jaw with her backhander. No, with my father it was altogether different, just give you a look, you know what I mean?'

'Well, he's a predikant, isn't he?'

'Too right,' Daniel nodded heavily, then suddenly thumped the table. 'Agh, man, he's so damned *useless*!'

'Useless?'

'Too damn holy, you know what I mean? As if he's got the keys of the pearly gates in his pockets. Agh, poor bugger. Useless!'

'I don't know about being useless,' said Mathias. 'He must have changed his ways from what I hear,' which was another innuendo that Daniel did not understand, but he covered by saying, 'Yes, well, I haven't seen him for almost three years, so how the hell should I know!'

'Well, you can't choose your parents, hey?'

'No.'

'My old man was a real bastard. You see this?' Mathias showed a small scar above his left eyebrow. 'He gave me that when he was drunk one night.'

'What did you do? Did you stand for that?'

'Agh, man, it's your father after all, hey?'

'Agh, for God's sake,' said Daniel, 'just let's sit and drink!'

After an hour, both men had drunk themselves into a state of glassy-eyed indifference. 'You know what I need?' Daniel said.

'You want some bitches?'

'No.'

'What, then?'

'Action.'

'You want to go up the mountain?'

'Now you're talking my language!'

'With the guns?'

'With the guns,' agreed Daniel.

'Why not, hey?'

'I'd like to shoot some buggers today, man.'

'Me, too,' said Mathias, nodding as if he were about to go off to sleep. 'I got guns at my place.'

'Right. Let's go.'

Daniel heaved himself to his feet; Mathias, still seated, offered an arm for support which was arrogantly waved away. Eventually, they walked, arm in arm, towards the door. A customer called, 'When your father next holds a church service, let me know, hey, Daniel?'

'You're too ugly,' Mathias shouted back and the two friends tumbled out into the street, weak with laughter. Once in the fresh air, they reeled senselessly, and giggled like young girls. Both had need to hold on to each other and, the blind leading the blind, some-how found their way to where Mathias lived, retrieved two hunting guns from beneath the bed and, with their pockets stuffed full of ammunition, they hired two horses from a livery stable and set off, singing, in the direction of Lion's Head.

3

Of all the Hennings, the only one to feel real concern for her father was Sybille. Sent to her room to pray, she took up pen and paper :

Beloved father,
    Tell me what you need. I will do anything to assist you. We are so anxious. Mother has prayed many hours for you, and Daniel, too. God in his mercy will protect you, I know it, dearest father. It is so long since we have seen you. I miss you with all my heart.
                                                    Yours to test
                                                        Sybille.

She folded it carefully and then paused, gazing out of the window which overlooked the Square; no one was about; an ominous still-ness had settled over the house.

Poor Sybille. She took everything so personally : if Daniel was scolded, she cried; her mother's misery she shared. Once more she took up the pen, re-opened the letter and wrote, 'God help you, father, if you should be made to suffer for my sins.'

Sins? Mischievous longings, girlish dreams, adolescent discomfort for which she felt that perhaps her father had been made to suffer. So delicate the line of sensibility, so strict her own moral censure to produce in her this rough-and-ready pain. A day-dream, no more : to be married, not to anyone in particular, just to be married. Not even carnal thoughts of the male animal entered her imaginings—her con-science was too strict a censor to allow that. But some notion had insisted itself, had nagged at her that life could be different, that an inward burden which she was unable to identify, a vague inertia,

47

could, she was certain, be dispelled; and this certainty of hope she associated with marriage. Not that the feeling of possibility was altogether pleasant, for here was the source of her guilt: the uncomfortable suspicion that she was really seeking a sinful, ungodly joy. She discussed the sentiments with her mother, was told first not to be silly, and second to pray. But hopes of marriage nourished in her expectations of being set free, and had come to represent deliverance, a kind of manumission from girlhood which, she convinced herself, she would go to any lengths to bring about. The conviction that all could be different, that there was a promise to be fulfilled, was indestructible and, for this meagre state of happiness, she felt her father had been made to pay. Now the happiness was dashed to pieces; the unidentifiable weight had returned and she suffered the agony her father suffered.

A parent as strict as Agatha was bound to produce secretiveness in her children. Sybille put on her bonnet with the blue ribbons and, hiding the letter under her shawl, walked into the dining-room. 'I'm going out for a walk, mother,' she said. Her mother did not even seem to hear; Sybille took advantage of this apparent indifference and crossed quickly to the front door, but, on opening it, was startled to see a hunchback dwarf with an enormous head and a perpetual frown as though his glasses were not powerful enough, holding up a shapeless hand as though he were about to knock.

'Mevrou Henning?' he said in a nasal, high-pitched voice, surprised at the door being opened.

'No,' Sybille replied. 'I'm her daughter.'

'Is your mother in?' he asked sharply.

Sybille called to Agatha who joined her and looked puzzled at the little man. 'What do you want?'

'My name is Bezuidenhout—big name for a little chap, hey? You've seen me in church, no doubt.'

'Who are you?'

'I'm the political commissioner to the *kerkraden*,' he explained. He was appointed by the government to protect its interests when the Church Consistories met: a watchdog to guard against religion intruding in Company affairs.

'What do you want with me?' asked Agatha.

'May I come in?'

Mother and daughter exchanged a nervous look. The dwarf's eyes seemed to twinkle behind his glasses, but in a cold, penetrating way.

'Come in, come in,' ordered Agatha but did not allow him to step further than the cramped narrow passage.

'Mevrou Henning, I am here on official business,' he began.

'Yes?'

'I would prefer to speak to you alone,' he said, glancing at Sybille.

'You may speak in front of my daughter. After all, you're from the Church.'

The dwarf shrugged modestly, and fingered the brim of his outsize hat. 'I'm afraid I have some bad news for you. Your husband—'

'I know about my husband,' interrupted Agatha.

'Ah! You know about it. That makes it easier.'

'Makes what easier?'

'It's a rather—a rather complicated story.' Again he looked uncomfortably at Sybille, and caught sight of a convex mirror above her head in which he saw himself, Agatha, Sybille, the passage, round, distant and distorted. 'You see, mevrou Henning, you're living here in Church property. Under the circumstances—'

'What circumstances?'

'The Kerkraad wish to avoid any unpleasantness—'

'Say what you have to say, mynheer Bezuidenhout,' Agatha commanded as if she were talking to a stammering child.

He cleared his throat, and then hummed a little nervously. 'I am instructed by the Kerkraad to ask you to vacate these premises within seven days.'

Agatha permitted herself no outward reaction. 'Why?' she demanded. 'Why are we being asked to leave?'

'I thought you knew about your husband—' said the dwarf, puzzled.

'I know he's a prisoner. That does not make him guilty.'

'But the nature of the charges—' said the dwarf, twisting his hat faster and faster in his little fingers.

'What is he supposed to have done?'

Bezuidenhout again cleared his throat and hummed. 'Disloyalty to the Company,' he said. It was as good a euphemism as any; he hoped he would have to explain no further.

'To the Company?' Agatha repeated incredulously, and with a sense of relief. 'But my husband's a predikant.'

'He's an employee of the Company nevertheless—'

'But he can't be disloyal to a company.' There was a note of scorn in her voice. The dwarf mumbled something. 'What did you say?' she demanded.

'I said disloyalty to the Church may come into it, too.'

Suddenly, Sybille intervened. 'I wish to see my father,' she cried.

'Sybille, be quiet!'

'I wish to see him!'

'I'm afraid that's not possible,' said the dwarf.

Obstinate as ever, Agatha took her daughter's part. 'Why isn't she allowed to see him?'

'I'll speak to Fiscal Berg.'

'I want to see my father—'

'She *insists* on seeing her father.'

'Yes, yes, I'll speak to the Fiscal—'

Agatha stepped towards him and, startled, he backed away but found himself against the wall and could go no further. 'You haven't told me what my husband's supposed to have done.'

Bezuidenhout addressed her in the mirror. 'It seems—I wish to be as delicate as possible—if your daughter will pardon me—and you, mevrou—it seems that your husband—that he is guilty—of—of immorality—'

With all her strength she cracked him hard across the face, knocking off his glasses. She watched him drop on to his knees, scuttling about like a frightened rat; involuntarily, Sybille went down on her knees to help. Agatha did not move.

'I can't see without my glasses—'

'We'll find them,' said Sybille, feeling on the floor with her hands.

'What do you mean "immorality"?' asked Agatha, her mouth drawn in a tight, hard line.

'I mean with black women, that's what I mean!' cried the dwarf.

Sybille froze. Agatha looked down at the little man with disgust, then walked quickly away and returned to her seat at the head of the dining-table; she placed both hands on the Bible.

'Could you look by the door?' Bezuidenhout asked Sybille who still had not moved. 'In the shadow, I can't see at all in the shadow—' he whined.

To cover her confusion, Sybille searched more keenly as if the information about her father and the dwarf's harsh tone had spurred her into greater activity. 'I have them,' she said, finding the glasses by the door. 'They're not broken.'

'Thank you—' and standing, he held out his hand to receive them.

While he slipped them back on his nose, he hobbled to the archway that led to the dining-room. 'Mevrou Henning, you have seven days to vacate these premises, do you understand? That's an order from the Kerkraad. Seven days and we want you out!'

As he made for the door, Sybille stepped in front of him, barring his way. She thrust the letter into his hands. 'Please, please see that my father gets this. I beg you.'

The dwarf hesitated, then took the letter and stuffed it into the pocket of his lopsided coat. 'Don't forget,' he said. 'Remind your mother: seven days. That's all.' And he was gone.

'Sybille?'

'Yes, mother?'

'Come here.'

Sybille wandered listlessly to where her mother sat. The girl was bewildered, dazed by what she had heard and the shock drained her of energy. She leaned against the table, at the furthest end from her mother.

'In future,' Agatha said, 'you will not mention your father's name in this house. Tell Daniel.'

4

Hunters

The story of Henning's disgrace, suitably embroidered, reached Market Square quickly. It was a little after one o'clock when Henrik Cornelius heard the tale and he was immediately more interested than most.

'Henning?' he said. 'I know the bugger. Right. Want to see me make a quick fifty?'

Cornelius was well-known, although he had only arrived in the Cape some three years before. But anyone who drank as much as he did was bound to gain a reputation. He had been imprisoned in the Tronk more than a score of times for disorderly behaviour, and once for stealing a dozen bottles of brandy from a Company store. Against authority he bore an eternal grudge, and, at the moment of hearing the scandal, he associated Henning with authority and decided to hit back; he had, in any event, nursed his resentment against the predikant for a long time.

No one quite knew what Cornelius did for a living, but he was forever hanging about the Castle, hoping, no doubt, to interest some official or other in schemes and deals. So when he presented himself at the gates, the sergeant on duty thought he was there on his regular visit.

'Who d'you want to see today, Henrik?'

Cornelius drew himself up to his full height, which was considerable, and said, 'Fiscal Berg, if you please.' But instead of being impressed, as Cornelius had hoped, the sergeant burst out laughing. 'What's so damn funny?'

'The Fiscal, no less, hey?' said the sergeant. 'Tomorrow it'll be the Commissioner-General, I suppose.'

Cornelius produced a flask from his back pocket and took a swig from it. 'Cut the jokes. You tell the Fiscal I'm here.'

'Piss off, Henrik, hey? See you tomorrow.'

'Listen, you want to lose your job?' He swayed a little as if the breeze bothered him.

'Go on, man, piss off.'

'Look, you listen to me and you listen with both ears: you tell the Fiscal that I have information regarding the Reverend Johannes Henning.' He took another swig.

'Who's he?' asked the sergeant, being cagey.

'Go play games with your own friends, don't waste my time!' said Cornelius with a wave of his hand.

'Come back tomorrow.'

'Listen, you tell the Fiscal I'm here. Unless you don't care whether there's a rebellion or not.'

The sergeant bristled with indecision. After a moment he said, 'Wait here.'

'That's better.'

The sergeant saw Berg's secretary and was, in turn, referred to the Assistant-Fiscal's office where he talked to Reenan's clerk, Malan. Malan asked the sergeant to wait and then went into his superior's office.

Reenan had not been out to lunch. He had been reading the evidence since early morning and was now only two-thirds of the way through. The interruption irritated him.

'Who?' Reenan asked, peering over his gold-rimmed glasses.

'A mynheer Cornelius.'

'Henrik Cornelius?'

'I think so,' said Malan doubtfully.

'Listen, boy, put him on to somebody else. I've no time to deal with drunks.'

'He's got information about Henning, he says.'

'Henrik has?'

'So the sergeant says.'

The sergeant was called in to explain; he passed on what Cornelius had told him, taking care to repeat the reference to rebellion. Reenan pushed his wig back and scratched his head. Rebellion, he wondered? Could that be what's behind all this? Like all officials, he did not like to take unnecessary risks.

'Bring Cornelius here. I'll give him ten minutes.'

The sergeant disappeared.

Presently, Cornelius was shown into the office. He looked disappointed. 'Mynheer Reenan?' he said. 'I thought I was to see Fiscal Berg.'

'You're seeing me.'

'That's all right by me, mynheer Reenan.' You could not help being attracted by his friendliness.

'You've got information about Henning?'

'Too right, mynheer Reenan. You don't by any chance have a drink, do you?'

'No.'

'Oh. Well, if you don't mind—' He produced his own flask.

'You've got ten minutes,' said Reenan.

'Can I sit down?' Reenan indicated a chair. Cornelius noticed Malan, pen poised, for the first time. 'Is he going to write down what I say?'

'Every word.'

'I don't think he's old enough to hear what I've got to tell you—'

'He's old enough. Now talk.'

'All right, mynheer Reenan. First of all we've got to fix a price. Fifty rixdollars, how's that?'

'Get out.'

'No, wait a moment, mynheer Reenan. Listen, we're businessmen, we can talk a price.'

'Ten if the information's any use to me. Otherwise nothing.'

'It'll be of use to you. Fifteen?'

'Ten.'

'All right, mynheer Reenan, but this is the last time I'm giving you information.'

'Good.'

'Fifteen?' Cornelius asked hopefully.

'Ten.'

'I've half a mind to get up and go.'

'Get up and go.'

'All right, mynheer Reenan. Ten.'

'What's the information?'

'In the first place, did you know that I was aboard the same ship that brought the Reverend Johannes Henning from Rotterdam to the Cape of Good Hope?'

'Oh?'

'I thought you'd be interested. Fifteen? All right, all right, mynheer Reenan, we fixed a price. I'm a gentleman. I'll stand by it. Yes. The *Zuylen* under the command of Captain Frischlin, a German, but a good sailor.

'So. There were a lot of passengers, me and my wife and of course, the Hennings. Have you met that wife of his? Mynheer Reenan, I'm telling you, she could sink a man o' war with a look. The time I'm talking of must be after six or seven weeks at sea. We'd left in winter and now it was raining heat, no wind, terrible. You can imagine, after that length of time, everybody hates each other, you all lie about the deck, you haven't got the energy to lift a hand—unless there's a glass in it, hey?' He gulped from his flask, and chuckled. 'Well, this fellow Henning, of course he conducted services on the foredeck and so on, but he kept to himself. Sometimes he'd stand in the full glare of the sun, at *noon*, until there was a puddle of sweat at his feet, I promise you. Always had the Bible in his hand, but he never seemed to read it. That wife of his, she kept to her cabin thank God. Mind you, I liked his daughter, she was very polite. But the son was a little worm, always hanging around the young girls.

'I'm going to tell you the truth now, mynheer Reenan, there wasn't much drink aboard and I was dry. My wife, she'd been ill for weeks. So I can tell you I was pretty low altogether. I tell you, when I swallowed it was like swallowing broken glass, that's how dry I was. But then something happened to cheer us all up. About three o'clock one afternoon, the look-out sighted a longboat on the port bow. With the naked eye, mynheer Reenan, it looked empty but when we drew alongside we saw it contained slaves, four females, four males, manacled in pairs. They didn't look too good, as though they'd been in the boat some time without food and water. I mean, I don't think they even knew we were there. The Captain guessed, just by looking at them, that they were from Guinea so he got hold of one of his sailors who could speak the language to question them. By now, we're all crowded round the boat rails to see what's going on, and I'm telling you it's like a circus.

'They were survivors of a shipwreck. Some slave ship had foundered in a storm and they were the only survivors. You should have heard the arguments: some said they were lying, because how could manacled slaves get hold of a longboat and survive for any time? You won't believe the theories: some said they'd probably murdered the crew and escaped, others that they'd been cast off because they were evil spirits. Half wanted them on board, like me, the other half wanted them left alone.

'But Frischlin, the Captain, he made up his own mind. "I claim these slaves in the name of the Company," he said, and he ordered two ropes to be lowered, side by side, so that the couples could climb on the deck. He wasn't going to risk one of his own men going down to help them. Well, you can imagine, mynheer Reenan, we all cheered and shouted as they began to come up. The first couple managed well, just like apes the way they got up those ropes. But the second, they were a bit older, lost their grip and fell into the sea; they drowned like stones. But the other two pairs got aboard safely. Frischlin ordered them washed and fed—more arguments, of course. Were they going to be taking our food, people asked? Now, the interesting thing is that Henning took no part in this at all, didn't watch or anything. I happened to glance back at one moment and saw him leaning against the mainmast, deep in prayer. That's by the by. The slaves were put into a dungeon and guarded day and night.

'Well, I can't tell you how it cheered us all up. Some of the passengers had never seen savages before, and, man, it was good sport to watch them fed between one and two. Some of the children threw titbits to them. But Henning, each day, he knelt outside the barred door and offered up prayers for their salvation. Some of the passengers didn't like that at all. Still, that's his business, I said. If he wants to pray for them that's his affair.

'Now, look here, mynheer Reenan, I'm coming to a bit of the story in which I was involved, I admit freely, which if you're a church-going man you may find ugly. But it was done in good faith. The sailor in charge of these slaves at night was a fellow called Grosse, another German. He came to me with the suggestion. He said to me, that if I wanted a bit of fun with the female slaves, you understand, he could arrange it. As I said, my wife was ill, and there's only one thing that's second best to drink, am I right? Well, on a couple of nights I went down to the dungeon and took my turn with the females. They were still manacled. Their men didn't mind or anything. We just did it, gave Grosse a few rixdollars and out we came. And these females, they just lay there like sacks, never said a word. It was a bit of fun, no more, no less.

'Then, if one of the females doesn't have to go and die. Too much for her, I suppose. Well, all hell broke loose. This fellow Frischlin, he had funny ideas about slaves. He questioned the crew because he suspected something was up, and then, Goddamn it, the whole story came out. My wife! If she'd have had a bottle she'd have broken it over my head! It wasn't funny. And what about Henning in all this? First, he insists on giving the female a Christian burial. He doesn't know whether she's baptised or not, just wants to give her a Christian end. Well! That caused an uproar. Everyone protested, even my wife. It made us look worse than we were! A slave is one thing, but a Christian's another. In the end, Henning won the day. Only nobody attended the service. Not a soul except the sailors who had to hold the body, the Captain and, of course, Henning. I could hear his voice droning away. "In the name of the Father" etcetera, etcetera. The following Sunday he preached to the full ship's company. God, what a sermon, I could almost feel the flames! He named every one of us who had been down there, and offered up special prayers for us. The embarrassment! My wife stood on my toes all through that service. But then came the climax, mynheer Reenan. Henning stood there and let us have it about slaves, all about our responsibilities and our duties. And he finished up by saying, this is the gospel truth, mynheer Reenan, he finished up by saying that slavery was a wicked abomination in the eyes of the Lord—like the Roman Mass, I think he said—and that if he had his way he would free all the Company slaves. Now, if that's not rebellion, I want to know what is!'

When Cornelius had finished, Reenan stood and wandered over to the window. Outside in the courtyard, he could hear the officials calling to each other as they returned from lunch. A troop of soldiers were drilling disconsolately, and somewhere distant he could hear the solitary violin playing a nervous, hurried tune. It was Cornelius who broke the silence.

'Don't you think that's worth fifteen?' he asked.

Without turning, Reenan said, 'Malan—' The clerk jumped to his feet. 'See this—this gentleman out.'

'How much are you going to give me, mynheer Reenan?'

'Ten.'

Cornelius stiffened to show his disappointment. 'I only hope, mynheer Reenan,' he said, 'that when they make you Fiscal because of this, you'll remember to give me the other five.'

Malan ushered him from the room, paid him as instructed and

then returned to the office. Reenan was again at his desk, reading the last of the statements. Seemingly engrossed, he said, 'Please ask mynheer Bezuidenhout to see me at three o'clock.'

'Yes, mynheer.' Malan turned to go.

'And Malan?'

'Mynheer?'

'After mynheer Bezuidenhout arrives, have the prisoner brought up. We'll both have questions for him.'

2

At the same time as Cornelius was being shown from the Assistant-Fiscal's office, Daniel Henning was clambering up a smooth, marbled-top rock face on Lion's Head. A few yards in front of him, on a narrow ledge, lay his friend Mathias Janssens signalling Daniel to join him, and to do so as quietly as possible.

The two young men had begun their hunt numbed by alcohol fumes; but now the effects were wearing off; with the assistance of the sun and the excess of ale, they were both sweating mercilessly with the result that Daniel found it difficult to gain the footholds, and his hands slipped as he tried to pull himself towards his friend. With his gun strapped to his back, he slowly edged his way upward, pausing after each exertion to regain his breath and to wipe his hands one at a time on his breeches. If he looked over his shoulder, he could see the ocean as if it had been hammered out by a silversmith, for it glittered like plate in the afternoon sun. Only the knowledge that they were closing in on their prey encouraged him to go on.

When he was close enough, Mathias held out a hand and hauled him on to the ledge. There Daniel rested, gulping water from a flask Mathias offered him.

'You make more noise than a whole army,' whispered Mathias.

'Man, I'm dying to piss.'

'Well you can't do it here!'

'I could do it over the ledge.'

'Are you mad? They could hear you pissing in Stellenbosch. Hold it in, for God's sake, man. You'll frighten away every damn thing on the mountain.'

'Any sign?' asked Daniel.

Mathias pointed to a clump of bushes, scrub, some fifty feet below them, blackened by the shadow of the ledge on which they lay.

'Do we go down?' asked Daniel.

'No. We wait.'

Nothing stirred, not even a leaf, for there was no breeze in the sheltered spot. The heat clung to the rocks and Daniel looked longingly towards the inviting sea where, out in the Bay, Robben Island trembled like a spoiled pancake. Beyond, he could see the mountains of Blauwberg Strand, aptly named, for in the haze they glowed bluer than the sea.

Suddenly, Mathias touched Daniel's arm and both men looked down into the shadows: a movement, a flicker in the bushes.

'He's keeping close to the ground,' said Mathias. 'He's crawling through the scrub.'

Daniel slipped the gun from his shoulder, but as he took aim, Mathias restrained him. 'We've got to get closer, don't be in such a hurry. I'll go to the left, you go to the right. I'll flush him out and he'll run your way, so be ready!'

Daniel nodded and moistened his lips. Slowly, his friend eased himself off the ledge, caught hold of an overhanging branch and swung himself to safety, landing on the steep downward slope, and running involuntarily into the shade of a boulder where he crouched for protection.

It was now Daniel's turn. Following the example of his companion, he lowered himself so that his feet dangled above the scrub where their quarry lay hidden. Then, swinging himself back and forth, back and forth, he gathered enough momentum to throw himself sideways and landed in a patch of soft earth, fifteen or so feet from the ledge. He waved to Mathias that he was unhurt and waited for a reply that would be the signal to begin the descent. Darting from the shelter of one rock to another, they began to close in on their quarry until they were no more than ten feet away from the spot where they had seen movement. Again Mathias signalled, this time to indicate that they must be still and wait once more for a sign of life.

Daniel felt better; the fallen rocks protected him from the sun, the pounding in his heart had ceased and he was breathing more easily. He held his gun at the ready and looked to see what Mathias was up to, but became alarmed to discover that he was no longer in view. Had he slipped? Had he fallen asleep? Where the hell was he?

Then he heard the shot to his left, and a frightened cry that came from the scrub which all at once seemed alive with movement.

Daniel swung his gun from one side to another trying to take aim.

'To your right!' cried Mathias from some hidden point.

Daniel spun round, saw a fleeting shape, fired and missed. How quick they are, he thought. He paused to reload while Mathias came running down at full tilt, passed in front of him and followed in the direction of the elusive prey. 'Cut up through the trees!' he shouted to Daniel who set off, finding the going difficult, having once more to fight the steep slope of the mountain.

He found himself in a small copse where the light played tricks: now he saw something move here, now there, thought he heard the snapping of dry twigs, was unnerved by the darkness and the quiet. Should he call to Mathias? Uncertainly, he plodded upwards, the pain in his chest returning, and an awful ache in his groin.

And then, for no reason that he knew, he looked upward, and there, staring down at him, crouching in the crook of a tree, was the quarry, a little wizened Bushman, no more than four feet high, his hair grizzled, his eyes wide with terror. As Daniel gazed up at him, he was aware that the soles of the Bushman's feet were cut and bleeding; it seemed like an eternity before Daniel found the strength to aim and fire. Without a sound, the old man slipped from the tree, plummeted to the ground like a bundle of wood at Daniel's feet, his brains splattered across the tree trunk. Daniel laughed foolishly, and then wet his trousers.

3

'He stinks!' said Reenan, opening the window.

'It's his wet clothes,' Malan explained.

'Take him out and have him washed. Get him something clean to wear.'

The smell was appalling: dampness and putrefaction which clung to the room long after Henning had been taken away by his two guards. Bezuidenhout had arrived some minutes before and did not notice the stench; he was too deeply engrossed in reading Cornelius' statement to notice anything.

Even the soldiers, who were used to foulness of every kind, marched some yards behind the prisoner, prodding him with their guns as they escorted him down the stairs. Henning made every effort to walk steadily, but his knees repeatedly gave way, so that he seemed to be partaking in some strange barbaric dance. The soldiers bustled him into the guard room where, in the corner, they ordered him to undress. This, too, he found difficult, his fingers fumbling with buttons and tapes until the sergeant could stand the irritating delays no longer. Using a small knife, he ripped at seams and stitching until he had torn the clothes off the man, who leaned against the wall, naked, hiding his face.

'It's a good size for a predikant,' said one of the soldiers leading him into an adjoining washroom. His companions crowded at the narrow doorway to watch the washing ceremony.

'The taller you are, the bigger it is,' said the sergeant as they flung cold water over the naked man.

'You know,' said another of the onlookers, 'I always thought a predikant's would be shrivelled up.'

'What are you talking about? Listen, man, in Rotterdam, I knew a predikant had eighteen children. Eighteen! Shrivelled up my foot!'

They handed Henning soap and he washed; then they threw more water to rinse it off. All the while he hid his face in his hands, and turned his back to the men, for he felt degraded at being naked in their presence.

'Give him a blanket,' said the sergeant, 'and let him stand out in the yard to dry.'

The soldiers began to speculate about the predikant's crime, none of them in possession of precise details, but what with the rumours and gossip and the few titbits they had gleaned from the escort who had accompanied the wagon to Cape Town, they knew enough to be intrigued.

'Just look at him! All skin and bone. You wouldn't think he had the strength.'

'These wiry fellows, they're tough.'

'Tough? He was making a pig of himself: three or four of the bitches at the same time!'

'Man, it's impossible. It's got to be one after the other, it can't be at the same time. You can see for yourself it's not forked.'

'All right, one after the other, what difference does it make? All night long, hey? *You* couldn't do it, I'm telling you.'

'With those black bitches? Just give me the chance.'

They dressed him in a pair of breeches and a coarse linen shirt borrowed from one of the men. Wearing shoes, but no stockings, Henning walked more securely now and, for the second time, followed his guards up the low tunnelled staircase that led to the private door of Reenan's office. Even with his breeches unbuckled at the knees, his bare calves white and scraggy, the shirt soaking up the dampness of his body in large, irregular stains, you could not accuse him of looking ridiculous or of lacking dignity; you had to admire the effort he was making to appear austere and formal. The crude bath had refreshed him and, perhaps because of the lack of food, his mind was acutely aware and alert. At intervals, he coughed painfully, although he tensed every muscle to control the discomfort.

The smile returned to Reenan's nervous lips. 'That's nicer, yes? You feel better now, dominee?'

Henning studied the two men who confronted him: both wearing glasses that obscured their eyes; the one hunchbacked and stunted, the other almost featureless.

'I think you know mynheer Bezuidenhout, the political commissioner.'

'He knows me,' said Bezuidenhout curtly.

'This young man is my clerk, Pierre Malan.' Malan stood and bowed formally. 'Won't you sit down, dominee?' Reenan said pleasantly.

'I prefer to stand.'

'We may be some time here.'

'I'll stand, thank you.'

'Write that down, Malan: the prisoner preferred to stand.' Reenan closed the shutters, saying, 'The light hurts my eyes,' and Malan's pen scratched away recording even that.

'Can I have some water?' asked Henning, his voice still hoarse and the cough troublesome.

Reenan glanced round the room. 'There doesn't seem to be any,' he said but without any hint of regret. Slowly he circled the prisoner, while Bezuidenhout clambered up to sit on a chair at the side of the desk.

'How old are you, dominee?' asked Reenan.

'He's forty-four,' answered Bezuidenhout without referring to any notes; he never once took his eyes off the prisoner, and noted how much Henning had aged since their last meeting two years before: his hair was prematurely white.

'What is to happen to me?' Henning asked as if the answer would not concern him.

'I cannot say,' replied Reenan. 'That is a matter for the Fiscal and the Commissioner-General. But there are some questions mynheer Bezuidenhout and I would like to ask—if that's all right by you.' So friendly and gentle.

'Have my wife and children been told?'

'Which wife and children?' asked Bezuidenhout thrusting forward his large head; he reeked of malice.

'They live in Church Square,' Henning answered wearily.

'Ah,' Reenan said, 'I believe it is being dealt with.'

'May I see them?'

'That is a matter for the Fiscal.'

'I trust they will still be looked after. They are blameless in this matter.'

'Yes, yes,' said Bezuidenhout with a flurry of fingers, 'they're being looked after.' He was about to hand the prisoner Sybille's letter, but changed his mind.

'Is there any news from Henningsdorp?'

Reenan did not reply but seated himself at his desk; he brushed imaginary crumbs off the edge. 'Are you sure you wouldn't prefer to sit?' he asked, disconcerted at having to look up to his prisoner; but Henning again refused, preferring to remain upright, although he swayed almost imperceptibly back and forth. 'What am I charged with?' he asked.

'What should you be charged with?' Reenan answered with an innocent, bland look.

So it is to be a game. 'Am I free to go then?' said Henning, but without any suggestion of playfulness; his voice sounded as if he were waking from a deep sleep.

'Let me say at once, dominee, that you are only here to help us with our enquiries into the affair at Henningsdorp. That's all. Any action that may be taken as a result, will only be done so in the light of the report I make. You understand?' This man oozed kindness.

'The landdrost van der Goes said I was to be banished without trial. That is why I am so anxious to see my family.'

'There's time enough for family affairs. You mustn't concern yourself with what the landdrost said. He's an impetuous man. Neither the Commissioner-General nor the Fiscal are obliged to accept his recommendations, you understand? All we want from you is your version of the events. Right?'

'They murdered my people,' Henning said.

'Whatever you say will be put in the report, I promise you,

dominee. I just want you to answer the allegations.'

'I think I would like to sit now.'

With a great show of politeness, Reenan hurried to him and held a chair in which Henning sat with difficulty; Reenan remained standing behind him. 'What . . . what did you say you wanted me to do?' asked Henning, looking anxiously from side to side, not knowing where his questioner was. Reenan tapped him on the shoulder causing the prisoner to jerk round sharply. 'Just answer the allegations,' said Reenan.

'My memory—I'm tired—I don't know if I shall be able to—to recall—' Henning stammered, lost, wanting reassurance.

'I'll help you to remember, dominee. That's what I'm here for: to help.'

Henning muttered his thanks, then without warning began to cry, biting his bottom lip in vain to control his tears which raced down his cheeks. 'They murdered my people,' he said. 'The landdrost murdered my people.'

'Why should he do that?' asked Bezuidenhout, his grating nasal tones disturbing the calm atmosphere Reenan had so carefully manufactured.

Henning shook his head, continuing to sob; but when he was more in control of himself, he said very softly, 'Christ have mercy.'

'Mynheer Reenan, let us begin,' said the dwarf, twisting uncomfortably on the chair and kicking his little legs petulantly.

Reenan, hands clasped behind his back, strolled lazily to the desk and, seated, faced the prisoner. 'Well now,' he said, fidgeting with the documents before him, 'where shall we start?'

'I have the first question,' Bezuidenhout said, his hands folded primly on his lap. 'What were the circumstances that led to your ministry at the Cape of Good Hope?'

BOOK TWO

5

The new arrival

Question: What were the circumstances that led to your ministry at the Cape of Good Hope?

I

These words:

'Of set purpose does Jesus use the expression *to all creatures*—in order to teach us that the Gospel must be brought to everyone who can bear the name of man—to the most ungodly heathen and the most barbaric nations, to the simplest and most ignorant. No exception may be made. Jesus has anticipated all excuses. His Gospel must be proclaimed to every human being, however savage, ignorant, degraded or sinful he be. No one can be too ignorant or too sinful for the Gospel to be offered to him: no one is so virtuous as not to need the Gospel. No man, whatever profession of virtue or innocence he may make, can do without the Gospel: to no man, however guilty and depraved he be, may the Gospel be refused.'

From a collection of sermons preached by a man of whom Henning had never previously heard: the Reverend Helperus Ritzema van Lier, delivered, he read with surprise, at the Cape of Good Hope on 17 May 1789. *To all creatures*.

2

He hungered for a wilderness, he said, for a savage, wild landscape which reduced all men to insignificance; a desert, in which he could hide from the sight of man and covet solitude with God. Was he not entitled to hope, he asked, in all humility that, like Jesus, the devil would leave him and he could lift up his eyes and cry, 'Behold the angels are come and they minister to me'?

The devil, he explained, creates evil in those who permit it. In his own case he licensed the subtle infusion of his soul with doubt, not

of faith, but of doctrine: the contention of knowing and not knowing, the conflict of two opposing rational thoughts: 'He is the God
of Vengeance; He is the God of Love' His spirit, he said, was like the
wasteland he so longed for, the desert in which the mirage of the
universal God was not only the promise of salvation but also the
forbidden fruit.

It is easy, he confessed, to trace this weakness, this admission of
the devil. His father-in-law, a predikant, van Breda, was right: 'You
are ill-suited to the ministry.' Doubt, as in Thomas, produces compassion for the doubts of others. Compassion robs man of absolute
certainty. 'You are a soul made at odds with your fellows, in sympathy with your fellows,' van Breda said. 'That is your Cross.'

The desire to enter God's ministry was not his, but his mother's.
Therein lies the first uncertainty. He would have preferred to work
on the family farm, in Brabant, like his father and grandfather before him. (Even now, at a distance of forty years, he could not bring
to mind his father's face; a presence, perhaps: remote, silent, brooding but formless.) There had been five sons; for each, the mother had
nursed a similar aspiration: to serve God, her God. Johannes was
the youngest, and the only one to survive beyond the age of six. One
so meek could not resist one so wilful. (His mother's image he still
carried in his mind: vivid, powerful, alive; she dominated every re-
membrance of childhood.)

The doubts of youth were suppressed in diligence. 'In my many
years at this University,' said the Professor of Theology, 'no student
has worked more conscientiously, none denied himself more the re-
creations and distractions to which young men are naturally prone.
I only pray that a greater sense of God's endless divinity and omni-
presence should take possession of your soul.' On the day before he
was ordained, his mother died. Grieved, he said, he entered on his
ministry.

In Delft, in the house of the Reverend Nikolas van Breda, the
crisis of maturity swelled and suppurated. The reaction to his
mother's death came late and savagely. The daughter of the house,
Agatha, older than he, heard his cries and sat by his bedside, reading
to him from the Psalms of David—he could not now remember
which. Then, she took him in her arms and lay on his bed, pushing
her breasts to his mouth, as if she meant to crush him with her
being. And so it was.

There is a thin dividing line, he said, between shame and sin.

Ashamed, you may face your Maker but not your fellow man; sin is the banishment of God in the presence of man. Shame was the nature of the young man's experience, and what widened the chasm of doubt was that it surprised him, shocked him to know that he felt no sense of sinfulness. ('If free of sin, then was I free of God, or the idea of God, or the inherited concept of God?')

Marriage overcame self-reproach, but not the entanglement of belief. His first two children caused him to glimpse, momentarily, the miraculous light of creation. Thereafter, the way was dark. He could no longer believe—if ever he did believe—in God's condemnation of man. He could no longer adhere to the doctrine of Divine selectivity. From the pulpit he declared that the Law of God's Love had been perverted by man; he was reprimanded for his leniency. The wandering began.

It was as if he needed proof that God loved his creatures and did not punish the innocent, so that when his third child, a girl, Paulina, was born misshapen he detected in her birth the sign for which he had been praying. 'A punishment for your sins,' said Agatha, 'for your weakness, for failing your Maker.' The accusing looks of the congregation; a monstrous birth concealed a monstrous crime. But, in his eyes, the deformity of the body was as much an abomination as the statues and relics of Rome, for it hid the true nature of the being; the soul of this child was as perfect as any in the sight of its Creator; so let it be with all men; the outward form was a blasphemy that defied Scripture.

Hitherto he had searched for proof; now he searched for corroboration. 'On the love of God, the Redeemer in Christ', he entitled his work, a direct affront to Calvin's 'On the knowledge of God, the Redeemer in Christ'. But it was a frustrating task; the established patterns of thought opposed him: He is the God of fear, of injustice. And then, a kindred spirit: van Lier, preaching a world away, liberated from the confines of the old immovable doctrines. *To all creatures.* To sinners and the Elect alike; to the strong and the weak. Was Calvin not in error to declare that sin perverted the excellent gifts of body and mind enjoyed by all humanity? Were those who did not enjoy those gifts damned?

When the child, the revelation of God's compassion, died, the father was immobilised by grief. In the stupor of bereavement, he lay long hours, alone, his prayers spattered with recriminations and wasted pleas to return the babe into his care. He could not work, and saw no meaning in either his doubts or his faith. But a determination to escape the world he knew and condemned hardened in him; the words of van Lier called. In secret, he wrote to one of the Elders of the Groningen Church, a mynheer Pretorius whose brother, Henning knew, was Secretary to the Council of Seventeen. The Elder was only too willing to be rid of this indifferent predikant; he whispered to his brother in Amsterdam; thus was all arranged.

'Is slavery also an abomination in the eyes of the Lord?' asked the dwarf, Bezuidenhout. The talk of deformity had soured him further and he was more morose than ever.

'The external forms that man applauds or derides are abhorrent in the eyes of the Lord.'

'Does the Lord deride slavery?' the dwarf asked.

'There is no foundation in Scripture that supports the belief that one man is different from another because of the accident of birth.'

'Accident?' repeated Bezuidenhout. 'God determines all things: from the loftiest thoughts of man to the most insignificant drop of rain. There is no such thing as an accident of birth.'

Henning narrowed his eyes, as if trying to pierce the ugliness of his questioner. 'Are you condemned,' he asked, 'because of your shape?'

'I am not here to be examined!' cried the dwarf, wriggling in his chair.

'You are not condemned, and nor is any man for the form in which God chooses to house your eternal soul—'

'Do I take it that you are an abolitionist?' asked Reenan, gentle as ever.

'I seek to give each man a truer understanding not of his own nature but of his fellow man's.'

'Who are you to seek to give man anything?' cried Bezuidenhout. 'You mock the forms and ceremonies of our Church. I suppose the sacrament of baptism is an abomination in the eyes of the Lord, too?'

'Why do you say that?' asked Henning, leaning forward unsteadily.

'I think mynheer Bezuidenhout is referring to an incident at sea—'

'Do you admit to giving Christian burial to one who was not baptised?' asked the dwarf.

70

'I admit to giving Christian burial at sea.'

'But was the creature whose body you committed to the deep a female slave?'

'She was.'

'And was she baptised?'

'She was!'

'How do you know?' demanded Bezuidenhout.

'*I* baptised her!' answered Henning. 'Each day, I visited the poor people in their cell and read to them from Scripture. At first they took no notice of me, for you must understand that I could not speak their language, nor they mine. But after a few days, one of the couples—they were manacled in pairs—seemed in some strange way to understand what I was doing; together they raised their conjoined hands and sweetly crossed themselves in unison. Never have I seen an act of faith attain such beauty; I wept. Thereafter, the others followed suit. I beckoned them to come as close to the bars as they could, then I made the Sign of the Cross upon their foreheads and baptised them all in the name of Christ Jesus.'

'You see? You see?' said Bezuidenhout. 'You just baptised them, just like that! It is a mockery of the sacrament! You did not ascertain whether they understood the precepts of the faith, or whether or not it was their wish to be baptised!' He could barely articulate.

'I took their own signal to be a profession of faith.'

'If that is so,' continued the dwarf, 'then why did you baptise them? If you believed they were already Christian why did you defile the Sacrament by administering it unnecessarily?'

'No sacrament is defiled if administered with true intentions. It was the only way to demonstrate that Christ was present in the cell with them, chained and suffering.'

'But the sacrament was improperly given. There was no immersion, was there?'

'I used spittle on my thumb.'

'A perversion!'

Reenan asked, 'Why did you not tell anyone of this so-called baptism?'

'Yes,' said Bezuidenhout, 'is it your custom to conduct your pastoral duties in secret like a thief in the night?'

'I told Captain Frischlin. But he insisted I remain silent on the matter since he had already claimed the slaves in the name of the Company. And, as you well know, it is forbidden to claim Christians in this manner. I said I would bide my time until we reached the Cape. But I became aware that the very act of baptism was not only a confession of faith before men but also an affirmation of the law of God's love that all souls are, in that moment, free of sin and created in bliss. Then, when one of the women died, it was learned that her body had been desecrated and misused. It was my duty to give her Christian burial.'

'I will take this matter up with the Classis in Amsterdam,' said Bezuidenhout. 'You are in direct contravention of their ordinances in these matters—'

Henning interrupted. 'Baptism is a weapon that dissolves all men's shackles—'

'A weapon? Are you thinking of waging war?' asked Reenan, smiling ingenuously.

'I war only against the enslavement of the soul.'

'The man's an abolitionist!' said Bezuidenhout. 'An admitted disciple of van Lier! I warned against van Lier. No one would listen to me. I said he was a danger. I said he would attract interfering do-gooders!'

'Are you an abolitionist?' asked Reenan again.

'I do not believe that one man, in the eyes of God, has the right to own another.'

'But you joined the Company's service,' continued Reenan, 'knowing that it owned vast numbers of slaves. Did you intend joining to overthrow the established order?'

'I intended to act in accordance with my conscience which I had informed with the love of God.'

'Your arrogance,' said Bezuidenhout, 'is out of place here!'

'Dominee,' said Reenan, his fingers tracing patterns on the desk, 'you were not one of the men who misused the female slave, were you?'

'I forgive you that question.'

'Don't you come the high-and-mighty with us!' cried the dwarf. 'We are here to ascertain the truth and I put nothing past you, so just answer the questions.'

'I have told you the truth.'

'Very well,' said Reenan. 'You arrived at the Cape in March '92. Please tell us how it came about that you were given a country parish to administer?'

72

Impressions:

The speed of events, the amorphous integration of memory, at times able to distil a single, essential recollection and then losing it once more in the tumble of new sights and sounds and people.

Dawn, and the look-out sighting land: the passengers, some already dressed, others still in their night-clothes, coming up on deck and crowding the port rail, chattering, laughing, looking south-eastwards. But a sudden mist embraces the ship and hovers protectively so that all are prevented from seeing the promised land. The chatter and laughter cease; only the creaking of the ship and the wind in the sails, like giant hands clapping, breaks in upon the silence; no one leaves the deck; they stand and wait. Then, the mist dissolves as abruptly as it materialised, and a great shout goes up as, far on the horizon, the diadem of mountains springs out of the sea.

Now the joy, the handshakes, the kissing, all past disagreements forgotten, all the irritations and distress of three months imprisonment at sea disappears. 'Give thanks, dominee,' someone cries and an old man overcome with emotion asks, 'Isn't that the most beautiful thing you've ever seen?' And the little boy asking, 'I can't see a lion's head, which mountain is the Lion's Head?'

A great circle of dancers, Daniel and Sybille among them, whooping and singing and whirling round and round the mainmast, hands held in brotherhood. And Henning, breaking through the circle, calling for silence which comes reluctantly. He falls on his knees and the others follow.

'Almighty and everloving God, forasmuch as it hath pleased Thee to bring us safely to our destination, we raise our voices and give joyous thanks with all our hearts for Thy great mercy. We dedicate ourselves to Thy service, to do Thy work in this our new land. And so we say with the Psalmist: "I am well pleased: that the Lord hath heard the voice of my prayer; That he hath inclined His ear unto me: therefore will I call upon him as long as I live." Through Jesus Christ, Thy Son, Our Lord, Amen.'

The quayside: searching strange faces, the anxiety of not knowing what to do or where to go, collecting trunks and chests, the distraction of brief farewells. 'Is no one here to meet us?' Two slaves, Ganymede and Mars, recognise the white clerical tabs at Henning's neck.

'You are the Reverend Henning? We got to take you to your house on orders of mynheer Bezuidenhout. Please follow.'

The relief, and with it renewed excitement. And Daniel and Sybille's laughter at the accents and comic slang the slaves use, here and there a word of Dutch, barely understandable. Agatha restrains them with a look, but temporarily, for they continue to giggle in secret.

Husband and wife, saying little, but wanting to share the pleasure of journey's end, unable, by nature, to share anything except the distance that separates them. The ride in the open carriage up the Heeregeracht punctuated by the children pointing, gasping, questioning from one end of the town to the other. At last, Church Square and the place where they will live. More prayers, asking God's blessing on their new home.

'Reverend Henning, tomorrow morning, nine hours, mynheer Bezuidenhout he wants to see you. That's his offices over there, just across the Square.'

'Who's mynheer Bezuidenhout?'

Ganymede pulls his ear lobe. 'I don't know for sure, but he's a big man for these parts, that's certain!' The slaves laugh, nudging each other. Henning gives them a rixdollar each and thanks them. They look puzzled but whether because of the money or the thanks is not clear; he is made to feel clumsy.

'Let's not unpack!' cries Sybille. 'Let's go out and walk, please, mother, let's just walk about before we do anything at all!' Daniel joins in; Agatha says, 'It's not up to me,' but although she sounds stern the children know her moods well enough to see that she is amenable.

'Will you come, dominee?' she asks her husband.

And so the first day is spent gathering these impressions: the friendliness of the inhabitants who bow to the newcomers as if they are old friends; the shabbiness of the buildings and the unswept streets; the high price of food and goods in the shops, on the market stalls; the number and variety of colour and shape of the slaves; the imposing mountains; the sea; the heat; and Henning's profound conviction that their new country has somehow bonded them together as a family for the first time in many a year, and full of expectancy and hope, he falls asleep, content, filled with anticipation for the morrow when he will meet the man who said the words *to all creatures*.

Morning, and the pace accelerates.

'Welcome, dear dominee, welcome. My name's Bezuidenhout—big name for a little chap.'

Pleasantries: the voyage, the arrival, the house; questions of health and of climate—

'I should like to meet dominee van Lier.'

'He is expecting you. But I thought we'd take this opportunity of becoming acquainted.'

Becoming acquainted means to Bezuidenhout sounding a warning: 'Remember this, dominee, whatever van Lier says. The colonists come first. You are going to be sent up-country where some of the people haven't had their children baptised. They travel for weeks just to attend the Lord's Supper at the nearest church. These are the important things: bring God to the people in the hinterland, instruct the children and conduct services. That's Company policy. The Kaffirs will have to wait. I warned van Lier, and he knows where we stand. So I'm just giving you some advice. This new missionary spirit that he talks about is not on my list of priorities.'

'God will guide me.'

'That's one way of looking at it. The savages are lazy and indolent. You don't know them as I do, dominee. They're happiest with a bottle of brandy and a good kick up the backside to make them work. They'll say amen to any prayer you care to utter; the next minute they'll be off dancing round the fire calling to the spirits of their ancestors. Our religion is our religion; they have their own gods, and they are happy that way. We have been chosen by the Lord to civilise this land, not they, because they couldn't do it if they tried. *We* have been chosen, that's all I say.'

'I keep an open mind.'

'That's it. Keep an open mind. But remember, what I am telling you is official Company policy. Where would it stop if we baptised the slaves? We'd have no slaves, and if we had no slaves we couldn't do God's work here! Remember: "Render unto Caesar" etcetera, etcetera!'

'I'll remember.'

'And now, van Lier.'

And now, the surprise: a boy, twenty-seven years old, short, round-faced, ghostly pale, bulging eyes, dark curly hair. Restless, as if pursued by unseen demons. His study littered with books and papers, on the chairs, on the window-sills, even on the floor. Henning's heart stops in the presence of such will and energy in a being that because of its constant movement appears to lack substance, like a will o' the wisp, flitting from thought to thought, driven by urgency, as if time was short. A man of passion, concludes Henning, and intimidating.

Van Lier's career has been meteoric : before the age of eighteen he had written and defended a dissertation which earned him the degree Master of Free Sciences and Doctor of Philosophy. Twenty-two years old on arrival at the Cape; a gold medal from the Hague Society of the Defence of Christianity for writing *The Importance of Religion for the Common Man*.

Bewildering. Henning stammers some details of his past. Van Lier seizes them like a tornado and tosses them aside, implanting himself in their place.

'Yes, yes, I, too, became a clergyman in deference to my parents' wishes. After I was ordained my spirit plummeted. Just like yours. My heart was filled with pride, self-righteousness and impure thoughts. But God's ways are not our ways. A death too brought conversion to me—the young lady to whom I was affianced. When she died I asked God to grant me a sudden death, too, so that I might follow her to the grave. At that very moment, it pleased the Lord to reveal himself to me. I saw, as clearly as though it were written before my eyes in letters of fire, that an unconditional obedience to God's commands must, in the future, be the law of my life.' All spoken so rapidly that Henning cannot keep pace, and spoken, too, with such feeling that the man seems to be reliving the agony.

Henning tries to tell van Lier of what the younger man has meant in his life—the sermon—the words, 'to all—'

'Yes, we must marshal our energies. There is stern opposition to my teachings, but is it not àlways the way when the truth is spoken ? We are not here by Divine Right, dominee, believe me. We are here for one purpose and one purpose only : to spread the Word of God to all men. It is the sin of pride to believe that only we are chosen to inherit the Kingdom. Take this thought to give you courage and strength, to help you endure the many cares and disappointments which are inseparable from an enterprise such as this : the great importance of the glory of God, of the extension of the Kingdom of Jesus, and of the salvation of so many thousands who are aliens from the commonwealth of Israel may be brought nigh by the blood and Spirit of our Saviour. God go with you, dominee, and pray to Him that we may meet again.'

'But where am I to work?'

Van Lier stops, looks astonished. 'Have you not been told?'

Words, maps, instructions follow in a torrent. A farmer, Le Roux, departs in two days by wagon for a place called Blauwzand. Be in Hottentot Square at dawn. Your wife and family are to remain here until you judge the time right for them to join you. 'It is an adventure into the Kingdom of Heaven on earth. Let Jesus be your guide.' Van Lier leads him to the door, more words, words, words. And Henning stands once again in Church Square, in the shadow of the Groote Kerk, clutching documents that tell him he is to minister to a parish two weeks' ride away, and letters of introduction: one to mynheer Le Roux, whose wagon will carry him north; the other, confirming his appointment, to Abraham van der Goes, the landdrost of Blauwzand.

6

The welcome

Extract from the statement made by the landdrost, Abraham van der Goes: 'We welcomed this predikant, this degenerate Henning, with open arms.'

I

Now he had to travel across the barrier of mountains which imprisons the town, escape the suffocating confines of busy lives, and burst out into the vast limitless sweep of country that lies beyond. (Why, he wondered, did men ever think there was a land beyond those mountains in the first place? What feats of imagination led them to believe that the Creation was not bound by the evidence of sight? There, if you like, was an act of faith.)

At dawn the wagons, drawn by ponderous oxen, depart from Cape Town, wending their way along the rough uneven roads that lead you to yet another barrier, another mountain range, the Hottentot's Holland which greets you first with an outcrop of gentle, seductive hills. The sun glowers from behind the taller distant peaks which, in silhouette, are black and forbidding, but just when you think there is no way through, the mountains suddenly part and you glimpse for the first time the great open plain they have been guarding; drawn by the oxen, you come upon it sluggishly; little by little, you are aware of a new measure of distance, until you can hardly breathe in the knowledge of such infinite space. Here there are streams of muddy yellow and rocks sheltering amidst the olive-green bushes and trees. All around you the mountains fall away in echoing curves, like gigantic petrified ripples and, as the sun rises higher, the landscape seems to blush a deep, unhealthy purple. For the first week of the journey, as the wagon crawls north-eastwards, the vista is unchanging and you may feel you have stumbled upon a world that, as you clap eyes on it, has just that moment been created. (Nowhere, he said, had he ever experienced a greater sense of the magnificence of God's creation, or the insignificance of his own place within it.)

His guide's name was Johannes Le Roux, a craggy-faced farmer who had recently gone bankrupt and now worked for the landdrost. Ordinarily, he did not speak much, but the coincidence that he and the predikant both had the same Christian name was a continuing source of wonder to him; at the beginning, hardly a day went by without his mentioning it.

'Were there other Johanneses in your family, then, dominee?'

'My grandfather was called Johannes.'

'No! But so was mine! My father, too, was called Johannes. My father, my grandfather, my great-grandfather and I don't know any further back than that. But who's to say they weren't all called Johannes, hey?'

Or: 'Johannes! Well I never! Agh, dominee, I can't get over it! Dominee, if you don't mind my saying so, I've never met a Johannes I haven't liked!' And so on. There was a further bond between them: they were both the same age in years, forty-three, although Le Roux was disappointed to learn that Henning was born in March while he had come into the world in October. 'Wouldn't it have been something if we'd both been born on the same day, hey, domi- nee? Now, that really would have been something, hey?'

At night, they camped wherever the fancy took them, but usually they tried to find a stream in which they could bathe. Le Roux in- sisted on a reading from Scripture before he slept so that each night when they lay down to sleep, tightly wrapped in their blankets, the fire dying, Le Roux would say, 'Well, dominee, I know we had the Book of Jonah last night, and the night before that come to think of it, but it's my favourite in the Holy Bible, so you wouldn't mind, please, reading it once more. I can't read, you see, dominee, and this'll be my best chance of hearing Jonah as often as I can. Just one chapter, hey?'

' "Now the word of the Lord came unto Jonah the son of Amittai, saying, Arise, go to Nineveh, that great city, and cry against it; for their wickedness is come before me." ' It took four successive nights to complete the book, and then Henning, to oblige his companion, would start all over again, wriggling forward to catch the last light of the fire. And if he made a mistake—

'And the Lord spake unto the flesh—'

'Unto the fish, dominee, unto the *fish*!'

'And the Lord spake unto the fish and it vomited out Jonah upon the dry land. Amen.'

'Amen. Chapter Three tomorrow, dominee? Good. I like him to be out on the dry land.'

And so, after a brief benediction, they would settle down to sleep, Le Roux snoring gently almost at once, and Henning gazing at the bright, crisp stars, feeling the icy wind of the veldt on his face. He experienced a contentment he had never known before; he was ready, he said, for the task to which he had been chosen. This solemn awareness that he had been specially prepared was constantly with him, and he faced the future with unaccustomed confidence. He understood better than he had ever done the oneness of God and man, and the Creation, bound by mutual love. At peace, he slept.

After a week, the panoply of broad valleys and plains unfold, and you have the feeling you are travelling along the base of a monstrous bowl, rimmed on all sides by the distant mountains. The colours, so harsh after what you have been used to in Europe, blend and transform themselves into the dull orange of the hills, the red clay of the earth and the khaki green of the scrub, a harmony you had not thought possible or pleasing, and yet now you cannot deny its beauty. (He felt what he had longed to feel, he said: lost and humble.)

It pleased Henning that he saw no sign of human life. At night, you could hear the cries of wild animals, and in the morning, the screeching of carrion birds, but of man, there was no evidence. His companion, he said, did not detract from the gift of such intense solitude.

On the second Sunday of their journey, after a break for a short service of prayer, they came at noon to the crown of a hill and saw in the compact valley below a small village, no more than a dozen buildings, shining white in the sun.

'That's Blauwzand,' said Le Roux. 'You see the large house on the rising ground beyond? That's van der Goes's place. We'll be there before nightfall.'

They did not pause for lunch. Henning, excited at the prospect of another journey done, took the reins and did his best to spur on the phlegmatic oxen, but they would not be hurried. Le Roux retired into the back of the wagon, and rested in the shade of the canvas canopy. He was just falling off to sleep when Henning shook him violently.

'Johannes, look!' cried Henning, agitated.

Le Roux peered over the predikant's shoulder: a horseman was riding towards them from the adjoining hill to the east, not from the town. As he drew nearer, they could see a gun nestling in the crook of his arm.

'Who is he? Do you know him?' asked Henning.

Le Roux said nothing, just watched the approaching rider. Presently, they could distinguish the features of a broad-faced man, with an impressive black beard shaped like a spade; he was no more than thirty and Henning had the impression of enormous strength.

'Pull up here, dominee,' barked Le Roux, tugging at the reins to assist Henning who was at once aware that his companion was trembling. By then, the rider had drawn level and, without a word, guided his horse to the rear of the wagon while he peered inside under the flap.

'It's all right, van Haarten,' called Le Roux in a reassuring singsong. 'Only food and supplies. No soldiers, nothing to worry about.'

Van Haarten trotted round to the front. 'Who's this?' he asked, with a jerk of the gun towards Henning.

'The new predikant, the Reverend Johannes Henning,' said Le Roux, trying to sound cheerful. 'We've got the same name. Johannes—'

Van Haarten closed one eye and regarded the predikant with the other. 'I haven't heard about any new predikant,' he said.

'Show him your letter, dominee, your letter to the landdrost.'

'Who is this man?' asked Henning.

'Never mind, just show him the letter, just to prove your identity, nothing more.'

But Henning resisted. 'He can see I'm a predikant,' he said.

Van Haarten eased the horse closer. He said, 'Just because you wear two white tabs at your neck doesn't make you a predikant. Show me the letter.'

'It's addressed to the landdrost,' Henning protested. 'And it's sealed.'

'Unseal it, then, and hand it to me slowly.' Henning hesitated but Le Roux nodded encouragingly, saying, 'Go on, dominee, please.'

Trying to show his reluctance at what he was doing, Henning slapped the letter, breaking the seal; then he handed it to van Haarten who asked, 'It's signed by van Lier, is it? Are you a van Lier man, then?'

81

Henning did not understand the question but Le Roux answered for him, 'Yes, yes, he's a van Lier man all right!'

'Shut up, Le Roux, he can answer for himself. Are you a van Lier man, I'm asking you again?'

'He has appointed me to this place.'

Van Haarten stared hard at Henning as if trying to assess his worth; then he tossed the letter into his lap, dug his heels into his horse and galloped off, back the way he had come, towards the adjacent hilltop.

Before Henning had time to ask any questions, Le Roux said, 'Nothing to worry about, dominee. He's quite harmless.'

'But who is he?'

'One of the renegades.'

'What d'you mean renegades?' demanded Henning, flicking the reins; the wagon rumbled forward once more.

'Just what I say.'

'Johannes,' said Henning, 'I want to know who that man is and why you were so frightened of him.'

'Me, frightened? Of van Haarten?'

'You were trembling.'

'Agh, dominee, forget it.'

But Henning persisted. 'You tell me who he is, Johannes, or else you get off the wagon and you walk.'

'Dominee, there's a whole settlement of them. About five days ride away to the north'—he pointed—'over the furthest hills at the back of the town.'

'A settlement? What kind of settlement?'

'Look, it's like this. Three years ago, maybe four, there was an argument with van der Goes. A dozen young farmers there were, hotheads, refusing to pay their taxes to the landdrost, you understand? So, what did they do? Just moved off, found themselves some good land to the north and settled there. They warned van der Goes that if he tried to collect, he'd end up with a bullet in his head. There was a lot of talk about rebellion and sending for soldiers from Cape Town, but nothing came of it. The landdrost preferred to let them carry on in their own way, don't ask me why. Now, they guard this road night and day, just in case van der Goes gets any ideas and changes his mind, you get my meaning? So everyone is stopped, wagons searched, just in case they've got soldiers hidden in the back or something.'

'But the landdrost has soldiers, hasn't he?'

'Hottentots, that's all, no match for van Haarten and his friends.'

The information troubled Henning; the idea of such blatant law-lessness was new to him and made him uneasy. 'But—but it's armed rebellion against the Company,' he said.

'Dominee, call it what you like. They don't do anybody any harm those fellows. Just don't pay their taxes, that's all.'

'But if it's as easy as that, why don't the rest of you join them and also stop paying your taxes.'

'What, and risk eternal fire?' Le Roux answered, genuinely shocked. 'Van der Goes laid it on the line. He's an educated man, the landdrost. Anyone who joins them lives out of the sight of God, he said. Three of them came back when they heard that. Van Haarten and the others stayed. Well, no wives, no family to think about, only themselves. Oh no, dominee, you can't risk a thing like eternal damnation. Look, if it wasn't for taxes I'd still have my own farm, so don't think I wouldn't have liked to join them because I would. But I'm strong in the Lord, I'm no antichrist. They've brought dam-nation on themsleves and there's not many of us who'd do the same.'

No more was said. Henning looked back towards the nearby hill where he saw the dark shape of van Haarten astride his horse, gaz-ing down on the winding track, guarding the approach from the south, and without knowing why, Henning prayed for him and the others and beseeched God to send them comfort.

2

They arrived in the fading light of afternoon. Blauwzand was not really a town or a village, but a haphazard collection of houses, a general store and an unfinished church lacking a roof. Behind the central cluster of buildings lived the slaves, all Khoikhoi, Hottentots, in huts and shacks of every mean description, which in turn were surrounded by a high wooden fence and a gate opened at dawn and locked at dusk. The only grand house, perfect in its gabled sym-metry, stood opposite the church; it belonged to van der Goes, and bore the date, 1784, above the front door. Word of Henning's ap-proach soon spread among the inhabitants and by the time the wagon had come to a halt by the church a crowd of forty or so gathered at the doors to greet him.

They welcomed him in silence, he said. Like statues, they stood, men and women with hard ageing faces, their children beside them, subdued and cowed by the occasion like the slaves, who stood apart, heads bowed, a gesture not of reverence but of tacit disapproval. It was a dark and sombre scene; the townspeople favoured blacks and browns and greys for their shawls and bonnets and tall hats; the sun was sinking fast and soon it would be night. The only splash of colour (and, because of his size, it was a large splash of colour) was provided by van der Goes, who came down the steps of his house clothed in a gaudy red velvet coat, edged in gold braid which gave him a military look. But when he drew close, Henning saw that the velvet was shiny and badly worn, and the gold braid tarnished.

In silence then, Henning descended from the wagon and, prompted by Le Roux, presented his letter of appointment to the landdrost who saw that the seal was broken, raised enquiring bushy eyebrows, received a nod of confirmation from Le Roux and then peered at the letter. It was evident that he knew who had read its contents before him.

'My friends,' van der Goes said at last in a booming voice. 'Let us give thanks to Almighty God for bringing safely to us Johannes Henning, His servant, who has come to minister among us. Until now, we have been without a true guide and if we have survived it is all thanks to the Almighty and to no one else.' He paused, turning to Henning. 'Dominee, we welcome you here to this place, where we have tamed the Hottentots, made our homes, and planted seeds in the earth and watched them grow. We know you are weary after your long journey, but we sincerely beg you to enter your church—' He glanced at Le Roux at that moment and in a more conversational tone, said, 'We must finish the roof,' and continued as before, 'Enter your church and conduct for us the Nagtmaal, so that we may have, for the first time in many a year, Communion with Our Lord and Saviour, Jesus Christ.'

Henning clasped his hands and rested his forehead upon them; he prayed for strength. A woman's voice rang out, singing the words of a hymn, 'The Servants of the Lord Stand on High'. One by one, the others joined in, van der Goes loudest of all, and tuneless. Some movement caused Henning to look up and, when he did so, he saw the Khoikhoi slaves dispersing without being told, and wandering aimlessly back towards their compound; he watched them disappear into the shadows; it was already night.

The hymn seemed endless but at last they voiced a full-blooded amen and Henning entered the unroofed church. There, open to the stars and a baleful moon, he conducted the Communion service, the Nagtmaal. (Was it fatigue or genuine emotion that made him feel he had, at last, found a home?) Consecrating the bread and the wine, he invoked the sacred communion of Christ's flesh and blood, transfusing life into the believers, uniting by the Spirit things which are separated in space, truly presenting His body and blood through these symbols. (Again, for the first time, he understood that, in the mystery of the Supper, a real participation of Him is enjoyed.)

For his sermon he took the text from Galatians, Chapter 5: 'Stand fast therefore in the liberty wherewith Christ hath made us free, and be not entangled again with the yoke of bondage.' His congregation, standing before him, took his words to mean that freedom of sin was synonymous with the independence of the spirit in which they all prided themselves—two of the older men thought he was pleading for less Government interference, a sentiment with which they heartily agreed. But Henning was preaching in his heart to the Khoikhoi, locked up in their compound behind the tall wooden gate and, unaccountably, to the man with the spade beard who had been told he was living outside the love of God. Be not entangled with the yoke of bondage. And, in the moment of silent prayer which followed the sermon, he earnestly dedicated himself to his mission. Then he blessed the congregation, beseeching the Lord to lift up His countenance upon them to give them peace.

Thus began his ministry.

'But the next day,' said Bezuidenhout, 'you did not go out and preach to the slaves. Or the next day. Or the next. Why not?'

'You are right to chastise me,' said Henning.

'I am not chastising you!' replied the dwarf angrily. 'I want to know what happened to your noble feelings,' he added, and looked at Reenan for approval.

'They were eaten by weakness.'

'So you openly disobeyed the instructions of your superior, the dominee van Lier, is that right?' asked the dwarf.

Henning did not reply. Reenan, sinewy and insinuating, said, 'Isn't it true, dominee, that you learned the lesson the hard way? It was all right for van Lier, wasn't it, to sit in his comfortable office, or stand in his pulpit and spout a lot of high-sounding phrases. Quite another to carry them out, isn't that so?'

'There is action in the expression of ideas,' said Henning. Van Lier, alone of all men, had the courage to bear witness to the love of God. He was Joshua at the walls of Jericho, but to his trumpet call the walls did not crumble. He beat his head against the stones, and he bled.

'And in your own case, dominee,' said Reenan, 'why did you abandon your fervour for the conversion to Christ of "all his creatures"?'

'Why? Because I ceased to see them. Because I had turned my back on Jericho.'

3

There is a virulent disease that is contagious in the Cape. Few escape the infection; those who do are the ones who leave before it is too late, or are made to leave, or are of such strength that they are immune—and they are not many. It is called the sickness of the blind eye. It is an insidious illness, for there are no symptoms, no pain, no fever. It is a creeping paralysis of the spirit, which, once attacked, seems to bask in its own inertia. There is no cure, except the conscious will, and that can be hard to come by.

At first, Henning explained, he was distracted by activity. Everything had to be done afresh, he told his questioners, from top to bottom. Elders and deacons had to be found; no point in holding an election, for only those who were literate were eligible, and those who were literate were few. On the first morning he baptised more than a score of children, some already two and three years old; that same afternoon he conducted two marriage services, and in the evening intoned prayers at the gravesides of four late inhabitants who had not enjoyed the blessing of an ordained predikant at their interment; one of the graves contained van der Goes's wife, Petronella.

There was a school to be organised—he gave lessons in Latin, Arithmetic and Scripture twice a week; on Saturdays, stripped to the waist, he climbed to the exposed beams of the Church and helped the men at work on the roof—the slaves were not permitted to assist in the building of the church. (He had never worked so hard, he said, or had less time to concern himself with his own inadequacies.)

Johannes Le Roux took a proprietary interest in Johannes Henning, acting as his guide and mentor, easing the newcomer into the settled ways of the population who were austere and stern. The

harshness of the land stamped its mark upon them; their faces reflected the barrenness of the landscape. They lived, most of them, on
their farms scattered in a twenty-mile radius from the town. Everyone seemed to be related to everyone else, and the land which, they
said, until their arrival belonged to no man, sprawled over great
distances, like monstrous patriarchal estates. Because the journey
was too long for many of them to make to Blauwzand, the predikant was obliged to visit each of the farms in turn. There he would
conduct the Nagtmaal in the presence of the farmer, his family and
as many of their neighbours as could attend. He would act as judge
and counsellor, for the people were quarrelsome and petty and expected from him Divine Justice. (Strange, he reflected, that with so
much land they would still dispute their boundaries.)

It seemed to him that the further from the town he travelled, the
fiercer the people of his parish. In one farm he found two Khoikhoi
slaves being starved to death as punishment. Their master reluctantly agreed to feed them at the insistence of the predikant, but
when they had eaten, both slaves suffered convulsions and died. The
farmer pointed to heaven. 'God is just,' he said, and later, 'We did
not come this far, dominee, to be told how to treat our slaves.'

On a neighbouring farm, he found the bodies of an aged couple
who had been dead for many weeks, their slaves fled into the hills;
on a third, a widowed farmer had not talked to another human being for more than a year and when he saw the predikant approach,
he hid in the house and many hours passed before he was persuaded
to come out; and when he did, he would not talk—or could not.

After Henning returned from his first visit to the outlying districts, with the help of Le Roux he organised 'The Ministry of
Sons': once a week, the son of a house was obliged to visit the
nearest neighbours who were without children of their own. In this
way he ensured that no one was isolated for a long period of time;
and the people thanked God for sending them a good and sincere
man.

The disease begins to do its work; yes, yes, the activity, the demands
of one half of your congregation, the plea is understandable, but
only as a temporary preoccupation; surely you will turn again to
your proclaimed mission with all your heart and soul and might.
Have you so quickly forgotten the words, 'to all creatures'? Were
the phrases you spoke so freely—'the Law of God's Love has been

perverted by man'—nothing more than grandiloquent self-glorifica-
tion? Had even the memory of Paulina vanished? Or does the sickness of the blind eye prevent you from perceiving the soul in bliss
and compel you to look only at the crippled body? And does it
erode compassion too?

Well, well, you answer, one is bound to feel—uneasy. Each time
you pass the slaves' compound and glance surreptitiously through
the wooden slats and see for yourself the desolation, you feel a
twinge of conscience. A twinge, but no more than that. Of course
you know they work them hard, sometimes seventeen, eighteen
hours a day, and reward them with maggot-ridden food and just
enough brandy to encourage them to work again tomorrow. And if
they do not work, they are punished, beaten with rods until their
bones are broken, or forcibly fed emetics to make them vomit what
little nourishment they have been given.

But look closer at the slaves; peer in through the slats; pause: are
they all as black as you first supposed? Are there not some lighter-
skinned, some who are the colour of dead grass? Ah, but now the
blind eye has you in its grip, like a vice. Even you shudder at this
distortion to nature, are repelled by this unfortunate admixture of
black and white, at this blatant offence to God's image. Yet, you
know as well as anyone how such hybrids come into being. Not
because you yourself partake, oh no, but because you can hear the
weekly ritual of van der Goes's pleasure—after all, you live in his
house and your rooms are adjoining. You know he has girls in there
with him, twelve and younger; children. And not only in the landdrost's home but also in a hundred others the men regard the
Khoikhoi women as objects to relieve their priapism; and so you
know the vile creation continues, the creation of this bi-generous
people who are cursed to spend their lives doing penance for their
fathers' sins.

Does the disease work so speedily? All this in six months?

Ah, but there are particular circumstances; there always are, and
in these, too, the blind eye thrives.

He found himself, Henning said, in an unusual position: for one
who had been accused all his life of serving his congregation indifferently, he was made welcome, more welcome than ever before.
('I think I may say I was respected, God help me.') How easily he rid
his mind of unpleasant thoughts, believing he had discovered contentment in a place of which he convinced himself he was an in-

tegral part. This is the disease at its most pernicious: its power to lull into false security, to provoke the hallucination that the land, like a mother, embraces you, to deceive you into believing that you are the favourite among her sons, and indispensable to her well-being. With lucid tranquillity you realise that there is no other place on earth to which you so readily belong.

His family, too, had receded into the distance. He wrote of his progress once a month and received a reply. That seemed sufficient contact. Agatha was managing as she always managed; Sybille was growing up; Daniel was employed by the Company. He had deposited all three people into pockets of unconcern. It may be said that he was badly infected; it may be said that there was little hope.

'What happened, then, dominee, to disturb your contentment?' asked Reenan gently.

'Certain events overtook me.'

Reenan glanced at the papers before him. 'Do we now come to the statement made by this man Johannes Le Roux?'

'I believe so,' answered the prisoner.

'Very well,' said Reenan, rising. 'We will adjourn for an hour so that you may be fed. We will resume again at nine.'

It was already night; the prisoner was given food by the soldiers in the guardroom. He asked if they could lend him a coat, for a wind from the south-east had risen and was buffeting the Castle walls as though besieging the fortress. He was cold and it pained him to cough. An old jacket was found which was much too large for him; at nine they returned him to his interrogators and the examination began again.

Out in Table Bay the wind whipped the sea into countless white horses, carried dust and dirt across the town, bent double the trees and covered the Table in a cloth of billowing cloud, pale blue in the racing moon.

The questioning continued until dawn; and then there were no more questions to be answered.

89

7

The renegades

Extract from the statement made by Johannes Le Roux: 'They kidnapped him. I missed him. He was my friend, you see.'

It was a simple plan. Henning was quartered in van der Goes's house, and although the landdrost had promised him his own home soon, few slaves could be spared to carry out the work. Van der Goes had needed all the able-bodied men he could lay hands on to combat the Xhosa cattle raids to the east. So he enlisted the Khoikhoi men into a kind of private army and led them on expeditions hoping to search out and punish the raiders who were draining his people of their wealth; for this reason, he was seldom in Blauwzand, leaving Henning to deal with any disputes that might arise. His own Council, the Heemraden, conducted the day-to-day affairs.

Early one bitter cold morning—it was already winter which can be harsh in the veld—Henning was woken from sleep by Le Roux.

'Dominee, urgent matters. A message from the Richter farm: the old man is dying and wants you with him—'

'Slowly, slowly—'

'Old man Richter is dying. He wants prayers. You've got to go at once. It's eight hours' hard ride, dominee.'

Henning tumbled out of bed. 'But I saw old Richter a week ago, he was felling trees. He was as fit as you or me.'

'The slave came with the message, that's all I know. I'm telling you, dominee, it's a morning for messages. The landdrost wants me to take as many Hottentots as I can out to him. He's having real trouble with those Xhosas. They've taken about three hundred head of cattle. So, you're on your own, dominee. Wrap up warm unless you want to be frozen.'

Henning dressed quickly. The landdrost's head slave, Mordecai, who lived in a hut in the yard behind the house, bustled round pre-

90

paring food for the journey, saddling the predikant's horse, and brewing strong coffee. In the dawn shadows he set off, riding hard towards the east and the formation of hills and rocks known as Blauwzand Pass.

For hours he followed the winding river and then, at noon, began the ascent that would take him through the hills to the Richter homestead which lay in the next valley. The going was hard, the horse stumbling on the loose falls of stone, and Henning himself was chilled to the bone. In the end, he dismounted and holding the rein, led the animal upwards through the pass.

'Go no further, dominee!' The voice echoed in the narrow place, overhung with jagged rock.

Startled, Henning looked up, but the pale sun was directly in his eyes and he could see nothing but blurred shapes and shadows.

'Tie your horse to the bush,' came the voice again. 'Now put your hands on your head where I can see them.'

Henning obeyed and waited; he felt no fear, but was strangely intrigued. Then, there was a rattle of stones and running footsteps; he swung round to see two men with their guns trained on him. One, with the black spade beard, he knew; the other was a stranger.

'Good afternoon, dominee,' said van Haarten. 'We've met before. Do you remember me?'

'Yes. I remember you.'

'This is a friend, Christiaan Basson.'

'I order you to let me pass,' said Henning. 'I am on a mission of mercy to a dying man.'

Basson, who was quite young, twenty perhaps, sniggered; he had the face of a mischievous angel and fair hair that was almost white.

'You mean old man Richter?' said van Haarten.

'He is dying and he has sent for me. Let me pass.'

'He's not dying. We sent that message, dominee!'

Henning lowered his hands. 'You? Why?'

Van Haarten seemed embarrassed by the question and glanced everywhere but at Henning. 'You'll see. All right, Chris, get on with it.'

Basson strode up to Henning and said, 'I'm not going to hurt you, dominee, just turn around if you please.'

'What do you want with me?' Henning demanded.

'Please, dominee, just do as I ask. Turn round. I wouldn't harm you for the world.'

The boy was obviously sincere, as if everything he said was spoken with profound reluctance. Henning turned and was, for the first time, frightened. Basson quickly bound the predikant's hands behind his back and then gently tied a kerchief round his eyes. 'Can you see anything, dominee?' the boy asked.

'No.'

'Right,' came van Haarten's voice. 'Now, I'm going to help you climb on your horse, dominee, so take it easy and don't do anything too sudden.'

They gripped Henning by each arm and led him to where the horse was tethered. 'Slowly does it,' said van Haarten.

'I told you we should have let him mount first and then tied him up,' Basson complained.

'Shut up, boy, and think about what you're doing.'

Somehow they managed to get Henning astride the horse, fixing his boots in the stirrup. 'Now hold on as best you can, dominee,' said van Haarten, 'because I'm taking the rein and I'm leading you, all right?'

They set off at a walk. Very soon, Henning lost all sense of time although he tried to feel the sun on his face and guess the hour. At intervals, one or other of the men would say, 'It's a bit steep, now, dominee, lean forward,' or 'We can take this bit at the trot, it's quite flat.' And every so often he would be asked, 'Are you all right, dominee?' or told 'It's not long now.'

Any fear he might previously have felt vanished. Two factors gave him confidence: there was something inept about his captors, and he was convinced that they were well-disposed towards him, their manner gentle and protective.

After what Henning judged to be some hours, he heard van Haarten call loudly, 'First Samuel, Two, thirty-five!' His voice echoed, and from somewhere high up, the answer came 'Pass!' Shortly afterwards, there followed a similar exchange, this time accompanied by what sounded like the moving of a large rock.

Henning puzzled over the reference to Samuel, which he was unable to identify without consulting his Bible. But it renewed his confidence, and amused him, to think that these renegades quoted Scripture as a password.

Soon, they halted. 'All right, dominee,' said van Haarten, 'We're here.'

Again they assisted him, this time to dismount, untied his hands and removed the blindfold. The light hurt his eyes but when he was able to focus he saw that he was in the centre of a small circular compound composed of rough wooden shacks, all within the shadow of a cluster of tall rocks with spikey peaks that formed a natural fortress. Some of the huts had roofs of wattle, reeds and straw, others were protected from the elements by canvas. Yet, there was nothing dingy or decaying about their appearance, for they were brightly painted and decorated with multi-coloured beads entwined round the lintels and windows, and grotesquely beautiful masks above the doors.

Then Henning noticed to his right, before a structure much larger than the others, a group of men, six or seven of them, all bearded like van Haarten, together with perhaps a dozen Khoikhoi women; there was something defiant about their look and the way they stood, so incongruously close together. The moment Henning glanced in their direction, one of the men, older than the others, his beard streaked with grey, stepped forward and raised his arms which was a signal for the group to burst into song, a curiously rhythmic tune, jaunty like a hornpipe, but interlaced with sudden, unexpected stops and Khoikhoi words that gave a wild, barbaric effect. Henning felt obliged to stand still, as though he were listening to a national anthem.

Van Haarten, who was standing just behind the predikant, whispered, 'It's a hymn. Muller composed it in your honour. It's called, "Now is my journey begun." '

'Why have you brought me here?' Henning asked.

But van Haarten did not answer; when the song was done, he said 'Just follow me, please, dominee,' and ushered Henning forward towards the choir. The Khoikhoi women giggled at their approach. (I noticed her at once, he said. She was the only one who did not laugh: a young and slender girl, naked but for a leather thong tied round her loins, her hair close-curled, her figure boyish, her breasts new-born, and her eyes huge like twin moons.)

Van Haarten indicated the conductor. 'This is Japie Muller,' he said. Muller had twinkling eyes, and when he removed his hat revealed a bald head; he was possessed, too, of broad, muscular shoulders. Further introductions followed—Joubert, Nel, Kruger—he could not catch them all. 'And these are our women.' Again, van Haarten rattled off a list of names, but full of clicking sounds, impossible to reproduce. One, however, he thought was called Afrika, and he listened especially hard for the name of the girl who had caught his attention but it was too difficult for him to remember.

'I want to know the reason for bringing me here,' said Henning.

Van Haarten pointed to the hut behind the group. 'That's the reason,' he said.

'This?'

'Make way for the predikant,' said Muller, his eyes dancing with pleasure and anticipation. The choir parted, making an aisle for Henning. 'Is this a trick or some sort of joke?' he asked.

'See for yourself,' replied van Haarten gruffly, and led the way, pushing open the wattle door. 'And take your hat off,' he said. 'It's a church.'

Even the ungodly know when they are in a holy place, Henning said (gazing coldly at his interrogators). The walls inside were painted white, the floor covered in rush matting, and furthest from the door stood the Lord's Table made from the wood of Cape beech trees. The lectern was a raised dais adorned by an eagle, savagely carved, to hold the Bible. But it was the light that abetted the impression of sanctity, a dull scarlet glow that filtered through the small square windows; and somewhere in the roof, a shaft of the sun's rays found a weakness and pierced a narrow, unintended opening, touching in a pale glow the plain wooden Table.

'We built it bigger than our homes,' explained van Haarten, 'out of respect.'

'Well, dominee?' asked Muller, full of expectation. 'What do you think? I carved the eagle out of one piece of wood, you know.'

'What do you want with me?' Henning said quietly, as if it pained him to speak.

'We want you,' said van Haarten, 'to consecrate this church.'

For some time, Henning barely moved, but closed his eyes and covered his face with his hands; he could sense van Haarten and Muller back away from him, as if to give him room to pray. 'You'll find a Bible in my saddle-bag,' he said at last.

'You agreed to consecrate that pig-sty?' cried Bezuidenhout, removing his glasses to polish them.

'I will never again enter so holy a place—'

'A Kaffir pig-sty!' insisted the dwarf. 'You're guilty of blasphemy, sure as I sit here!'

'Did you not realise that you were giving aid and comfort to rebels against the legally constituted authority?' asked Reenan.

'It did not enter my mind.'

'Well, what *did* enter your mind in that pig-sty? Man, you disgust me!'

First: a cry of despair: the sudden unasked-for knowledge that your beliefs are without roots, nothing more than conscious fantasies, like chaff in the wind. O Christ have mercy.

Second: the vision of your own inadequacy, of coming face to face with your own lies, of hearing yourself indulge in a lifetime of lip-service. O Christ, save me.

Third: the prayer, Guide me O God and I will serve you unto martyrdom. Christ, teach me.

Fourth: surrender to His Will. Christ, lead me. Amen.

'Are you telling us,' continued Bezuidenhout, 'that God *instructed* you to sanctify that dirty hovel?'

'I am telling you there was no denying Him in that place. I had denied Him long enough.'

After the ceremony of consecration, he performed the service of Communion, the Nagtmaal, and when Basson came to receive the bread and wine, Henning saw tears streaming down the boy's face, and he wept, too.

During the service, the Khoikhoi women prepared a feast in honour of the visitor, a great ox was roasted on the spit, and the men called the feast the *braaivleis*. The wine flowed, and the atmosphere was seductive. Van Haarten said, 'Dominee, we have never been so happy as tonight. We thank you.'

As the evening wore on, Henning asked a good many questions and bit by bit he pieced together their story. Van der Goes, it appeared, was out to drain them dry, as he did everyone else. They had owned good farmland down there in Blauwzand and each time van der Goes had visited them he told them that the taxes had been raised. When they asked for proof—a document, a signature, anything—he would utter threats, tell them soldiers would be sent from Cape Town if they did not pay. So, they paid, until they refused to pay any more. Van der Goes sent his Khoikhoi soldiers but they were easy game and soon retreated. The landdrost declared a war of attrition: people were forbidden to trade with the rebels and, in the end, the men had no alternative but to take to the hills.

'Van der Goes confiscated our land,' Muller explained, 'but that was his mistake. Instead of telling the Company, he kept quiet about it; kept the farms for himself, you see.'

'As if he didn't own enough already,' said Basson. 'He's a hard man, is van der Goes.'

'More than half the farms in his own district are his,' van Haarten said. 'He's the biggest landowner by far. When the people can't pay their taxes, he allows them to stay on their farms, but he collars eighty per cent of the profit. We weren't going to stand for that.'

'But why don't they report him?'

'Oh, you're an innocent, dominee, if you don't mind my saying so. What do you think he's got that Hottentot army for? Just to fight the Xhosa? No, of course not. Anybody who doesn't do as they're told . . .'

'He met his match in us,' said Basson proudly.

'We wouldn't stay on our farms on his terms,' said Muller. 'We held meetings, but saw no way out. We trekked north. And if it gets rough here, we'll trek a little further. We can thank God it's a big country.'

'But you're near enough to Blauwzand for him to send soldiers against you,' said Henning.

'I told you he'd made a mistake, dominee. When we found out he'd taken our farms for himself, we sent him a letter. We agreed not to tell the Company if he agreed to let us live our lives in peace. That's why we guard the road to Blauwzand. He's a treacherous man, van der Goes. He'll find an excuse to change his mind.'

So now they lived here in this settlement, and farmed one communal farm producing just enough for their needs, and a little more to sell secretly behind van der Goes's broad back. 'Just so we can purchase the stuff we can't make ourselves,' said Muller.

'And we paid no attention to his threat that we were living outside the sight of God,' cried Basson fiercely. 'And when van Haarten told us you'd arrived, dominee, we began to build our church. And now it's a proper place of worship. So what did van der Goes mean? God wouldn't have allowed that if He was angry with us, would he, dominee?'

'And what of these women?' asked Henning and, although he did not mean to sound disapproving, he could not keep the tones of censure from his voice.

'Heathen, the lot of them,' said Muller happily, putting his arm affectionately round the one they called Afrika.

Basson crawled over to van Haarten. 'Ask him, go on, ask him.'

'Ask me what?'

'To convert them,' van Haarten replied.

'Make decent Christians of them,' said Muller.

'Will you, dominee?' asked Basson.

'Disgraceful!' cried the dwarf. 'All those Kaffirs there were guilty of fornication, and still you agreed to baptise them?'

'Yes, but I forbade the men to cohabit until the women were baptised.'

'And then what?'

'Then I would see to it that they married, though I did not say so then.'

Married? screeched the dwarf. 'Didn't you know there exists the Ordinance of 1682 that forbids marriage between Europeans and freed slaves of full colour? Didn't you know that? It's prohibited by law!'

'But these women weren't freed slaves, they had never been slaves.'

'Don't you play the lawyer with me!' warned Bezuidenhout, waggling his finger at Henning.

'But, dominee,' said Reenan, pouring oil, 'in the end it didn't work out like that, did it?'

'Well? Did it?'

The young girl Henning had noticed when he first arrived at the compound understood Dutch reasonably well, and talked it a little; she was aware that they were discussing the women and crept towards Muller to whisper in his ear; he chuckled. 'She wants to ask you a question, dominee.'

'Me?' He was embarrassed; her nakedness embarrassed him.

'She wants to know if you can pronounce her name.'

'No, I don't think I can.'

'Try.' Muller said the tongue-twister for Henning to imitate but all the predikant could manage was, 'Alala.' This caused some laughter. 'That's a good name for her,' said Muller, gently caressing her cheek. 'That's what we'll call you from now on: Alala.' And the girl was pleased; she sat back on her haunches and gazed at Henning with unconcealed admiration, which caused him further embarrassment. To overcome his discomfort, he turned to van Haarten and said, 'It is late. I must return now to Blauwzand.' But he was howled down. Muller said, 'We're not done with you yet, dominee,' and began to clap his hands in a steady rhythm. Two of the women rose and moving slowly, with clumsy shuffling steps, danced round the fire, their movements like marionettes and in no way sensual. When they were done, Alala brought Henning a special dish of corn and milk that the others insisted he taste, and then she sang for him. In a weird, high-pitched voice she intoned her song, the words clicking as though her throat were some strange stringed instrument being plucked. Muller translated:

> The jackal will catch the hare,
> That evil hare
> Who takes away
> Our wish to wake
> When we are dead.
> The Moon will catch him, too,
> She throws the branch of a tree
> Like a spear
> And splits his lip, that stupid hare,
> Who takes away our wish to wake, so fast,
> So fast he runs that evil hare.
> But the jackal will catch him, be sure.

Henning thanked her, and she replied, 'You are heartily welcome,' in Dutch.

'You can't go back to Blauwzand now,' said van Haarten. 'Better to sleep here, dominee.'

'No. I must get back.'

'But you'll need a guide.'

'One of you—'

'No, no, dominee, it's too late,' said Basson. 'You'd do better to stay here.'

He was given, after much protest, van Haarten's bed; van Haarten lay on the floor, insisting he could sleep standing if necessary. In the dark, he said, 'And when will you come again, dominee?'

'I will have to arrange my visits carefully.'

'How often will you come to instruct the women?'

'Two, three times a month. I'll try.'

'That's good.'

In the flickering light of a shrunken candle, Henning opened his Bible to read before sleep.

'Would you read to me, please, dominee?'

Henning tried to decide on a fitting passage, and then remembered the password van Haarten had used. Out of curiosity he turned to First Samuel, Two, thirty-five:

'And I will raise me up a faithful priest, that shall do according to that which is in my heart and in my mind: and I will build him a sure house; and he shall walk before mine anointed forever.'

Van Haarten heaved himself up on one elbow and grinned, 'Apt, hey, dominee?'

'Very.'

'Yes. You can't fault Muller for Scripture.'

Henning extinguished the candle, closed his eyes but could not sleep. He struggled with a confusion of images he could not shake free. Christ, he saw, astride the winged eagle, and Agatha dancing with Alala; he consecrated corn and milk into blood and flesh, and the monstrous van der Goes took the young, firm breasts of the girl and devoured them, and Jesus fought with the hare, and the jackal devoured them both and sang the words 'Who takes away/Our wish to wake/When we are dead.'

8

Alala

Extract from the statement made by the landdrost, Abraham van der Goes: 'He lived a lie, that's all there is to it. He lived two lives.'

I

Now when he passed the slaves' compound in Blauwzand, he felt no twinge of conscience at all. He had two worlds to inhabit, the one feeding the other with contentment, but the trick was to keep them separate.

Henning told no one of his sojourn with the renegades. When he returned to Blauwzand he met Le Roux, who asked after old man Richter. Henning took the opportunity to complain that old man Richter had not been ill at all.

'Then it must have been a hoax,' said Le Roux.

'Yes. A hoax. Very probably.'

And it amused Le Roux no end that the predikant had been the victim of a practical joke.

His ministry in Blauwzand continued much as before. He baptised the new-born, taught the children—though he reduced their classes to only one a week—visited the sick and comforted the dying. The church roof was finished and the landdrost went off on yet another expedition to punish the cattle-thieving Xhosa.

Henning was welcome in every home, respected and trusted. He was the object of attention of a score of fussing, fussy women, the recipient of sweetmeats and wild flowers, fruit and vegetables; he enjoyed their well-meaning ways, and the gruff affection of their silent men. And he could even agree to all their sentiments without a pang of self-reproach:

'They will share heaven with horses and oxen.'

'They're lazy good-for-nothing liars!'

'They'd rather dance than work.'

'Dominee, they breed like flies!'

He could nod and condone because he had a secret place which appeased his disquiet. It made him almost smug. Was he not fulfilling van Lier's injunction? Was he not also serving the Company who employed him? True, he might not be bringing the Gospel to all God's creatures but, at least, he was doing *something*. The contentment of these days, he argued, helped him to work with renewed fervour for both his congregations, the lawful one and the one outside the law. (The sickness had not left him, nor had it yet reached the crisis, but he was, at that time, in the clutches of the most crippling stage of the disease: self-justification.) His visits to the encampment were easily arranged. On the pretext of journeying to the remoter farms in the outlying districts, he would make a detour and climb the steep Blauwzand Pass, cross the great expanse of veld by the trail van Haarten had shown him, and come at last to the haven. Be it there or in Blauwzand, Henning admitted that for the first time in his life he was truly at peace. (But I had deluded myself, he said. God was at chess, and I was his pawn.)

2

The conversion of the twelve Khoikhoi women took many months, and much patience, but it was the most comforting and rewarding of all his work.

In the beginning he learned that the Khoikhoi had little religion of their own, and no religious customs; they sang and danced, not in celebration of the mysteries of existence but out of the joyfulness of life itself. The secret, Henning said, was to fuse their primitive beliefs, such as they were, with the fervour of Christ in Glory, and then to sublimate that union.

He came to them, he said, in love, to make them acquainted with their Saviour Jesus Christ; and the one they called Afrika replied that it was good. He asked them if they knew that there was a great God who had made the heaven and the earth and all that was therein; and Alala it was who replied that they called heaven *Muma*. 'And what,' Henning asked, 'do you call the great God who made us all?' and she replied '*Tui'qua.*' Whereupon he cried, 'Oh my dear people, this *Tui'qua* is our Saviour. He became man, and for us men He died upon the Cross.'

And so, in *Tui'qua*'s good time, Henning perceived that the acceptance of God's word had brought light, and he ministered the rite of baptism to them, and admitted them to full membership of the visible Church of Christ.

And when the ceremony was over, the men came to him and said they would call the place Henningsdorp.

3

Of Alala, these things he remembered: her pleasure at his visits; her shining face alive with happiness seeing him ride into the encampment. She was constantly by his side and angry if she had to leave him. Her meekness and modesty, her joy in prayer and in Christ, these too, he remembered. She could not do enough for him, washing his dusty clothes after the long ride, or preparing food, or even when he slept in the afternoon, she sat beside him, as if on guard.

And this: one night, late, around the dying fire, listening to tales told by the men of the hunt, she sat by his side, her eyes heavy with sleep, the stars aflame in the dark summer sky; she rested her head upon his shoulder and he, intuitively, gave her the protection and affection of his arm (and the older women smiled, and the men nodded knowingly).

And this: walking with her by the stream, seeing a hare scamper through the scrub out of sight, and her fear: the hare is the messenger of *Gauna*, she said. There is no *Gauna*, he is powerless against the love of Jesus Christ. But she would not be stilled. The hare is *Gauna*'s messenger to rob man of the hope that he will awake after death. Then *Gauna* is Satan, he said, and Christ conquers him, *Tui'qua* is Christ. You, she said, are *Tui'qua*. And her fear was transformed into fervour, she trembled and shook and gazed upwards towards heaven which she called *Muma*. He comforted her, soothed her, lay down with her, and she took his forefinger in her mouth, and her teeth were gentle, also her tongue, and it was her way of making known her love; and he was moved to kiss her; her eyes, her lips, her breasts; and they were as one; and God was at chess.

Bezuidenhout left the room and vomited; they could hear him retching in the corridor and then calling in a broken voice for the night slaves to clean up the mess, before being sick again. When he returned to Reenan's office, he was shivering and his teeth chattered uncontrollably. He climbed back on to his chair and shuffled papers with nervous little fingers. Outside, the south-easter howled round the Castle and, in the courtyard below, soldiers were bolting doors and shutters, securing windows against the fierce wind.

'Are you ready to continue, mynheer Bezuidenhout?' asked Reenan. The dwarf did not reply, nor did he immediately respond to Reenan's second enquiry which was, 'Have you any questions of the prisoner or may we go on to the next statement?' But when the Assistant-Fiscal began to read 'This is the statement made by the Hottentot woman known as Afrika—' Bezuidenhout interrupted.

'Yes, I have questions.' His voice was harsh. Reenan leant back, bland as ever, and waited while the dwarf collected his thoughts. Far away, across the town, a relay of frightened dogs barked a message of alarm into the wind.

'Prisoner,' said Bezuidenhout, 'I want you to be aware of the depth of your degeneracy. I'm talking first about this so-called Christian instruction you gave. It's a disgrace, what you've told us: all you did was to grovel before their heathen practices. Now just you understand what I'm saying! I'm saying that we're not going to admit for one moment that you converted those Hottentots to Christ. Just understand that now! Get it into your skull! Those Hottentots were heathens and they remained heathens!'

'They were baptised—'

'Don't argue with me now, Henning.' A dangerously calm note crept into the dwarf's voice, but his fists were tightly clenched. 'I'm not here to argue, I'm here to tell you. Next, and listen hard now, Henning: you can disguise your actions in any words you like, but I can see through your lies. You are a whoremonger, understand? You're a pervert! You try to make us think there's love in this filth, like using your spit for baptism—well, I'm here to tell you that you copulated with that bitch because you're eaten with lust and you know what that word means, lust? It means you're an *animal*!' The deliberateness vanished and he spat his next words at Henning: 'You think I don't know that they've got grease all over their bodies, and they've got the stench of pigs, and that they're dirty and diseased, and that they're put there by Satan to trap us, you think I don't know that? Just you understand that I know every word that you're talking about, because I can see *through* it, just you understand that!'

Malan's pen continued to squeak long after the dwarf had concluded his brief tirade; now the little man sat, breathing noisily through his nose, squeaking like the pigs he disparaged. When Reenan tried once more to pass on to the next statement, Bezuidenhout again interrupted: 'I've still got questions,' he said sharply, fidgeting with his notes. 'Now, I'm going to prove what I say. Earlier, Henning, you told us that you intended to make these renegades marry the Hottentots after you got through with them. You remember that? All right. Now you answer me this: did you marry them to these bitches?'

'I married Muller to Afrika—'

'Yes, Afrika!' cried the dwarf. 'A fine name for a Christian! Yes, and the others?'

'No. I did not marry them.'

'Why not?' asked Bezuidenhout feigning wide-eyed surprise.

Henning bowed his head. 'They were reluctant—'

' "Reluctant?" ' repeated the dwarf in a playful sing-song way. 'Now why were they reluctant do you think?'

'When the time came only Muller agreed.'

'Yes, yes, but what was the reason that the others refused to marry the bitches?'

'It was never stated.'

'But why didn't you pursue the matter, you the great Christian, why didn't you compel them to marry these souls in bliss?' Bezuidenhout was enjoying himself, for he had manoeuvred Henning into an untenable position, and both knew it.

'I—I could not compel them,' the prisoner stammered.

'Oh, you could not, I see. Why was that?'

4

Do not think, he said, that I was free from self-reproach, bitter as aloes. The warring factions of guilt and remorse sounded their battle cries; he could not endure the burden of sin Alala represented. He struggled to transmute the meaning of their relationship, to justify its continuance. The plea that love graced the very earth in which it had flourished was to him hollow and insufficient, for even love, Calvin taught, can be illicit. But worse: the spectre of his lawful wife, Agatha, distorted each and every day-dream of uncertain quietude which he was able on rare occasions to achieve. But what course was open to him? Could he find the strength to set Alala aside forever? Could he live without touching her again, this fragile, modest girl whom he loved? Could he ever make her understand that denial, too, was a supreme Christian virtue? Sinking into the morass of inertia, he admitted to settling for the coward's way out:

he would never again return to the encampment; but even then he continued to be haunted by the mystery of that oneness with the girl—for he saw it now, and then, as an event born of inspiration, like a vision—and he had the sense of a profound communion; for weeks his soul was in turn racked by the separation he had enforced, and eased by the belief that he had acted out of motives of self-denial. (I was, although I may not have known it, he said, settling for life within my lawful congregation.)

Then a letter came from Sybille:

23rd March, Anno Domini 1793

Beloved Father,

I write to you with a heavy heart. Two days ago, that great good man the Reverend Helperus Ritzema van Lier entered into his rest, aged twenty-eight years. The last scenes of his life were pathetic in the extreme. His sorrowing wife and four little children stood by his bed. Many friends and members of his congregation visited the sick-chamber, among whom mother, Daniel and I were honoured to be numbered. For many minutes he talked of nothing but his profound hopes for his Society and Seminary for the Propagation of the Christian Religion among Heathen and Mohammedans. He beseeched us all to work for its formation and eventual success. Then, from all of us he took his farewell and was especially affectionate towards our family, commending me most earnestly to communicate to you his love and respect with these words: 'Do right and God will be thy Shield.' With that, he commended you to the Almighty in his prayers. His slaves were not forgotten, but were summoned to the bedside to receive their master's parting charge. He invoked the Divine blessing upon the land of his adoption, upon the Church which he held so dear, and upon the heathen who have not as yet been gathered to one fold. During the spasms of pain he earnestly besought God for relief, and when relief came he was filled with gratitude and his lips overflowed with expressions of joy and holy rapture. In the early hours of the morning, he passed to his eternal reward.

These are sad days; and no man is so widely mourned. It is said that only the good die young. I pray God for his soul and that we might see you soon.

Your daughter
Sybille.

His reaction to van Lier's death was savage and instinctive, and no amount of reason could temper the agony he suffered. (It was, he recalled, the torment of even greater remorse. God had brought me face to face with my own treachery.)

His little world of neat, separate compartments was shattered without warning. The will to extricate himself from his personal dilemma, by turning his back on it, cruelly evaporated. In the church in Blauwzand he prayed for many hours after reading his daughter's letter and tried to bring reason to his confusion, but the notion of betrayal, like a poison, impaired his intellect. Betrayal of God, of van Lier, of self, of his family, of the people of Blauwzand, of the renegades, of Alala; he could discover no cause, no person with whom he had kept faith. And this particular terror was uppermost: that, not having carried out with all his might van Lier's injunctions, he had contributed to the young man's death. In the face of such mighty opposition, before the walls of Jericho, friendless, had not van Lier hurled himself against the stones and died? Was that to be the fate of every man who sought to sound the trumpet before the city of resistance? Even unto martyrdom, Henning had vowed.

As if to cleanse his beggarly spirit, Henning prostrated himself in the shadowy, cool church and determined, like a soldier of Christ before the battle, to bring together into one universe the twin spheres of his existence.

But the impulse to harmonise, born in an empty church, was blunted by the onslaught of reality. Perhaps he should have dedicated himself not to conquering the confusion of his life, but to bridging the less finite worlds of intention and action. He was prevented, he said, from translating into deeds the will of the spirit. God had ordained it otherwise, and was about to sacrifice His pawn.

5

On a day in late April, while the sun swaddled the earth in a blanket of heat Henning led his horse through the narrow, burning confines of Blauwzand Pass, the rocks like hot coals. (The heat in the Pass, he said, was like the fiery furnace because he would not any longer bow down his head and worship the comfortable paths a man may take.) His head held high, believing the spirit of the Lord was all about him, Henning plodded onwards, inspired by the noble feelings of righteousness. A glowing vision of what he could achieve, like a shimmering goal, was constantly before him. He would compel the men to marry the women, for he would not connive at a community of sinners. Today, he would have it out with them; today, they must acquiesce. And once they were married, he would preach in Blauwzand, and hold them before the people as a living and true community, proclaimers of tolerance. And he would enforce all this by his own example of self-denial which he now knew was the right course : not by avoiding a confrontation, but by meeting it head on. He resolved that he would, before the world, put aside the creature he loved in the cause of the Greater Good, blessed by Christ in Mercy. And so, filled with the determined passion of van Lier's dying wishes, he approached Henningsdorp.

But he knew, the moment he entered the encampment, that all was not well : Alala was nowhere to be seen and, because he was so accustomed to her bright, welcoming eyes, her absence on this day caused panic to rise, as though he anticipated catastrophe; then he saw Muller emerge from his hut.

'Where's Alala?' Henning asked, dismounting.

'She's not—not well,' replied the older man, but not in a sombre way. 'Come, I'll take you to her.' And as they walked, he continued, 'Van Haarten's on guard duty today. He was going to get a message to you, but we knew you would come, sooner or later.'

Henning was surprised to find that he was being led towards his own hut, near the church. 'Why is she in my hut?' he asked.

'It's cooler there,' said Muller, scratching his beard.

'Is it serious, this illness?' asked Henning, but they were already at the door and, instead of replying, Muller pushed it open and stood aside for the other man.

A puzzling sight greeted Henning : Alala sat, her legs curled under her, in the centre of a close circle formed by the other women, and all but she were chattering and laughing animatedly. At the entrance of Henning, they fell silent, but their eyes continued to laugh. Alala gazed at the floor, never once looking up, the inclination of her head, the attitude of her whole body signifying sadness. Muller's wife, Afrika, rose and bowed. In Dutch she said, 'You are welcome, master,' and then unleashed a torrent in her own tongue.

'What does she say?' Henning asked anxiously. Muller, who stood half in, half out of the hut, as if reluctant fully to enter, replied, 'It's best you come out now, dominee, and I'll explain.'

Henning, suddenly overcome with sympathy for the forlorn girl seated in the centre, took a step towards her, but this seemed to

107

alarm the other women, especially Afrika, who held up a hand, fingers spread wide, as though to create a barrier. All the while, Alala had not taken her eyes off the ground, but sat quite still.

'What's the matter with her?' Henning asked the moment he emerged again into the heat.

Muller said, 'I don't know what you're going to think, dominee, but your woman is with child, your child, you understand?'

(I do not know what I felt, he said. Whether pain or shock or horror: I do not know. I left Muller standing in the noon sun and walked, as if in a dream, towards the little church I so loved. Before the simple Table of the Lord, I went down on my knees and asked God to forgive me.)

6

His resolution to insist on marriage between the renegades and the Khoikhoi women was, of course, swept away. Two factors caused the change of heart, and the first he called compassion: how could he now banish Alala from his presence and proclaim that the intimacy between them was ended? (I did not possess the strength for such cruelty, he said.) The second he called the loss of the righteous ally: he could not now chastise the men for their sinfulness when the evidence of his own grew daily in size. The girl's pregnancy robbed him of moral superiority. He was in no position to preach hell fire to anyone but himself.

And so, receiving the congratulations of the men, and displaying false happiness and pride, he returned to Blauwzand. (I think they understood my position better than I did, he said. They knew quite well that I could not enforce marriage between them and the Khoikhoi, and this knowledge lightened their hearts.)

Men are made mad, he said, by the times they live in. Where previously he had sought to merge his two worlds, he now contrived to avoid collision. Wild, disturbing fantasies proliferated like weeds: he would find a way of having the child aborted—were there not living in the hills old, sour Khoikhoi hags who mixed foul-smelling potions that would serve the purpose? Or: he would find a way of having the settlement attacked, sweep it away as though it never existed. Or: he would himself become a renegade. Or: he would mount his horse and ride north, north, north until he could ride no more. As the time of the birth drew nearer, desperation increased by feeding upon itself. The times, he said, were against him.

9

Birth and rebirth

Extract from the statement made by the Hottentot woman, known as Afrika: 'They came; we were praying in the church; the soldiers came.'

I

The spring, the season of promise, severs winter and summer with startling abruptness: there is no more rain, no more cold, spring lasts a week, and it is summer.

On a blazing Christmas Day, 1793, Henning preached on the message of the Saviour's birth, but in his mind he carried the image of Alala and the child she was about to bear. The following day news reached Blauwzand of an Xhosa raid to the north-east; three hundred cattle, it was said, had been spirited away in a night. His ragged army of Khoikhoi soldiers formed up behind him, landdrost van der Goes set off on what he liked to call 'a punitive expedition'.

Then, shortly after New Year's Day, 1794, the head slave of the landdrost's household, Mordecai, woke Henning early and thrust into the startled predikant's hand a piece of crumpled paper.

'What's this?' asked Henning, still half asleep.

'You read it, master,' said Mordecai, clearly nervous and watching the door as if he expected the landdrost to enter at any moment.

'But who gave it to you?' Henning said, opening the shutters and flooding the room with pillars of light.

'I go now, master. You say nothing to no one please, master. I go now.'

Henning unfolded the paper and read:

1st Samuel, 2, xxxv.
Come at once. It is time.

Shortly before evening he arrived at Henningsdorp. From far off, he saw van Haarten and Muller waving to him. When he drew near, both, bubbling with excitement, ran towards him and cried in unison, 'It's a boy! It's a boy!' They took him to see his son.

Curious, he thought, that when it is your own, there is no offence against nature: what beauty he now perceived in that indeterminate pallor, neither black nor white, and in the flat nose and full lips, in the tight screws of hair, the colour of over-ripe corn. What joy it was for him to hold the squawking bundle in his arms, feel its warmth and marvel at its perfection. And then to see Alala, incandescent with pride, and to kiss her gently, and to utter thanks.

His sojourn lasted a week; days of happiness shared by the men and by the Khoikhoi women, the feasting and the dancing. (The cares of the last months, he said, fell from me and I was young again.) Towards the end of his stay, on the Sunday, he baptised his son, and called him Adam, which means in Hebrew 'of the earth'.

On the journey back to Blauwzand the conflicts returned with renewed violence. Twice he cried, tears racing down his cheeks. What life could that child expect? What pain would he have to endure? The vision of the slaves' compound was never far from his mind. Now it seemed that there was no alternative but to shatter the tranquillity of his position in Blauwzand. Go up into the pulpit and confess. Lay bare your soul before the Christians of your congregation, fall on their mercy, pray for their compassion upon you. Do this for your son.

2

God, he said, has commanded man to trust in Him: 'with all thine heart; and lean not unto thine own understanding. Be not wise in thine own eyes: fear the Lord, and depart from evil'. Subjection to the Divine Will was the most difficult lesson and the most painful.

When you ride from Henningsdorp, after you have descended the rocky Pass, you come again to gently rising ground from which you can see Blauwzand beckoning to you. From this vantage point, Henning looked down on the place where he intended publicly to confess, prayed for courage, and was about to begin the last miles of the journey when his attention was drawn to a cloud of rising dust on the far horizon. From time to time, the dust cloud settled and he glimpsed horsemen; they too were approaching Blauwzand but from the opposite direction. The nearer Henning came to the town, the nearer came the column of riders. At last, when he was no more than an hour away, he caught sight of van der Goes's red coat and the gold braid twinkling in the last rays of the sun. He could also see the Khoikhoi army, twenty men on horseback, like a curling tail straggling behind but, in their midst, bound together with ropes, a dozen men on foot being driven forward. A sense of urgency overtook Henning, he did not know why, but he spurred his horse to greater effort and rode as if his life depended on it. He had, however, misjudged the distance, and when he entered Blauwzand van der Goes's column had arrived before him and were dismounted before the church. Most of the inhabitants had come out to greet the returning general and his army, and to gloat over the collection of prisoners they had brought back in triumph.

By the time Henning reached the church, a scene of horror greeted him: two of the prisoners, old Xhosa men, were hanging by their necks from a tree, still emitting terrible choking sounds. The rest were being trussed and made ready for similar treatment. But it was one prisoner in particular who captured Henning's gaze: a young half-caste boy, eleven years old, no more, who was screaming and kicking and crying out in terror while the soldiers bound his arms behind his back.

'Come on,' van der Goes was shouting, 'get the rope around the little bugger's neck.'

Le Roux saw Henning and ran towards him. 'Good sport here, dominee,' the old man said. 'The landdrost's caught the lot of them. Not only Xhosa, Hottentot too, they were in it together. The herdsmen were *giving* the cattle away!'

But Henning barely heard the explanation; his eyes were fixed on the boy who was sobbing in unbearable torment as the soldiers grabbed his legs and tied them tight. Henning pushed his way through the knot of townsmen and cried, 'Stop! Stop this at once!'

'Keep away, dominee,' growled van der Goes. 'These men are guilty of cattle-stealing and are being punished.'

Henning ran forward, brushing past van der Goes whom he knocked to one side, and caught hold of the soldier struggling with the boy. Desperately, Henning tried to untie the knots, to loosen the ropes but the landdrost saw what was happening and shouted, 'Grab the predikant! Go on, grab him!'

Two soldiers took Henning by the arms and held him while four more ropes were slung over a sturdy branch. Impotent, he watched the Khoikhoi soldiers jam the nooses round the necks of the condemned men, and of the boy, the colour of his son, whom he had tried to save. Now, they pulled hard on the ropes, jerking the prisoners off their feet, their cries trapped in their throats. The people cheered, and the bodies swung to and fro, with twitching feet, their faces showing blotches of blood beneath the skin. When they had lost consciousness and struggled no more, the solders released Henning and he stood and stared at the dead men, with but one thought running through his brain: he had witnessed the desecration of God's image, of the child Alala had borne, the strangled soul in the body of the dead boy hanging from the tree.

The people did not disperse, for they were now aware of van der Goes approaching the predikant; the landdrost was purple in the face, rumbling like a volcano about to erupt.

'Dominee,' he said, 'as long as you are predikant here, never again interfere with my duty, is that understood? I have to keep the peace in these parts, I have to keep law and order and I will not be undermined! You get that through your head now and we'll stay friends for a long time. Those dirty Xhosa and Hottentots are thieves and scavengers, you understand? They're too damned lazy to work, so they steal! And if they steal they get hanged for it. They know it, and we know it, and there's no argument! This is not a Church affair, this is a Government affair, and in these parts, I am the Government!'

Night fell; the people returned to their homes; the slaves were locked up in their compound; the bodies hung from the trees, and still Henning did not move. And then, from the compound, he heard a familiar sound, a Khoikhoi song, 'Who takes from us/The will to wake/When we are dead'.

Henning mounted his horse and with a loud cry galloped full pelt towards the slaves' compound.

'Open these gates!' he ordered the Khoikhoi guard, who hesitated and then began to shake from top to toe. 'Open the gates!' Henning cried again but the man was too fearful to obey. So Henning himself loosed the wooden bolt, threw open the gates and galloped from hut to hut calling to the slaves, 'I will give you Christ!' he cried. 'I will bring to you your Saviour! Follow me, good people, follow me!'

But none followed.

Henning rode round and round the enclosure, as one demented, calling on them to be free, ordering them to run away.

But none obeyed.

By then the alarm had been given and the church bell rang out a warning. Somewhere a shot was fired and then Henning saw, in the light of approaching torches, van der Goes heaving through the gates surrounded by soldiers who began to fire indiscriminately. Henning's horse reared and bolted, leaping the rough fence that formed the limits of the cage. When he looked back he could see the flickering torches, hear the shooting and the cries of the women.

3

His recollections of what followed, he said, were embroidered with the shapes and shadows of a nightmare.

Riding hard, and looking back to see the column of pursuers, their torches flickering like a rivulet of fire in the darkness, wending its way towards him; the dangerous ascent up Blauwzand Pass and then, Henningsdorp.

Explanations, confusion, panic.

'You freed the slaves?'

'Are you mad?'

'Yes, mad.'

'They'll destroy us!'

'Yes, they will destroy us.'

The women are herded—no, gathered—into the little church; he carries his son Adam in his arms, while Afrika cares for Alala. Van Haarten and Muller order the other men to vantage points on the crags and ledges surrounding the encampment. Basson climbs to the highest point, from where he will be able to signal the approach of van der Goes's army. The sky is beginning almost imperceptibly to lighten. Now, in the church: the women kneel; Henning stands at the lectern, his Bible resting on the eagle's wings. The light of a single candle seems to burn unnaturally still; the murmured prayers, the amens.

Van Haarten and Muller enter, their guns desecrating the holy place. They station themselves at the small windows and watch for the invader.

Now Henning kneels and prays, but the boy dangling from the rope intrudes and shatters his communion. Adam begins to cry. A dreadful sense of loss overpowers him, and even the absolute certainty of his love is besieged. He is moved and he speaks, turning to his congregation, remaining on his knees like a penitent.

'My brothers and sisters in Christ: Ask me not whether anything can be done against God's Will. I say this: nothing is or can be done which He may not impede if He so pleases. His word declares unto us what He approves and what He condemns. That is sufficient and by that we rule our lives, leaving the secrets to God, as by Moses we are taught to do.

'Calvin affirms that the pride of those shall be punished who, not content with the revealed Will of God, to which they will not be obedient, delight to mount and fly above the skies, there to seek the *secret* will of the Almighty. We flatter ourselves in sin to think that, in committing iniquity, we obey God's will. We here have vomited blasphemies, crying, Let us do evil that good may come of it, let us abide sin that grace may abound. But the paths of righteousness are strict. We cannot, in our blindness, cry that, even when we sin, we obey God's will.

'God has not given His law in vain by which we may distinguish good from evil. We are commanded that no man steal or defraud his brother; that none commit adultery, fornication or filthiness but that every man keep his own vessel in sanctity and honour. We know that if we do these things and others which are commanded, and abstain from that which is forbidden, then we obey the will of God. And if we do not do so, we cannot be acceptable to Him.

'Christ have mercy.

'I hold marriage a blessed bond; for Christ Himself maintained it, and approved it and made it free to all men. One, and only one among us, has found it in his heart to enter that holy state. But I and the others have refrained. O good women, forgive us our trespasses. We have taken men's daughters and refused the bond God has made. We are guilty of sin, for we have looked on you as less than God's creatures—'

'No!' cried van Haarten. 'No!'

'As *less* than God's creatures, for God never forbade marriage to any man or any woman, of whatever state or degree. There are no half-measures in godliness. We are guilty of preferring comfort to the harsh bed of righteousness, compromise to the rack of purity. We must either enter fully into our enterprises or we are damned. Either we believe, as that great and good man van Lier taught us to believe, that God's word is a blessing to all creatures, or we believe it is a blessing to none.

'I accuse my own life. I have sought to justify my deeds in the arrogant knowledge of God's will to which I believed I held the secrets. I look now at this woman, Alala; I have wronged her, she whom I love. *For love does not absolve sin!* I have played God tricks, argued in and out, yet knowing that out of sin no virtue can ever be born.

'We, who have love in our hearts, are in constant danger of damnation. We who love are commanded to walk the straitest and the narrowest path.

'Submit, good people, submit. I know I must die once and therefore as Christ said to Judas, "What thou doest, do quickly." But this I say before you and before my God: mine is the greatest sin, for I, in my own wickedness, turned my back on the promise of Christ in this place and defiled it with my poverty of spirit and I sinned. Mine is the sin of compromise. Amen.'

Dawn, and the sun sped higher into the heavens.

The waiting continued and Henning sat on the floor of the church, leaning against the wall, his face deep in shadow. Muller disturbed him, sitting beside him, whispering, 'Dominee, I am guilty, too. I just want you to know that.'

'You?'

'Yes. After Afrika and me took the vows, the moment you said we were man and wife, I never touched her again, I never went near her.'

'But why?'

Muller lowered his head and murmured, 'I didn't want children who'd end up as slaves. No, I never touched her again. Agh, dominee, we're all cowards.'

Then, they heard the shots and Muller returned to the window, beside van Haarten who called over his shoulder, 'What do you want us to do, dominee? Do we surrender? I can see van der Goes already. What's the path of righteousness now, dominee?'

But he was answered by the landdrost's voice.

'Van Haarten!' called van der Goes. 'All we want from you is the predikant. If you are sheltering him, hand him over, and we'll leave you in peace!'

'*Who* is it you want?' answered van Haarten innocently.

Then Muller hissed: 'Look! He's got the boys from the town with him, the Europeans. He means business!' There were ten or twelve of them, laughing and calling to each other as they wandered carelessly round the compound.

'Van Haarten, don't play games with me,' said van der Goes. 'We know he's here. He's guilty of a criminal offence. I don't want to start quoting the law at you but you know the penalty for harbouring criminals, hey? Just hand him over and we'll go.'

It was then Muller saw the smoke: 'They're burning our houses!' he said and, bewildered, he turned to the frightened women and to the predikant seated in the shadows. 'They're burning our houses,' he said again.

('Make haste, O God, to deliver me; make haste to help me, O Lord. Let them be ashamed and confounded that seek after my soul: Let them be turned backward, and put to confusion, that desire my hurt.')

Van der Goes turned angrily to one of the young men standing beside him. 'Stop them. I've told them we came for the predikant, and that's all.'

But it was too late: the fire was already spreading from one hut to the other. Muller, in desperation, lifted his hand and the women began to sing. (What is this hymn, wondered Henning? They had sung it the first day he set foot in the place. A journey—but begun or ended, he could not now remember.)

From the rocks above, shots rang out as the look-outs, seeing the smoke, opened fire on the invaders. The army scattered, taking cover and returning fire. Van der Goes, frightened at being under attack, rushed forward bursting into the church, followed by a handful of his men. As they did so, Alala began to dance, a wild barbaric expression of fear. Henning and Muller grabbed hold of her naked body, but she slipped out of their grasp and made for the Lord's Table, circling it, hands upstretched. Van Haarten confronted the intruders, as if defying them to take another step into the hallowed place. The women sang, and Alala danced, and the men stood as still as statues.

Then one of the Khoikhoi soldiers came to the door and said, 'Landdrost, no more shots, no. All dead up there. All dead.'

The women's song turned to wailing and van der Goes bellowed for silence. 'I arrest you all in the name of the Government of the Cape of Good Hope, and of the United East India Company!' he cried. 'Lay down your arms, you are outnumbered.'

Henning remembered Alala holding her baby; he putting his arm round Alala; emerging into the morning sun from the church; the ropes dangling from the branches of the trees; the absence of terror; the need to speak:

'We have committed no crime.'

'No crime? You've broken every law in the book!'

'I may have sinned but I have committed no crime and nor have these men.'

'Man, you've just booked a passage to hell!'

And this: the questioning of the Khoikhoi women; the disgust on van der Goes's face; the burning of the little church.

'Hey, you fellows, pull down your ropes. We can't hang them. This is more serious than I thought.'

More details are told van der Goes: the nature of the life in Henningsdorp; the marriage of Muller and Afrika; Henning and Alala's child; baptism; sin.

'Agh, man, we've stumbled on a pig-sty. This is something for the Fiscal.'

And this: Henning is separated from the others, and bound hand and foot; the rest are guarded by the Khoikhoi soldiers; Alala feeding Adam on the breast; two of the women taken from the group and raped by the Khoikhoi men for everyone to see; the smell of brandy on van der Goes's breath as the day wears on; the stench of burning; nightfall; van der Goes snoring.

'Dominee . . .?' van Haarten whispers, crawling close. 'They're all half-drunk. Now's our chance. We can get away.'

'No,' Henning says. 'You go. Take Alala and the baby.'

'But what about you?'

'No. I cannot. No more.'

The silent tread of shadows.

(I think the baby was brought to me, he said. But I do not remember. I think Alala kissed me but I am not sure.)

And he was left, alone, amidst the smouldering ashes of Henningsdorp.

'But how do you know it was not God's will that you should escape?' The Assistant-Fiscal said, offering his sickly smile.

'No,' said Henning with finality. 'My soul was in need of confinement. His laws are strict.'

'With that,' said the dwarf, Bezuidenhout, 'I wholeheartedly concur.'

(Henning, the records show, was then returned to his cell, while the political commissioner and the Assistant-Fiscal considered, in the light of what they had heard, their recommendations.)

BOOK THREE

10

Beginnings

Extract from the findings of mynheer Bezuidenhout and mynheer Reenan: '... that it be known that the said Reverend Johannes Henning is guilty of gross misconduct, both as a minister and as a Christian.'

I

The south-easter blew itself out by morning, leaving a fine layer of dust over the town. The cloth of cloud rolled off Table Mountain which, with its two cohorts either side, seemed to loom larger and nearer. It was Friday, 6 February 1794.

Daniel Henning, after his hunting expedition up Lion's Head, had arranged to meet his friend Mathias Janssens at daybreak. Accordingly, he rose early and stole out of the house in Church Square, leaving his mother and sister sleeping. He was the first to arrive at the jetty, near Green Point, where the Robben Island ferry began its outward journey.

Presently, Mathias arrived on horseback with a bundle wrapped in a grey blanket slung over the animal's rump. Together the two friends heaved their load aboard the boat which would take them across the narrow stretch of water, to the small island out in the bay.

The boatman said, 'So, you've found another one, have you? I don't know how you fellows do it.'

'You've got to know where to look,' said Mathias.

'I suppose so. Still, not like the old times. We were taking across thirty, forty a day not long ago.'

There was no mist; the wind had seen to that. And soon, the little boat, encouraged by the currents and a stiff breeze, reached its destination. Daniel and Mathias brought their cargo ashore and carried it into an office, situated in a small complex of Government buildings that clustered near the harbour. From the island, the mountains of the town once more assumed their majestic stature, like a throne waiting to be filled.

A clerk, Leibrandt, weary and elderly, knew the two friends well. 'Hello, boys,' he said. 'Not another one! God, I don't know where you fellows find them. Let's have a look.'

He beckoned them through a door leading off his office and they laid the bundle on a wooden trestle table that stood in the centre of a bare, dingy room.

Leibrandt flicked back the blanket to reveal the dead Bushman. 'Good work, boys, but don't go mad, hey? If you get all these little buggers they'll close this office down, and then where would I be?'

'I thought that was the point,' said Daniel. 'To get all the little buggers.'

'Ja, ja,' sighed Leibrandt, 'so it is, so it is. Come on, hold out your hands and I'll pay you. How you going to split this, fifty-fifty?'

'Yes, right down the middle,' said Mathias, as the clerk slapped the rixdollars on to his open hand.

'All right, boys,' said Leibrandt, 'the boat doesn't leave till after lunch. You can spend some of that at the bar, hey? A man's got to make a living.'

So, the boys, content with their payment for delivering the dead Bushman, bought brandy from the clerk and hungrily devoured as many sausages as he could cook. By afternoon they were back in Cape Town but, on his return home, Daniel was greeted with news of his father's fate.

2

Fiscal Willem Berg arrived at the Castle on the stroke of eight. His first act that morning was to summon the Assistant-Fiscal, Danie Reenan, to his office. But when the secretary returned to say that Reenan was not in his office, Berg exploded like a jumping fire-cracker.

'Does nobody work round here?' he demanded. 'It's eight o'clock. Where is everybody?'

'Mynheer Reenan had a late night, Fiscal, they were questioning the prisoner Henning until dawn. He's home to bed. But his clerk, Malan, was still there. He's just finishing the report. He said he'd bring it down as soon as he's done.'

The information appeared to satisfy the Fiscal for the moment; he turned his attention, albeit perfunctorily, to other matters, to uncollected taxes, to familiarising himself with the cases he would have to prosecute that day, to the thousand-and-one details sent to plague him. When Malan finally appeared, red-eyed and exhausted, carrying the weighty report, the Fiscal said, 'You've kept me waiting. I just want the recommendation—don't bother me with the evidence —just hand me the recommendation.'

Malan obliged, bowed and shuffled off, his task done. The Fiscal read his minions' conclusions quickly—they were no great length— and then, highly delighted, requested an interview with the Commissioner-General.

The recommendations were brief because both Reenan and Bezuidenhout had been hungry for sleep. There was no doubt how they would find; they came to agreement speedily, discussed the wording and directed Malan accordingly. After shaking hands on a job well done, they set off for their respective homes: Reenan in time to breakfast with his wife and four children, Bezuidenhout to his solitary room off Market Square where he lived alone. It was as he was undressing, emptying his pockets, that he found Sybille's letter to her father. The dwarf gazed at the rounded, elaborate hand and wondered what to do. At length, he sat down and wrote:

To the Fiscal,
The Castle.

Revered Sir:
    The enclosed letter was given to me yesterday by the prisoner Henning's daughter. I have not read the contents. Whether it should be delivered or not, I leave entirely to you.
                                        Yours respectfully,
                                        E. A. Bezuidenhout.

He summoned his slave and instructed him to take the note at once; then the dwarf hauled himself onto his bed, was too tired even to pray, and soon was fast asleep.

3

The Commissioner-General signed the order of banishment at noon, and then set off for his farm near Stellenbosch. Berg returned to his own office, still blowing dry the ink, and ordered the prisoner to be brought to him. He also instituted enquiries into the movement of ships to Batavia.

While he was waiting for Henning to appear before him,

Bezuidenhout's note was delivered together with Sybille's letter of affection to her father. Berg read them both, was irritated first by Bezuidenhout's failure to act on his own initiative, and then by the sickly tones of the girl's message. He pushed both to one side.

His secretary entered. 'What now?' barked the Fiscal.

'The landdrost of Blauwzand is here, Fiscal.'

'Yes, yes, yes, show him in.'

Van der Goes strode through the narrow doorway. 'What's the verdict?' he asked at once.

'Banishment.'

'Good, good, good!' and he rubbed his hands to emphasise his delight. 'May I see the report?'

'It's very long,' said Berg, pushing the pile of documents towards his visitor. Van der Goes immediately turned to the last pages, for he wanted to read Henning's account of the arrest in the church, and he was thus occupied when Henning himself was marched into the office, escorted by two guards who had to hold him up, for he was in danger of collapsing. He was ill; his treatment the previous day, principally the length of time he had been forced to spend in damp clothing, had weakened him. A high fever raged, and his chest ached: it felt as though he were breathing fire. Henning heard, or thought he heard, the Fiscal say, 'Are you the Reverend Johannes Henning?'

'I ... I am.'

'Yes, yes, that's him all right,' muttered van der Goes, still reading intently.

'I will now inform you of the recommendations made to the Commissioner-General by the Political Commissioner and the Assistant-Fiscal. Do you understand?'

'Yes.'

' "We, the undersigned, recommend that the Reverend Johannes Henning, being a minister of the Reformed Church of the Netherlands, be banished from the Cape of Good Hope, and that it be known that the said Reverend Johannes Henning is guilty of gross misconduct both as a minister and as a Christian, being guilty of bestiality and blasphemy." Signed, etcetera, etcetera. Accordingly, His Excellency the Commissioner-General has signed an executive order to the effect that the recommendation be carried out forthwith.' So devoid of reaction was the prisoner, that Berg asked, 'Did you understand?'

'Yes. May—may I see—may I take my leave—of my family?'

'No. That is forbidden in these cases,' Berg said, but hesitated, glancing once more at Sybille's letter. 'This daughter of yours . . .'

'Yes?'

'She's a harmless sort of girl, is she?'

'A good girl, Sybille.'

'I don't allow families in these cases because they start getting up petitions and such-like—especially wives. Now, I'll give permission for this girl to see you on condition that she undertakes to draw up no complaints, etcetera, etcetera.'

'Thank you.'

'I do this so you can understand the meaning of Christian charity.'

'Thank you.'

'Quite right,' said van der Goes.

'Take him away.'

'Thank you.'

With Henning gone, van der Goes said, 'Now we can all breathe easier.'

'You must excuse me, landdrost,' said Berg, 'but I have an important letter to write to the Classis in Amsterdam.'

'Understood.' He rose. 'Fiscal, have you read all this?'

'Not yet, I've been with the Commissioner-General, I—'

'Well, you read it. Because, I'm telling you, if fellows like that have their way, we'll all end up in the pig-sty. He was preaching to people without souls! To think I gave him the hospitality of my house!'

When the landdrost had taken his leave, Berg dictated a letter to the Classis in Amsterdam, outlining the case against the predikant and the sentence passed upon him. He was grateful to van der Goes for providing the phrase 'without souls.' That, it may be said, was the only theological matter he touched on: there was no mention of baptism or of Christ; no mention of attempting to free the enslaved; he was guilty, the letter said, of bestiality and blasphemy.

4

Although Agatha Henning forbade Sybille to visit her father, the girl, usually so meek and obedient, rebelled. Not that it was easy for her, but her desire to see her father was stronger, more deeply-felt, than the fear of her mother, and she left the house whimpering, partly with relief, partly with anxiety, and set off for the Castle.

When Daniel returned from his boat trip to Robben Island, he found his mother sobbing. He could not remember ever having seen her cry before, and in his clumsy, bovine way, tried to comfort her.

'Agh mother,' he said, 'it's not so bad.'

'Not bad? Banishment? Like a thief in the night? Not bad?'

He tried her own remedy. 'It's God's will, mother.'

'But where's it leading us?' she asked. All her life she had been able to discern the pattern; now she was at a loss. 'Oh, the disgrace!' she sobbed. 'I'm not talking about people, I don't care about people. I'm talking about our disgrace before the Lord.'

Awkwardly, Daniel put his arms around her. 'Mother, mother, stop this crying. It doesn't help. It makes me want to cry, too. Please, mother, stop it.'

She made every effort to control her tears, but some resistance in her had been broken, a knot, pulled tight over a lifetime, had been severed, and she was defenceless against the tide of emotion.

'Try the Bible, mother. Go on. Turn a page, go on, mother.'

'I've tried!'

'Try again. Please, for my sake, mother.'

Sniffing and shuddering, she pulled the book towards her. 'O God,' she said, 'help me, help me!' Then she opened and pointed to the last Psalm:

'Praise ye the Lord. Praise God in his sanctuary: praise him in the firmament of his power.'

She looked helplessly at her son. 'Yes, yes,' she said, 'praise the Lord.'

After a long while, Daniel said, 'We're better off without him.'

The Fiscal's secretary said, 'You have been given permission to see the prisoner on condition that you make no complaint as to his condition, nor write nor publish nor cause to be published any matter concerning your visit. Do you agree?'

'Yes, I agree.'

'Sign here.'

The next few minutes were the most frightening of her young life: down the cold, dark passage that led to the dungeons, along the rat-infested corridor, following the sickly torch of the guard. When they came to the cell door, the soldier slid open the panel and called 'Prisoner Henning?' and she heard her father's voice answer.

'You have a visitor. Come on, stand up. Come to the door.' The soldier turned to Sybille. 'Stand here, talk to him through this hole.'

'But am I not to be allowed to see him?'

'Talk through the hole.'

'But—but it's too high for me. I can't reach.'

'I can't help that. I've got my orders,' and he stood a few paces away, holding the torch towards the girl.

Already near to tears, Sybille stood on tip-toe. 'Father? Can you hear me?'

'Who is that?'

'Sybille.'

'Who?'

'Your daughter.' She sobbed now.

'Is Adam with you?'

'Who?'

'Where's your brother?'

'Daniel? He's with mother.'

'Find Adam.'

'Oh father, what's to become of you?'

'I am ill.'

'Dominee, I shall pray for you as long as I have breath.'

'*Hurry it up now, you've only a few more minutes.*'

'Yes, pray for me.'

'I will, I will.'

'And find Adam. And his mother. We'll meet in Henningsdorp.'

'What, father?'

'Yes, yes, we'll meet there, in the church, I promise. Find your brother, and we'll meet.'

'I don't know what you mean, father—'

'*Time's up!*'

'Yes, you remember, child, Adam!'

'No, father—'

'*That's enough, now!*'

'Oh Christ! I am guilty of love!'

'Goodbye, dominee, goodbye!'

'Oh Christ!'

'Father, I have to go now!'

'Oh Christ!'

At midnight on 6 February, Henning was taken, by a coach that bore neither the Company's emblem nor the Colony's coat of arms, to the harbour and given into the charge of Captain Schmidt of the East Indiaman, *'t Goede Hoop*. He was bound in chains and committed to the ship's dungeon. An hour later, the Captain ordered the anchor to be raised, cast off and set sail for Batavia.

From the Captain's log:

The twenty-third day at sea.
In the forenoon I was summoned to the dungeon by my second officer, mynheer Louw. The prisoner Henning was delirious and could not be calmed. I ordered laudanum to be administered and a close watch kept on his condition. Towards evening I was again summoned to the dungeon where I was informed that the prisoner was dead. I committed his body to the deep and, although cognisant of his crimes, I prayed for the resurrection of the body, when the Sea shall give up her dead and the life of the world to come, through Jesus Christ.

5

Bezuidenhout, the dwarf, observed the activity from the window of his office across Church Square. Standing on a three-legged stool, his head reaching just above the raised sill, he watched the trunks and packing cases being carried out and roughly placed on the hand-cart that stood on the dusty sidewalk, close to the Hennings' front door. He saw Sybille hovering, fluttering, one moment appearing in the doorway issuing instructions or nervous pleas to the pair of Company slaves, the next vanishing once more into the house. Then, when the cart was piled high and the two slaves were slinging and tying ropes to secure the load, Daniel Henning emerged into the sunlight with his mother. Even Bezuidenhout was shocked by the change events had wrought in her. Less than a week before he had confronted a woman carved out of granite; now she seemed shrunken, hesitant, lost, as though by some trick of time she had aged too quickly and was entering the shadows of senility. Tightly gripping Daniel's hand, she shuffled, small, imperceptible steps, the short distance from door to cart. At last, Sybille, wrapped in a blue cloak despite the heat, and carrying another of olive-green over her arm, stepped outside, hesitated and glanced up towards Bezuidenhout's office as if she knew, unaccountably, that the little man was witnessing their humiliation. He, for his part, felt a sharp prick of uneasiness and withdrew into the shadows of his musty room, but still managed to gaze down on the scene across the Square.

Daniel called to one of the slaves, 'Give me a hand with my mother,' but Agatha shook her head violently, her chin pressed to her chest as if she dared not look up. 'No!' she rasped. 'Not him, not him, not that one!'

'You know him then?' Daniel asked, full of aggressive suspicion. Agatha remained silent; her son turned to the second slave who was busily knotting the ropes, and ordered him to help. Again Agatha declined, this time flailing her arms as though she were warding off a physical assault. 'Keep them away from me!' she barked.

Daniel said, 'Agh, mother, can you get on the cart by yourself?'

To answer him, she edged forward once more, grabbed hold of the cart but then appeared to be stuck, locked, immobile. She looked helplessly at her son who placed his hands under her arm-pits and clumsily heaved her on to the back end of the cart with such ease that she gave the impression of weightlessness. Her legs dangled over the edge, swinging to and fro, like a dreaming child's, while Daniel seated himself beside her, holding her awkwardly around the shoulders in case she slipped.

'Where shall I sit?' asked Sybille.

Daniel glanced backwards, saw there was no room, and answered, 'You'll have to walk.'

And so, with the two slaves dragging the cart, with Agatha and Daniel nestling uncomfortably amidst the untidy pile of the family's belongings, and with Sybille trailing forlornly behind, the sad little procession moved off. From his vantage-point, Bezuidenhout experienced a sense of relief and of satisfaction. It passed through his oversized head that justice had been done and that he had been the instrument of that Divine pattern, so pleasing in its perfect symmetry. The family of the antichrist were obviously humbled, their spirit oppressed, their pride shattered: what more could this mis-shapen Christian have done in order to bear witness to his love of God? (Had he looked closer, had he been able to scrutinise Sybille's face, had he searched those pale eyes, he would have perceived a disturbing light: no broken spirit here, no penitent, but one aflame with spiritual exaltation however humble her demeanour. Had he stood face to face with her, the dwarf would not have been so smug.)

He watched them disappear in the direction of the Grand Parade before hopping down off the stool. He sat at his desk and wrote the concluding paragraph of a letter to his cousin in Amsterdam:

Today the family of the degenerate, whose name I cannot bring myself to write, were justly evicted from Church property. If I had my way I would have deported them too, since his sins are a stain on our community of which it is best not to be reminded. But the charity of Jesus Christ prevailed, and one must pray that God's wrath will be subdued and that these people may deal more kindly with us than their criminal father did. I will pray for them. I can do no more.

II

Obsessions

It may be said that Sybille protected the tender, painful memory of her last meeting with her father, Johannes Henning, in the nebulous glow of sickly religious sentiment, and transformed his parting words into a litany. ('Yes, pray for me/And find Adam, and his mother, we'll meet in Henningsdorp/We'll meet there, in the church, I promise, find your brother and we'll meet/Remember, child, Adam/Oh Christ, I am guilty of love/Oh Christ/Oh Christ!') She recalled that dreadful interview as though she were remembering a vision, intensified his presence by passionate concentration as she was accustomed to do when in prayer, and heard his disembodied voice as though it echoed in a sepulchre. She thought of little else; indeed, she thought of nothing else, so that her father's memory represented strength and will, love and hope. It was his presence within her that brought a fierceness to her eye and caused those she met to speak mistakenly of her loss of reason. It was these same people who could not understand that anyone, having to suffer the hardships heaped upon Sybille, could endure them with apparent indifference, could smile and exude peace, and face a forbidding future with such meekness. They could not know what fortified her: the incoherent murmurs of a condemned man.

The memory itself was so full of life to her, for it contained puzzles and conundrums that cried out to be solved. His words, like a coded message, so beloved of prophets, were burdened with supplication, pleas for prayer, mysterious names, but above all with the promise of a second coming, a future, mystical réunion—'We'll meet in Henningsdorp! We'll meet there, in the church, I promise'—

which offered the girl a hopeful reality and enabled her to ignore the painful present. But she was mindful that he had made conditions as all holy men do: 'Find Adam, and his mother, pray for me/Find your brother/Henningsdorp.' And so it was she took a solemn, secret vow to fulfil her father's parting wishes in the knowledge that she would see him again; this knowledge was more certain even than her belief in Christ's Resurrection.

The painful present: two rooms in a wooden house near the Parade; sharing a bed with her mother whose right side had become immobile, particularly noticeable about her face and especially the mouth, dragged down at the corner into a grim, almost sardonic scowl. Agatha spoke little, voicing only her physical needs to which her daughter ministered selflessly. At night, when the two women lay together, Sybille would sleep like an innocent child, lulled, it seemed, by her mother's harsh, regular moaning. In the morning, Sybille would be first at the market stalls, buying cheap food and even stealing when money was short, justified by the necessity of having to keep her vow. (She had grown alarmingly thin and her face was dominated more than ever by two staring eyes.)

From the market she would wend her way to Hottentot Square, there to greet the wagons bearing newcomers from the hinterland. 'Any here know Henningsdorp?' she would ask, 'or Blauwzand?' Once, a blind man, old with scarred eyeballs, answered, 'I'm from Blauwzand.'

'Do you know Henningsdorp?' Sybille asked, her throat constricting with excitement.

'Who wants to know?' demanded the man, turning his head sharply so that his ear was close to the girl's face.

'My name is Henning,' answered Sybille. 'My father was predikant in Blauwzand.'

The blind man raised his head and spat at Sybille's feet. 'Keep away from me,' he cried. 'I'm cursed as it is!'

But Sybille ignored the insult. 'When you return, take me with you,' she pleaded. 'I won't be any trouble, I'll work for you, I won't be a burden, please—'

'Gert! Gert!' called the man and moments later he was joined by his son. 'There's a woman, here, Henning's daughter. Bundle her off, man, bundle her off!'

'Get away from here!' the son shouted, raising his hand to slap her. 'We're good people! You're from the devil!'

Soon, a small knot of onlookers gathered, threatening Sybille as though she were a dangerous animal. Several swore at her, others stamped their feet as if performing a ritual dance, and one small boy threw a stone that glanced off her shoulder. She had no choice but to retire; the next day, however, she was there again. And the next, and the next.

By noon she would return to her mother, cook lunch, wash and repair their threadbare clothes, read from the Bible and pray for the soul of her dead father. Thus each day passed in expectation of the one that was to follow; she lived in time future, an exercise that rendered time present meaningless.

To her brother Daniel, however, time present was an insoluble problem. The day following his father's deportation he had been dismissed from the Company's service. For two weeks he sought employment but found none. His name, with its recent disgraceful associations, hung round his neck like a noose. In the end, he threw his despairing lot in with Mathias Janssens, stealing here, selling there, seeking out the right official to bribe, obtaining information, smuggling, pimping, anything that came his way. At first, he had accepted the responsibility of his mother and sister willingly; he felt that he and they had in a genuine way been cemented together by their misfortune, bound by the mutual need to survive in the face of their disgrace. But he soon lost heart : setback followed setback and scraping a living was harder than he had ever imagined. Then too, he could not bear to see his mother decline so rapidly before his eyes. When she first became ill he regarded her condition as recuperative but as time wore on her debility became a serious drain on their meagre resources, and he resented with growing bitterness the visits by the doctor and the medicines that were prescribed. As for Sybille, he did his best to ignore her, believing the common gossip that she was demented. He regarded her with growing suspicion which, in no time at all, generated a dull, brooding hatred.

And so we may leave him for the moment, this surly, grim youth, leave him to pick his unthinking way through life, leave him to become a dynast, to found a family, to sire respectability. He, even more than the community in which he lived, had rejected utterly and savagely his father's existence. Daniel will become his own ancestor; and we will return to him at the proper place. But it is his sister who is our present concern, who gives birth to a mystical, at times reluctant and mistaken, spirit of independence and renewal which is at odds with the inexorable force of times past.

2

In the first weeks of 1795 Sybille, it appeared from her diary, had lost contact with the everyday world around her, and had begun to centre her entire being in that universe created by her dead father's spirit, in which Henningsdorp loomed as large as do Mecca or Jerusalem to earthly pilgrims. Certain it is she was given encouragement in these flights of fervour, to soar in ethereal domains which comforted her; in so doing she was able to neglect, with a good conscience, the demands of her more mundane existence. The entry for 11 January:

> God's greatness is revealed! A friend from Henningsdorp. Now I am certain, certain, certain! Mother worse. Doctor here. Foul. Soon I will be free. Our spirits shall be conjoined. Praise be to God for sending me the messenger.

She had, as was her daily habit, climbed the steep slope to Hottentot Square, wandered from wagon to wagon asking if any hailed from Blauwzand, or knew Henningsdorp. Although in the town she had felt the heat, up here on the hill it was cooler, the breeze gently buffeting her bonnet. She had no especial premonition that today would be marked as the revelation of God's will, for each and every day she greeted the dawn with the hope that her life would be transformed from ordinariness into bliss.

'Are you from Blauwzand?' she asked, peering into the rear of the covered wagons. No, from Graaff-Reinet or Tulbàgh or Swellendam. And then the longed-for answer: 'Yes, I'm from Blauwzand.'

A man, difficult to say how old, his face lined like a well-worn map, grizzled hair and eyes perpetually narrowed as though constantly scanning the horizon.

'Do you know of a place called Henningsdorp?'

He was clearly taken by surprise, for he glanced nervously from side to side as if afraid she had been overheard.

'Who wants to know?' he asked, quiet but gruff.

'I do.'

'What's your name?'

'Answer my question first,' said Sybille. Her earlier experience with the blind man had taught her caution.

134

Then, unexpectedly, the man looked at her more closely, closing one eye and squinting out the other. 'Don't I know you?'

'We've not met,' answered Sybille, blushing and studying the ground at her feet.

'Something familiar about you,' said the man pointing his fore-finger as if to accuse her of mischief.

'You have not answered my question,' said Sybille. 'Do you know of a place called Henningsdorp?'

'Ssh! Keep your voice down.' Again the nervous glances from side to side. 'Tell me first who you are.'

Sensing she would get nowhere unless she obliged him, she said, 'My name is Henning. Sybille Henning.' She raised her chin, squared her shoulders, prepared to brave any assault. Instead the man's eyes grew large, his mouth opened a little: he could not believe what he had just heard. 'Johannes Henning's daughter?' he asked in an awed whisper.

'Yes,' she answered tentatively.

'I knew I recognised you,' said the man. 'You're the spitting im-age of him—except he had bigger ears.' He was genuinely delighted. 'Agh, I knew at once I'd seen you before, I just couldn't put my finger on it, that's all.'

'We haven't met!' Sybille insisted.

'No, no, that's true. But I knew your father well and I could see his likeness stamped on you. Something about the eyes. Yes, I knew your father. We had the same Christian name: Johannes. My other name's Le Roux.'

They became friends at once. He helped her into the back of his wagon, brewed coffee, folded a blanket for her to sit on and chat-tered away, marvelling at the coincidence, as he saw it, of their meeting.

'I'm a great believer in coincidence,' Le Roux said. 'It was the same with your father: both our Christian names the same. That's why we liked each other. And now you and me, meeting just like this, out of the blue. Agh, you can't beat coincidence.'

'Mynheer Le Roux, I have a favour to ask.'

'Ask away. Nothing would be too great for the daughter of the dominee, my old friend, nothing.' Tears sprang up in his eyes.

'You must answer some questions,' said Sybille.

'Agh, it would be a pleasure,' Le Roux said, searching for a hand-kerchief.

'When I last saw my father ...' her voice faltered, 'when I last saw him, he begged me to find someone called Adam, to find him and his mother and to meet in the church in Henningsdorp. Do you know anyone called Adam?' As she spoke, Sybille detected a sudden change in Le Roux's demeanour, an abrupt cooling of the warmth he had shown her. He shifted uncomfortably, filled his pipe and lit it, blowing thin funnels of smoke through tightly compressed lips. 'Do you know anyone called Adam?' she repeated.

'Adam, Adam,' he murmured. 'What surname?'

'I don't know, that's just it, if I knew—'

'Adam. I knew old Adam van Wijk—'

'Yes?'

'No. He's been dead five years at least and I don't think the dominee ever met him. No. Before the dominee's time, I'm certain of it. I never knew his mother, that's for sure.'

'Perhaps they live in Henningsdorp,' Sybille suggested.

'Agh, I don't know Henningsdorp well. More of a Blauwzand man myself.' He was not at ease telling lies.

'But there is a church in Henningsdorp?'

'Agh, now you have me. A church? Yes, I think there is. I really can't say. I—I don't know the place well, you understand. It's—it's not my line of country, you may say.' No pipe ever needed more attention.

'Mynheer Le Roux, I beg you to help me,' Sybille said earnestly.

'I'm doing my best, mejuvrou, but you ask such difficult questions.'

'No, I mean in another sense.'

'How?'

Sybille paused, considering the best way to frame her requests. She began by asking, 'It is far to Henningsdorp, is it not?'

'Well, I don't go that way,' answered Le Roux unable to conceal his discomfort. 'I couldn't say.'

'To Blauwzand, then. It is a long way.'

'Yes, certainly. Two weeks at least.'

The reply seemed to satisfy her momentarily. 'I mean it is not a journey for a young woman to undertake unless she had good cause.'

'No, no, certainly not. I wouldn't advise any young woman to head that way, no, certainly not.' He answered a little too eagerly.

'Very well, then,' said Sybille. 'When do you return to Blauw-zand?'

He became hesitant once more. 'Difficult to say. Funny thing, though, my meeting you today of all days. You see, I'm here to collect the new predikant just as I collected your father a couple of years back. Seems like yesterday. Well, I'll be heading back the moment the new man shows up. It could be any minute. My orders are to wait here for him.'

'I see,' said Sybille. 'Good. And when will you return again to Cape Town?'

'Now that's a poser. Certainly in the next year. I come at least once a year.'

'But maybe sooner?'

'Oh yes, yes, maybe sooner. You never know. Landdrost van der Goes always has business in Cape Town and if he doesn't feel like riding, or if I have to collect slaves for him, no you can never know when I'll be back.'

'Then I must ask you this,' Sybille said, her eyes fixed on the man's face. 'When you go back to Blauwzand find out all you can about this person Adam and his mother. Perhaps the new predikant can help. He will get to know the church in Henningsdorp, won't he, perhaps he could make enquiries there for me. When you have information try to come back to Cape Town as quickly as possible. I come here every morning so I shan't miss you. Please, for my father's sake, find out all you can.'

The request was less binding than Le Roux had expected. After all, he could promise now and when he next returned pretend he had discovered nothing. With relief he answered, 'Agh, certainly mejuvrou Henning, I'll do that for you with pleasure. That's no trouble at all.'

'Good,' said Sybille. 'And if you do have news for me, I shall ask you to take me to Henningsdorp. I promised my father.'

She was about to rise but Le Roux stopped her. 'Listen to an old man,' he said evenly. 'Don't come near the place. Stay here. If another Henning shows their face in Blauwzand, God knows what would happen. Van der Goes was no friend of your father's. Take my advice, mejuvrou: forget about Henningsdorp.'

But Sybille did not hear what she did not wish to hear. She rose, saying, 'Find out all you can. I look forward to your return.'

God's greatness is revealed! At last the girl was able to feel that she had taken the first faltering steps along the road that would lead her to Paradise. How wise of God to send her father's former friend, how loving and compassionate! Filled with His glory, she returned home to find Doctor Mauser at her mother's bedside.

'Your brother Daniel sent for me,' he explained. Sybille untied her bonnet, smiled vaguely and looked disinterested; her mind was full of other matters.

'Did *you* not notice the stench?' asked Mauser.

'What stench?'

'Oh come, mejuvrou, smell the air: it's putrid!'

Sybille sniffed. 'I don't smell anything,' she said. She wondered why the doctor held a cloth to his nose.

'Your brother says he has complained to you about the smell for the past week. Why did you not call me?'

'I don't recall Daniel complaining,' Sybille said, opening her diary and beginning to write.

'Her stomach's swollen,' Mauser said, crossing to the window and opening it wide.

'Doctor!' said Sybille, looking up. 'You told us to allow no draughts!'

'Never mind the draughts! If you do not want me to become asphyxiated, I must have some air!' He poked his head out of the window and breathed deeply.

Sybille glanced at him with a pitying look and returned to her diary. In the bed Agatha was snoring gently.

'Come here to the window, mejuvrou,' said Mauser.

'I tell you honestly, doctor, I can smell nothing.' She continued to write.

'Whether you smell it or not is of no interest to me, mejuvrou. I can barely breathe in here and that is proof enough. Now, do as I say and come here to the window.'

As if humouring a child, Sybille obliged. 'Mother's just the same as she always was—'

'When did she last move her bowels?' Mauser asked.

Sybille's cheeks coloured; such matters embarrassed her and, as was her habit whenever her sensibility was assaulted, she locked her hands tightly and moved her lips in prayer.

'Look here, mejuvrou, it's no good praying to the Almighty, He won't know the answer to my questions, He's not interested in her bowels! Come along now, think!'

138

'She sleeps a great deal,' said Sybille nervously, desperately trying to change the subject from matters which were abhorrent to her.

'I'm not surprised!' replied Mauser. 'She's in a sort of coma. I've tried twice to wake her without effect. Your mother is a very ill woman. How could you be with her daily and not notice that she is in a decline?'

'I thought sleep was good for her—'

'Never mind that. When did your mother last open her bowels?'

Sybille shuddered, answering, 'I don't know, I can't say, I—'

'Don't you put her on the pan?' Mauser demanded gruffly.

'When she asks,' Sybille said.

'Well, when was the last time?'

'I don't remember . . .'

'You don't remember,' the doctor repeated, mocking her by imitating her faraway tone of voice. 'Was it a week ago, ten days, a month?'

'A week, ten days . . .' Sybille said as though the words were meaningless to her.

'Well, it wasn't yesterday then?'

'No.'

'Or the day before?'

'No.'

'All right then, it must be more than two days ago, am I right?'

'Yes.'

'Well, mejuvrou, a person can't go for two days without getting rid of the waste inside them, you understand?'

Sybille appeared not to hear him; she said, 'I don't remember. I try not to think about time like that. We all live in God's plan of—'

'Look,' interrupted the doctor. 'God's plan includes opening your bowels every day.'

'Come to think of it,' said Sybille, 'she has not asked for the—for the pan for a long time,' and smiled.

He nodded, resigned to Sybille's irritating manner and, placing the handkerchief once more over his nose, returned to Agatha's side.

'Mevrou Henning,' he said. 'You must sit on the pan.' Then to Sybille: 'Fetch the pan, mejuvrou.'

'But mother's asleep,' argued Sybille.

'We are going to wake her!' Gently, he slapped the invalid's face, then forced her eyelids back. 'Come along, come along, mevrou, come along, wake up, wake up!' Agatha groaned and then quite suddenly opened her eyes of her own accord, looking first at the doctor then at her daughter.

'Can you hear me?' Mauser asked.

'Of course.' The voice was strained but there was no doubting she understood; Mauser was concerned, for he thought she was too aware of what was going on around her.

'Mevrou, when did you last move your bowels?'

Now Agatha shook her head violently, as though once begun she had no power to stop it.

'What's the matter, mevrou?' Mauser asked, trying to calm her with one hand, while still keeping the handkerchief to his nose with the other.

'Where's Daniel?' Agatha cried out.

'Your son's out, mevrou, he's not here—'

'Leave me alone—'

'Mevrou, try and understand what I'm telling you: you must sit on the pan—'

'No!'

'You will do as I say! Your whole body will become poisoned!'

She made a rasping, hissing sound like a cornered animal. 'No, no, no!' she cried.

'Mevrou, you will open your bowels!'

'I will not!' Agatha growled, her face distorted by paralysis and vehemence. 'No! I—will—not! I will not—I will not shit and I will not piss!'

Sybille cried out involuntarily, buried her face in her hands and muttered fervently prayers of forgiveness.

'Oh, it's like that is it?' said Mauser. 'You listen to me, woman, don't play tricks like that with me. You get on the pan and you let out the dirt inside you. Mejuvrou, bring the pan here!'

But Sybille did not move. Agatha said, 'I will not *shit*!' The word seemed to give her secret pleasure.

'I can play games too, mevrou Henning. I've got medicines that will make you do it, do you hear?' And from his bag he took a jar, and from the jar he poured into the cup a dark brown liquid. 'Come on, open your mouth and take this.' He leaned over her, but, as he did so, Agatha raised her good left arm and dashed the cup from his hand, causing the medicine to spill over his waistcoat. He rose angrily. 'I'm not standing for this!' he cried. 'You stupid old witch! You can rot to death for all I care! God Almighty, no one can pay

me enough to smell the smell that's coming from you!' To Sybille:
'I'll leave the medicine here. Get it down her if you can, and take
my advice; go sleep in the other room—'

'With my brother?' Sybille asked, eyes wide.

'You won't die from immodesty, mejuvrou,' Mauser growled. 'But
you may well die from this stench!' He marched to the door. 'Pay
me now,' he said, holding out his hand. Sybille hesitated, then hurried to the chest of drawers where she kept the money.

Mauser said, 'I've known cases like this before. They swell with
their own waste, you understand? They rot from the inside out,
God knows why! When the pain gets too bad she'll take the medicine, don't worry,' and clutching the money, he ran from the room
out into the fresh air.

When he had gone, Sybille said, 'You're a wicked girl, very, very
wicked. I shall be in the next room. Call me if you want your medicine.'

But Agatha did not call. As if to be revenged on her mortality, she
refused to rid herself of her own waste. The stench of decay emanated from every pore of her body. She yelled obscenities at her
daughter, called for her son, and cursed her dead husband. After
three days, she declined into a deep, morose stupor, her stomach
swollen with putrefaction. Sybille called the doctor once more but
he did not come. Daniel held his mother's hand and wept; his sister
prayed. On the fourth day, at dawn, Agatha died.

12

Farewells

A month after Agatha's death, Daniel abandoned his sister; the two children of Johannes Henning never saw each other again. Two weeks after that, a neighbour, who lived in the same house, found Sybille semi-conscious, unkempt, half-starved. It appeared she had not eaten since Daniel's departure and was now seriously ill. Early in February 1795, she was admitted to the Hospital, an institution under the jurisdiction of the Company and shamefully neglected by those whose special responsibility it was.

The ward, intended for ten beds, now housed thirty women. There were approximately twelve new admissions a week, which corresponded, more or less, to the death rate. The patients were attended by slaves for their day-to-day needs, and by doctors when the doctors could spare the time. The subject of cockroaches was twice raised by voluntary workers, and twice action was promised by the appropriate officials. To enter the hospital, some said, was the same as being fitted for a coffin.

But, at least, Sybille was fed, and her strength soon returned. However, she now became the subject of a dispute between the Hospital and the Orphan Chamber. The Hospital, ever anxious to make room for newcomers, discovered to its dismay that Sybille had no means of support. The details of her case were at once passed to the Orphan Chamber, who rejected her claim to their charity. At what age, they asked, did a person cease to be an orphan? Could a girl in her early twenties qualify for aid from a fund intended for children? The argument passed back and forth; meanwhile, Sybille remained in the care of the medical authorities.

Although her physical needs were being taken care of, spiritually it was not a comfortable time. She was haunted by the thought that, because of her illness, she had missed meeting up with Le Roux in Hottentot Square. She was convinced the man had come again to Cape Town, with news of Adam and his mother, waited to inform her and, when she had not appeared, had returned to Blauwzand. These misgivings would not have played so prominent a part had Sybille the physical strength to believe that her illness was as much a part of the Divine scheme as any other event in her life. Doubt too, she realised long afterwards, was one of God's weapons.

As her strength returned, so she took more interest in the life of the ward and the world around her. On 8 May, she was able to record:

> They say the French will occupy the Cape any day now. The women are all afeared, for we know how the French treat women. God help us all.

And two days later:

> There is a rumour that Prince William has invaded France and is at the gates of Paris. God be praised. We are to be saved from all manner of indecencies.

But on 16 May:

> The rumour is false. The Prince is still in England. They say the French have already put to sea with an army of ruffians. Many people, so Dr Mauser says, are leaving for the interior. If only I were well, I could perhaps find a wagon for Blauwzand.

The reason for all the speculation was real enough. The revolutionary French, who had shorn themselves of the Bourbons, found unexpected sympathy among republican Dutchmen whose anglophile Prince William of Orange had fled to England. The English and the exiled Prince, temporarily resident at Kew, were convinced that the vile French had designs on the sea route to India. The question was how could they be prevented? For the first time in its history, the Cape became the centrepiece of international politics, and this unaccustomed role threw the population into a ferment of rumour and exaggeration. It is indicative of Sybille's state of mind that, apart from the above entries in her diary with their fears for her virtue, she mentioned the events but once more, on 30 May:

Dr Mauser says we must pray that King George gives our Prince an army to conquer the murdering French. But one of the women says the English are not to be trusted. Her husband was English. We are in the hands of God.

But, for the most part, she writes:

Could I but find a way of escaping this prison. I know, *know* that Le Roux has come and gone. I feel it to be so in every bone of my body. I pray that he may find me. My only hope is that if the French take the Cape, they will move us north, nearer to Blauw-zand. God please will it so. Yes, yes, I feel it deeply, deeply. Le Roux is here and looking for me. He is close. God help me to meet him again.

In one respect, at least, she was right: Le Roux was in Cape Town, but he was not looking for Sybille.

2

On 10 June the Hospital was the centre of a great flurry of activity: a personage of some importance had been admitted to a private room. No one knew his name for certain, but some said it was the Commissioner-General, others that it was Fiscal Berg. Later that day, both the Commissioner-General and the Fiscal were seen visiting the patient, which re-opened the door to new theories. The women in Sybille's ward did their best to find out his identity, but to no avail; all they could learn for certain was that the man was near to death.

Late in the afternoon of that day Sybille, who was well enough to assist the nurses with the less fortunate patients, rose from her bed and made her way to the kitchens to help with the preparation of the evening meal. Walking along one of the interminable corridors, she chanced to pass an open door through which she saw a minister of the Reformed Church praying at the bedside of a patient. She guessed at once that this was the dying man. She could not see his face, but she was struck by his enormous bulk and she later re-marked that it looked as though a wine vat had been put to bed. The predikant, seeing her hovering in the doorway, waved her away, and then shut the door. Having collected the food from the kitchen, a chore which took almost an hour, she returned to her ward and again had occasion to pass the room. Once more the door was open, but this time the bed was empty. She knew that the patient had died.

At midnight, when all was quiet but for the groans and snores of the women, the ward was woken by dreadful screams. Candles were lit, the slaves hurried back and forth, there were urgent whispers and still more screams which grew louder and louder.

'Here!' called one of the women, peering out of the window behind her bed. Those who were well enough, Sybille among them, swarmed to her side and saw, down below in the courtyard, a Malay woman struggling furiously with three or four of the hospital staff.

'Open the window,' said a patient, 'we'll hear what's going on.'

'I must see him!' the Malay woman was shouting. 'He's my friend! Tell him! Tell him who I am. My name is Tantira! Tell him!'

Now, from the Hospital itself, came two men, nightshirts showing beneath their coats. A spirited conversation followed which the women in the ward were unable to hear, but in the midst of it, the Malay woman gave vent to a terrible, agonising scream and collapsed on the cobble stones.

From Sybille's diary:

A dreadful commotion: the Malay was brought, struggling as though the D-v-l possessed her, into our ward. Several of the women objected. Mevrou de Wet complained loudest of all, protesting that a Malay woman should be allowed in the same ward as she. Yet, to tell the truth, mevrou de Wet is herself of a much darker complexion than the Malay, Tantira. When they had managed to hold her down on the bed, laudanum was called for and administered. Soon, the woman became quiet. We were ordered to sleep and our candles were extinguished. With everything quiet once more, Old Martha, whose bed is next to mine, and Willi Janssen rose and tip-toed to Tantira's bed. She was not yet asleep, although the laudanum had begun to make her drowsy. At first, I thought they meant to do her injury, and shut my eyes tight for fear of seeing anything untoward, but instead, Old Martha and Willi questioned Tantira, and her answers caused me the utmost disquiet. 'What was all the fuss about?' Old Martha asked. 'He owes me money,' answered Tantira. 'Who does?' asked Willi. 'The landdrost,' came the reply. 'Is he the one who died?' This question alarmed Tantira. She struggled up on one elbow, her eyes starting. 'Is he dead?' she asked. 'Oh Allah, now he'll never pay me!' Then her story tumbled out in fits and starts. This landdrost was in the habit of visiting a bar called the Haarlem, where Tantira worked, each time he visited Cape Town. On this particular day, he and Tantira were in conversation in her room when her husband burst in, drunk and savage, and stabbed the landdrost eight or nine times. Tantira had come to the hospital to demand money from the wounded man for some service or other she had rendered him. How callous are these Malays!

By now she was nearly asleep, but as she began to lose consciousness, she said something that caused me to sit bolt upright. 'I suppose,' Tantira said, 'I shall have to go to Blauwzand to collect . . .'

I sprang from the bed and rushed to her side. Shaking her, I demanded, 'Was he the landdrost of Blauwzand? Was his name van der Goes?' 'Yes, yes, yes,' she answered, 'van der Goes, van der Goes . . .'

Several of the women tried to restrain Sybille from leaving the Hospital then and there. But she could not be argued with. Uppermost in her mind was the thought that Le Roux might be in Hottentot Square or, worse, on his way back to Blauwzand. She was convinced that she must go and see for herself, now, in the night, or else miss forever the opportunity for which she had waited so long.

She dressed in the dark but was delayed twice by having to clamber back into her bed, pretending to be asleep, while two Company soldiers entered the ward and made for Tantira's bed. They chained her wrists to the bedstead; she was a vital witness whose evidence would be needed against the landdrost's murderer, and they were not going to allow her to escape. The delay strained every nerve in Sybille's body, but at last, when all was again peaceful, she bade farewell to her companions and set off for Hottentot Square.

A dull, tepid drizzle was falling, and heavy clouds shrouded the Table and Lion's Head. Yet, the air was cold and by the time Sybille began to clamber up the hill towards the Square, her teeth were chattering uncontrollably. She could see the torchlight from some way off, and the sight of the flames, yellow smudges against the sky, caused her to quicken her pace.

When she reached the cluster of wagons, she knew at once that she had been right to come, for they were loading the body of Abraham van der Goes into the rear of Johannes Le Roux's wagon. The minister of the Reformed Church, the one Sybille had seen at the dying man's bedside, was in attendance, reciting Psalm 51, 'Have mercy upon me, O God, according to thy loving kindness.' Sybille was quite unaffected by the solemnity of the macabre ceremony; she had waited too long for this moment to be cautious. As the land-drost's bloated remains were being heaved on to the tailboard, she rushed forward, crying, 'Mynheer Le Roux! Mynheer Le Roux! I have come!'

Gravity gave way to absurdity: the bearers of that heavy load paused, their cargo half in, half out of the wagon; the astonished face of Le Roux appeared over the linen shroud, and the predikant broke off the Psalm at the words, 'Purge me with hyssop—.' All turned to look incredulously at the pale, thin girl who held out her arms as though she expected to be embraced; for a moment, they were still and silent, disturbed only by the drizzle gently rapping the canvas of the wagon canopies.

Then, everyone acted at once. Le Roux, recognising her, darted out of sight; the men carrying van der Goes pulled in opposite direc-tions; a soldier stepped out of the shadows and challenged Sybille, threatening her with his gun; the predikant marched towards her. Sybille seemed not to notice any of this, but ran straight on, ducking under the bulky cortège, and clambered into the wagon to find Le Roux. It was then that the predikant collected his thoughts, called loudly for order, and clumsily pulled the girl off the tailboard on to the ground.

Explanations tumbled out. 'He must, he must take me to Blauw-zand!' she cried, 'He must, he must, he must!'

Le Roux said, 'Who is she?' in a nervous, frightened way, al-though he remembered her well.

'I am Johannes Henning's daughter! You promised to take me to Blauwzand, you promised—!'

The name Henning caused the predikant to stiffen, and while Le Roux continued to protest that he had never seen the girl before, the minister ordered the soldier to place her under arrest. In the mean-time the pall-bearers had shoved the landdrost's body into the wagon and were standing in a semi-circle observing the dispute.

'Mount up and get going, Le Roux,' commanded the minister, and gratefully Le Roux obeyed.

It was all over very quickly: the oxen heaved forward and the wagon began to rumble over the uneven ground, towards the far side of the square. Sybille started to scream and to run forward, but the soldier grabbed hold of her and held her back. Watching the wagon depart without her, she was numbed by desperation. It passed through her mind that God's displeasure would kill her, for how could she bear to live knowing that the one chance she had suffered so much to create was now slipping through her fingers? Le Roux's wagon, van der Goes's hearse, soon disappeared from sight.

The soldier said, 'Dominee, do you want me to take this woman in and charge her?'

The predikant considered the matter, shook his head and walked off; others, who had partaken in, or watched the strange charade, also dispersed. Sybille walked aimlessly, a few steps in this direction, a few steps in that, now stopping, now turning; the soldier fell in beside her.

'Hey, girlie,' he said. 'If you've nothing to do for the next couple of hours, you can come and keep me company, hey?'

'Why did He desert me?' cried Sybille.

'Who? Was that your husband? Who?'

'He who watches over us all.'

'Listen, girlie, I don't know about that. I'm talking about a little fun in the guardroom, that's all.'

'What shall I do now?' she asked in a vague, distant voice.

'That's what I'm talking about,' answered the soldier. 'If you want to keep out of the rain and at the same time have a little fun, what about it?'

'I'm cold,' she said.

'It's warm in my box.' And, putting his arm around her waist, he led her to the wooden hut which stood on rising ground with a fine view of the Square, and of the Ocean beyond; the drizzle had ceased, and the sombre clouds were falling back behind Blauwberg; it promised to be one of those unexpected winter days, clear and cool.

The warmth of the little hut melted Sybille's bewilderment and sense of loss. No sooner was she inside than the exertions of the night took their toll, and she sank down on the floor, sobbing gently at first but then more painfully, more loudly.

'What's the matter with you, hey?' asked the soldier, already un-buckling his belt, and loosening the collar of his tunic.

'O Christ, what's to happen to me?' she cried.

'Hey, wait a minute,' said the soldier, suspicious that he was about to be disappointed. 'You agreed to come here with me—'

'Save me, save me,' she moaned, hands clasped, eyes to Heaven, and then began to writhe on the bare floor as the spirit of prayer and helplessness conjoined in her.

The soldier, looking down at the twisting body, felt his mouth become dry. 'Is this the game?' he asked in a hoarse whisper. 'Is it now I'm to do it? Is it now?' And, without waiting for a reply, he dropped down on his knees beside her, throwing back her skirts, clumsily pulling at her undergarments and at her bodice, while she implored God to show her the way to Blauwzand. And when the soldier turned her on her back, her eyes were glazed and sightless, her whole body shuddering.

'Keep still, keep still,' he cried. 'I can't get in, I can't get in!'

'God, make the way clear,' Sybille said.

'Just keep still, that's all!'

'Sweet Jesus, I deliver myself into Thy hands!'

'I can't get in!'

'My heart is open to Thy love!'

'Never mind your fucking heart, open your legs, you stupid bitch!'

'Christ, O Christ, take me to Blauwzand!'

'If you don't—Christ Almighty—I'm coming—I'll come all over —O Christ!'

'O Sweet Jesus!'

'Christ!'

'Blauwzand!'

'Stupid, fucking bitch, I've come!' He slapped her hard across the face.

He rose and dressed, while she continued to lie on the floor in an intense ecstasy of communion, praying God to transport her to Blauwzand.

'You're mad in the head, you know that? I knew a girl had fits like you. They locked her up, you get my meaning? They locked her up in the mad-house. That's where you should be. Now, get out of here, I don't want to see your face again, go on, clear off, get out!'

Throwing open the rickety door, and grabbing her by the arm, he tried to tumble her out of the hut. But as he stood in the open doorway, he was suddenly alerted by two events which occurred almost simultaneously. The first puzzled him; the second caused alarm. Out in the bay, beyond Robben Island, he saw a cluster of ships, ten in all, men o' war, in a formation that was both threatening and sinister. At the same moment, his attention was drawn to the far side of the Square, to the sight of his sergeant and six men, haring towards him. The sergeant was shouting but the soldier could not make out the words. Overcome by panic, he turned to Sybille and hissed, 'Get up, we're for it now, my sergeant's here, Christ, I'll be for it!' Somehow, he managed to pull her into the corner which would be obscured by the door when open. He grabbed a blanket and the Company flag and threw them over her. 'Keep still now, otherwise we're lost. Don't move for God's sake!'

By then, the sergeant had reached them and his words were plain. 'The French have invaded! Fall in, fall in! The French have come!'

3

But it was not the French.

Aboard the leading ship, Admiral Sir George Keith Elphinstone stood at the rail, telescope to his eye, and surveyed the panorama which his fellow-countryman, Francis Drake, had described two hundred years before as 'a most stately thing, and the fairest cape that we saw in the whole circumference of the earth'. But Sir George had little eye for beauty; he appraised the topography of a place only for its strategic advantages. Turning to the man beside him, the Admiral said, 'Dashed inconvenient for a landing.'

The remark was addressed to Major-General James Henry Craig, tall and elegant, known to his men as 'Gentle Jimmy', more of a diplomat than a fighting soldier. 'I daresay we'll find somewhere,' he said.

The two men had left England in April. The Admiral was in command of the entire expedition, two squadrons of six and four ships; the smaller squadron was commanded by Commodore Blankett, a stern disciplinarian, nicknamed 'Wet'. The combined squadrons carried sixteen hundred men under Craig's command; they were not to be regarded as an invasion force, but rather as a symbol of British authority. Their presence was not aggressive, but diplomatic. Unfortunately, the inhabitants of the Cape were not to know their true intentions.

By eight o'clock on that Thursday, 11 June, panic and confusion had swept through the town like the south-east wind. In a hundred households emergency measures were taken: guns were primed and loaded, windows shuttered, doors barred, barricades erected. A discord of bugles sounded over the town; horsemen galloped wildly down the streets; the slave bells tolled; all was chaos. The rumours of the past months had served, it seemed, to catch the population unawares. Many families were already packing their belongings, locking their houses and fleeing into the interior. One such was the family de Mist.

Henrik de Mist had six good reasons for leaving Cape Town: six daughters, aged between sixteen and twenty-four. Visions of French soldiers raping his beloved brood plagued his thoughts and he was determined to prevent so hideous a prospect. (He discounted the idea that the French would be interested in his wife, Maria, although she was by far the most attractive of the females in his household.) De Mist was, at the best of times, nervous and fidgety, with a tic that made him bare his teeth as though he were leering; on this day, he could hardly keep still, rushing from one member of his family to another, scolding, chivvying, hurrying, and the tic occurred with such frequency that he gave the impression of a mad terrier with a perpetual snarl.

His wife, Maria, tall and buxom but with a wonderfully pretty face perfectly heart-shaped, remained calm; she packed the clothes and linen, smiling serenely, as though she were setting off for a day in the country. Her attitude enraged her husband who mistook her tranquillity for indifference.

'Hurry, hurry, Maria, I implore you. The world is crashing about our heads and you smile!'

'Now then, mynheer de Mist, they have not landed yet. There is plenty of time. After all, they will not know to come straight to this house the moment they set foot ashore.'

'You're certain of that, are you?' said de Mist viciously. 'Do you not think they have had spies in the town these past months? Do you not think they know—' he lowered his voice—'where to find creatures for their pleasure? They are French! You forget, I have been in Paris!'

The six daughters bubbled with excitement; nothing quite so dramatic had ever occurred in their young lives. Although the true reason for their sudden departure was kept secret from them, they nevertheless sensed that something faintly indecent was the cause, and this excited them further.

Just before noon they were ready. De Mist paid off his slaves and urged them to hide in the cellar. With wife and daughters perched atop packing-cases and furniture, which, in turn, were piled on an open cart, de Mist flicked the reins and drove his horses in the direction of Hottentot Square in the hope of purchasing a covered wagon to carry them, he prayed, to safety.

4

The soldier had forgotten all about Sybille:

I felt as though I could not breathe. I was aware of much activity outside and, in the end, I could endure my concealment no longer. My body ached, especially my shoulders and my thighs, but I knew that God had prevented the vile soldier from harming me and I thanked Him for entering my spirit and for comforting me when I was most in need. Having thrown off my covering, I crawled to the narrow door, opened it a crack and peered out. The sight that greeted my eyes was utterly bewildering: Hottentot Square was filled with people running this way and that, shouting and calling to each other, scolding children who were crying, and generally causing a shifting, continuous confusion. At that end of the Square where I had last seen Le Roux, there were a great many wagons, more than a score, all trying to take the road at the same time, each making it impossible for any other to move, so that, apart from men and women bustling to and fro, trying to sort matters out everything had come to a standstill. I made my way towards the beleaguered wagons, asking as I went what the cause was of the commotion. 'The French have invaded,' I was told, and this caused me to fear for my safety and my virtue.

The scene at the bottleneck was quite frightening. Men were fighting with each other and the curses that rent the air were of such a blasphemous nature as to give the D-v-l comfort.

At first it was impossible to see the exact cause of the impasse, but when I had pushed and squeezed my way through I soon discovered the reason: a long line of carts of every description filled the road in the opposite direction, so that those wanting to enter the Square were blocked head-on by those wanting to leave it.

Without knowing why, but doubtless spurred by fear, I started to run along the road, passing cart after cart filled with goods and people hoping to reach the Square. The further I ran, the greater grew my fear, until, before long, I had reached the last vehicle. There were still a great many people struggling up the hill on foot, and just as I was about to turn off on to one of the side roads that lead back to the town, I saw yet another open cart rumbling up the dusty track. I felt suddenly compelled to warn them of what lay ahead. 'Go no further!' I cried. 'The Square is blocked, and all the road that leads to it. You'd do better to take the lower road along the coast!' I was, by then, level with the driver, a man of middle years, neat as a pin, but with an alarming grimace that afflicted his face from time to time. On the back were seven women, obviously his wife and their daughters.

The wife, a kindly woman, called to me, 'Where are your parents, child? Have you lost them?' I replied that both my parents were dead and that I was seeking a way to escape the French. 'One more won't make any difference,' she said with a welcoming smile, offered her hand and pulled me aboard. 'Turn the cart round, mynheer de Mist,' she ordered, and her husband tugged at the reins and turned the cart. In a short while we descended from the high road and were proceeding north through the town in the direction of Stellenbosch. We had not gone very far before a horseman overtook us, crying, 'It is the British, not the French, the British!' But mynheer de Mist did not believe him, saying that it was a trick, for the French were cunning and wicked and would stoop low to achieve their evil ends. I thank God that He has sent so wise a man to protect me.

By evening we came to a small farm. After much bargaining, mynheer de Mist was able to purchase a covered wagon together with a span of oxen. I helped the family transfer their goods and, this done, we set off once more, mynheer de Mist at the reins, we women now under cover.

It seemed that we were making for Swellendam where the family had an uncle. Although it is not Blauwzand, at least we were travelling north, and I knew, just knew, that God would not fail me and that somehow, with His help, I would reach my appointed goal. In all things one may discern His hand, even in wickedness, for had the soldier not been rough with me, had the French not invaded, I should be helpless and alone in Hottentot Square. God be praised. Hallelujah.

5

Two days after dropping anchor off Simonstown in False Bay, Admiral Elphinstone sent ashore one Captain William Bull-Davis with orders to demand an audience of the Commissioner-General Abraham Sluysken, the officer administrating the government of the Cape on behalf of the Dutch East India Company. Captain Bull-Davis carried an important document, a letter signed under seal by Prince William of Orange enjoining Sluysken to surrender the Colony to Great Britain, as a protective measure against the French, the Colony to be returned under solemn pledge as soon as independence and 'its ancient and established Form of Government' had been restored to the Prince's afflicted country. Captain Bull-Davis, admitted to Sluysken's presence, requested admission for the British force in the name of His Majesty King George III, and then returned to his ship.

'Admit the British,' said Fiscal Berg, 'and you can say farewell to the Company.'

'What is the alternative?' asked Sluysken.

'Fight! Fight! Fight!' thundered the Fiscal.

The Council lasted far into the night; the atmosphere was tense, for all present sensed that a vital moment in the Cape's history had arrived, and there is nothing more likely to cause politicians to act and speak irrationally than the feeling that they are concerned with making history.

'How many men do they have?' asked Sluysken, weary and dispirited.

'Approximately sixteen hundred,' replied Commandant Laube, a Westphalian, in charge of the troop of German mercenaries. 'We can match them man for man.'

But Sluysken was less confident. He knew that, though he might well command a force of equal numbers to the British, his mercenaries, burgher militia, Hottentot Pandours and Malays were no match for the highly-trained fighting machine aboard the ships in False Bay.

'I wonder if I may make a legal point?' said Reenan, the Assistant-Fiscal. 'Are we not duty bound to accept this letter from His Highness? Is he not legally the nominal head of the Company?'

Fiscal Berg answered in his best telegraphic style. 'Legality? Bah! Reality? Ja! The Dutch are allied with the French. No match for the British. Prince's position doubtful. Exiled in England, no authority. We must act only in best interests of Company. History demands!'

Laube, sly and subtle, said, 'Also, we cannot afford to make mistakes. If we back the wrong side . . .'

'What do you mean by that?' demanded Berg.

'I mean this, Fiscal: if we admit the British without a shot being fired, and tomorrow in sail the Dutch and the French, how will they regard us? As traitors! We must not back the wrong horse.'

A long silence ensued, each man trying to find a solution to these complex problems. At last, Sluysken spoke. 'We must not back either horse,' he said. 'Our only weapon is delay.'

It was fortunate that both Elphinstone and Craig had expected Sluysken to react in the way he did, although they were greatly annoyed that he had not welcomed them with open arms.

'We cannot take the Cape with our present force,' said Craig, seated at the table in the Admiral's cabin. Across from him sat Commodore Blankett, depressed and baleful. They waited for the Admiral to speak but he was busily pacing the cabin as though he were measuring it: up, across, down, across, up, heel to toe, heel to toe.

Blankett said, 'Sluysken's hoping for the French to save his bacon. And if they turn up in any strength, by God, sir, they will!'

'Without cavalry, without field guns, we simply must not be drawn into a fight,' said Craig. 'We must exert pressure of another kind.'

Elphinstone stopped pacing; he turned to his subordinates. 'What d'you mean, sir, pressure of another kind?'

'We must make them understand that we can bring good government and prosperity far superior to the damned Company.'

'They won't buy it, Craig. Your Dutchman's an obstinate beast, pig-headed. These men here, these Capers, damned weaklings, sir. What they respect is strength.'

'But we have no strength, sir,' said Blankett. He was not known as 'Wet' for nothing.

'Then, by God, sir, we'll get some!' said Elphinstone, and continued to measure his cabin.

'What d'you mean, sir? Reinforcements?' asked Craig, puzzled.

'Precisely,' replied Elphinstone, coming to a halt and balancing precariously on the balls of his feet as though on a tightrope. 'To-night, when it is dark, we will despatch a fast sloop to Major-General Clarke at San Salvador in Brazil. He has five thousand men under his command. We will urge his instant departure for the Cape. In the meantime, General, you may do your damnedest to persuade these Capers to do what's best for 'em: surrender without a fight.'

For two weeks a terse correspondence ensued between ship and shore, both playing a waiting game: Elphinstone hoping that Clarke would arrive with reinforcements, and Sluysken hoping that the French would sail into Table Bay and blast the British out of the water.

Sluysken gained the first advantage. At the end of June, definite news reached him that the French and Dutch had formed an alliance to which, *de facto*, he owed his allegiance. Prince William of Orange, as far as the government of the Cape was concerned, had no legal authority. At once, the Commissioner-General broke off negotiations with the British, and withdrew all the forces under his command to a strongly fortified position at Muizenberg, which lies at the foot of gentle hills on the eastern side of the Peninsula, and whose white and smooth sands are gently lapped by the Indian Ocean. Furthermore, he issued orders that the sale of fresh provisions to the British must be stopped.

In no time at all, two hundred of Craig's soldiers fell ill with scurvy. The position was becoming untenable; all hope of a friendly occupation was ended, and it was decided that they must act now, without further delay. On 7 August, having gradually landed his troops, Craig launched an attack on Muizenberg, supported by a barrage of the ships' guns. By nightfall the well-trained British soldiers held fast, and the German mercenaries fled into the hills. Sluysken sounded the retreat, taking up position along the tract of land that lay betwen Muizenberg and Table Bay, across the breadth of the narrow peninsula. If the British were to occupy the Cape, they would have to risk a frontal attack on Cape Town itself. It was a course of action that neither Craig nor Elphinstone would risk, but with a small force they continued to harass the Dutch in an effort to break through their lines; twice, at Retreat and Steenberg, they engaged the enemy, and twice they were driven back.

August lingered and died; the first days of September were uncommonly hot, a warning of what was to come. Aboard the British ships there was an atmosphere of unreality, as though they were becalmed. Then, at dawn on 3 September, the look-out sighted fourteen men o' war on the horizon: Major-General Alured Clarke sailed into Table Bay with his army of five thousand. Thirteen days later, after much threatening and little fighting, the Dutch wisely surrendered. The inhabitants of the Cape Colony were required to take an oath of allegiance to His Majesty King George III 'for so long a time as His said Majesty shall continue in possession of this colony.'

'A temporary measure, my dear Sluysken,' said Elphinstone as the two men emerged from the signing of the surrender. 'A temporary measure.'

Sluysken smiled wryly, and said nothing.

'General Craig will assume the government at once,' said Elphinstone and saluted the former Commissioner-General; then, he turned to join Craig who was waiting for him in an open carriage.

It was a pleasant ride into Cape Town; the day was warm and sunny, the British flag already fluttered happily over the Castle.

'Yes, yes,' said Elphinstone. 'A temporary measure.' He seemed regretful.

Craig looked up at the mountains. 'It really is very beautiful, is it not, sir?'

Elphinstone frowned. 'No need to talk like a poet,' he said.

The British had conquered. The temporary measure, with a short interval of three years, lasted for more than a century and a half. The United East India Company of the Netherlands had been swept into the sea.

13

Reunion

I

Three years after leaving Cape Town, Sybille Henning found herself not in Blauwzand, but in a village called Swellendam, some two hundred miles equidistant from both the place she had left and the place she most wanted to be. Her life had settled into a serene and uneventful mould, played out within the orderly confines of a tightly-knit family; to many she was known as Sybille de Mist.

All had gone well for the family. Swellendam was small but prosperous. Like Blauwzand, it had grown up to serve the vast cattle ranches that sprawled for miles around and, on arrival, de Mist entered into partnership with his cousin, Danie, in a general store which stood in the main street, and was the only one of its kind in the town.

Within a year of their arrival, the three eldest de Mist girls married. The second, Elizabeth, who was Sybille's immediate contemporary, and closest friend, did best for herself, marrying Paul Gelderhuis, the owner of the largest ranch in the district, a member of the local Heemraden, a man of importance and wealth. The only drawback was that Elizabeth now lived some four days' ride from the town which meant that Sybille saw her rarely.

Mynheer de Mist accepted Sybille more by default than by inclination. Not that he treated her any differently from his daughters, for he saw to it that she worked for her keep, as they did, serving in the store and helping in the home. But he never warmed to her; he found her too strange, too fey for his liking. He preferred practical women, busy women, and nothing irritated him more than when that certain vague and distant look clouded Sybille's eyes, and she appeared abstracted from the present. 'Stop dreaming,' he would say, and she would oblige for the moment, busy herself with the task in hand; but, after a while, the look would return.

Maria de Mist held the girl in genuine affection. Sybille was so unlike her own children who were, on the whole, boisterous and noisy, as is the way with large families. She liked the girl's stillness, her solitariness, and that very quality which de Mist found so annoying, the ability to detach herself from the tumult around; it led Maria to believe that the girl had an inner life, and that fascinated and intrigued her; she was forever asking questions, trying to discover the cause.

Sybille found a contentment she had never known before. She was not used to the unembarrassed affection which the de Mists displayed amongst themselves; she never quite overcame the thrill of being embraced without warning, or of being kissed goodnight and blessed before sleep. If she had not exactly lost faith with the memory of her father and the words he had last spoken to her, then it would be true to say they had receded into the distance. What she thought about in those moments of detachment, when that distant expression seemed to alter her very being, was not her father; another man occupied her mind:

My feeling of shame and guilt is uppermost, yet I cannot prevent my thoughts from returning to him. I see him so clearly, for he invades my mind with such violence and always unexpectedly. It is ever the same, ever that moment when his face is closest to mine, with his body pressing down on my body, his words smothering my prayers. Oh, soldier boy, God forgive my memories of you whose name I do not know.

Three years passed. The world of politics, of government, of war, was not her world. She saw the British flag hoisted over the Drostdy, heard that it had been torn down and ripped to pieces the next day, took the oath of allegiance to King George, heard of the Kaffir cattle-raids into the Colony, shuddered at the stories of their murderous assaults upon the settlers, but was not deeply affected by any of it. Sybille's reality, as Maria de Mist had detected, was secret and inward, a universe inhabited by fractured memories, by frail longings and attachments; it was a world into which she retreated from habit and by preference; it needed the rude and brutal hand of another reality to extricate her from her fantasies.

On the first day of February 1799, Elizabeth Gelderhuis visited her family in Swellendam, and a week later returned to her husband's farm, taking with her Sybille for company. They travelled in style, for Elizabeth had her own carriage, upholstered in velvet and fitted with curtains and brightly-coloured cushions. The last three days of the journey were spent travelling across her husband's land.

The girls had much to talk about, and spent their days gossiping. For Sybille it was luxury the like of which she had never known: she awoke late, was served breakfast in her bedroom, washed in hot water which was heated by slaves and partook of the lazy, rich life as to the manner born. Elizabeth was generous and gay, and liked nothing better than to rummage in her cavernous oak wardrobe to find Sybille dresses and shawls and bonnets and capes of which she had tired. It was all very exciting, and novel, and refreshing. There was but one dark shadow over Sybille's wholehearted enjoyment, and that was her host, Paul Gelderhuis. It seemed to her that he did not welcome company for his wife, that he found Sybille's presence unbearably obtrusive and, although the house was large and the two hardly ever saw each other except at meals, when they did meet, he found it difficult to be relaxed or civil. Several times Sybille heard Elizabeth remonstrating with him for his manner towards their guest, and on each occasion he cut his wife short by storming out of the house, be it night or day, and riding off on his horse. There were other things about the Gelderhuis farm that disturbed Sybille:

I asked Elizabeth if she thought it proper that a Madagascan slave woman should be allowed to attend to mynheer Gelderhuis in his bedroom, heating his water for him, shaving him and so on. To this she replied, 'Oh, Syb, you are a child!' and laughed. A day or so later, I happen to pass mynheer's bedroom and to my horror saw the creature asleep in his bed. I reported the indecency to Elizabeth at once, and she became very serious and bade me walk with her out of doors. What she told me was deeply shocking, and against all the teachings of Christ Jesus. It seems that this Madagascan is a second wife to mynheer, a state of affairs which Elizabeth encourages. 'It would never please me, Syb,' she said, 'for mynheer to interest himself in me too often. He is very brutal and selfish in his habits and he is welcome to have other interests.' All this said with some passion, that embarrassed me deeply and caused me to blush, but not her. 'What,' I asked, 'if she should have a child by him?' Elizabeth replied, 'But she has! They all do!' and when I asked what she meant, she took me by the hand and led me towards the slave compound. There, behind the wooden fence, six or seven children played, all a most hideous mixture of colours, some light brown, others rather dark, quite horrible to look at, an offence against nature. At our arrival, they pushed their flat, ugly noses through the slats and greeted us warmly. I turned away near to fainting, but Elizabeth actually patted their *krillikops* and pinched their sallow cheeks affectionately. On the way back to the house she confessed without any shame that they were all sired by mynheer. 'You mustn't be shocked, Syb,' she said. 'All the men hereabouts do the same. It is the custom.' But I could not conceal my disapproval, for I know that I sleep in an adulterous house and I fear that God will punish them.

Even so, she was able to report with some pleasure:

I am to stay an extra two weeks at least. Mynheer Gelderhuis is to be away from the house on commando, and I thank God for his absence, although Elizabeth and I are quite frightened in the evenings without him. The Kaffirs have become bold and impudent, stealing many head of cattle. Worse still, they have murdered a farmer and his family who lived some forty miles away. Commandos have been organised from far afield as Graaff-Reinet. I even heard Blauwzand mentioned, and my heart quickened again. Mynheer Gelderhuis leads the farmers from these parts and they have gone to punish the Kaffirs for their crimes. I am thankful. The house is pleasanter without his sinful presence.

Not long after that entry into her diary, Sybille would have welcomed mynheer Gelderhuis back with open arms. On a Friday evening, ten days after his departure, the two women were about to retire to bed when they were disturbed by a loud knocking on the front door.

'Mevrou Gelderhuis! Mevrou Gelderhuis!' called a voice; Elizabeth and Sybille, nervous as kittens, stood at the door and, as they had been told always to do, asked who was there. On learning that it was their neighbour's son, they admitted Jan van Niekerk whose clothes were stained with blood; he was near to fainting.

They sat him down on a settle in the hallway and called for the slaves to bring water and bandages, while van Niekerk explained what had happened. 'The Kaffir raiding parties are running wild. We engaged some of them about a hundred miles to the east—'

'Is my husband all right?' demanded Elizabeth. 'What has happened to my husband?'

'He's well. When I last saw him, he was well. He sent me to warn you. A commando is coming this way to protect the farms, but if the Kaffirs get here first, you must defend yourselves. The savages!' He winced with pain as Elizabeth dabbed at a wound in his shoulder. 'The commando should be here soon, but the Kaffirs advance like locusts. Oh Christ!'

'Syb, you bathe his wounds. I'll round up the boys and—' She broke off and turned back to van Niekerk. 'Do I give the slaves guns?' she asked in a matter-of-fact way, as though she were discussing their food rations.

'Of course you give them guns, mevrou!' answered van Niekerk. 'But only the best boys, mind. When you've collected them, bring them here to me.'

Elizabeth went off and sounded the slave bell, a curiously ominous clanging in the still night air. Cursing and complaining, the slaves rubbed sleep from their eyes, pulled on their shirts and trousers, and wandered slowly, lethargically, towards the rear of the farmhouse. They seemed to take an age, and Elizabeth continued to toll the bell with growing insistence, until, at last, the slaves were all gathered before her. Hurriedly, she chose a dozen of the youngest and strongest; the remainder she sent back to the compound with instructions to remain there: on no account were they to leave.

'Right, Ahab,' she said, addressing one of the Malays. 'You are head boy for tonight, understand?'

'Yes, madam,' he answered dutifully, mystified as to what was happening, but servile enough not to ask too many questions.

Elizabeth raised her voice so that all could hear. 'We are expecting an attack from the Kaffirs. Help is on the way, but if the savages should get here first, we must be ready to defend ourselves. I am going to give you guns. You must only use them against the Kaffirs.' Then she led them to her husband's office, unlocked the stout cupboard that served as an arsenal, and handed out two guns to each man, one to fire while one was being loaded.

With her small army, Elizabeth returned to the hall to find Sybille binding van Niekerk's wound. The Madagascan woman, Esther she was called, had brought brandy, and he was calmer now, able to take command.

'Listen boys,' he said. 'The Kaffirs are on their way. They move in bands of twenty or thirty, so if we're ready for them they'll have no chance against us. One of you must go on to the kopje and keep watch. If you see anything you fire a shot to warn us, then you tear back to the house as if you'd seen the devil, understood?' He was answered by murmurs of assent. Ahab chose one of the men and sent him off. Van Niekerk continued, 'Now I want a man front and back, and at either side, upstairs and downstairs, understood? You don't fire until you hear the warning shot and then only when you see something to fire at, you get it?' He turned to Esther. 'You collect up some of your women to load the guns, one woman to each man.'

Elizabeth said, 'I can fire a gun.'

'And I can load for her,' said Sybille.

'If you wish, mevrou, but I'd prefer you to take shelter in the cellar.'

'This is my house,' said Elizabeth cheerfully.

'Very well. Take the front windows upstairs. The more the merrier.'

The hours of waiting were terrible. An awesome stillness enveloped the house; here and there you could hear whispers between the men and the women loaders; someone laughed; another yawned noisily. Van Niekerk went from station to station, kept the men alert and gave them encouragement. When he went to check the look-out on the hillock behind the house, he took Ahab with him; all was well.

Elizabeth and Sybille did not say much to each other, and when they did speak the conversation was always much the same.

'Can you see anything, Liz?'

'No. Just the night.'

'I hope the commando gets here soon.'

'I hope so.'

'I'm praying all the time that God will deliver us.'

'So am I, Syb.'

'Can you see anything?'

'No.'

The warning shot was fired just as the first pink streak of dawn showed above the distant hills. 'Hold your fire,' van Niekerk called. 'It may be the commando.'

But it was not; the Kaffir war-cries were suddenly near, dangerous, savage, terrifying. To those in the house, it was as if they were already surrounded and certain of defeat. Still, they opened fire, each shot like the sound of cannon, reverberating in the closeness of the wooden house.

'I can't see anything, I can't see anything!' Elizabeth cried, firing blindly. The noise shut out all thought; you did what you had to do: you loaded or you fired, that was all, no time to think of death or even victory, you loaded and you fired, that was all.

Screams of pain, and the sound of breaking glass. A spear splintering the woodwork, the smell of burning, flames leaping from the slaves' compound, the pain of children and, most terrible of all, the war-cries inside the very house itself.

Sybille remembered this: loading for Elizabeth, and looking up, unaccountably, to see a Kaffir warrior standing at the head of the stairs, his face painted, his hand raised, and in his hand a spear dripping blood. She cannot speak or think or act. Then, as he advances, she stands, gets the gun to her shoulder, sees the spear flying towards her, feels pain, fires, and then nothing, darkness, oblivion. When she next opens her eyes, she has the impression of movement, as though she is travelling; she tries to speak but cannot; she hears a voice say 'laudanum', is reassured and sleeps. Does she dream or does she see Le Roux? A dream it must be, for the soldier-boy is there too, her soldier-boy, his face close to hers, his hands pressing her shoulders which ache. It is a nightmare surely, for now her mother is with her, 'I will not shit,' she says; but where, where is father, where? If only the pain in her arm would cease. 'More laudanum.'

She opened her eyes and found herself in a strange room with a man she did not know sitting on her bed looking down at her; he had a broad face with a large black beard, square, like a spade.

'Who—who are—where—'

'Quietly. You are safe. My commando rescued you.'

'Where's Elizabeth?'

'Safe, too. Her husband took her back to Swellendam a week ago. You were too ill to move. I'm afraid their house was burned to the ground so they have gone to her parents.'

'My arm hurts.'

'Yes, you were wounded but it is healing well.'

'But where am I? Who are you? Where is this place?'

'You are among friends. My name is van Haarten and you are in my house. I am the landdrost of Blauwzand.'

3

I thank God for bringing me to the appointed place. I repent; O God forgive me for being diverted from my true course, for allowing myself to fall into the ways of the wicked. I renounce the paths I have of late trodden. I renounce comfort both of body and spirit. I renounce all manner of things except that which binds me to Thy Everlasting Spirit. I shut from my mind all thoughts of home, family and friends. All evil visions which I have made welcome. I have not kept faith with Thee, O God, as Thou hast kept faith with me. I am reunited with my true self, set upon my true purpose. Your hand guided the landdrost to rescue me; in Thy arms was I transported hither. Blessed is the name of the Lord. Through Jesus Christ. Amen.

Thus, Sybille returned to the mysteries which shrouded her father's last words to her. It did not seem to her in any way fortuitous that the commando party which rescued her and Elizabeth should be led by the new landdrost of Blauwzand; God's hand alone was the instrument of her salvation, both physical and spiritual. Her strength returned rapidly, the wound caused by the Kaffir spear healed, and her soul was enriched by rediscovering its sense of purpose.

Sybille learned something of what had happened from van Haarten himself, and from his young, pretty wife, Wilhelmina. Daily, one or the other visited her and gradually she pieced together the story of her rescue. The Kaffir warrior who speared Sybille was, it seemed, the only one to gain the upstairs. His fellows had set fire to the house and it was burning fiercely by the time the commando arrived. Van Haarten himself braved the flames and rescued the two women who, apart from the look-out, were alone in being saved; all the rest perished, either murdered or burned. Elizabeth suffered no injury except minor burns on her legs and so recovered more quickly than her friend. Both were taken by wagon to Blauwzand where mynheer Gelderhuis joined them. As soon as Elizabeth was well, she and her husband made the return journey to Swellendam, leaving Sybille in the care of the landdrost. One act of kindness touched the invalid: mynheer Gelderhuis had given money to van Haarten for Sybille's needs such as clothes, medical attention and, when she would be well enough, transport back to the de Mist home.

But she had resolved never to return to her adopted family until her mission to Blauwzand, and more particularly to Henningsdorp, had been satisfactorily completed. From the very beginning of her convalescence, when taking a mid-day walk with Wilhelmina, or when the landdrost visited her alone, at every available opportunity, she asked questions.

Now, you must know that she had never before heard of van Haarten; she did not know that he had led the rebels at Hennings-dorp, that he had returned from the hills after van der Goes's death and been appointed landdrost by the British precisely because he had resisted the corruption of the Company's regime. You must also know he never told her that he had known her father.

Three conversations determined Sybille's future. The first was with Wilhelmina van Haarten as they picked their way among the bricks and trenches of the new school that was being built.

'Mevrou, how far is it to Henningsdorp?' Sybille asked.

'To where?'

'Henningsdorp.'

'A town with your name?' Wilhelmina asked, amused by the idea that anyone as strange and insignificant as Sybille should have a town named after her.

'Yes, but not a large place, I think. More likely a village. It has a church, I'm sure.'

'I've never heard of it.'

'But I believe it's very near Blauwzand.'

'It may be,' answered Wilhelmina, 'but I have only lived here a year. I come originally from Graaff-Reinet. You must ask one of the locals, they may know the place.'

'Well, do you know a man Le Roux?'

Wilhelmina paused and turned to her companion, eyebrows arched in astonishment. 'Do *you* know that old devil?'

'I met him once, just briefly,' Sybille explained. 'He knew my father, you see. Does he still live here?'

'Don't mention his name in front of my husband, will you?'

'Why ever not?'

'Oh, the landdrost had such trouble with him. He's a drunken lazy thief—yes, and a liar! He accused my husband of terrible, unspeakable things. The landdrost ran him out of the town. He's gone to seed, that one, he lives with the Hottentots in the hills. What do you want with Le Roux, anyway?'

'Oh nothing. Just that—well, he knows where Henningsdorp is, that's all,' Sybille said.

'My advice is to forget about Le Roux. He's a terrible sinner, and remember what I said, don't talk to the landdrost about him, please—'

'No, I won't, I promise.'

'You ask the head slave, Mordecai, about Henningsdorp. He knows the district well.'

And when, that evening, Sybille asked Mordecai, he was frightened and trembled.

'But what's the matter, Mordecai, all I asked was if you knew the place?'

'Ask the landdrost,' replied the slave.

'But why can you not tell me?'

He held a hand to his mouth and spoke through the fingers. 'Landdrost no like talk of these things.'

'Does the landdrost know Henningsdorp, then?'

'Oh, yes,' blurted out the slave. 'He lived there. But I say no more, no more. You talk to him.'

At the first opportunity, which was at breakfast the following morning, Sybille raised the subject with van Haarten.

'Henningsdorp?' repeated the landdrost, scratching his beard. 'Henningsdorp. Named after your father, you say? No. Never heard of it. You must have misunderstood.'

'I told you there was no such place,' said Wilhelmina.

Sybille made no response; her mind was racing, formulating a plan, for she knew the landdrost was lying. She gazed at her empty plate as if the words of God were written there.

'No need to look so sad,' said Wilhelmina. 'You've made a mistake, that's all. This place Henningsdorp must be somewhere else.'

During their walk that day, Sybille managed to lose Wilhelmina twice. On both occasions, she enquired of casual passers-by the whereabouts of Henningsdorp; she received either evasions or silence. By evening her mind was made up.

'Landdrost,' she said at dinner. 'Could I have some of the money mynheer Gelderhuis left for me? I wish to buy myself a new dress tomorrow.'

'How exciting,' said Wilhelmina. 'May I come with you and help you choose?'

'Of course. I should like it.'

After the landdrost had given her ten rixdollars, she complained of a headache and retired. 'I hope that won't prevent us from shopping tomorrow,' said Wilhelmina.

'I hope not,' answered Sybille, slipping out of the room. She went straight to the kitchen and took Mordecai aside; the slave was terrified.

'Tonight,' she said urgently. 'You have two horses ready, and you take me to Le Roux.'

Mordecai's eyes grew large with fear. 'I cannot, I cannot!' he cried.

'You can and you will. In one hour's time. You be there!'

'I cannot, please, don't make me, madam, don't make me!'

'Here,' she said and thrust the ten rixdollars into his hand; he had never had so much money in all his life. At the appointed time he brought the horses to the rear of the house and led her through the night up into the hills.

4

The caves lie to the north of Blauwzand, hidden among the barren outcrop of rocks that lead to Blauwzand Pass. Dark, putrid holes they are, fashioned by wind and sun. By day they are ovens; at night, the water freezes and like glistening slime coats the jagged walls.

When they reached the first of the caves, Mordecai dismounted and ordered Sybille to wait; then he disappeared into a black hole from which the sound of singing came, an unmelodious chant. Sybille was not frightened; the certainty that she was doing right, and that her life was in God's care, brought courage.

Mordecai rejoined her and begged her not to go on, but she would not listen. 'Have you found out where Le Roux is?' she asked.

'We must go a little further. But, madam, please, go back. They are smoking *dagga*, the wild hemp that makes them dangerous.'

'Lead. I'll follow.'

They found Le Roux crouched by a fire, with two or three Khoikhoi women; they were passing a long clay pipe from one to the other, and Sybille could smell the spicy stench of the drug. She barely recognised him; he had grown thin and aged, and his hair was matted with filth.

'Johannes Le Roux?' said Sybille.

It was only then that the group became aware of her. The women giggled inanely, and the old man narrowed his eyes, trying to focus on her in the firelight.

'You remember me?' she asked. 'Sybille Henning. Johannes Henning's daughter.'

He allowed his head to loll from side to side. 'Henning?' he repeated. 'Henning? We had the same name.'

'I'm his daughter.'

'Oh, lady, lady, you come too late.' He began to snivel, then to cry until tears coursed down his cheeks.

'You must take me to Henningsdorp,' she said.

'No such place,' he muttered between sobs.

'There is! There is! I know there is!' she cried. 'Henningsdorp, where the church is!'

At the mention of the place, one of the Khoikhoi women rose to her feet and came closer; although the smell from her was foul, Sybille held her ground. The woman said nothing but stared at the pale young girl as though she were a vision. Sybille continued to address Le Roux. 'You must take me to the church, you must find Adam for me, and his mother, do you understand?'

It was the Khoikhoi woman who spoke next. 'Adam?' she repeated, and then in Dutch, 'You have Adam?'

Sybille thought she would faint. 'No,' she replied. 'But do you know him? Where is he? Who is he?'

'Come,' said the woman and beckoned Sybille to follow. As she went, Le Roux called after her, 'Too late, lady, you've come too late!'

The woman led Sybille up a precarious, slippery path where the stones were loose and dangerous.

'In here,' said the woman.

It took Sybille a few moments to adjust her eyes to the pale light that came from the dying embers of a fire. The cave was small and horribly cold. There was but one occupant, a woman, fat and bloated, snoring. By her side empty casks of brandy, and in her hand a pipe. The smell of *dagga* clung to the rocks like incense in a church.

169

The first Khoikhoi woman woke the sleeper and talked to her rapidly in their own language. Then, turning to Sybille, she said, 'This woman is Adam's mother. Her name Alala.'

'You have my baby? You have my son?' Alala asked, her words slurred.

'No. Where is he? I have come to find him,' Sybille cried.

'They took him, they took him,' she answered in a plaintive singsong.

'I am Henning's daughter,' said Sybille. 'Does that mean anything to you? Henning, Henningsdorp, does it mean anything to you?'

Alala struggled up on to her hands and knees and, as if it cost her much effort, she crawled towards Sybille. When she drew close, Sybille saw for the first time that she was quite young but that her face was swollen and her eyes dazed. Sybille was overwhelmed, though she did not know why, by a feeling of pity, and even more so when Alala asked so helplessly, 'Where is Henning? Where is my man?'

'I am his daughter,' Sybille said.

'He is my man.'

'Your priest, is that what you mean, your predikant?'

'*Tui'qua*,' Alala said. 'He is Christ *Tui'qua*.'

'Yes, yes, the predikant,' answered Sybille. 'That is he, my father!'

'Why he go? Where? Why he not come?'

'They took him,' said Sybille.

'Yes. The Fat One.' She meant van der Goes.

'He is dead.'

'Where is my son?'

'I do not know. You must tell me.'

Alala sank back on her haunches and, as though she were blind, felt on the ground for the pipe. Then she took a glowing ember from the fire and held it to the bowl, and puffed deeply. She said in a far-off voice, 'We make the house of *Tui'qua*, the Christ who kill *Gauna*. And we call the house Henningsdorp for Henning who is *Tui'qua*. And *Tui'qua* he comes to me, for blood and bread, for wine and flesh, I drink and eat his finger, and here on my head is the Cross. And my child comes and the *Tui'qua* is joyful. And my son is Adam, and also the Cross is on his head. And then comes the Fat One who is *Gauna*, the hare, and *Tui'qua* leaves to go with him and there is no *Tui'qua*, there is no Christ. Only *Gauna*, the hare. Then van Haarten says he is *Tui'qua* and he takes Afrika and me and

Adam far, far away. And his finger is in my mouth, but he is also *Gauna*, he is not *Tui'qua*. Then he leaves us too, but returns with men and guns to kill. Afrika he kills and Muller his friend. But not me and not Adam. And then, after many days and many suns, other men come and take Adam to work, my little son. And me they leave.'

A movement behind her caused Sybille to turn. In the narrow opening of the cave stood Le Roux, swaying.

'That van Haarten,' he said, 'that one, he's Satan! When he heard that van der Goes was dead he went back to Blauwzand. Yes, oh yes, the British made him landdrost all right. So what does he do? Goes back and kills his women and his friends. Man, if you're a landdrost, you've got to be a good Englishman! No Hottentot women, no! Kill the bloody lot and become lord high almighty. Bless King George and piss on Henningsdorp.'

'There is no Christ *Tui'qua*,' said Alala, the pipe slipping from her hand.

'And look at me!' cried Le Roux. 'I knew all about him, you see. I'd seen him at Henningsdorp! He'd have killed me, too.'

'But where, where is Adam?' pleaded Sybille.

'Taken for a slave and him only six years old.'

And Alala sang:

> Now is my journey begun,
> The light of the Lord will guide me,
> The Devil I will shun,
> Christ rides beside me.
>
> Now is my journey begun,
> Over rivers, over the land,
> From Satan I will run,
> Christ takes my hand.

5

I have not understood all. God reveals, not man. I left the pitiful place weighed down by sadness, though I knew not why. The woman, Alala, slept deeply, in mourning for her son. If it is her son, for the truth is hard to discover, but of this I am certain: she partook of the mystery of God, communed with Christ at the hand of my father, Johannes Henning, who took her to his heart and bade me find her and her son, Adam, my brother in Christ.

After leaving the cave, I ordered Mordecai to take me to Henningsdorp, but he refused and rode back to Blauwzand leaving me with these tormented people. But I persuaded Le Roux in exchange for the promise that I would tell the British about van Haarten. While it was still dark, we set off, and at noon the following day, came upon a desolate spot where, Le Roux said, had once stood Henningsdorp. He showed me where my father had built the church; there was nothing but burnt wood and weeds. There I knelt and spoke these words: 'Lord God, I take this oath in Thy sight: I shall not rest till I have found my brother Adam. My life I dedicate to that purpose, and to doing Thy work, through Jesus Christ, Our Lord, Amen.'

Continuum:
The family historian

Continuum:
The family historian

They have relaxed the restrictions surrounding his confinement: he may now leave the house from nine until noon, but he does not take advantage of the concession. One letter and one alone is delivered and although he knows it to be written by his Uncle Jacobus, the Minister of Justice, he refuses to open it. He prefers to ferret underground following the dark burrowings of the mole.

He reads what he has written, discerns nothing but the betrayal of man by man, and his heart is heavy. And yet, he perceives a glimmer of light, for he must now discover how Sybille's diary came to be found on an English farm near Grahamstown, in the eastern Cape Province. What circumstances led to it being there so that his grandfather Dawid, the Judge, could find it?

He is interrupted from time to time by his friend, the kind policeman.

'Go away.'

'Don't you know you're allowed out now, man?'

'Go away.'

'Here's another van der Merwe story for you.'

'Go away.'

'This is really good. Van der Merwe's been managing a mine up in Zambia, you understand? And he comes back to Pretoria and who should he meet in the street but the Prime Minister. "Where have you been, van der Merwe?" asks the Prime Minister—they were at school together, you see. "I've been up in Zambia, managing a mine. What have *you* been up to?" "Well, I'm now the Prime Minister." "Agh, man," says van der Merwe, "where I've been they've got a kaffir doing that job!" '

To find the link between Sybille and the Thompson family, that is the task the prisoner now sets himself. Sybille, who screwed her life to an impossible cross, nailed to it with the words of a dead man, condemned to an endless journey. Where, where, O God, will she find her Adam? How many miles will she have to travel to find him who cannot be found, a boy, lost among the lost, faceless among the faceless, one of a race that is not a race, not black or white or yellow, but simply coloured.

Then, like a faded photograph, a memory from childhood returns to plague the prisoner day and night, in and out of focus and, contained within the elusive images, he knows there lies the clue for which he is searching, the link. Struggling to fix the print of past events firmly in his mind, he scrawls:

Seven or eight years old. Seven, yes seven candles on the cake, my birthday party and my mother at my shoulder urging me to blow: *Een, twee, drie!* Faces of children, can't remember any of them, but Granny Victoria and Oupa Dawid are there, standing, watching the candles. Oupa, sucking on a pipe: blown-out-birthday-candle-smoke-lost-in-pipe-tobacco-clouds. And a jelly wobbling with our excitement. A row, but much later, the same evening. Suffocating heat. In bed with after-party over-tiredness, playing with a—with a toy ambulance; supper on the oval tray uneaten, soft-boiled egg, and crustless whitebread soldiers, and the leftover jelly. Grown-up voices outside, yes, a row, an argument, anger. Oupa Dawid's voice like thunder and Granny Victoria crying.

Barefoot across the bare wooden floor, sticky with wax polish, and looking down from the upstairs balcony through the *fleur-de-lis* balustrade at the *braaivleis*, the charcoal fire, the Native boys turning the steaks, and Oupa Dawid shouting, 'Smuts!' in a way that makes them know he hates Smuts; and Granny Victoria hates . . . but impossible to remember who. Oupa Dawid turns and storms into the house, returning minutes later with a sheaf of rolled-up papers, thick as a tallow-candle and, in his anger, tosses it on to the glowing coals. The Native boys, eyes wide, jump back as Granny Victoria rushes to rescue the roll of papers, which she does, blowing at the already charred crimped edges. And then Oupa Dawid turns once more and shouts . . . and shouts . . .

But what? All the prisoner can remember is his grandfather's mouth moving, but the words do not escape. And yet, the prisoner knows with absolute certainty that in the childhood recollection a clue is locked, a clue to Sybille Henning and the Thompson family. (He calls this the instinct of solitude.)

Again and again he forces the memory through the sieve of adult perception, to test whether or not he has deluded himself with a dream or a fantasy. But still he cannot hear the words Oupa Dawid shouted and the more he persists in trying, the longer they elude him. He sees the paper thrown on the fire, sees Granny Victoria snatch it from the coals, sees Oupa Dawid turn ... sees his mouth move ... and that is all.

And then, after a week, two perhaps, in the waking hours of morning when he is neither asleep nor awake, but in the silhouetted world of pleasurable semi-consciousness, his grandfather's voice resounds in his ear like a rasping thunderclap: 'DISHONEST AND ENGLISH! Dishonest and English like your father Michael Thompson! Let it burn, Victoria, because that's all he's good for: ashes!' And now fragments of other things ... Chamberlain and Munich, Daladier and ... 'Leave it to burn! The English have jelly for spines!'

The prisoner rises from his bed at once. Gowned and slippered he shuffles along the passage to the room which his grandmother Victoria occupied, and where he has not thought to look since his incarceration. But there, in her old leather trunk bearing the initials V. T., he finds the roll of paper, the edges burned as it was on his seventh birthday all those years ago. There are some forty sheets in all and, at first, the prisoner is puzzled for although the handwriting is Victoria's, the words are plainly not hers. It takes him a little time to realise that he is reading the garbled recollections of Victoria's father, Michael Thompson, a document damned by Dawid 'Dishonest and English.'

Deep into the night he works, Mpobe at his desk, reading, studying, piecing together the jig-saw, turning the pages of Sybille's diary and Michael Thompson's dishonest and English testament. And in that charred document, this passage:

And I was with Miss Henning when she died peacefully in her sleep. I am glad I was there. I owe the world to her. Everyone called her mad with all her talk about God and her lost brother— or was it a son? whoever it was. But she touched my heart with her stories and even now I cry to think of her wandering all over the place in search of some coloured boy. A good woman. She taught me everything.

Had the spirit of Henning, of van Lier been transmitted like an echo through space and time? 'She taught me everything . . .' Did Sybille in her turn pass on some fragile hope to Michael Thompson?

With infinite patience the prisoner begins to fashion the next link in the chain. Mpobe has once more gone to ground.

BOOK FOUR

14

The link

1

'Our English family ties, of which we are intensely proud, were brought about by the daughter of Johannes Henning, one Sybille, of whom, I hasten to add, we are less proud. The truth is that she reveals a mental weakness in our family which, thankfully, has not reproduced itself in subsequent generations—at any rate, not to my knowledge! She was, what we would nowadays call, a misfit and yet, because of her anti-social mode of living, she caused the Hennings to meet the Thompsons.'

From the official family history by Dawid Henning, the Judge.

2

Through space and time. Across the barren subcontinent, over mountain ranges and fast-flowing rivers, crawling ant-like through the arid, sprawling monotonous scrubland of the Karoo, a solitary, lonely being they call the wagon-woman relentlessly pursues her quarry. True to her sacred vow, she searches for her father's son, the coloured boy, Adam. Time: a life sentence. Thirty years without remission. Time enough to age, to weary, but never to betray. Transfigured from avenging angel to abandoned soul, yet forever faithful to that ephemeral moment of dedication in a ruined and desecrated church.

Difficult to pin her down, confine her, hold her still even for a moment. Yet, across the pages of her diary, careless of chronology, haphazard, are scrawled place names and occasional dates, signifying pauses in her travels, time caught, adding to the confusion. Distance is meaningless, towns and villages irrelevant, occupations various: in Tulbagh she nurses an old rich widow; she is midwife in Graaff-Reinet; in Beaufort West she teaches in a school; an English lawyer employs her as interpreter in George, and in Uitenhage she is paid by a local printer to balance his accounts. Sometimes, she remains a few weeks; at others, more than a year. Impossible, at first, to penetrate the logic, to discern the pattern.

Then, curious repetitions: Bethelsdorp, Hepzibah, Bethesda, Bethelsdorp, Bethany, Hepzibah, Theopolis, Bethelsdorp, Theopolis, Bethany. The names of mission-stations, dotted like oases throughout the Colony. But why return time and time again? Was it simply because they offered rest and sanctuary, an opportunity to refresh not only her frail body but also her flagging spirit? Or was there a deeper purpose, one that brought real hope of expiation? Certain it was that Sybille Henning was not the only one to return to these places; she was not alone in seeking rest and sanctuary; there were others, even more in need: men, women and children, the unwanted, mottled offspring of miscegenation, among whom she was obliged to spend her life if ever she was to find her father's son.

Hottentots, they were now known as by the Colonists who fathered them: thirty thousand Hottentots, half-caste, one for each Colonist. They were without cattle and too poor to buy land—even if that had been legally allowed. Untaught, ill-used, neglected, not having even the recourse to law that slaves had, they took to the land, wandering at large in gangs, plundering, whoring, pimping, existing. And never far behind followed Sybille Henning, a vagrant, in search of vagrants.

Governments came and went. The British ended their first occupation in 1803. For three years after that the Colony was administered by the Batavian Republic, a remnant of the Dutch East India Company. Two Commissioners, de Mist and Janssens, men of reforming zeal, sought to sweep away injustice but were themselves swept away by the return of the British in 1806, when the French had again posed a threat to the sea-route, and the Cape was reoccupied on a more permanent basis. Each administration in its turn tried to deal with the Hottentot problem. And when, in the early years of the new century, the slave trade was abolished, the Hottentots were seen as heaven-sent to take the place of imported labour who were, it was commonly said, dangerous and degrading to morals. Codes of conduct towards them were drawn up: do not put them in chains and do not chastise them except after a fair trial; a modest gain, one might think, after decades of tacit enslavement.

And then came Christian soldiers: the missionaries marching as to war, building barracks for the homeless, the old, the destitute, and why not Hottentots? Suffer little Hottentots to come unto institutions, but do not exempt them from military service or hard labour for public services. Pragmatism poisons good intentions.

But still the sore suppurated; for what no government could do was answer the one question that cried out for an answer: who were they, these people? What were they? Control them, said the farmers, they are slaves, and we need them on our land. Free them, cried the missionaries, they are souls, and we need them in our churches. To balance the scale of conflicting definitions, the Government issued one of their own: 'We deem it necessary ... that Hottentots in the same manner as the other Inhabitants, should be subject to proper regularity in regard to their places of abode and occupations, but also that they should find an encouragement for preferring the service of the Inhabitants to leading an indolent life.' (Who, you may ask, would reconcile the Government's definition?) Hottentots, therefore, shall have a fixed place of abode. To protect them, contracts shall run a year, to be registered in triplicate and, in case of a dispute, favour the Hottentot. Wages to be duly paid, but not in kind: wine and brandy do not rank as the necessities of life.

Now, for it: the fixed place of abode for a Hottentot was to be registered with the landdrost, and if the Hottentot wanted to move he must first obtain a certificate, a 'pass', as it was known, and, if he failed to do so, he would be arrested as a vagabond and treated accordingly. Immobilised, he could not even seek the best market for his labour. The new century gave birth to these opposing forces: to the missionary spirit of freedom for all men in the name Christ; to the hunger for labour in the name of necessity. Who can reconcile the irreconcilable?

A politically agile missionary, Dr John Philip, of the London Missionary Society, now entered the list as the Hottentots' champion. Knowing well the minds of his fellow-countrymen, he mounted a two-pronged attack; first, was to solve the intricate maze of Whitehall corridors and batter his way to the Colonial Secretary's door; second, and by far the more effective, was to form an alliance with the traditional fountainhead of British power: uninformed public opinion. The English can smell an underdog even at a distance of six thousand miles. On 17 July 1828, Ordinance 50 was promulgated which abolished the pass laws, repealed all former proclamations and enactments, and stated categorically that 'free persons of colour' were at liberty to move around the Colony, to search for higher wages, to own land and to abstain from work. Man may legislate, but God ordains. Who were these arrogant English with their soft and sentimental souls to impose their will on God's Elect? The new law could not alter the unalterable: the Dutch in the Cape Colony were the lords of the earth in need of beasts of burden, and that, like it or not, was the reality of the times. The age of enlightenment may have dawned elsewhere, but its rays did not warm the people of the Cape. The Hottentots took to wandering the land again under the semblance of freedom; nothing changed but the law.

And so, Sybille wandered with them: Bethelsdorp, Bethesda, Bethany, Hepzibah, Theopolis, not for regeneration, but to gather information that would lead her to Alala's child.

Then, three mis-spelled and cryptic entries in her neglected diaries are of significance:

November 183?
Bethelsdp. Met a Malay, Fathma. News of Adam. Paid her. Did not stop. Never been to Gramestown. All those English.

12 Nov.
Grahams Town. Babel. A leaf. He'll see. Must stay here. Must.

Saturday
T. English. Sick Child. I'll stay. Will find Adam through Fathma.

3

What happened was this: late one November evening, her wagon entered the confines of the Bethelsdorp mission station and rumbled into the courtyard adjacent to the chapel; the sun had just set, and in the rose-glow of a brief dusk, the pale shadows disappeared quickly, giving way to night. There were few people about. In the centre of the yard, four women stood chattering, drawing water from the well and, beyond them, near an open doorway illuminated by the sallow light of a hurricane lamp, a clutch of children played a skipping game to the accompaniment of nasal voices from somewhere distant, practising a Christmas hymn, one phrase over and over again: ' "The child! The child!" the Three Kings cried.'

Sybille, tired and stiff, eased her back, stretched and then climbed down to unharness the ox from the wagon. The women at the well noticed her and began to talk in earnest whispers, punctuated by raucous screams of laughter. Sybille paid no attention, continuing with her task but, as she led the animal towards the water-trough, one of the women called on her to stop, which she did, turning to see a Malay, swinging an empty pitcher, lazily walking towards her to the boisterous encouragement of her companions.

'You talking to me?' Sybille asked, her manner suspicious, almost belligerent. The Malay woman drew nearer, resting her pitcher on the ox's scrawny rump, and patting him reassuringly. Even in the diminishing light, Sybille could see that she was remarkably handsome: high, proud cheekbones and playful, mischievous eyes.

'Are jou the wagon-woman?' the Malay asked.

'What d'you want with me?'

'Are jou the one looking for thet boy Arram?'

'You know him?' Sybille asked, the weariness of travel vanishing.

'I know him,' the Malay said. (At this, her three companions at the well screamed with delight.)

'Where is he?' Sybille demanded. 'Where's Adam?'

The woman looked back at her friends. 'Agh, stop it, demmit,' she called. 'Can't you see I'm talking to a lady?' Which was greeted with more laughter.

'Never mind them,' said Sybille. 'You tell me about Adam!' Her whole being was charged with urgency.

The woman traced patterns with her forefinger on the ox's hide. 'I dunno if it's right. Jou'll make trouble for him. They'll put him in the tronk.'

'I don't want to make trouble for him,' said Sybille. 'I just want to find him.'

'Ja, but if I tell jou where he is, and jou find him, and he gets to hear about it, he may come looking for me, and I don't want no trouble,' the Malay said in her strange, plaintive insinuating singsong.

Sybille nodded several times, then turned her back on the woman. Looking from side to side, making sure she was unobserved, she thrust a hand into her skirts and withdrew a draw-string purse; from this she took two coins and once more faced the woman. 'What's your name?' Sybille asked.

'Fathma,' came the reply, reluctant.

'All right, Fathma. You tell me where Adam is and I'll pay good money.' She held up the coins for Fathma to see.

'You pay me first, then I tell.'

Slowly, Sybille shook her head. 'No. First, you tell me.'

Fathma leaned across the ox. 'Grahamstown,' she said. 'He's going to be working the Kaffir Fair there.'

'How d'you know?'

'Agh, 'cos I'll be there, too.'

'Are you meeting him there?'

'Ja, I go to earn my living. I work for thet Arram of jours, j'unnerstan'? I give him half everyt'ing I earn.'

'Is he in Grahamstown now?'

'Sure. He's there. He's got girls there, they work the fair. They all give him half what they earn, j'unnerstan'? He's no blarry good thet Arram of jours!'

Sybille considered for a moment. 'Fathma, one thing: don't you dare tell Adam I'm on the look-out for him. You have to promise.'

'Agh, don't jou worry. I won't say nothing. I promise.'

'Here,' said Sybille, handing over the coins. 'If I find him in Grahamstown, I'll give you more.'

Fathma snatched the coins and ran back to her friends; their amusement was unrestrained, and from the mission a voice shouted to them to be quiet. Like birds frightened by a shot, they dispersed, running towards the open door where the children played, and disappeared inside.

In the courtyard, Sybille allowed her ox to drink then led him back to the wagon. Shortly afterwards, full of expectation, she set off on the road north, towards Grahamstown, acting on the information of an indolent Malay whore.

4

When you enter for the first time, as Sybille did, the district then known as Albany, you are aware at once of a savage landscape which has been tamed by man. Crossing the Bushmans River at Jagers Drift, you leave behind the dusty, parched plains, and enter a region where the rolling grass-covered hills are sprinkled with mimosa trees, with thickets and densely wooded forests lolling on the slopes. You will see cacti and aloes, and irregular clumps of the dull green *doringboom*, and high on the hills trees cluster tightly as if for safety. You may hear an elephant trumpet, or the thudding of a rhinoceros, and it is a common sight to witness the hippopotamus wallowing in the deep river pools. Buffalo and wild boar are plentiful but, most of all, there are the antelopes rich in their variety: koodoo, eland, wildebeest, hartebeest, springbok. At night, all the terrors of the wilderness assail you, for the leopards, the wild dogs and the hyenas are drawn to the warmth of the camp fire, and you may hear a rustle of snakes slithering through the undergrowth to prey on a million crawling things.

But soon, it becomes apparent that all the insouciance of nature has been marshalled and kept at bay. For now, miraculously, there are ploughed fields and fences. Roads and paths criss-cross the wooded slopes, and bridges span the rivers. No miracle of creation this, but the work of four thousand immigrants, English, Welsh, Scots and Irish who became known as the 1820 Settlers, and no group of men ever stood higher in the canon of Cape pioneers.

From the shadows of the dark satanic mills of England, from the crowded bustling cities, from sleepy market towns and villages, men, women and children set out to subdue a territory which had hardly ever felt the presence of man. 'Frontier fodder' someone called them, for the area they were to inhabit up to the Great Fish River formed the eastern boundary of the Cape Colony, formerly the hunting ground of the mighty Xhosa nation, known to the white man as Kaffirs.

Successive governments discovered a limit to their ingenuity in dealing with the aggressive, marauding Kaffir. Peaceful persuasion and diplomacy failed. It took a Colonel John Graham and an army of highly trained soldiers to drive the enemy across the Fish in 1811–12, and, in so doing, found the frontier town named after him. But driving the Kaffir back was one thing: keeping him back was quite another. It became obvious that the border population had to be increased in order to resist invasion and maintain the frontier. Easier said than done. Farmers knew, by bitter experience, that the closer they lived to the frontier, the more likely they were to lose their cattle, their farms, even their lives to the black savages. It fell to an effete British Governor, Lord Charles Somerset, to formulate a plan which became known as The Albany Settlement, a scheme for attracting his fellow-countrymen to the Cape of Good Hope.

At first, the costly idea was resisted in official circles. It took another invasion, in broad daylight this time, by ten thousand Kaffirs for all misgivings to be laid aside. The British army won a famous victory, for they not only drove the enemy across the Fish, but also pursued him north, forcing him back further than ever before, beyond the Keiskama River, thirty miles to the east. Now a buffer was created between the Fish and the Keiskama, known as the Neutral Territory, and it was controlled by a military post, Fort Wiltshire, on the west bank of the Keiskama. Six months later, twenty-one emigrant ships set sail from England with the four thousand hopeful settlers aboard. They gazed with heavy hearts on their new homeland and, in the face of the terrible hardship, Government indifference, repeated Kaffir invasion, somehow they survived and prospered.

But still it is a time of doubt and uncertainty. There, beyond the Keiskama, the Kaffir waits for the moment to strike again, to take back what was his. The newcomer is immediately aware of the impermanence of frontiers. The people go armed and watchful; they have made this corner of the earth a prize and are ever on guard to protect what they have created. Outnumbered ten to one, they have little choice but to draw strength from a source that has traditionally ignored the weight of numbers : they put their faith in God, and pray to Him in heaven to destroy their enemy; and, far, far away, across the Keiskama, the enemy prays, too.

5

Sybille entered the environs of Grahamstown towards evening one Friday in November. Her wagon lumbered down the broad main street, lined on either side by trees and bland white houses, towards the surprising space of Market Square. People paid her little attention, which was unusual for her : further south, she had seen children hide in terror as she rumbled past—'the wagon-woman's here, the wagon-woman's here'—and heard their parents call on Jesus Christ to protect them from the evil spirits, which, they said, possessed her. Although the sky was stuffed with grey clouds, and the day close and airless, the wagon-woman, as if oblivious to the oppressive heat, wore a colourful shawl of her own making, a patchwork affair, an intricate mosaic of brightly-coloured hexagonal and diamond-shaped pieces, and a quilt of similar design round her legs. She looked straight ahead with narrowed eyes, as though her destination lay at some point in the furthest distance, beyond the possibility of sight.

Sybille then, long past fifty, on that grey afternoon : gone was the pale, insipid girl who feared her mother's presence; this woman feared no one. Gone was the innocent, modest look; this woman had seen much in thirty years. Her face had aged markedly, scarred with deep lines, especially about the mouth; her hair was grey as ash; her once vacant eyes appeared to be a darker blue, and she stared fiercely. But the most noticeable change of all was her complexion, once so delicate and fair : the sun and wind had tanned and roughened her skin, and it was as though every particle of dust from her long journey had settled on her face : like a weathered statue she looked, carved from agate. Yet, there was little about her that spoke of neglect : her clothes were worn and patched, but they were clean, and her hair was scraped back neatly in a bun; only her hands were uncared for, the palms calloused, the nails cracked and grimy. But anyone who knew her as a young girl would know her still, by her voice which, soft and breathless, belied the austerity of her appearance.

It was her custom, when coming to a new town, to visit first the dominee. His position put him on intimate terms with his parishioners' affairs and, whatever Sybille's problem, he would usually know who the best person was to solve it. This day, she wanted the dominee to find her a place of work, for she intended to stay until she discovered Adam's whereabouts. But here, in Grahamstown, she was doubtful and uneasy : would an English town possess a Dutch minister? If not, would the English dominee be helpful? With these concerns uppermost, she entered Market Square, brought her wagon to a halt, dismounted, and looked about for a Reformed Church.

She stood for a moment, lost. The shopkeepers were shutting up for the day, and people were hurrying home from work. There were, too, many soldiers about, for Grahamstown was the army's headquarters, and Sybille had, understandably, a fear of soldiers. Feeling strange and foreign, she was uncertain what to do; finally, taking courage, she approached the first woman who passed and asked, in English, if there was a Reformed Church in the vicinity. But the woman, unduly startled by Sybille's fierce manner, shook her head and hands to signify she did not understand. Sybille, confused, tried Dutch on one of the shopkeepers, a butcher, who smiled and shrugged apologetically, saying, 'Ich praat only English, verstaan? Ich nie praat die taal, kan nie Hollands praat, you understand what I'm saying?' It was Sybille's turn to shrug. At last, she spied a little black boy, eight or nine years old, dancing on the sidewalk for a small audience who were clapping an unhelpful rhythm to accompany his sinewy movements. As she had done with Fathma, Sybille reached into her skirts and withdrew her draw-string purse, taking from it a coin. Then, she approached the dancing boy and said, in Xhosa, 'If you stop dancing and tell me something, I'll give you this.' The boy left off at once, and his face shone with pleasure. He did not seem in the least astonished at being spoken to in his own tongue by a white woman. His audience, however, was clearly annoyed that the performance should be interrupted, and one of the men was about to remonstrate with Sybille, but his wife restrained him with a firm hand on his arm, and sniffed haughtily, as if to imply she would not demean herself by arguing.

Sybille gripped the little boy by the hand and led him into an alleyway. He did not take his eyes off the coin which she continued to hold enticingly. 'Do you live here?' she asked, managing well the clicks and stops required by the strident, muscular tongue.

'I live here, madam,' the boy replied.

'And do you know what a church is?'

'Oh yes, madam,' he said, grinning and licking his lips. 'You can get food there sometimes.'

'I want you to take me to the church. To the minister.' She used the Xhosa word *iqgira*, which means diviner.

'It is not far, madam,' the boy said, beckoning Sybille to follow; he led her down the twisting network of alleyways, coming at last to a small, unimposing house that looked too run-down to be the home of a predikant.

'Are you sure the *iqgira* lives here?'

'Sure, madam,' said the boy, standing on tip-toe to reach the heavy iron door knocker. 'You pay me now.'

Sybille handed over the coin and the boy ran off. She waited and, presently, heard heavy footsteps and a deep male voice humming. The door was opened by a tall, handsome man, with black eyebrows and grey hair. He said, in English, 'Good evening, can I help you?'

Sybille retreated a step or two, all at once confused and tongue-tied: she had expected a Reformed minister and was now being studied by a pair of gentle, puzzled eyes belonging to the Reverend John Ayliff, a name which Sybille would record phonetically in her diary as 'a leaf'. After the first embarrassed explanations had been overcome, Sybille introduced herself and was invited indoors but she declined. 'I—I don't know if you can help me,' she said, playing with the ends of her shawl.

'Is it food you want, or a lodging?'

'No, no,' Sybille answered gruffly. The man's sympathetic manner confused her: the ministers she knew were made of sterner stuff. 'I want—I want—' she stammered, but ground to a halt, unable to find the words.

'Do come in,' Ayliff said. 'We can talk more comfortably indoors.'

Again Sybille refused. 'No,' she said, 'I don't like rooms.'

'If you would tell me what it is you want—?'

'Work. I need work.'

'What sort of work?'

Sybille reeled off a list of the jobs she had undertaken over the years, explaining, 'You see, I have to stay here in Grahamstown for a bit. I can't say how long. I'm looking for someone and I won't go till I find him.'

'I see. I cannot think of anyone off hand who may have need of your services—'

Sybille's manner became urgent and intense. 'I'll do anything, anything,' she said. 'I have to stay in these parts. Have to!'

'I'll see if I can think of anyone—'

Abruptly, Sybille changed the subject. 'What days are the Kaffir Fair?'

Taken aback, Ayliff smiled vaguely and answered, 'Er—Wednesdays and Saturdays.'

'I see, I see,' murmured Sybille. 'Well? Can you help me?'

Ayliff considered for a moment, studying his visitor, a little suspicious of her unsettling manner. At last he said, 'I will give the matter some thought. Call upon me again tomorrow morning early, and I hope then I will be able to help you.'

Without another word, Sybille shuffled off into the night trying to find her way back to Market Square, leaving the Reverend John Ayliff to shake his head, shrug and close his front door. He had just entered his small dining-room where his wife was about to serve the evening meal when a thought struck him. 'Of course!' he cried. 'Mr Thompson!'

6

On the following morning, Mr John Ayliff presented Sybille with a letter of introduction to Richard Thompson Esquire, of Safehaven, in the Albany district of the eastern Cape Colony:

Dear Mr Thompson,

I have taken it upon myself to write this letter which will introduce to you the bearer, Miss Sybille Henning.

Miss Henning is presently visiting Grahamstown for an unspecified period of time, and is desirous of finding temporary employment to support her sojourn in these parts. To this end, I have suggested to her that she might well be of assistance to you in your present extremity. She has a wide experience and, as far as your particular needs are concerned, it will interest you to know that she has, on several ocasions, nursed the sick. It has occurred to me, and to Mrs Ayliff, that she may be the answer to all our prayers. I have little doubt that she is of an upright character, sober in her habits and conscientious in all she undertakes. I cannot believe that a better opportunity will present itself, and it is my most fervent hope that you will employ her as nurse and tutor to Michael. This cannot but ease your own labours.

I pray daily for Michael's recovery.

> Yours sincerely and with the love of Christ,
> John Ayliff.

15

Father and son

It was a cheerless place: the farmhouse was long and narrow, and stood at the threshold of a small and confined valley, guarded at the rear by modest hills, called *kopjes*, and looking out on land that sloped imperceptibly towards a muddy stream, a weakling tributary of the Kowie River. To the north-west stood Grahamstown, three hours' ride away; fifty miles to the east flowed the Great Fish.

The man at work in the orchard looked up and saw the wagon approaching. He was busily repairing fences with the help of two Hottentot slaves and broke off with a weary sigh. 'Not another bloody trader,' he said, then, cupping his hands over his mouth, shouted, ' 'Ere! You can't come through 'ere! It's private property!' But the wagon did not turn or stop. 'It'll be one of 'em Boars, you mark my words,' he said. 'They never will understand the Queen's English! *Go away!*' And with another sigh, he set off up the path that bordered the orchard.

He had the air and look of a defeated man. His whole demeanour spoke of failure. His eyes were watery, his long nose drooped mournfully, and his narrow little shoulders were so stooped and bent they seemed to carry all the weight of the world upon them; and despite his red, sunburned, weathered complexion, there was no concealing the sickly, yellowish pallor of a Londoner, born and bred. As he trudged upwards, he gazed at the cloudless blue sky and wished it would rain.

He was about to shout again, and more obscenely this time, when he saw there was a woman at the reins. He scratched his head and waited for the wagon to draw level.

'And what can I do for you, ma'am?' he asked.

'Are you Mr Thompson?'

'I am.'

'And is this Safehaven?'

'It is.'

'Then this is for you.' She handed him the letter from John Ayliff.

He read it with growing excitement, muttering 'Well, I never!' and 'Would you believe it?' At last, smiling, he looked up at Sybille and said, 'Welcome to Safehaven, Miss 'Enning, and I mean that with all my 'eart.'

'Am I to look after your boy, then?' she asked, surprised by the warmth of his greeting.

'Well, if Mr Ayliff says you're suitable that's good enough for me.'

'What's the matter with your son?'

'Chest,' Thompson replied, tapping his own.

'And it's bad, is it?'

Tears welled up in the Englishman's eyes. 'He ain't got long,' he said, shuddering at the thought of it.

'And I'm to teach him, too, Mr Ayliff said.'

'Just to keep 'is mind occupied, if you follow my meanin'. I don't think 'e 'as much time left for a great deal of learnin'.'

'I'll do what I can,' said Sybille.

'No one can do more. It's been 'ard for me, Miss—er—' he referred to the letter again, 'Miss 'Enning, tied day and night to the 'ouse. I never thought we'd find anybody willin' to undertake such a miserable task. But Mr Ayliff said to 'ave faith, and now me prayers've been answered. Oh, you are welcome, and I can't say more.'

Abruptly, Sybille changed course. 'What will you pay?' she asked.

Thompson hesitated, not having given the matter much thought, and a brief exchange of offers and counter-offers ensued until they settled on ten rixdollars a week. 'Come,' said Thompson, offering her a hand, 'let's shake on it, and I'll take you now to the boy. Michael's his name, poor little blighter.'

They shook hands and Sybille, like a woman half her age, hopped down. Thompson said, 'I've a nice little room for you, Miss 'Enning—'

Sybille turned on him sharply. 'I sleep in my wagon. I don't like rooms. Rooms poison people. My mother died of a poisoned room.'

'Oh well. There you are then,' replied Thompson, hurriedly suppressing any disquiet her last remark may have caused.

They continued towards the house. 'One thing,' said Sybille, 'I must have two afternoons off a week. Wednesdays and Saturdays would be best.'

'Wednesdays *and* Saturdays,' Thompson repeated doubtfully.

'I have to go to the Kaffir Fair.'

'The Kaffir Fair? And what would a lady like you be doin' at the Kaffir Fair?'

'I'm looking for someone,' she explained, as though the quest were immediate and urgent. 'He keeps one jump ahead of me all the time, but I'm going to find him in Grahamstown, I'm certain of it!'

All sorts of theories passed quickly through Thompson's head: was she looking for an errant husband or a lover? was she seeking revenge? He felt it best not to pursue the subject, and said, 'Well, you're welcome to them Kaffir Fairs. I 'ate 'em. You get all the scum of the earth at them fairs. Shady white traders, Kaffir scoundrels and worst of all them Hottentots, roaming around in gangs, scroungin' and stealin'! No, not for me, Miss 'Enning. And if you'll pardon me mentionin' the subject, them women who stand round Market Square of a Saturday, foul they are. I avoids Market Square of a Saturday. Them women and their bullies leerin' at you, and the smell of them! Sweet and sickly!' He grimaced. By then, they had mounted the three wooden steps to the verandah and stood at the front door. 'I'll take you to Michael,' Thompson said.

Sybille paused. 'Then it's all right, is it?' she asked. 'Wednesdays and Saturdays?'

'Agreed,' replied Thompson. 'I'll lead the way.'

It was as cheerless inside as out, colourless, lacking a woman's touch. There was one main room which ran the length of more than half the house; it was sparsely furnished yet appeared cluttered, and the home-made chairs and tables had an impermanent look about them. Here, alone, Thompson sat in the evening, ate his meals, and did his paperwork. A short, narrow passage led to the kitchen and to the bedrooms, one of which was occupied day and night by his son, Michael.

The boy was half asleep when his father and Sybille entered, his gaunt face turned away from the window and the sunlight, so that his cheeks seemed unnaturally hollow and pinched. 'Michael,' said

Thompson quietly, 'there's someone to see you.'

Michael opened his eyes and focused upon the two figures standing at the foot of his bed. Almost at once, he began to cough and splutter. With open mouth, he struggled for breath, twisting from side to side. In no time at all, he was fighting a massive, desperate spasm, and soon lapsed into unconsciousness.

2

There were reasons for Michael's sudden and terrible attack, and not all of them were physical. He had first begun to show symptoms of a weakness in his chest shortly after his third birthday. By the time he was six, he was regarded as a chronic invalid who was unlikely, the doctor said, to reach puberty. It seemed to all a harsh diagnosis, for the boy had known little joy in his life: his mother had died giving birth to him, and there was not even a portrait to remember her by. Being motherless and solitary, he was treated with the utmost care and solicitude, and possessed that special and peculiar inwardness that comes from being indulged, from self-reliance, and from habitual loneliness. Thus, he perceived more than he was given credit for, and understood events and relationships far beyond the experience of his years. He also developed a certain cunning as far as the adults in his life were concerned, an ability to take advantage of their weaknesses, to misuse his illness in order to get his own way. This produced in him an outward show of maturity—'old-fashioned' it was called—which prompted everyone from his father to the servants to treat him as a man when, in one vital respect, he was still a child, and that was a painful longing he felt for his dead mother, a constant ache he believed only she could dispel. And, although the grown-up part of him, the one he presented to the world, knew quite well that she was dead, he nevertheless nursed the forlorn conviction that she would one day return to take him in her arms and that, in her embrace, his illness would vanish. These longings he confided to no one, but wrote them down each day in a letter beginning, 'My dearest Ma.'

From his bedroom window he could see the upper part of the orchard, the long straight lines of apple trees looking like Grenadiers on parade. A cool breeze nudged the flimsy curtains, and the boy welcomed it, for the sun was high and the heat clung to his room like a poisonous gas. In the kitchen, Gwali, four years Michael's senior, scrubbed the floor; the scraping noise of his brush against the stone blocks was the only sound to disturb the auspicious morning quietude.

The boy dozed in fits and starts; somewhere distant he heard his father's voice calling but the words were indistinct; unaccountably, the sudden reminder of his father filled him with apprehension. Not that Michael feared the man: the boy knew too well every twist and turn of mind, and how easy it was to play him like a fish at the end of a line, intuitively acknowledging the helplessness the older man suffered when confronted with his son's illness. No, there was another reason for his unease: on several occasions recently, when Michael's father had been filled with self-pity, cursing his lot, questioning his misfortune, he had taken pleasure in repeating the same threat: 'I'll take a wife, so 'elp me I will, and see 'ow you make do with a step-mother!' The fear of a domineering cruel harridan haunted Michael; the idea that some awful woman would come in, take over the household and turn his father against him was a perpetual terror. ('My dearest Ma, I do not want a step-mother. Please prevent it, please!') It frightened Michael that his father would, on a whim, present him with this witch. Would, one day, they come riding back together? Would his father say, 'Meet your new mother, Michael'? Would today be the day? And in a curious, perverse way, it was a fear he often encouraged, and secretly enjoyed.

So it was understandable that when Michael stirred from his broken sleep, and saw, at the foot of his bed, his father and a woman with a penetrating gaze standing there, he should at once think that the witch had become reality. He did not speak and there was no time to hear explanations. His chest began to heave up and down in ever-increasing convulsions, a terrible choking sound came from his throat as he gulped desperately for air, and a noise like a concertina played out of tune emanated from his chest. Terror of the attack fed the attack, and in a short time he was writhing in agony, imagining that each impossible breath he took was his last. He heard his father cry, 'Gwali, go for Dr Clarke!' and then the woman saying, 'Doctors won't cure him!' and his father: 'There is no cure!' and the woman: 'There is always a cure!'

3

For three days, Michael's attack raged; on the third day, Dr Clarke shook his head sadly and said the boy would not live through the night. Mr and Mrs Filmore, the Thompsons' oldest friends and nearest neighbours, came to visit with their youngest daughter, Alice. Thompson sat on one of the home-made chairs, staring out at the orchard, and saw Malgaia, an old Khoikhoi woman, plucking the ripe fruit from the trees, a simple, ordinary act which so clearly seemed to echo his own situation, that he wept openly for his dying son. Sybille kept to her wagon which stood at the rear of the house in the shade of a small copse. Although she had suggested she remain with the boy, Thompson refused, and kept the vigil at the bedside himself; Sybille, feeling strange in her new surroundings, did not insist: things would have to be desperate for her to do that. Now she sat reading her family Bible, and singing a curious atonal melody that did not belong in any Christian hymnal. It was the singing of this song that drew the Xhosa boy, Gwali, to her covered wagon; he sat cross-legged, his head resting against a tree trunk, as if on guard.

At eleven, Dr Clarke left the house, head bowed, and marched quickly to his horse and cart.

'Are you the doctor?'

The stooped, scholarly man turned to see Sybille advancing on him, with Gwali a short distance behind her.

'I do not believe I have had the pleasure,' he said, tipping his hat.

'I'm here to teach the boy, Michael,' she said.

'Oh yes. Thompson did say he'd found someone,' he answered, looking at her over his eye-glasses, which made him feel superior.

'How is the boy?' Sybille asked.

'I fear your employment will be terminated tonight,' the doctor replied.

'He's dying,' Sybille stated bluntly, but wanting confirmation.

Clarke winced at such indelicacy: he preferred euphemisms such as 'no hope' or 'not long' or 'God's will be done'. He said, 'He is dangerously, nay, gravely ill, madam.'

'And you can do nothing.' Another statement.

'I have done all I can. God's will be done.'

She nodded as if to dismiss him, and, taking his cue, he touched his hat once more and mounted up. She waited until horse and cart were out of sight, then turned to Gwali and spoke to him rapidly in Xhosa, issuing instructions. The boy's eyes, which in ordinary circumstances were unusually large and expressive, seemed to grow to twice their size: he shook his head, terrified; Sybille spoke again, more sternly this time, and, without waiting for a reply walked purposefully towards the house, Gwali following reluctantly at a safe distance.

The scene inside had an air of unreality. Thompson was seated, his gaunt cheeks stained with tears. From time to time, he made observations directed at no one in particular. John Filmore was at a rickety table, shuffling and re-shuffling playing-cards, though he never laid them out in any game; he, too, uttered occasionally. His daughter, Alice, conducted a continuous conversation, in a loud voice, with an imaginary being called Hopeless, now and then reporting his remarks to the others. Mrs Filmore spent most of her time with the patient and appeared in the main room only to issue alarming bulletins on Michael's state and to reprimand her child.

'Just when I thought 'e was gettin' better,' said Thompson.

'Hopeless says that Jesus Christ was born in Port Elizabeth, don't you, Hopeless?'

'That's blasphemy,' said her father.

'I can't help what Hopeless says.'

'Be quiet, child.'

'Oh, I *did* pray . . .' Thompson said fervently, but his voice trailed off; and, then, as though a threat: 'If 'e goes, if 'e goes . . .'

'Control yourself, man,' said Filmore, easily embarrassed.

'Hopeless, that's rude! You're not to say things like that again. Mama will spank you!'

Mrs Filmore, round and bustling, entered. 'The elixir isn't doing any good. Poor little mite. It'll be a happy release, God help him. And Alice, stop your chattering, Mama will spank you.'

She was about to return to the sick-room when Sybille appeared, grim and determined; Gwali clung to the lintel as though it were a magnet. Mrs Filmore hovered, intrigued by Sybille's look of purpose. (This was a scene the Englishwoman repeated countless times. 'I don't know what made me stay . . .' she always began.)

'Mr Thompson,' said Sybille, 'the doctor tells me your son is going to die.'

'Hush, woman,' said Filmore, furiously shuffling the cards.

'Have you called a preacher?' Sybille demanded.

Thompson's face clouded with alarm; it had never occurred to him to send for the minister, and no one had thought to remind him.

Mrs Filmore said, 'Oh Lord, how did we forget!'

Thompson addressed Gwali. 'Go for Mr Ayliff at once,' he ordered.

'Not Gwali,' said Sybille. 'I need him. Send someone else.' In Xhosa, she gave instructions to the boy who ran off, and returned moments later.

'Hopeless says Mr Ayliff knows Jesus,' said Alice. 'That's blasphemy,' said her father.

'Alice!' cried Mrs Filmore.

Sybille took a step towards Thompson, who cowered involuntarily. 'You are all to come into the sick-room and pray!' she announced.

Behind her back, Mrs Filmore was signalling her disapproval to Thompson, but the man chose not to notice. 'I can't see as 'ow it would do any 'arm,' he murmured, sniffing tears. 'I should've summoned the minister. I just didn't think.'

Sybille called over her shoulder, 'Gwali!' The boy did not move. She called his name again and with eyes downcast, Gwali padded quickly across the room, transferring his allegiance from the lintel to her skirt. Then, taking him by the hand, Sybille advanced on the doorway that led to the passage where Mrs Filmore stood guard; Sybille pushed past.

' 'Ere!' called Thompson, stirring for the first time from his mournful lethargy. 'Where's the Kaffir going?'

Mrs Filmore felt bound to champion this sentiment. 'The Kaffir can't go in there!' she declared. 'Michael's too ill, poor little soul,' but by then, Sybille, with Gwali in tow, had entered the sick-room. 'Well, I never!' exclaimed Mrs Filmore, and from Alice, 'Hopeless says that's blasphemy!'

'Come along!' Sybille called. Thompson, feeling decidedly foolish, shuffled into the room, followed by the Filmores and their daughter.

For most of the time, apart from when he fell into an exhausted sleep, Michael sat on the edge of his bed, hands tucked beneath his buttocks, rocking to and fro; it was the only position which seemed to ease the pain. The wheezing, like a resonant whistle, filled the room. He glanced up at the assembly and feebly shook his head as if to say that he did not want them there. His face was pinched, and contorted with the difficulty of breathing, and two dull pink patches gave an unhealthy glow to his cheeks. Sybille sat beside him on the bed and, to everyone's annoyance, whispered into his ear.

'God loves you,' she said.

The boy looked frightened or surprised, impossible to say which.

'What's she telling him?' demanded Mrs Filmore, but Sybille silenced her with a withering stare, and once more into the boy's ear, said the words, 'God loves you.' Gently, she helped the invalid to lie down; at once, his breathing accelerated, 'There, there,' she said, 'try to sleep,' and turning to the others, 'We must kneel.'

Alice did as she was told, but the adults, embarrassed by the proceedings, stood about uncomfortably, not knowing what was expected of them. Gwali, too: he did not leave go of Sybille's hand and she, turning to him, suddenly intoned, '*Uku-nqulu!*'

The boy shook his head; the woman repeated her command.

' 'Ere, what are you sayin'?' said Thompson, fearful that some heathen spell was about to be cast over his son.

'I have told Gwali to call on his ancestors for help. *Uku-nqulu* means to pray.'

An argument erupted at once: Mrs Filmore had never heard anything so disgraceful and Thompson, under her influence, flatly refused to continue with the farce; Mr Filmore was already on his way out of the room. All the while, Michael lay on his back, struggling for breath.

'God listens in any language,' said Sybille, widening the chasm between herself and the others who were of the opinion that God, being an Englishman, had difficulty understanding even Dutch, let alone Xhosa. But Sybille could not be moved from her course. Dismissing Thompson's and Mrs Filmore's protests simply by ignoring them, she once more ordered Gwali to pray. Terrified the boy turned away from them, but began to chant. '*Uthixo!*' he called in a faint unsteady voice, and once he had embarked on his liturgy, Sybille herself, as though to accompany him, sang, in Dutch,

'O God, let us see Thy glorious light,
Shine, O Lord, shine!
Thou art our comfort by day and by night,
Thou art mine, O Lord, mine, O Lord, mine!'

Thompson and Mrs Filmore fell silent as the strange harmony of sound enveloped them. They looked helplessly at each other, but Mrs Filmore, overwhelmed by a conviction not to be outdone, fell on her knees, muttering, 'Our Father, who art in Heaven, hallowed be Thy name,' and, after a moment, the men joined her. Alice watched with a blank expression, as though the grown-ups had taken leave of their senses.

Gwali chanted, Sybille sang, the others beseeched their god to forgive them their trespasses.

> 'O God, bless us now and forever more!
> Say, O Lord, say!
> We will live by Thy word, the holiest law,
> Let us pray, O Lord, pray, O Lord, pray!'

The Lord's Prayer finished first, then the Xhosa chant. Sybille, oblivious, rendered one more verse:

> 'O God, art Thou there in Heav'n above?
> Shine, O Lord, shine!
> We rejoice, we give thanks for Thy perfect love,
> We are Thine, O Lord, Thine, O Lord, Thine!'

When she finished, she turned her attention to Michael, uttering soothing sounds to the boy, who fought for breath as though he were wrestling with an unseen adversary.

Thompson and the Filmores gradually regained their composure, but avoided each other's looks guiltily, for all of them felt they had been caught up, against their will, in some madness or other. Flushed and tearful, Mrs Filmore rose and hurried out, followed by her husband. Thompson, before leaving the room, raised a warning finger at Sybille, 'If 'e goes,' he said, 'if 'e goes . . .'

She remained with Michael and, some hours later, when the Reverend John Ayliff arrived to offer up prayers for the dying boy, she was able to report that he was sleeping, and that his breathing was easier. She retired to her wagon and confided to her diary that all was well:

M. better. The power of God in all. Can see T. from here, on verandah, smoking. He sings a song about the sea.

4

'Anchors away, me lads, anchors away!
The great ship's cast off her ropes!
Three months and a day, me lads, three months and a day!
She'll carry me home with high hopes!

For England's our port, me lads, England's our port!
We'll soon have the anchor at rest!
And we'll have been taught, me lads, we'll have been taught
That England's the place we love best!'

Thus sang Richard Thompson on the night his son's attack abated. Chair tilted back, his feet resting on the flimsy wooden porch rail, he puffed on his pipe and looked out at the wisps of cloud chasing the crescent moon. For the first time in many years he was experiencing a deep contentment, not because of Michael's recovery, but because a secret hope he had been nourishing ever since his arrival in the Colony at last seemed possible of fulfilment, a hope born out of his hatred for the Cape and everyone in it. Now, as he sat gazing out at the night, his thoughts floated free: his mind detached itself from his body and from his physical surroundings and wandered into other worlds, other places he knew and loved. Smells invaded his nostrils, old familiar smells that nourished nostalgia: the perfume of sweet hay and clover from Stratford, from Bow and Romford, and Whitechapel Market: now that was a market, not a Kaffir Fair! Urchins scuttling under carts and wagons to gather up fallen produce; the fine joints of meat hanging in Butcher Market; the butchers themselves, rubbing their hands with cold and satisfaction, crying out, 'What do you buy, buy, buy?' In the London of his mind's eye it was always cold, always busy, crowded, airless, suffocating, lovely. People, hundreds of people, muffled and gloved, stamping their feet at street corners or warming their hands at the braziers of the chestnut sellers, and a bitter north wind, and a good fall of snow. That was his last memory of England: winter, September 1819.

September, and a severe frost; what with two or three heavy falls of snow the whole way through Whitechapel to Milk Lane was covered in frozen sleet. And being out of work, which was a new malady but soon to grow stale. And Mary, Mary Mason. The Red Lion near Brick Lane. Mary: prattling on about their wedding plans, her dress, the veil, the guests, the cost. He didn't dare tell her he'd been laid off from the warehouse; he didn't dare tell her he'd only ten pounds saved. Ten pounds: how far would that go in a bitter winter; with coal and food and rent and taxes?

And Mary's brother, Charlie, with a map, pointing to a spot that meant nothing and still meant nothing. 'That's a long way off,

Charlie'—he could hear his own voice—and Charlie's, worse luck:
' 'Course it's a long way off. Affrikay ain't on Stepney Green,
y'know!'

'I know that, Charlie. But I've got a feelin' you mean Botany Bay.'

'Don't talk daft! The Cape of Good 'Ope is wot I'm talkin' abaht.
That's as far away from Botany Bay as Affrikay is from Bow!'

'I don't wanna go, Charlie. Them people out there are called Boars
an' Hotnetots and Kafferees. I don't wanna be eaten up alive by
them cannerbils!'

'Give over! My old man was at the takin' of the Cape, Richard. 'E
saw plenty of Dutchmen and Dutchwomen, too, white as you 'n me.
We won't 'ave to pay no bleedin' taxes in the Cape of Good 'Ope,
and we'll 'ave servants of our own, instead of bein' bleedin' servants
to others, me old son! And the bleedin' sun shines all day and ev'ry
bleedin' day!'

And meetings all over the East End. Times were bad. Cape Fever
they called it: busy, self-important, little men coming to explain the
terms. The Zuurveld, that was the place: free passage, keep during
the voyage, and a grant of a hundred acres to every head of family.
There'd be clergymen and doctors and churches and schools. Paradise.

In the end, it was Richard who went and Charlie who stayed at
home. Mary and Richard were married in November. In December
they boarded the ship at a place called Deptford. Colder than ever.
The Thames frozen as hard as the pavements in Cheapside, and they
roasted an ox on the ice.

19 January 1820. Quarter past three. Heart heavy as the anchor.
The ship loosened from its moorings. Mary crying, and he too,
howling like a baby when he said farewell to Gravesend, the utmost
limit of his knowledge of the civilised world. Seasickness, and the
terrible, useless regret. Only one thing did he clearly now remember
of that long sea-voyage: some weeks from Table Bay, the look-out
sighted land, and everyone rushed to the rail to see a grim lump of
rock rising, out of the sea. Is this the Cape of Good Hope, they
asked. Is this where we're to live?

'You see that rock,' said a sailor. 'Thank Almighty God for its
existence. Upon that rock, so 'elp me, resides the Devil 'imself. That
rock, friends, is called St 'Elena.'

They sang hymns of thanksgiving, and the clergyman aboard
offered up prayers for England's deliverance from the tyrant. But

Thompson did not sing. He gazed out at the stark, forbidding island and felt a terrible, desolate sympathy for the Emperor exiled from his homeland whose prison it was.

And now he gazed out at his own prison: the Cape, with its heat and sickly, olive-green scrub; the space, the endless space, and those dull, lifeless Boers, and that grating, ugly *taal* they spoke that made them sound as though they were perpetually choking. He refused to learn it; all the English had refused to learn it. Let the bloody Boers speak a civilised tongue instead of this Kaffir-Dutch which gave you a sore throat to listen to. Misfortune, that was all he had ever reaped here, and cruel misfortune at that. A sweet wife dead before she was five-and-twenty; a wheat crop that failed three successive years, two hundred head of cattle stolen by marauding Kaffirs and a dozen friends lost to their assegais. And this abominable loneliness. The Cape offered you happiness with one hand and snatched it away with the other. And Michael, his only child, who they said would die before his tenth birthday.

But dare he hope? Dare he believe that this strange nurse, this Sybille Henning, who conducted prayers in Dutch, Kaffir and English, dare he believe that she might hold the answer to Michael's health? If it were so, then his ambition could be realised: to quit the Cape, if only for a few months, to see his beloved London once more, that's all he asked, just once more before he died; and, sitting there, singing to himself, oblivious of the dark night, he had already made the decision:

'Anchors away, me lads, anchors away,
See the white cliffs, proud and white!
Let the wind play, me lads, let the wind play,
And I'll sleep in England tonight!'

5

Some days after the prayers at his son's bedside, Thompson entered the room to find Sybille reading to Michael from the Bible. Full of good cheer and wanting to share his decision with them, he announced his intention of returning to England for a short holiday. The news came as a profound shock to the boy, and he smarted at the pain of rejection which his father's plans represented. In a matter of hours, he had worked himself up into such a state of self-pity and resentment, that he was seized by another attack. For two days he suffered. Thompson pleaded with Sybille to pray once more for Michael, but she declined, well aware of Michael's culpability in the matter. 'There is nothing I can do!' she said. 'It will pass.' And it did. Nevertheless, Thompson decided to postpone his journey.

Little boys soon learn who is susceptible to their wiles, and who is not. To his father, he continued to present the face of illness; to Sybille he offered recalcitrance, ill-temper and a grudging obedience. In time, however, even this facet of his capricious temperament receded when he understood he had more to gain by being well than by remaining ill, although he soon realised that it is as painful for chronic invalids who are cured to surrender to health, as it is for healthy men to submit to chronic illness.

Michael's acceptance of the change was a gradual process and no single dramatic moment heralded the transformation. Miss Henning became a fixture in his life, and one he increasingly relied on. His father, who continued to work hard on the farm, indulged Michael in small ways and invariably took his son's part in any dispute with Miss Henning.

The climax to full health was reached one birthday, his ninth or tenth, he was not certain which. But he liked to think of 16 February as the day his childhood began in earnest, for on the previous night, a mighty thunderstorm had raged and let loose torrential rain. So severe was it, that Sybille was forced to abandon her wagon and take shelter inside the house. But the next morning, the dust of a dry summer had been laid, and a cloudless sky trumpeted one of those perfect Cape days when every tree and plant is refreshed, the earth warm, and all living things content and heartened.

His father presented him with an ornate pen and ink stand, imported from England. 'Thank you, Dada,' said Michael, weakly. 'I have much time to write while I lie in bed here.' Thompson blinked back tears and left the house; by ten o'clock he was hard at work, bundling hay and cursing the heat as he did so.

The only other gift Michael received was from Sybille:

'Get dressed,' she said. 'You're going down to the stream. Happy Birthday.'

At first, he did not believe her: the promise of such an excursion had been held out to him so many times before, and always for some reason or another denied, that he had grown suspicious and, in his heart, believed he would never venture further than the shadows of the verandah. But this day, the promise was fulfilled. Dressed in a suit that was sizes too small for him, he took his first uncertain steps into the sunlight, doing his utmost to suppress an irresistible urge to cough.

It was, to begin with, easy going: the orchard sloped casually down to a screen of bushes and trees, beyond which lay the stream. Half-way down the orchard, Michael rested, Sybille standing over him, watching his chest closely: she saw that he was panting and Gwali was deputed to carry Michael pick-a-back the rest of the way.

Strange and wonderful impressions consumed him: the pleasure in prodding Gwali with his heels to make him run faster, Miss Henning trotting to keep up with them, the still wet leaves against his face as they galloped through the bushes, a branch scratching his forehead, and the sight of the stream itself, yellow and muddy and feeble, but to him, a great, surging expression of well-being and freedom. The smell of drying earth and of pine needles, of his own sweat and Gwali's, these were the sensations of health. And in the cycle of passing months, there were always specific moments and incidents that stood out, as though time travelled at speed, and was abruptly halted at important, memorable signposts.

Sybille and Gwali, always together, inseparable, speaking Xhosa, excluded Michael.

'What do you talk about?' Michael asked one day.

'We talk about Our Lord and Saviour Jesus Christ.'

'You talk about God in Kaffir?'

'No,' said Sybille. 'In Xhosa.'

'Same thing. What d'you want to do that for?'

'Gwali is to become a Christian, Michael, like you and me.'

Michael bridled at this new bond between them, resented every moment they spent together. And he was aware of Gwali's eyes bursting with wonder at the story of the Resurrection, and understanding and believing in a way that was alien to Michael. 'But master Michael,' Gwali said, 'they touched the wounds of the risen *uthixo* and there was blood on their fingers!' And his excitement at learning that Sybille's father had been a priest. 'My uncle, too, is *iqgira*.' (Little was known of Gwali and how he came to be employed on the Thompson farm. His parents, it was said, had been captured on a cattle raid, and the little boy had wandered into the Colony in search of them. They came, he said, from the Great House, which was the line of Xhosa chiefs.)

And Michael determined in his heart to drive a wedge between them, to capture Sybille from Gwali, whom he saw now as his rival in her affections. He chose the moment when he and Miss Henning were sitting in the shadow of a rock cluster, on one of the *kopjes* that overlooked the grazing fields; Gwali was herding sheep into a pen, running after strays, whistling, expertly controlling the flock.

'I want to learn Kaffir,' Michael said solemnly. And her surprise, her pleasure, a wise, knowing look, and not asking him why, but beginning lessons that night. He regretted what he had done, but persisted: painful, evening hours when he wished that he was ill again, learning to click his tongue round impossible words, to capture the exact rise and fall of voice, to force his throat to contract with the shocks of the strange, new tones. Pastoral words at first —*igusha* for merino sheep, *inkomo* for head of cattle, *ubisi*, milk, *inca*, grass—and then, with Gwali, entering the world of prayer and magic: *iqgira*, diviner; *uku-nqulu*, to shout to your ancestors; *uthixo*, supreme being. (And the pleasure, at first reluctant, later wholehearted, at finding it possible to master this athletic African tongue.)

And the journey to Grahamstown: sitting beside Gwali on the tailboard of Miss Henning's wagon. Gwali, dressed in one of Michael's suits, shining with cleanliness. The Reverend John Ayliff anointing the black brow, baptising him with the names Miss Henning had chosen, Johannes Daniel, in the name of the Father, and of the Son, and of the Holy Ghost. But still they called him Gwali, and still he herded the sheep, and ran messages, and scrubbed the kitchen floor, and did as he was told. And Michael was secretly glad of that. (But how he envied the gold cross Miss Henning gave the new Christian, which he wore round his neck and swore never to lose. Once, Michael tried to steal it while Gwali was asleep, but the boy woke.)

Her stories, too, and her voice, the distant look, the impish smile. 'Oh, boys, there was a soldier loved me once. Handsome and strong and brave. Noble he was, too. D'you know what he did? When the French invaded the Cape, he smuggled me out in a wagon, although he knew he would never see me again. That's real sacrifice. God would bless him for that.'

'But Miss Henning, the French never invaded the Cape.'

'Well, whoever it was then.' And her laugh, raucous as a crow.

'When was that, Miss Henning?'

'Oh, when you were playing with the monkeys on Table Mountain.'

And gathering his courage to ask, 'What do you do on Wednesdays and Saturdays, Miss Henning?'

'Never you mind!' How sharp her voice could be: her eyes like stones, her mouth tight as a sprung trap.

'But where, Miss Henning?'

'It's my business! I don't tell anyone!'

Which was a lie: because she took Gwali once, and every week after that, and when Michael questioned him, he said. 'We go to the Kaffir Fair in Grahamstown.'

'What for?' Michael asked.

'To look for someone.' After that he became as silent as Miss Henning, and closed his eyes, and would not speak, no matter how hard Michael bullied, or threatened or cajoled.

And the impression her moods made: for days she could be ordinary and nice and kind. But after her excursions into Grahamstown and the Kaffir Fair, she would be angry, invaded by demons that made her restless, anxious and driven.

Most important of all:

'You must think of Our Saviour Jesus Christ as standing on the peak of a high mountain. And, at His feet, stretching all the way down to the ground, are the gods of other men, wanting to be one with Him. I have travelled and I have seen, and I know, as surely as I do His love, that all men seek the way to our Lord and Saviour. And we, who are his Elect, his chosen ones, must lead all others up the mountain's side, to the feet of the true God, so that all souls may come to Christ Jesus.' (And it was an image of Christ, Michael later claimed, he carried all his life.)

16

Departure

I

Sybille's sojourn in the Thompson household was brief but stormy.
In the months that followed Michael's recovery, a tense, explosive
relationship developed between herself and the boy she had somehow helped to cure. The cause lay in Sybille's unashamed preference
for Gwali, not inverted prejudice this, because none but Michael's
father would argue that the Xhosa boy was by far the more likeable
of the two.

Michael was a bully. His return to health uncovered a disturbing
energy that had previously, by circumstance, been concealed. His
father put it down to boyish exuberance, but it was wilder, more
savage than that. In the first place, there was something unmistakably English about his arrogance: not an aristocrat's *hauteur*,
but what seemed an inbred certitude of his own importance, which
he flaunted towards both Sybille and Gwali. But since neither his
teacher nor his servant were easily intimidated, Michael was forced
to assert himself in other ways; he might believe in the matchless
quality of his birthright, they did not. He was obliged, by the very
nature of his troubled personality, to feel he had always the upper
hand, and this, in turn, reflected itself in his desire to be noticed and
made much of. Sybille became the battleground, a territory to be
conquered.

By contrast, Gwali was the kind of boy teachers cherish, for he
made no demands, but was both responsive and giving. He enjoyed
learning, and he was instinctively aware of powers and forces outside the confines of his own being, as if the mysteries of the universe
were gifts to be savoured. Michael's belligerence he appeared not to
notice, and refused to partake in the one-sided war for Sybille's

affections, this disregard only serving to exacerbate the white boy's aggression.

The conflict came to a head shortly after the first anniversary of Sybille's arrival and it coincided with a series of events that were to presage her sudden departure. On a golden day in the first week of December, Sybille sat in the shade of a *doringboom* near her wagon, making one of those patchwork shawls intended as a Christmas present for Gwali. Mr Thompson was at work with two or three of the Hottentot farm boys, casual labourers, harvesting the wheat.

Michael and Gwali played by the river bank. They sat side by side, idly tossing stones into the stream and then, by throwing on as flat a trajectory as possible, skimmed them across the water so that they bounced two or three times and then sank. Gwali was content with the activity in itself, but Michael insisted on turning the game into a competition, to see whose stones would bounce the most. After one of Gwali's stones had attained a 'four-bounce', Michael grew irritated. 'I'm sick of this,' he said. 'Let's play Kaffirs.' This was a game of his own invention in which he was the certain winner, for it involved Gwali crossing to the opposite bank of the stream, which they pretended was the Great Fish River, to assume the role of Hintza, the Xhosa chieftain. Michael, of course, was the British Governor or the commander-in-chief, whichever took his fancy. The object was for Gwali to storm across the stream, 'invade the Colony', and then allow himself to be driven back by the superior British army. It was a game they had played many times and it had always ended in a fight that was something more than friendly. This day, when Michael suggested it, Gwali at first declined, but sensing the obstinacy of the white boy's mood, shrugged to show his indifference, and dutifully crossed to the far bank.

Meanwhile, Michael clambered up a small cluster of rocks that overlooked the stream; strategically, it was a commanding position, and Gwali was not slow to appreciate the fact.

'Master Michael,' he said, 'why don't you attack me for a change?'

'No,' said Michael, 'the Kaffirs always attack. They take us by surprise and kill all the English babies.'

'Yes, but master Michael, sometimes the English attack, too.'

'Never. Now go on: hide.'

Resigned, Gwali took cover behind some bushes, crouching low, and looked for some new way to surprise the enemy; but the game did not really fire his imagination. After a few moments, he stood and, waving his arms half-heartedly, ran into the shallow stream. Michael's response first astonished, then angered him, for Gwali was surprised to find himself being pelted with stones and rocks, some as large as his fists, which exploded all round him as they hit the water.

'Stop that, master Michael!' Gwali called, but to no effect. The white boy continued to hurl the missiles, accompanying each delivery by simulating the sound of exploding cannon.

'Go on, retreat!' yelled Michael. 'Retreat!'

Gwali hesitated, backed away a few steps and was about to turn when a small sharp stone caught him just above the left eye, drawing blood. He winced. 'You've hurt me, master Michael,' he shouted, holding the cut, but the bombardment continued.

'We've won! We've won!' shouted Michael, letting loose another hail of stones, and imitating the cavalry's bugle call to advance. Standing, with a rock in either hand, he prepared to charge, but was suddenly arrested by the sight of Gwali, climbing purposefully out of the river and, with a menacing look, advancing towards the British position.

'Get back,' yelled Michael, 'or I'll let you have it!' and he prepared to hurl the stone.

Gwali did not heed the warning: he was furious, enraged by the cut to his forehead which was bleeding freely now. Up, up, he went, eyes blazing.

Sensing the danger, Michael dropped the stones and ran, but Gwali was much the more agile, and caught him easily. Michael struggled to no avail, for the older boy was stronger and more determined. Taking hold of Michael from behind in a bear hug, Gwali dragged him down towards the stream and then, with a violent twist, sent him headlong into the river. Michael spluttered for air, wiping the water from his eyes, terrified of a further attack. Gwali stood on the bank, hands on hips, legs apart, like a Colossus. 'I won this time, master Michael!' he called, still angry. 'And that's where you belong, in the sea where you came from!'

'I'm going to tell Miss Henning!' Michael cried.

'Tell who you like, I don't care!'

Then Michael burst into tears, blubbering, 'You know I'm not supposed to get wet!' Gwali did not hear; he was marching back towards the house.

Michael, true to his threat, reported the incident to Sybille but received no satisfaction. 'You've got to punish him,' he said.

'No, first I want to hear what Gwali has to say.'

'You *always* take his side!' Michael shouted and ran off to find his father; there, he could be certain of justice.

Mr Thompson came up trumps, accepting his son's version of events without question: Gwali was punished by being locked in one of the outhouses and starved for two days. Sybille intervened, pleading her favourite's cause, but she was forbidden to see him. In her diary, she wrote:

> *Night.* G. cries like a woman in childbirth. No one can sleep.
> Mr T. on *stoep* smoking pipe. G. quieter now.
> *Dawn.* To stream to wash, but see M. near shed where G. is. Hide and watch. M. talks through window—slides bundle under door —returns to house. I talk to G. Ask what M. has given him. Bread and jam, he says. There is good in all.

It is her last entry written on the farm, for later that morning, the second of Gwali's imprisonment, John Filmore arrived at the house with an urgent summons for Thompson. The two men talked in whispers, Filmore without dismounting from his foam-flecked, snorting horse. When they had done, Thompson ordered his own horse saddled and called for Michael and Sybille.

'I 'ave to go to Grahamstown on important business,' he explained. 'I don't know when I'll be back. You can let Gwali out tomorrow morning.'

As the two men rode off, Michael called, 'Is it the Kaffirs, dada?' but either his father did not hear or chose not to answer.

A gloom hung over the farm all day. Sybille insisted on Michael doing his lessons as usual, but the boy found it impossible to concentrate, his thoughts concerned alternately with Gwali, and the prospect of a new Kaffir invasion which, he had convinced himself was the reason for his father's sudden departure for Grahamstown. Sybille, too, was concerned, but only for Gwali.

'It was nice of you to give him food this morning, Michael,' she said.

The boy flushed guiltily. 'I didn't, I didn't,' he cried.

'But I saw you!'

Cornered, he replied, 'Well, you're not to let him out! Not until tomorrow morning! My dada said so!'

Sybille did not pursue the subject; secretly, she planned to release

213

Gwali during the night, when Michael was asleep. 'Go and play,' she said.

'But what if the Kaffirs have invaded?'

'You send them to me. I'll talk to them,' she answered lightly to reassure him.

But Michael was not reassured. Frontiersmen and their families lived in daily fear of their lives, and it was not unusual, when the strain became too great, to hear of hysterical women and children arriving in Grahamstown, convinced that a massacre was imminent. Michael, his imagination boiling with scenes of carnage, saw black warriors behind every bush and the slightest unexpected noise filled him with terror.

And so it was predictable that when, after lunch, he was at the stream floating paper boats, racing them against the gentle currents, and saw the black man staring at him from the opposite bank, his panic should erupt so convulsively. He had waded barefoot into the water to retrieve one of his home-made craft which had trapped itself between two well-worn stones, when he became aware of eyes watching him. It was then that he looked up and saw the man, whom he had not heard, but who was just there, suddenly. For one awful, alarming moment, Michael stood stock still, his hand frozen in the action of retrieving the boat; then, the intruder was joined by three or four others who appeared from behind bushes and trees, like silent hunters. In that instant, Michael's panic erupted; he turned and ran back towards the house; but more frightening still was the sight of the men pursuing him.

Up through the orchard, Michael ran, bounding breathless on to the verandah, and looking back to see the men crouching in the shadows of the apple trees.

'Miss Henning! Miss Henning!' Michael cried. 'The Kaffirs! The Kaffirs!'

Sybille answered his call quickly, and came striding out to where Michael stood, at the verandah rail, pointing.

'What, Michael? Where?'

'There,' he whispered. 'In the orchard!—Kaffirs! They're going to kill us!'

Sybille narrowed her eyes and raised a hand to shield them from the sun; Michael watched her intently, waiting, hoping for her to formulate a plan of action that would save them all. Instead, she smiled.

'Oranje!' she called, and beckoned.

The black man whom Michael had seen first emerged from the orchard and walked slowly towards them; Michael hugged Sybille round the waist, burying his face in her skirts. 'Stop that,' she said, 'he's my friend.'

The man she called Oranje whistled, and presently was joined by the others. Surrounding Sybille, all smiling happily, they talked in a tongue that was neither Xhosa nor the *taal*. Oranje was their spokesman, and he gesticulated urgently, pointing to the hills; the others nodded, endorsing what he had to say. Sybille's expression turned from one of friendly welcome to one of intense concentration. For some time she listened, and Michael noticed that her neck had flushed an ugly purple, and her hands fidgeted incessantly. When Oranje had finished speaking, Sybille sent Michael to fetch her string bag. While they waited for the boy's return nothing was said: Sybille had that distant look in her eyes, and she breathed deeply as though suppressing an inner excitement. Oranje and his friends stood in a tight little knot, waiting. They were dressed in rags and each carried a cudgel; Oranje was the only one with a knife, tucked into a belt of rope around his waist. Their skins revealed the strains of every human colour, from the ebony of Oranje to the dirty yellow-white of one of the boys. They were Hottentots.

When Michael returned, Sybille paid them and ordered them to leave. She clasped each of their hands in turn and then the ragged band disappeared as suddenly as they had come. Like strange animals, they looked, loping across the fields, hurdling the fences and stone walls, until they were quickly lost to sight.

Sybille was about to re-enter the house when she paused, seeing Michael; she bit her lip, as if she had only just remembered that he was there.

'I have to make a journey,' she said. 'We must go to Fort Wiltshire . . .' her voice trailed off and she pressed a hand tightly to her brow, as if in an effort to think clearly.

'To Fort Wiltshire?' Michael repeated in astonishment. 'That's three, four days away, Miss Henning.'

She made no comment, but, chin thrust forward, marched into the house, through the kitchen and out into the garden towards the shed in which Gwali was imprisoned. She unbolted the door.

'You can't do that, Miss Henning,' Michael cried. 'My dada said—'

'Be quiet!' she commanded and Michael was stilled at once, for he had never seen her so tormented and drawn.

Gwali stumbled into the light but was given no time to recover. In Xhosa, Sybille said, 'We have to go to Fort Wiltshire, to the Kaffir Fair. They brought me news. He'll be there!' And she set off towards her wagon, Michael running after her, with Gwali, a step or two behind, confused and weak.

The ox was harnessed in no time at all and while Sybille was collecting her belongings together and bundling them into the wagon, Gwali hovered near, waiting for an opportunity to speak. 'Miss Henning,' he said as she glanced round to see if she had forgotten anything, 'I'm hungry.'

'Well, eat!' she barked. 'Go into the house and take bread, some cheese, fruit, anything.' Gwali ran off.

'But that's stealing!' Michael cried.

'That's right,' she answered, with a little laugh.

Michael was frightened of her in her present mood, so wild and unnatural, and he dared not question or argue with her further, but stood watching the proceedings, desperately trying to think of a way to stop her.

It was not to be: when Gwali returned with a basket of food, she said, 'We'll take this one'—meaning Michael—'to his dada in Grahamstown. Then you and me'll go on alone.'

The ox-wagon rumbled towards Grahamstown, Sybille guiding the frail animal, with Gwali and Michael sitting behind in the shade of the patched canvas canopy.

'Why does she want to go to Fort Wiltshire?' asked Michael.

'We are to find someone,' Gwali said, stuffing bread into his mouth.

'Who?'

'Someone.'

'Tell me, Gwali,' he ordered, but Sybille heard and intervened. 'Mind your own business, boy!' she called over her shoulder.

They reached the market square at dusk, and Sybille sent Gwali to van Rensberg's tavern and waited impatiently for his return; the boy was an age and when he came running back he drew Sybille aside and delivered his message in a whisper, for her ear alone.

'Your father's busy,' she said curtly to Michael. 'He cannot be disturbed. You'll have to come with us. Gwali's told him where we're going.'

They remounted the wagon and Sybille swung the ox towards the northern exit of the square.

'Wasn't my father angry?' Michael asked Gwali as they watched the town disappearing from view behind the darkening hills.

'No,' replied Gwali, 'he was too busy.'

2

The reason for Richard Thompson's unexpected journey to Grahamstown was politics. Many years before, shortly after his arrival at the Cape, he had been persuaded by John Filmore to join the Grahamstown Friendship Society, founded in 1823 so that 'men of English and Dutch descent may meet together.' Two years later, the Society, which had boasted a large membership, found itself left with a handful of regular members, all of whom were English. One by one, the Boers had ceased to attend, not because of any major disagreement, but because the English seemed unable to learn Dutch, and the Boers resented having to speak English. For a while it had become a social club where the few members drank themselves into a monthly stupor, but even that stopped. The Society was never formally dissolved but fell into neglect. Then, out of the blue, John Filmore, the last Chairman, was approached by a well-known Boer, a leader of his community named Piet Retief, who asked for an Extraordinary General Meeting to be convened which would prove 'of the utmost importance to every man, woman and child in the Colony.' Such an injunction was too urgent to ignore and Filmore dutifully persuaded as many of the old members as he could quickly muster to attend. In the event, he was only moderately successful: ten of his colleagues collected at van Rensberg's tavern to learn what the Boers had in mind.

The room in which they met took up the whole of the top floor of the tavern, one of the oldest buildings in the town. A long, highly polished mahogany table stretched from one end to the other and, arranged on either side of it, were a score of gilt chairs, upholstered in red plush which was worn, stained and shiny. Dotted all over the walls were framed samplers—the work of the landlord's daughter, Miss Petronella van Rensberg—proclaiming, in Dutch, eternal truths and quotations from Scripture. ('*Die Here welcom u*'—'God welcomes you'—in pride of place.)

Thompson and Filmore were the last to arrive; they entered the large room to find the English sitting one side of the table, the Boers on the other, as though ready to negotiate a treaty. They talked among themselves but never to each other; even physically the difference was marked: the Boers intense, bearded men, with the piercing eyes of fanatics; the English frailer, less formidable; and they laughed more; they laughed a great deal.

There were not only superficial differences. The Boers had a uniformity about them, a bleak similarity the one to the other. The English were unashamedly individual and stubbornly aloof, as though determined not to be contaminated by those sitting across the table from them. The Boers were rooted in the land, heart and soul; the English had a flair, almost a genius, for daring and enterprise. The Boers served the Cape; the English served the Crown. (You could make a Boer turn pale by saying, 'She's your Queen, too, you know.')

When the Boers left the Society they had made no secret of the fact that the chief difference was one of language. But, in truth, they were more disturbed by something subtler and insidious: the English had brought a new equivocal atmosphere into the Colony which seemed to strike at the very foundations of Dutch life. They could feel it in the air, for they lived now in a Colony basking in the harsh glare of the Imperial British sun. The age of moral severity had given way to the era of elegant objectivity. The British threatened to conquer not by crushing their foes in battle but by being indifferent to their presence; it was as if looking around the Colony they were surprised to find anyone else about. The Boers did not take kindly to being treated as the servants of English country gentlemen, especially by men, like those seated around the table, who were not English country gentlemen. It did not please them that, in the new vocabulary, the pronoun 'they' no longer meant only men of darker colour; it now referred to all those who were not English.

And what, in all conscience, could these stern Boers have in common with Governors who built hunting lodges instead of churches? What sympathy could their womenfolk have for ladies who discarded shapeless sacking for bows and frills, silks and lace? What possible meeting-point was there between these practical, thrifty men who demanded a government which would face reality, and Lord Charles Somerset, who had bidden farewell to the elegant silk-lined drawing-rooms of Whig and Tory England, passed under the ceilings and through the doorways delicately painted by Angelica

Kauffmann, and arrived at the Cape as though by Divine Right only to introduce horse-racing? What meaning could they perceive in such frivolity? And more difficult still, how were they to worship a friendlier God?

Yet, on this day in van Rensberg's tavern, the Boers had sought to enlist the aid of their English neighbours and it was to this end that their leader, Piet Retief, opened the proceedings by saying, 'My friends, we are gathered not to rake up old differences which are trivial and unimportant. We are here to unite against a common enemy: the Government of this Colony. Yes, my friends, we are here to talk politics!'

Now politics, as the word was understood by the world at large, had a quite different meaning to the Boers in the Cape Colony. If, in other countries, politics was conceived as the science by which a society orders its progress for the greatest good, then the Boers had deliberately and wholeheartedly rejected the definition. It was possible, of course, to apply the theory that in all nations, in all human institutions, the common denominator of politics was simply the pursuit of power, but that would be to take the cynic's view, and to underestimate the intensity of feeling which drives some men towards achieving their ideals, however misconceived they may seem to others. In the Cape, almost from its very inception, politics were founded not on a doctrine, but on a creed, fervently believed, zealously guarded; not on slogans or social theories or principles of government, but on a single article of faith: the inalienable right of the white man to treat the black man as he saw fit, *without interference from outsiders*. This was the fountainhead of the Boers' history; all else was irrelevant.

So it was that Retief, fiftyish, with dark, restless eyes, did his best to infect his audience with some of his own bitterness and resentment. He was no stranger to the English members. Many of them remembered him as a kindly man who had helped to settle them in their flimsy, temporary homesteads in the eastern frontier, carrying supplies, giving advice. Now he stood, in van Rensberg's upper room, speaking in his calm, reasonable voice, stirring in his listeners memories of their early disappointments and hardships. Who, among the English, could not rekindle the dreadful humiliation of their first years in the Colony? Who could not recall Somerset's calumny that the disastrous blight of the wheat crop in three successive years had well served the turn of the settlers by furnishing them with additional means of fomenting discontent? (Radicals he had called them when they petitioned him for assistance.) Who could not, with justification, accuse the government of indifference and neglect? Upon these sentiments Retief now played, but he had misjudged the mood and temperament of his audience. For, when he developed his theme, it became clear that the Boers were not so much angered by the Government's indifference, as by its *concern*. At the heart of his plea was an age-old sentiment: the outrage the Boers felt at being told how to treat their slaves. And the proposed response to authority was also age-old and traditional: if you desired independence, you packed your belongings and moved out of reach. That was what the Boers had always done, and would continue to do: it was called *trekking* and it implied a journey with a purpose.

But the English had short memories. Their enemy was no longer the Government; they had but one enemy—the Kaffir, bellicose, aggressive, barbarous. The Kaffir who swarmed across the border time and time again, destroying, raping, pillaging. True, the Government did not do as much as the settlers would have liked, but then they had a different tradition of dealing with recalcitrant administrations: they published articles in newspapers, drew up petitions, memorials, used the law to defeat the lawyers. The Englishmen fought for their rights according to the rules. Anarchy, rebellion, trekking, all were foreign to them.

Retief, sensing the restlessness among the English, catalogued what he believed to be their shared grievances: the encouragement of Hottentots to complain about their treatment, the repeal by the hated Fiftieth Ordinance of the Pass System which enabled scoundrels to move freely about the Colony and, most terrible prospect of all, the movement to abolish slavery. And then he came to his peroration: 'It is proposed,' he said, lowering his voice, 'that three parties of exploration be organised, to the north-west, north and east. I welcome volunteers. We must move, trek, away from the hateful hand of this meddling administration, and we must move *now*. I beg you, my brothers, to join us. There is no other course of action open to us, and I must stress the need for absolute secrecy in our affairs. Confide only to God.'

John Filmore closed the proceedings, promising that Retief's words would be carefully considered. The members of the Friendship Society then adjourned to the downstairs bar to indulge in more pleasurable business. Retief and his friends politely declined to join them; they had another meeting to attend that day.

Left to themselves the English discussed the Retief proposals. The reaction was typical: sympathy with the cause, disapproval of the means, but this attitude was merely symptomatic of a disease that attacked the British and no one else; painless, comfortable, soporific in the early stages, but with a dangerous proclivity to rot, like a cancer, the whole body: it is called the disease of secret condonation. To be fair it did not attack all the British; it was powerless against those few with a sincere belief in justice or Christian morality, that peculiar breed of high-minded Englishman, devoid of cynicism, whose greatest virtue is his obstinacy. But it fed on the great majority, men like Thompson and Filmore and Fielding who, coming as they did from the humblest strata of their own society, saw in their adopted home, for the first time in their lives, a genus of mankind below them: black, heathen and savage. Justice and Christian morality were precariously balanced against the demands of personal advancement, and against an endemic awareness of class. Secret condonation acted like a pernicious balm.

'Yeah, but them Boers 'ave 'ad their bellyful, 'an' no mistake,' said Thompson.

'Aye, but the law's the law,' argued Filmore.

'But we're English, John,' declared Tommy Fielding. 'Them Boers is 'alf way to bein' savages themselves.'

'True,' Filmore agreed smugly.

'I've seen the way they whip them 'Ottys. Work 'em to death, they do.'

'The Boers 'ave their own way of dealin' with things. Best not to get involved.'

'Yeah, best not to interfere.'

And so the discussion spun in ever-decreasing circles with the men concluding that what was right for the Boers was not necessarily right for the English. ('Best to do nothing,' advised Filmore.) And, later, when drink had clouded their modesty, Thompson was able to assert with a good conscience that the English were the most superior people on earth, a sentiment the others had no hesitation endorsing heartily. (These are the early symptoms.)

'Fuck the Cape!' cried Thompson.

' 'Ear, 'ear!' cried Fielding.

'Fuck the fuckin' Cape!'

'Give us a poem, Richard!' cried Filmore, banging the table with his tankard.

'Yes, give us a poem!' came the chorus, and Thompson stood, his eyes glazed with drink and sentiment. In a passionate voice, like an actor in a melodrama, he launched forth:

> 'I love thee, O my native Isle,
> Dear as my mother's earliest smile,
> Sweet as my father's voice to me,
> Is all I hear and all I see.
> I love thee, when I see thee stand,
> The Hope of every other land;
> A sea mark in the tide of time,
> Raising to heaven thy brow sublime.
> I love thee, next to heaven above,
> Land of my fathers! *Thee* I love,
> And rail thy slanderers as they will,
> With all thy faults I love thee still.'

The others cheered and Thompson cried. Then they all joined Tommy Fielding in two choruses of *Hearts of Oak*. By evening, only Thompson and Filmore were left; the others had either passed out or found their way home. The two survivors were very drunk, both in confessional mood.

'You know what I fancy now, don't you, Richard?' said Filmore, cupping a hand to his mouth to preserve intimacy.

'I do, I do, John,' Thompson said fervently. 'But I beg you for Gawd's sake, don't go on about it!'

'I hear old Ma Matenje has got two little sweet ones in from Bathurst—'

'Don't go on, for Gawd's sake,' pleaded Thompson.

'Virgins, Richard, but won't be for long if we don't get over there now.'

Thompson suddenly looked at his companion with an expression of outrage. 'I don't like virgins!' he said, raising his voice.

'Ssh!'

'What made you think I liked virgins?'

'I never said you did! *I* like them!' confessed Filmore.

'I don't like virgins,' continued Thompson. ' 'Orrid, messy things, they are. No, not virgins, not me.'

Without warning, Filmore covered his eyes and began to cry. 'O God,' he said. 'O God.'

'What's up, John, old son? Don't cry, for pity's sake, you know 'ow easy it is to set me off.'

'I've got to tell somebody!' Filmore said.

'Tell 'em what?' asked Thompson, finding it difficult to raise his tankard to his lips.

'I've got two bastards!' cried Filmore passionately.

'Two what?' asked Thompson.

'Two bastards!'

'Who are?'

'I have.'

'Me 'n you, d'you mean?'

'No! I've sired two bastards, that's what I mean!'

'Who 'as?'

'I have!'

'Gawd.'

'Sold them off to the Portuguese.'

'You did?'

'Ma Matenje did.'

'Gawd.'

A long silence followed. Then Thompson said, 'I was fuckin' an 'Otty the night Michael was born.'

'No!'

'S'help me! The night Mary died I was up an 'Otty!'

'Blimey!'

'True. Well, I didn't know Mary was goin' t'die!'

'Ssh!'

'Well, did I?'

'No, course you didn't.'

'Course I didn't.'

'Impossible.'

'That's why I'm bein' punished, y'see John. That's why the Lord above 'as got it in for me.'

'I see.'

'That's why Michael's an invalid.'

'Who told you that?'

'The Boers' predikant, dominee Burger!'

'How the hell would he know?'

' 'E was there!'

'Where?'

'At Ma Matenje's.'

'Who, the dominee was?'

' 'E'd 'ad the 'Otty before me!'

'Blimey!'

'So I'll never know whose bastard it is: 'is or mine!'

And they began to laugh, until too weak to utter a sound. After a while they rose.

'Where we goin'?' asked Thompson.

'Ma Matenje's,' said Filmore.

'But I took an oath!'

'What for?'

'To please the dominee.'

'What did you swear?'

'That I kept off 'Ottys until Michael was either dead or better!'

'Well, he's better, isn't he?'

'True.'

'So what you worried about then?'

'I'm not worried, who the 'ell said I was worried?'

'Come on, then!'

They staggered out of the tavern, found the turning off Market Square, weaved their way through a network of alleyways until they came, at last, to Ma Matenje's house. Later, when it was dark, Thompson had the impression that Gwali was standing over him, but thought it must be a dream.

3

Meanwhile, Michael was experiencing the most exciting adventure of his young life. They travelled east, and the darkness of the night was frightening and absolute. Hills and rocky gorges loomed like ghosts out of nothingness, and, at every turn, he heard the threatening cries of the hyenas, and the high-pitched gibbering of monkeys. They made camp by a stream, lit a fire to keep the wild animals off, and Michael slept, for the first time, on the veldt, his face exposed to the stabbing cold. And strangely, he discovered, he felt no fear and cared little about the discomfort: all he could sense was an overwhelming pleasure at being there, looking up at the distant stars, resplendent in the summer night, and, as was his custom in recent months, he prayed before sleep: 'Dear God, thank you for making me well.'

Mid-morning the next day, they crossed the Great Fish River, the border of the Cape Colony, and Michael learned how useful the ox was in this terrain: whether forging the broad river at its shallowest point, or pulling the wagon upwards over the *kopjes* and rocky slopes, the animal persisted with the same dogged determination, and Sybille drove him hard.

Soon, Michael became aware of the changing colours of the land. Here, the countryside was bleak and forbidding, with great cracks scarring the dry, dusty earth. He had been used to green hills, and cultivated fields, an orderly, gentle background, but now his eye beheld a more savage, desolate landscape dipped in bleached ochre, and grey.

Perhaps most intimidating of all was the sight of Xhosa tribesmen, wild and fierce, huddled in their distinctive red blankets, herding their cattle, stolen cattle, leading the animals to find new grazing ground. None of them interfered with the travellers, or impeded their progress. Indeed, many seemed to know Sybille and they exchanged greetings with her.

The second night was again spent on the veld. Sybille said, 'We should reach Fort Wiltshire by noon tomorrow.'

While Gwali was collecting firewood, Michael asked, 'Tell me why we are going there.'

'To meet someone,' was all she would say, and, as Michael settled down to sleep, he saw her close to the fire, scribbling furiously.

'Tell us a story before sleep,' he said.

'In a moment.'

Sybille was writing in her diary; it was one of the few entries of the period:

O God, let me find him. Let this wandering be done. Let me nurse him, and bless him, and hold him as my own. Let him be at Fort Wiltshire. He was never at the Fair in Grahamstown, yet Fathma said he would be there, Adam, she said, would be there!

'Please tell us a story, Miss Henning,' Michael said, and Gwali, to encourage her, smiled.

She paused, reading what she had written, then put away the book in her bag.

'Settle down, and I will tell you,' she said in Xhosa.

'Slowly please,' said Michael, 'so I can understand.'

'Once, a young girl, one of the Nguni, was asked by her parents to guard her brother who was only a babe in arms. She loved the baby, and held him tightly, taking him down to the river to bathe him. Now the river was deep and there was no way across. While she sat

225

there on the bank, she heard a voice, far-away and mysterious, telling her to throw the baby into the water and, if she did so, the waters would part, she could walk across the dry bed, and on the other side, she would be re-united with her brother, and they would bring home untold wealth for their parents.

'So the girl threw the baby into the river, and, indeed, the waters parted to let her across. But when she reached the other side, she could not find her little brother. Oh, she was frightened, but she ran quickly home and told her parents what had happened. Then, her father said she must go away and never come back until she had found the baby again. She set off through the forest.

'All at once, she met a lion who was bleeding from a hunter's spear. "Let me pass, lion," she said. "First you must bind my wounds." This she did, and the lion let her pass. Next, she met a leopard with a thorn in its eye. "Let me pass, leopard," she said. "First you must take the thorn from my eye," which she did, and he let her pass. Last she met a hunter, Sawoye was his name, and his whole body was disfigured by a terrible disease of the skin. "Let me pass, Sawoye," said the girl. "First, you must cure my disease." "But how shall I do that?" asked the girl. "You must kiss me," said Sawoye, "and lie in my arms." And so, remembering her baby brother whom she had to find, she kissed Sawoye and lay in his arms, and his skin was perfect once more. "Now," said Sawoye, "I will reward you for your goodness to me. I will take you to a place where the road divides and you will hear a voice on the one side saying *mbo* and on the other side *ndi*. You must take the first."

'All this soon came to pass and she followed the road where the voice had said *mbo*. And she came to a hut where an old woman lived. "Is my brother here?" asked the girl. "He is here," said the woman. And she led the girl inside and showed her not one baby, but many, all extremely beautiful. She recognised, or thought she recognised, her brother and chose him. "Now speed home," said the old woman.

'Holding the baby tightly once more, she ran back the way she had come, but when she reached the forked roads, she looked down at the child and saw that he was wretched, diseased, crippled. Frightened, she turned to go back but who should be standing there but Sawoye—'

Her voice trailed off. She looked down at the boys: both were asleep, and she did not finish the story.

17

Lost boys

I

Fort Wiltshire nestled at the foot of a humble *kopje*, on the banks of the Keiskama River. With the Great Fish to the south, and the Keiskama to the north, the vast tract of land was the neutral territory, forbidden to Xhosa and colonists alike, a result of a treaty between Gaika, the Xhosa chief, and Lord Charles Somerset, after the defeat of the former's warriors in 1819. In order to police the territory, and to see that its neutrality was observed, a small military post was maintained, and here, on Mondays, Wednesdays and Fridays, a Kaffir Fair was held.

It was an orderly gathering, supervised by the military—white officers, Hottentot troops—and specially appointed officials. Here the Xhosa came with their ivory and ostrich feathers, their hides and gum, and here the colonists, with their beads and trinkets, spades and hoes. Any bargain struck had to be approved by an official, and any dispute settled by the military in the person of Captain Arthur Jones, of the Cape Corps of Hottentots, a soldier bred, but not born.

Captain Jones was a Cardiff man; in 1820 he arrived at the Albany settlement; by 1821, he was destitute. While his fellow settlers struggled on, Arthur Jones joined the militia and, in a short space of time, was promoted to Captain, and given the least sought-after command in the Cape Colony: Officer Commanding, Fort Wiltshire.

Captain Jones took his profession seriously: he walked in a soldierly fashion, he talked in a soldierly fashion and, in all but one respect, he conducted himself in a soldierly fashion. Each hair on his head seemed to be on parade, and his eyes shone like polished buttons. There was something of the caricature about him, as if he had too often studied military portraits, or too often read descriptions of the Duke of Wellington, for everything about him seemed so strained: the way he heaved his shoulders back so that his chest bulged like a fighting cock's, or the effort he made to disguise his Welsh accent, did not come easily to him. And what made matters worse was that Captain Jones was only five foot three.

The one blot on his military character was Lokai, a Hottentot girl whom he liked to describe as Javanese; before that, it had been Yasmina ('Polynesian, I assure you'), and before that, Roxane ('Touch of the Persian, I fancy'). It was the only flaw in his military bearing, for it encouraged his subordinates to seek similar companionship, and prompted Sir Lowry Cole, the present Governor of the Cape, to describe Fort Wiltshire as 'that randy little Welshman's knocking-shop.'

To all outward appearances, then, the Kaffir Fair was a model of organised trade. But, behind the neat rows of wagons, other bargains were struck, and on the barrack-room beds no official was required to witness or approve the transaction.

At four o'clock on that Friday in March, Captain Jones emerged from his quarters, having ordered Lokai to leave by another door—he liked to preserve the fiction that no one knew of his liaisons—and surveyed his domain. Facing him, was the open space of the parade ground, empty now but for the guards at the outer corners; beyond, on sloping ground, the settlers' wagons were drawn up and trade, which had been brisk that day, was beginning to slacken. To his right, along the paths that led towards the river, the Xhosa were wending their way homeward, many of them carrying their purchases in bundles on their heads. Captain Jones was well satisfied: the day had gone off peacefully. (Later, when he was obliged to make a full report of events, he omitted any incriminating details.)

Shoulder-blades meeting, a swagger-stick under his arm, Captain Jones marched across the parade ground which was the signal for Sergeant Veraker, a Dutchman and an old Company soldier, to appear from the duty-room and salute.

'Commerce will cease at five o'clock sharp, sergeant.'

'Sir.'

'And I want the barracks empty and the beds made by six.'

'Sir.'

'See to it, sergeant.'

'Sir.'

He was about to dismiss Veraker, when something on the southern hills caught his eye, a puff of dust, a flash of white.

'Now what?' he said through his teeth.

'Beg pardon, sir?'

'Over there.' Jones indicated with his chin.

'Looks like a wagon, sir,' said the sergeant.

'I'm not having any late trade here,' replied Jones. 'Turn them back.'

'Sir.' But Veraker did not obey the order at once; he took a closer look at the approaching wagon.

'What are you waiting for?' Jones demanded.

'No need to turn it back, sir,' said Veraker. 'Belongs to the wagon-woman, sir.'

'What the hell is she doing up here?'

'The usual, sir,' said Veraker, knowingly.

Just then, as the wagon began to negotiate the last few hundred yards to the Fair site, a horde of children surrounded it, and shouting and laughing, escorted the ox the rest of the way. Jones bristled with indignation and alarm.

'Sergeant!'

'Sir!'

'Get those urchins out of sight!'

'Sir!'

The reason for the Captain's annoyance, was that these children were known locally as 'Officer Bastards' (four of them were fathered by Jones himself), and he disliked them showing themselves on Fair days. They were made to play in the woods to the west of the outpost, but as the day wore on, it was their custom to wander back to see if there were any pickings from generous or careless traders.

While Sergeant Veraker set about obeying the Captain's latest order, Jones busied himself with other matters: he discussed the day's official business with one of the appointed clerks, Mr Martin, and learned that a record number of transactions had been recorded; and the same was true of the unofficial business, as he learned from his adjutant, Lieutenant Codley, whose special responsibility it was to exact payment for use of the barrack-room beds from those traders who wished to avail themselves of the service; Jones took sixty per cent: his savings were growing fast.

Near the wagons, a Coloured girl was dancing, surrounded by a group of onlookers clapping in time to the music which was played on a violin by one of the traders. Jones was about to join them, when he heard someone screaming. Everyone heard it: the violin ceased abruptly; the dancer paused, hands on hips, pouting; two or three men ran across the open fields, and the urchins, the Officer Bastards, appeared once more from nowhere and, like a flock of carrion birds, descended on the scene of the commotion. Captain Jones braced himself, his jaw set firm, and marched smartly to join them.

He was greeted by an astonishing sight. In the back of one of the wagons Sybille Henning and a handsome Malay girl he knew as Fathma were locked in combat, holding each other by the hair and pulling with all their might; Fathma was screaming more or less continuously. To add to the confusion, a Xhosa boy was trying to drag them free, and the owner of the wagon, a Dutchman called Marais who was rather aged, was screaming 'That's my wagon! They're destroying my wagon!'

Just then, the two combatants rolled off the tailboard on to the ground, scratching and tearing each other. The ragged linen blouse Fathma had been wearing was now ripped from her and, for a moment, Captain Jones was fascinated by the sight of the Malay's amber breasts, at one moment squashed flat, the next bouncing free; the sight roused him.

Michael was also witness to the scene, but obtained no pleasure from the spectacle. Seeing Captain Jones, he pushed his way through the large crowd that had now gathered, and pulled at the officer's tunic. 'Stop them, sir, please, stop them!' Jones brushed him aside, just as three Hottentot soldiers arrived and quickly pried the women apart. Fathma wailed and screamed as though at a graveside, and Sybille struggled to free herself of the soldiers, crying, 'She knows where he is, the whore! She knows where he is! Whore! Slut! Where have you hidden him? Where is he?'

'Guard-house!' yelled Sergeant Veraker who appeared at the Captain's elbow. In a cloud of dust and obscenities, the prisoners were frog-marched towards the barracks, Captain Jones bringing up the rear; it was all over in a matter of seconds.

Michael and Gwali ran after them. 'We're with Miss Henning,' Michael said, near to tears. 'Both of us! She brought us here, oh, what's going to happen?'

But Captain Jones did not answer them directly; instead, he ordered a corporal to take the two boys into custody for the time being.

Once in his office, his rage exploded. He summoned Sergeant Veraker, who had been waiting outside the door, and gave vent to his anger. 'Did I not order you, Sergeant, to turn that bloody woman away?'

'Sir.'

'Well, then, why the hell don't you obey my bloody orders, you bloody Hottentot!'

'Sir—'

'Don't argue with me, you incompetent twot! I run the best Kaffir Fair in the colony and you go and allow something like this to happen!' His voice had lapsed into its native Welsh; he was almost singing. The reprimand continued like a tenor aria. 'I tell you what you're going to do now, boy, you're going to put that Henning woman with those two little bastard boys and send them back where they've come from. Then, you'll bring that bloody Malay girl to me, 'cos I want to have words with her, you get me?' But events overtook him: he was interrupted by a sharp knock on the door. 'What?' he bellowed.

A nervous orderly entered, holding a document. 'Excuse me, sir. A despatch from Grahamstown. Urgent.'

Captain Jones broke the seal with his fist, muttering to himself. But when he read the contents of the document, all his fury vanished. 'Bloody hell,' he said quietly. 'I've got the two of them in custody already.'

2

The despatch was signed by the Chief Magistrate of Grahamstown:

To whom it may concern:

Last Wednesday, in the district of Albany, mejuvrou Sybille Henning, presently of Safehaven in the said district, did, in the company of a Kaffir youth, Gwali, abduct from his home, the aforementioned Safehaven, an English youth, one Michael Thompson, against his will. Officers commanding the militia into whose district the aforementioned mejuvrou Henning proceeds, will apprehend her and take her in custody. Such action being taken, the said Officer will return the prisoner, under escort, together with the Kaffir, Gwali, and the boy, Michael Thompson, to Grahamstown and into the jurisdiction of this Court.

Accordingly, Captain Jones summoned Sybille into his presence and read her the contents of the communiqué. Though still smarting from the fight, and a little afraid of the Welshman, Sybille laughed scornfully. 'Abducted?' she repeated. 'Rubbish!'

'This document, madam, is issued by the Chief Magistrate of Grahamstown.'

'It's still rubbish.' She tried to explain the circumstances that led up to Michael accompanying her on the journey, how they had sought out his father but found him otherwise engaged.

'If you did not abduct him,' said Jones, 'what caused you to make the journey in the first place?'

'Information,' she replied.

'What information?'

'About a man I'm looking for.'

'What man?'

'Adam, he's called, Adam Henning, same name as me.'

'A relative?'

Sybille parried his question with one of her own. 'Do you know him? He has a scar above the right eye.'

'Is he a trader?'

'No!'

'Why were you fighting with that Malay?'

'She's been living with Adam, that's why.'

'So why fight with her?'

'Because she's keeping him from me.'

'Is he your husband, then?'

'No!'

'Who is he?'

'That's my business.'

'Why should this woman keep him from you?'

'Ask her.'

'I will.'

'Whore, that's what she is, lying whore!'

'Now cut that out!' ordered the Captain. 'This Adam fellow, is he a Hottentot?'

'If you like.'

'Well, is he or isn't he?'

'His mother was Khoikhoi!'

'What the hell's Khoikhoi? You mean this chappie's a Hottentot, that's all there is to it, what?'

232

Sybille did not answer, but growled impatiently. Then, she said, 'Let me have ten minutes with that woman, please, captain, I must find out!'

' 'Fraid not. I want no more trouble from you. You can tell your story to the Magistrate.'

Sybille stepped towards him, 'I beg of you, captain, please. Long years I've been looking for Adam. I was waiting for him in Grahamstown a whole year now. But he never came. Each week I went to the Kaffir Fair, looking for him, but no sign, not of him, not of his woman. They go to the Kaffir Fairs, you see, because that's where she does her trade, you understand me, captain? She's a whore!'

'And this Adam chap lives off her, then?'

'I don't know, I've got to find out, I've got to find him.'

'But why? What do you want with a Hottentot whore and her pimp?'

'Not saying,' replied Sybille.

'Guard!' called Jones. Veraker entered with two soldiers, received his orders and, taking Sybille by the arms, led her towards the door.

'Let me talk to that woman!' she cried, struggling once more. 'I've got to talk to her.'

Jones heard her screams continue as they bound her hand and foot. He then sent for Michael. The boy was so overwhelmed by events, so awed by Jones' uniform and authority, that he could barely articulate, but in fits and starts, his story tumbled out. True, he was confused and bewildered, but that did not prevent him from introducing a malicious note into his testimony. 'It was both of them, sir,' he said. 'Miss Henning and the Kaffir. They took me, forced me to go with them,' and he recounted the facts of Gwali's imprisonment, and of how Miss Henning had freed him. (It fed Michael's self-importance to be the centre of attraction.)

'What are you saying, boy?' asked Jones, narrowing his eyes. 'These two kidnapped you, because they didn't want a witness?'

'I expect so, sir.'

'But they'd done nothing wrong, had they?'

'I couldn't say, sir,' Michael said, as if he was keeping something back.

Jones dismissed him. The Captain sat at his desk puzzled and concerned, and soon convinced himself there was more to the case than met the eye. Once more he studied the warrant, and was struck by

233

its ambiguity. Did it mean that the Officer Commanding who apprehended the woman was to escort her back to Grahamstown personally? 'The said Officer will return the prisoner, under escort ...' Captain Jones, being a letter-of-the-law man, did not like to take chances. He decided to command the escort himself. And any excuse for a trip to Grahamstown was always welcome.

Two wagons were made ready. One contained Sybille and Gwali; the other Michael and the woman, Fathma. Captain Jones mounted up and ordered the escort forward, the wagons lumbered across the parade ground towards the southern hills.

Michael sat beside the driver of his wagon, a Hottentot corporal whose nose had been eaten away by disease. In the back, bound hand and foot, lay Fathma. No one had bothered to dress her, and she was still naked from the waist up. Michael, who had never seen a woman's breasts before, kept peeking back at her, and, if she caught his eye, he turned away hurriedly, blushing. The corporal beside him grinned. Once, Fathma licked her lips in a way the boy found deeply disturbing.

As night was falling, Captain Jones rode up alongside Michael.

'All well, young man?'

'Yes, thank you, sir.'

'That's the way. Soon have you home safe and sound.' Then he muttered something in the *taal* to the corporal, who nodded, pulling tight the reins and bringing the wagon to a halt. Michael thought that they would now make camp for the night, but, presently, Captain Jones hitched his horse to the tailboard, and climbed into the wagon; the journey continued.

'Just going to question the prisoner, Fathma,' he explained, and drew the canvas curtain that divided the driver's seat from the occupants in the rear. Michael heard their voices and, through a narrow gap, could see Fathma's legs, bound together, and he saw Captain Jones' hands undoing the bond.

'You've been a naughty girl, Fathma, what?' Jones said.

'Me? I done nothing. It's that blarry woman! She med, captin, med!' And when her legs were free, she thanked him.

'Where's this chap Adam, then?'

'I don' know no Adam, Captin!'

'She says you do.'

Fathma mumbled something.

'What? Speak up!'

'It's like this, my captin: I jused to know that woman, years ago, in the mission stations down south. She was med, then, captin. She jused to ask quesh'ns about this Adam. My captin, she jused to pay good money for news! Captin, we made up all sorts of stories. We jused to send her jere and there, all over the place. Then, my captin, one day in Bethelsdorp I needed some coin, so I just told her that this Adam was friendly with me, j'unnerstan', and that we'd be workin' the Grahamstown Fair. *Just made it up, j'unnerstan'?* My captin, she's been followin' me all jover the place! True! Ev'ry demn Hottentot from jere to Cape Town tells her stories, Captin. She gives good coin. She's med, captin, med, she believes every demn one of them!' She changed her position, and, again, her breasts were visible.

'And you've never seen or heard of this man?'

'No! I made it all up!'

'I trust she didn't hurt you in the fight,' Jones said gallantly and Michael, terrified and fascinated, could just see his fingers examining her ample breasts as though for bruises.

'Agh, captin,' Fathma cried raucously, 'if I'm sore, will jou kiss me better?'

He squeezed her nipple hard. 'Sore?' he asked.

'Real sore,' she answered, wincing.

'Then I'd better kiss it better!' he said playfully.

'Ah ... captin ... jou's got the lips of a baby.'

'Ah ...' he sighed between kisses, 'my little Balinese.' Michael stared straight ahead, not daring to look any more; the noseless Corporal flicked his reins and urged the ox onward.

3

Over the camp fire, on the second night, Michael asked, 'Who is that woman, Miss Henning?' meaning Fathma.

But Sybille was in no state to answer: she cried silently, and he could see tears streaking her cheeks.

Two further incidents on the journey remained in Michael's memory. The first was when one of the Hottentot guards noticed the gold cross round Gwali's neck and tried to snap the chain. Sybille spoke then. 'Touch that chain and you will be dead!' she warned in Khoikhoi. The soldier hesitated. 'That is the cross of *Tui'qua* and he will strike you dead!' The soldier slapped her face, but did not take the cross.

And later, she said, 'Now, I have to start all over again. They say they have settled the Hottentots near the Kat River to the north, a whole district just for them. I must go there. Will I ever be allowed to rest?'

4

Mr Thompson, it appeared, had lost his head. When he discovered that Michael was not at home, he had returned to the town and made desperate enquiries. Several people had seen the boy in the back of Miss Henning's wagon. Panic-stricken, he could think of no satisfactory reason why Sybille should go off with Michael and, in no time at all, came to the fearful conclusion that for reasons best known to herself the irrational creature had abducted his beloved son. The Magistrate was half asleep when the report was made, and he issued the warrant without asking questions. Now, while Thompson waited for news of his lost boy, he suffered terrible anxiety on two accounts.

The first was, of course, for Michael's safety and well-being; that was a genuine concern which brought real pain to the pit of his stomach. But the second cause was not quite so selfless: he could not rid his mind of the vague image of Gwali trying to give him a message in Ma Matenje's. At first he had thought it a dream conjured up by alcohol; but misgivings soon set in. What if it *did* happen, and Gwali *had* tried to tell him something, something that explained the sudden journey? A brief visit to the establishment confirmed his worst suspicions: yes, Ma Matenje remembered the boy; yes, he had tried to wake Thompson with a message.

The days of waiting were spent in agony. The Magistrate's clerk, a Mr Jervis, having taken statements from Thompson and other witnesses who claimed to have seen Michael in Sybille's wagon, said, 'A nice little case, most unusual. Now, we'll have to wait for the return of the boys, and see what they have to say.' This innocent remark had set the fires of apprehension raging. Thompson knew quite well what Gwali would have to say. There would be a scandal; Thompson would be disgraced. He would have to resign from his Friendship Society, he'd be ostracised by his neighbours, oh, the consequences of such revelations would be unbearable. He confided to Filmore, and by the time the party returned under escort from Fort Wiltshire they had come to a decision. Once he had embraced Michael with relief, and seen him safely to bed, he returned with Filmore to

236

Grahamstown and they made their way to Mr Jervis's office. They were only just in time, for in the small, ill-lit waiting room sat Sybille and because of Michael's statement, Gwali too, guarded by soldiers. As they entered, Sybille half rose, showing him her manacled hands. 'Tell them it's all a mistake, Mr Thompson, and even if you've got it in for me, though God knows why you should, Gwali had nothing to do with it! Please, tell them!'

Mr Thompson could hardly bring himself to look at either prisoner; he said nothing, but knocked and walked quickly into Jervis' office, followed by Filmore.

'Ah, Mr Thompson, Mr Filmore, how very opportune! I am about to question the prisoners. I have no objection to your being present, none at all,' Mr Jervis said.

'Well, no, that is,' stammered Thompson, 'it's not that at all, Mr Jervis: I want to drop the charges.'

'Drop the charges?' Mr Jervis fished for his snuff box, and took a liberal pinch.

'That's right, it's all been explained t'me, y'see, quite innocent really, nothin' criminal implied, 'pon my word, there ain't.'

'Drop the charges,' Jervis repeated, wiping his nose with a handkerchief.

'I was wrong, y'see, Mr Jervis, quite wrong. There was no abduction intended, all 'armless and above board. It's not too late, is it, to drop charges.'

'Never too late, except after a hanging,' the clerk answered cheerfully. 'Well! How extraordinary! There's nothing more to be done!' and he wrote out a document which ordered the prisoners' release.

Outside in the street, Sybille thanked Thompson. 'I knew they'd understand,' she said. 'I hope Michael has not been too upset. The soldiers behaved so rudely.'

'Michael's fine,' Filmore answered; Thompson was unable to find his voice.

'Where is he? At home?'

'No. At my house,' replied Filmore.

'Oh, shall we go there first to get him, before going home?'

They came to her wagon. Thompson reached into his wallet, removed some notes and thrust them into her hands all in one quick, nervous movement. 'I don't want you 'ome,' he mumbled. 'You and Gwali, I don't want you about, is that understood? Both of you, I want you out of 'ere, out of Grahamstown, please. I've done you a favour, now you do me one: just go.'

And without giving her time to answer, the two men crossed the street to van Rensberg's tavern and disappeared inside. But the moment indoors, they put their faces to the window and watched to see what would happen.

It was noon, and the day pale and chill. Sybille and Gwali stood for some time looking in the direction of the tavern and, momentarily, Thompson and Filmore feared she might come to find them, but she did not. She heaved Gwali up into the back of the wagon, then slowly shuffled round to the front and mounted to the driver's bench. The wagon moved off and disappeared amidst the bustle of Market Square.

It took Thompson several tankards of ale to wash the unpleasant taste from his mouth.

Continuum:
The family historian

Continuum:
The family historian

It is winter in prison, June, the month of tepid rain and blustery wind. There is no one to tell him jokes any more: the kind policeman has been posted elsewhere and did not bother to say goodbye; for many days now, the prisoner has seen nothing but his own reflection, in mirrors and window panes, as he tries to draw comfort from the mountains which seem so distant in the dull mist of yet another day.

The intrusion occurred when he was about to begin work on Michael Thompson's adolescence and manhood, when trying to decipher the pencil-faint hand in which the document judged 'dishonest and English' was written. Suddenly, without warning, the prisoner hears the front door open and the wooden hall floor bombarded by boots. Four policemen enter, all boyish, as though in the midst of a painful adolescence, their faces proliferating with pimples and inexperience. A heavy, thick-set sergeant pushes his way through and stands before the prisoner.

'All right,' says the sergeant, addressing his youthful squad. 'I'll keep an eye on him, you search the house from top to bottom. You know what you're looking for.'

'Yes, sergeant,' the quartet answers and, as one, turn and march back into the hall to obey orders. The prisoner can hear them clumping about overhead, opening drawers, cupboards, wardrobes.

The prisoner asks, 'What are you looking for?' but the sergeant, after a moment's hesitation, does not reply. He stands, like a caricature, at ease, hands behind back, rocking on his heels.

The prisoner pretends to work, but listens to the clumsy, careless boys on the floor above. He is frightened, although he knows he has

nothing to hide but his manuscript, and they are obviously not looking for that; but for what?

After a half hour or so, the youths return and lay their finds before the sergeant: four candlesticks, a statuette—in bronze, of
Justice with her scales—carving knives, a meat cleaver, an assortment of fire irons.

'What about glassware?' asks the sergeant.

'The cupboards are full of it, sergeant,' answers one of the policemen, his voice not yet broken. 'We'll need a removal van for all that
stuff.'

The sergeant considers for a moment, stroking his many chins.
'Okay,' he says at last. 'De Wat, you stay with him for the rest of
the day. I'll get someone to relieve you this evening.'

'I'm to have a guard with me night and day?' the prisoner asks.

'That's right,' says the sergeant cheerfully. 'All right, boys, out
with this stuff.'

'But what is this all about?' the prisoner says, confused and unsettled.

The sergeant waits for the haul to be removed, then, looking
about, as if to make sure he is not being overheard, says, 'We're
taking away all likely weapons,' and points an accusing finger at the
prisoner.

'But why? Are you afraid I'm going to commit suicide?'

'Boy,' says the sergeant, 'you wouldn't do us the favour. No,
it's on the Minister's orders.'

'My uncle?'

'We've had word he's coming to visit you. We can't risk an attack on him.'

'By me?'

'Well, there's no one else in this house.'

'When's he coming?'

'You'll be informed.'

At that moment, the one called de Wat returns. 'Okay,' says the
sergeant. 'Now, de Wat, no talking to this one, hey? You just watch
him. You don't take your eyes off him, you understand?' and he
marches out, solid-footed, across the hall.

De Wat takes his orders seriously: he stares at the prisoner as
though playing a children's game to see who will look away first.
The presence of the boy, the knowledge of his uncle's impending
visit, injects an urgency into the prisoner. Several times, since his

incarceration, he has felt time to be precious and now he works, frantic, close to that despair which he knows to be the enemy of reason.

'Dishonest and English'; he comes to these words:

'I wrote to Miss Henning, thanking her. For the second time I had to thank her. Did I say she brought me back to health when I was a child? I do not know if she ever received my letter. I had to thank her for my health, that was the first time, and then for this introduction to Brownlee, that was the second. It was in my mind to ask her the last time I saw her, to ask her if ever she received my letter, on her deathbed that was in her wagon. Did I mention I was with her when she died? She was over eighty, just before the dreadful business with the Xhosa, in fact she warned me of it. I did my duty. I have always done my duty.'

Mpobe, guarded, reaches down the mole run.

BOOK FIVE

18

The god

He grew to manhood with the secret belief that he was to be singled out, and called to some great task which would confirm an important place for him in the Colony. He countered the disappointment and the setbacks of his youth by keeping faith with that powerful and undeniable sense of his own destiny which revealed itself in his appearance and manner: the gaunt, sunken cheeks, the veiled, inward expression of the eyes, and, about the lips, a smirk, all-knowing, self-confident, as though he could not bring himself to dispute with lesser mortals; the years had not made him any more likeable.

After Sybille Henning's departure, he was considered well enough to attend school in Bathurst. His lessons he treated with disdain, giving the impression there was nothing he could be taught, but the chief attribute which seemed to set him apart was his knowledge of the Xhosa language and this, in turn, caused him to be teased unmercifully. His only friend at this period was a handsome flamboyant boy called Logan Stanley who displayed an early, and some said unhealthy, interest in anatomy, and later became a doctor. Logan it was who first kissed Alice Filmore, the prettiest of the girls, and boasted about it so much that John Filmore, Alice's father, got to hear about the incident and insisted that the Principal cane Logan before the entire school. Privately, Michael rejoiced at Logan's humiliation, for he, too, nursed a secret love for Alice, though he never dared declare it openly.

His schooldays passed as though an unnecessary weight had been hung around his neck to delay him, and the solitariness of his early childhood continued, like a bad habit, into adolescence. Yet, with Logan's help, this period of his life passed with the usual pranks and incidents of boyhood: they smoked tobacco in the fields, spied on the Hottentot women undressing, hoped to see them making love, and furtively boasted of their sexual appetites.

His father's thoughts of returning to England were once more placed in abeyance, but he never gave up the hope of seeing his native land again before he died. But now, he had to face realities: he could not leave the Colony until Michael was old enough and his health stable enough to risk a long absence. Their curious dependence on each other continued, but it was never an easy, demonstrative relationship, although one devoid of serious conflicts. They did not have much in common: Michael's interests lay buried in himself, in his ambitions, his plans for the future; Mr Thompson toiled from dawn until dusk on the farm and, in the evenings, read all he could lay hands on about Napoleon Bonaparte.

Michael, being a first-generation Colonial, took an interest in his country: he thrilled at seeing public figures or high-ranking officers about their business; he was impressed by events, and discovered a keen excitement when witnessing official ceremonies.

I remember Jacob Uys, the patriarch of the great Boer trek, and his party camping near Grahamstown. We English presented him with the largest Bible I have ever seen, inscribed to him and his departing fellow-countrymen. And I thought that one day I might do as much for my people—as Uys had done for his, I mean.

And then, the dreadful shock of reading one morning in the *Grahamstown Journal*, the frontier newspaper, the words of Piet Retief, the local leader:

As we desire to stand high in the estimation of our brethren, be it known *inter alia* that we are resolved, wherever we go, that we will uphold the just principle of liberty; but whilst we will take care that no one shall be in a state of slavery, it is our determination to maintain such regulations as may suppress crime and preserve proper relations between master and servant ... We quit this Colony under the full assurance that the English Government has nothing more to require of us, and will allow us to govern ourselves without interference in future.

The English were stunned by events: before their eyes the white frontier population was reduced: ox-drawn covered wagons set off into the unknown hinterland with little but faith to fortify them. And Michael remembered how the news reached Grahamstown of Retief's death: how the treacherous Dingaan, king of the great Zulu nation, had signed the document ceding Port Natal to Retief and his Voortrekkers as they had become known; how Dingaan had invited them to enter his camp unarmed; how two Zulu regiments encircled the Boers in a war dance, moving the dusty earth with their feet to reveal hidden weapons buried underneath. No one was spared. And how the massacre was revenged at the Battle of Blood River, when three thousand Zulus died, and not one white, and people talked of Cortez and Montezuma. Then, the Voortrekkers covenanted with God to build Him a church wherever He so pleased, and they promised to celebrate their victory, they and their descendents, as a day of thanksgiving.

(Abolish slaves, convert the heathen, raise up the poor: what concerns the world is meaningless here. The message had been sent, the words unequivocal: allow us to govern ourselves without interference. We are masters, they our servants.)

2

'I was not strong enough to follow in my father's footsteps and become a farmer, and, in any case, I did not think farming a suitable occupation for one of my particular talents.'

Particular talents: for restlessness, for changing jobs from clerk to apprentice cartographer to draper's assistant, all in the space of a year:

'Of the various employment I experienced, the work I enjoyed most was in the warehouse, for I had no one to bother me. I was in charge of some eight or nine Hottentot boys and I believe I did my work well. But with the appointment of mynheer Prinsloo as manager everything changed. He was typical of the more unintelligent Boer type, with a very narrow forehead indicating a small brain. It would have been best if he had done my work and I his, and I believe he thought so too, for he was always picking on me and making life disagreeable. He felt I was a threat to his authority. Even the Hottentot boys disliked him and he treated them no better than he did me. Then, because of the scandal, I became more settled but only for a brief time.'

The scandal concerned Logan Stanley. The son of a prosperous cattle-farmer, Logan had studied medicine at Edinburgh University and, on his return to Grahamstown, announced his engagement to his childhood sweetheart, Alice Filmore. Three months after the announcement, Logan was accused by one of his patients, a married woman, of indecently assaulting her. A brief but succulent feast of rumour and gossip was devoured by all and, at dead of night, Logan Stanley departed for Cape Town and the army, leaving Alice inconsolable:

'I used to visit her, sit with her, comfort her. Often no word would pass between us, but she found comfort just in my presence. What a change had come over her, she, who used to be so lively. She just sat and stared and even her golden hair seemed dulled. It was difficult for her, you see. In those days—I'm talking about the 1850s or thereabouts—people were still strict, people cared about such things. Somehow, Logan's behaviour had brushed off on Alice. Even going to church was a painful experience. People would point and whisper and give her room to pass as though she had the pox. I do not remember now how marriage came to be discussed between us. All I know is that I used to see her often, two, three times a month, and the subject must have arisen naturally. I think it must have been a year after Logan's departure that Alice and I were married ... Although her parents were bitterly opposed at first—not so much to me, as to Alice marrying so soon after her disappointment. John Filmore appointed me assistant manager at one of his granaries, which position I occupied for three years. All in all, I was congratulated on having made a good match.'

And so it was: John Filmore, with foresight and vigour, persisted with his wheat crop when many another was turning to cattle or sheep or fruit. By 1850, he owned several farms, and three granaries: he had become a man of substance. Alice's marriage was opposed not for the reason Michael suggested but because Filmore envisaged a brighter future for his daughter; instead, he saw himself having to support a son-in-law who appeared aimless and idle. Richard Thompson, sensing the Filmores' disappointment in the marriage, invited the couple to live at Safehaven until they could afford a home of their own; the offer was accepted.

'I must put the record straight. I must, though I am sorry to speak of such things, they embarrass me but I must set down my side of events. Our wedding night was spent in my old bedroom at Safehaven, the one where I had endured the sick and painful hours of my childhood. Father had refurnished the room, giving us his own large bed, the one in which I was born and Mother died. I apologise once more for speaking of such things, but, on our wedding night, on our wedding night I questioned Alice Thompson, *née* Filmore, about her innocence, purity, call it what you will and she explained that because she had ridden a horse from an early age she was not intact. I accepted her story. I am not proud of my gullibility, but then I myself was innocent on my wedding night. I will not pursue the subject, but I must put my side. A marriage which begins in deceit ends in deceit.'

3

It was the English who brought to the Colony a sense of community. Their churches were not only houses of worship but also meeting places; their lives were dedicated not just to taming the land and the savages, but to a wider more inclusive concept of the social fabric. Gone was the dour and sober life the Dutch had created; in its place, a new vitality insisted itself. The poor who left Britain in 1820 found themselves, thirty years later, a dozen rungs up the social ladder: they had attained the middle class; above them were the aristocrats who ruled by right; below them, the easily identifiable mass of black humanity. It was the age of lip-service: convert the heathen, educate them, but do not dignify them; clamour for the abolition of slavery, but retain slaves. Service to the community was construed as service to the English; secret condonation was still rampant.

The new bourgeoisie published newspapers and fought for the freedom of the press; they interested themselves in public affairs from the parish to the capital; they wrote books and journals, and celebrated the landscape in paint and verse. They coveted, too, the small coinage of their new society: manners, gossip, conversation. With the passage of time, their communal roots reached deeper and deeper into the soil, and all this was achieved in the face of a common enemy: the Kaffir. Eight times the Colony was invaded; eight times the Xhosa warriors crossed the Great Fish and, like a locust storm, ravaged all before them. But the English, with their genius for surviving against indecent odds, resisted and stood firm. It was not to a victory of arms they owed their continued existence, but to a triumph of will, a smug confidence that they could not be beaten. True, battles were won in the field by an outnumbered Colonial army with superior weapons, but the covert strife between the English and the Kaffir was a contest of inner resources not of physical strength, a conflict of more profound realities between Christ Jesus and *uthixo*, the supreme being.

Yet, despite the growing confidence of the young community, Michael Thompson felt excluded from that mystic circle of fellowship in which some men stand so easily, and readily, while others do not. He wanted a special place within it, a parting of the ranks so that he could march proudly into its midst, be recognised and accepted. And, as though by willing it, insisting on it, this too was brought about but by means Michael could not have foreseen or planned.

On mild spring evening in 1854, a messenger arrived at the Thompson farm with an official letter for Michael, bearing the coat of arms of the Colony. With trembling hands he opened the envelope, while Alice and his father, themselves made nervous by this unexpected intrusion, waited impatiently for the contents to be revealed. Michael looked up from the letter. 'I don't understand,' he said.

'Read it, for pity's sake,' implored Alice.

'Put us out of our misery, son,' said Mr Thompson poking tobacco deeper and deeper into the bowl of his pipe.

' "Dear Mr Thompson," ' Michael read, ' "If you are the Mr Thompson who was once a pupil of Miss Sybille Henning, I would be obliged if you would call at my office at your earliest convenience. Yours faithfully, Charles Brownlee, Gaika Commissioner." '

A flurry of speculation ensued which ended with Mr Thompson insisting that the old woman had probably died and left Michael something in her will. The theory satisfied them for the time being, but it was way off the mark, as Michael was to learn the next morning when he presented himself at the office of the Gaika Commissioner.

Brownlee could easily have been mistaken for a poet. The carelessness of his dress, the wildness of his hair, the far-away look in his eyes, all conformed to the popular, romantic image of a sensitive, absent-minded literary man. He was possessed, too, of a restful, mellow voice which enhanced the impression. But behind the dreamy exterior, there lurked a shrewd, practical intelligence, and an energy that was seemingly inexhaustible.

He had been a missionary, but his temperament was too vigorous, too impatient to suit that calling. However, the years he had spent seeking to convert the Xhosa—he never called them Kaffirs—were not wasted: he had acquired a thorough knowledge of their language, a profound understanding of their customs and way of life, and most important of all, a deep love of the people. When the post of Gaika Commissioner was created, he was the obvious choice.

He greeted Michael warmly. 'My dear boy,' he said, 'I cannot tell you how pleased I am to meet you. Pray, be seated.' The interview took place in Brownlee's modest office near Market Square. A large map of the British Kaffraria hung on the wall behind his desk, while the other three walls were decorated with tribal carvings, masks, and an assortment of Xhosa weaponry; it had the atmosphere of a hunter's trophy-room.

When Michael was seated, Brownlee, his eyes twinkling, said, 'Now we shall see if she was right,' and, leaning across the desk, said in Xhosa, 'You speak the language of the people, is that right?'

'I do,' answered Michael, mildly put out by the older man's playful manner.

'And how are you presently employed?' Brownlee continued.

Haltingly, Michael told him of his work at the granary, but ended by asking, 'Please tell me, sir, what Miss Henning has to do with my being here?'

Brownlee perched on the corner of his desk. 'All most extraordinary,' he said and launched forth into an account of his meeting with Sybille Henning and all she had told him.

On an expedition to the Kat River Settlement, where large numbers of Hottentots had been settled by a despairing government, Brownlee met for the first and only time the white woman whose life was spent among the half-castes. She had opened a school to teach adults to read and write, and there Brownlee spent three days while seeking to recover cattle which had, for once, been stolen from the Xhosa by a gang of Hottentots. During the course of a conversation with Sybille, he mentioned that for months he had been searching for a bilingual assistant, believing that the speaking of Xhosa was an essential qualification for the work of ministering to the people's needs. At once her eyes glowed fervently and she talked of Michael Thompson of Safehaven in the Albany District, a boy of driving energy whom she herself had taught the tongue. 'Oh, Mr Brownlee,' she said, 'the hand of God, the hand of God! If only He would intervene on my behalf as He has done on yours!' She made Brownlee promise to interview Michael and he had kept his word.

'An assistant?' Michael said.

'An assistant-commissioner,' corrected Brownlee more gravely. They discussed the post and what it would entail: regular journeys to Kaffraria; being judge, jury, advocate, medical officer to the people placed in his care, the writing of reports, 'and above all,' Brownlee said, raising his forefinger, 'learning to love those less fortunate than yourself.'

<h1 style="text-align:center">4</h1>

'Alice was against it. So was her father. He was furious at the thought of me leaving his employ to become a "Kaffir clerk" as he called it. "Working among kaffirs?" was all Alice could say. My own father was more enthusiastic. "Assistant-Commissioner," he said, almost with reverence. The night after my interview with Mr Brownlee I slept hardly at all, although I knew what my answer would be; I could not rid my mind of Sybille Henning's face, as I had known it in childhood. The next day I wrote to Mr Brownlee telling him that I would accept the offer, though I very nearly withdrew it when he informed me that I would have to spend some six weeks in Cape Town learning the ways of government departments. "What is there to learn?" I asked. "I speak their language, surely that is enough?" It was my first encounter with bureaucracy and after some heart-searching, I agreed. In due course, much to Alice's displeasure, I set off and spent six wretched weeks learning to fill in forms and what special language to use when writing reports. I was instructed, for the most part, by second-rate men whose chief interest, it seemed, lay in commas and semi-colons; I kept to myself, did what I was told and acquitted myself well. On my return to Grahamstown, I presented myself once more to Brownlee, expecting to take up my new post at once. But an irritating delay followed, almost a month, before I received an official letter appointing me Assistant-Commissioner for Gaika Affairs ... I later learned the reason for the delay when I accidentally came upon a report on my conduct in Cape Town. Some tuppence-halfpenny clerk had written to Brownlee saying I was difficult, insulting, and arrogant. I am happy to say Brownlee did not accept the charges.'

He did not, because he could not: where would he find another young man with that one essential qualification? To Sybille he wrote a letter of thanks. 'I account him a man of modest competence,' but he crossed out those words and replaced them with, 'I account him modest and competent.' Then, he crossed out the word 'modest.'

5

The turning-point in Michael's life occurred after his first visit to British Kaffraria. Brownlee should have accompanied him, to introduce him to the Xhosa chief, but the Commissioner was taken ill with influenza two days before the departure date. In the event, Michael was placed under the guidance of Sergeant Tromp who, with an escort of four soldiers, led Michael across the Great Fish River into the Xhosa homeland. He remembered it as though recalling a dream:

'Red blankets, that's what I saw first, their red blankets from afar. And when we drew near, the whole village collected in the centre of the *kraal*, their chief at the head. I cannot remember all I did that day but flashes, incidents return and I will never forget the whole village, the chief included, bowing to me, falling on hands and knees in obeisance. I sat on a chair, Tromp to one side of me, the four soldiers behind like a guard of honour. I remember the chief greeting me and then laying before me gifts of beads and pottery. I did my work, I suppose—listened to their complaints, arbitrated disputes, advised, promised action. I say "suppose" because I cannot truly remember. My lasting impression is of those people on their knees to me, doing obeisance. That evening, on our return to the Colony, Sergeant Tromp must have observed the impression the day's events had made on me, for I rode as if in a daze, unaware of the changing countryside. Then, and I shall never forget this, the Sergeant made an awesome remark. I can hear his voice as though it were yesterday. "Yes, sir, that's the way it is. Among these people you are god." '

From that day forward, a change was wrought in Michael. He would endure the insults that his new position attracted, 'Kaffir-clerk' or 'Kaffir-lover' it mattered not; he would endure his self-imposed exclusion from his own community, endure anonymity, for he possessed a secret that nourished and supported him. Michael Thompson had come into his own : among these people, he was god. (This is the recurring malady for all : the divided life of the soul.)

19

The warning

In the course of time, Michael and Alice moved from Safehaven to a small house in Grahamstown and there, in January 1856, Victoria, who was to be their only child, first saw the light of day. The satisfaction Michael received from his work was mirrored in his appearance: he had put on weight, and lost the irritating smirk. His manner, in the Colony, at least, was less abrasive: a certain unctuousness had crept into his demeanour, as though to imply that by working among the Kaffirs he had earned a small degree of sanctity, which others called self-righteousness.

1856 was an important year for the Thompsons: in February, Victoria was born; in July, Richard announced that he had sold his farm to John Filmore and had purchased a ticket for England. 'I'll see 'ow I goes, but I've made me will, Michael, my boy, so if anythin' 'appens to me, the loot's all yours!' Shortly after his departure, in September—he wanted to spend the winter in London—the third, and, as far as Michael was concerned, most important event occurred.

Husband and wife were finishing supper. They were a little late that evening because six-month-old Victoria had not settled immediately after being fed, and Alice had insisted on getting the baby off to sleep before she herself sat down to eat.

Over mutton stew, husband and wife discussed their day. Alice, who had become nervous and fidgety since her child's birth, prattled on in her high-pitched nasal voice about the baby's wind which was a problem, and about her bowel movements which were not. She talked compulsively, as if afraid of silence, straining to remember all the details she could. Michael appeared to listen attentively, nodding or shaking his head, whichever seemed the most appropriate. She informed him that her mother, Mrs Filmore, had visited in the afternoon, bringing a bonnet for Victoria, and a set of six claret glasses for them, 'though I told her we cannot afford claret to go in them, oh, Michael, I do wish you'd find something better-paid to do, and the bonnet is quite lovely and *does* suit the little baby so, though mother thought—where are you going, dear?'

'I have to finish my report,' he said, rising.

'Can you not write down here for a change?' she asked earnestly. 'I'll sew, I won't say a word, I promise.'

'I need my map and my books,' he explained, with an apologetic, sickly smile, and left her alone.

He retired to a small upstairs room into which he had managed to fit a roll-top desk and a swivel stool. On the wall hung a map of the Colony, showing the Neutral Territory and the area beyond where the Xhosa lived, British Kaffraria, marked with crosses in red, green and blue. Here the Gaika lived, an estimated 70,000 souls, who were Michael's special concern. The Gaika were an important branch of the Xhosa people, a clan within a nation, though not the most important: the senior tribe were the Gcaleka, but they lived outside the jurisdiction of the British Government.

His chief duty was to visit the area three times a year; hence, the crosses on the map: red denoted his most recent journeys, green those villages he had not seen for six months, and blue the areas he had badly neglected. Next year, he would hang up a new map and begin all over again.

He enjoyed writing his reports for Mr Brownlee. On this particular evening he was formulating an assessment on overcrowding. The moment before starting was the one to be savoured: settling down at the desk, arranging his papers, sharpening his quill pens. A wind had arisen and was rattling the window panes; from the window, he saw a man and a woman in the narrow street below, struggling against the stiff breeze when a sudden sharp gust caught her crinoline which billowed to reveal frilled pantaloons. From downstairs he heard faint colic-cries from Victoria, and Alice's voice attempting to soothe. He sometimes wondered if Alice woke the baby deliberately just for company, but he quickly pushed the thought from his mind, and, in no time at all, lost all sense of his surroundings and immersed himself as best he could in the problems of the people who were his especial concern and that world which was his Olympus. He wrote:

'Their villages, or *kraals* as they are called, are now crowded upon one another, in such a manner that there is scarcely sufficient pasture for their cattle, a state of affairs that must lead to them desiring more land from the Colony. In the past this has led to military invasions and bloody conflict. On my recent travels, however, I have noticed that the people live in a depressed state, their morale shattered by the defeat of 1853 which makes any war-like action unlikely, unless some change in the present—'

He was interrupted by Alice. She stood half-in, half-out the room, trying not to make too much of her presence; she had Victoria perched over her shoulder and was repeatedly patting the baby's back.

'What is it?' Michael asked; he made no effort to conceal his irritability.

'There's a Kaffir downstairs wants to see you,' she said. 'I told him you were busy but he insisted. He said to tell you that his name was Gwali and that you'd remember, but I said—'

'Gwali,' Michael repeated, swivelling a little from side to side on his stool. 'Gwali . . .'

'He's at the back door,' Alice continued, patting away as though her hand were a mechanical toy. 'I do wish they wouldn't trouble you at home, I've told him—'

All at once, Michael stood. 'Gwali!' he cried, and without explanations, pushed past Alice and bounded down the narrow stairs two at a time. He paused on the landing, for, through a high, narrow window he could see the back yard, and, standing at the entrance was an old wagon, the canvas canopy patched and re-patched; he recognised it instantly, and took the last few steps in one stride, running, stumbling to the back door.

'Gwali!' Michael said again, seeing the squat, powerful man framed in the doorway. They were about the same age, but Michael looked years older, almost fatherly in comparison to his visitor.

'I am glad you remember me, master Michael,' Gwali whispered, but he did not smile or show any pleasure at the reunion.

Michael's astonishment soon gave way to a sharp sense of remoteness, as if he had deliberately put a distance between himself and the other man, aware of his position, and the barriers that separated them. Yet, in that instant, associations and memories tumbled across Michael's mind in confusion: Gwali: the little gold cross round his neck, the night on the veld, the journey back from Fort Wiltshire and, inevitably, 'Miss Henning!' Michael cried. 'Where is she?'

Gwali lowered his eyes. 'She's in the back,' he said, indicating the wagon. 'She is dying, master.'

Michael did not take in the news at first. 'I want to see her,' he said, his face alight at the prospect. Together the two men climbed on to the tailboard and raised the canvas flap, shredded with age. The sight that met Michael's eyes stilled him, and his excitement plummeted.

She lay covered by threadbare shawls, once multi-coloured, now a uniform grimy orange. Michael knelt beside her and studied her aged face: he could barely recognise the woman he had known twenty years earlier. He said, 'It's me, Miss Henning, Michael Thompson, do you know me?'

She did not open her eyes, but held out an unsteady, trembling hand which he took in his, and shuddered at the feel of it: wrinkled flesh, fragile bone, and cold. Her hair was white, but so thin and sparse, he could see her scalp beneath, and the mass of lines and creases on her face seemed to proliferate, then and there, as he looked at her. He had the impression of a dry, brittle leaf.

Gwali said, 'She wanted to see you, master, before—before—' he could not finish.

'Where have you come from?' Michael asked.

'The Kat River. Many miles.' Then, his whole body trembled. 'Oh, master!' he cried, covering his face with both hands, 'What am I to do?'

'Stop it, boy,' Michael said in a quiet decisive tone that he reserved for black men. 'Fetch a doctor.'

'But the madam hates doctors!' Gwali protested.

'Don't argue with me, boy, just go and get Dr Allan behind St George's. Tell him it's for me.'

'But I must be with her, master. If she should die—'

'Did you hear what I said, boy?'

Gwali hesitated, and then obeyed.

Alone, Michael sat with her, trying to remember her as she was, but her present appearance, crumbling, so it seemed, before his eyes, impinged too powerfully upon his senses and, try as he might, he could bring no other picture of her to mind. After some minutes she suddenly opened her eyes. In a voice so clear it startled him, she said, in Xhosa, 'Danger,' and in Xhosa, he answered her, 'You are safe here, my teacher.' The words of childhood came naturally to him.

'Danger!' she said once more, becoming agitated. 'The people prepare.'

'For what?'

'To kill.'

'Are they to invade again?' he asked, incredulous.

'To kill.'

'Are the warriors ready?' This, to humour her.

'Yes. To die. Tell Brownlee.'

He knew it could not be so, and had just said as much in his report. He assumed her mind must have wandered to an earlier time. He whispered, 'All is well, my teacher.' His words appeared to calm her, and she lapsed once more into sleep or semi-consciousness.

Watching her approaching death, Michael was numbed by a feeling of helplessness; he could not bring himself to hold or comfort her, although he felt the need to do both, but either the stench of decay or the revulsion he experienced on touching her prevented him. And then he heard Alice, in the courtyard, calling to him; he poked his head out of the wagon.

'Who's in there?' Alice asked, trying to keep the wind from her hair, so that it looked as if she was covering both ears with her hands.

'It's Miss Henning,' Michael replied.

'Who?'

'You remember Miss Henning. She nursed me for a bit, years ago.'

'The wagon-woman!' Alice exclaimed, remembering.

'That's her.'

'I used to be frightened of her,' Alice said as though the fear was still with her.

'She's dying,' Michael said. 'Do you want to see her?'

Instinctively, Alice took a step backwards. 'No,' she answered at once. 'I shall go indoors and I shall pray for her.'

When Michael returned to Sybille's side, she was moaning on each exhalation of breath, and somehow he knew that the end was at hand. Leaning close, he whispered, 'Our Father, Who art in heaven, hallowed be Thy name,' but he could not continue, for his eyes had welled up with tears; stifling a sob, he said, 'God, show me how to thank her,' and, after a brief pause, fighting nausea, he bent

261

over and kissed her gently on her forehead. Some minutes later, she died.

When Gwali returned with the doctor, Michael left him with the body, and arranged for the undertaker to come as soon as possible. 'I'll see to it,' said the doctor. 'I'm sorry I could not get here sooner, but I assure you there would have been nothing I could do to save her. She was very old.'

As Michael returned to the house, he heard Gwali's voice intoning a prayer. He paused and listened. Later, he would recall this moment, and understand why the sound disturbed him, but for the present he was puzzled not hearing the name of Jesus Christ, although he knew Gwali to be a Christian, but the word *uthixo*, which means supreme being, repeated over and over again. And it occurred to him to ask Gwali what Miss Henning had meant by her confused warning.

That night, when the sky was streaked with racing clouds, Michael and Alice prayed for the departed soul, and some time after that, Gwali, tear-stained and solemn, came to tell them that the undertaker had arrived.

2

'Will you be the only one at the funeral?' Alice asked over breakfast; the thought appalled her.

'Well, Gwali will be there,' Michael replied, trying clumsily to operate a pair of egg-scissors.

'What? Just you and a Kaffir? Doesn't seem right.'

'No one else knew her.'

'Ma and Pa did.'

'I don't like to ask—' he confessed.

'It's your Christian duty!' Alice cried. 'How would you like to be buried alone? You wouldn't like it at all. *I'd* attend, but I cannot leave Victoria alone. I'm sure that's why Miss Henning came back here, because she had friends, and there you are denying her the pleasure of being buried among those she knew. It's too bad of you, Mr Thompson, really too bad—'

'Nonsense—'

'It's *not* nonsense! Oh, you *are* aggravating! You must invite Ma and Pa!' she cried as though she were discussing a fancy-dress ball.

'I don't think so.'

'Ask them!'

'I'll think about it.'

But he knew, as he walked to the office, that Alice was right. The picture of Sybille Henning, frail and enfeebled, alone in the wagon, had remained with him all through the night, and it was as if he could still feel her wrinkled skin touching his lips as he bent to kiss her. He was strangely moved by that image of her loneliness. Yes, he thought, she deserves more than a solitary mourner and, though still hesitant, he decided to follow his wife's wishes.

John Filmore had been at work for more than an hour when Michael entered. His ground-floor office, which had once been a hardware store, was fronted by an enormous window bearing the words, in gothic letters, 'J. Filmore, Provision Merchant.' Commerce suited the owner: he had built up the business into a thriving enter-prise. He had a passion for hard work, and despised idleness in others, expecially in his son-in-law whose departure from the granary to the Gaika Commission Filmore had taken as a personal insult. Michael, on his part, always saw to it that their relations were as untroubled as possible, partly because of Filmore's wealth, which he respected, but chiefly because Michael had recently been initiated into the Grahamstown Lodge No. 3, born out of the old Friendship Society, and of which Filmore was Grand Master. The higher ideals of Freemasonry escaped the notice of the younger man; he had joined the Lodge only because he believed that, in some way, being a Mason would secretly advance his career.

The office, from which you could see the entrance to St George's Church, was unnaturally tidy. Filmore was hard at work: he sat at a large trestle table on which were neatly placed mountains of let-ters, dockets, *pro formas*; on either side of him sat two young clerks who scratched away at ledgers, eyes perpetually downcast.

'Two minutes to nine,' said Filmore with mock wonder. 'You bet-ter be careful, Michael; you don't want to give the Government more than they pay for.'

Michael affected to laugh. Filmore returned to his papers. 'Are you going to watch me all morning?' he asked.

'No, I've—I've come to ask a favour.'

'Oh! What bad luck!' cried Filmore. 'I've lost the key to the safe.'

'No, no, no, sir, it's—it's not money.'

'Oh God, Michael, where's yer sense of 'umour?' said the older man as though he were going to cry.

'Well, what I have to say,' Michael replied sharply, 'is not much

263

of a laughing matter.' And, he went on to tell about Sybille's return the previous evening, and her death.

Filmore was genuinely saddened by the news. 'May she rest in peace,' he said. 'What a long time ago it all was . . .'

'I've come to ask you, sir, to attend the funeral. Alice thinks, and I agree, it doesn't seem proper to bury her alone.'

Filmore nodded. 'Yes, of course. And I'll have a message sent to Mrs Filmore. She'd want to be there, too, I'm certain of it.'

At five o'clock they gathered in the Reformed Church. The Filmores and Michael occupied the front pew, Sybille's coffin filling the narrow aisle. At the back of the church sat Gwali, fingering the little gold cross round his neck, his lips moving incessantly. At the grave-side, dominee Burger intoned the final prayers—'I didn't understand a word of it,' said Mrs Filmore, 'but I expect dust to dust and hellfire came into it!'—and when it was all over, the small funeral party laid their home-made wreaths beside the grave and then left the cemetery. Michael looked back and saw Gwali, standing with his head bowed, watching the grave-diggers shovelling the earth. He had waited for everyone to leave before paying his last respects, as though he had not wanted to intrude; yet it was he who had known her best.

Outside the cemetery gates, dominee Burger said, 'You're good people. You English are kind. I only wish your Government was made up of people like you.'

'Will you join us at van Rensberg's for a drink, dominee?' asked Filmore.

'Thank you, no,' said the dominee sternly, then drew Michael aside. 'Mr Thompson, any truth in the rumours?'

'What rumours?' asked Michael.

'They say the Kaffirs are going to invade again.'

'I've heard nothing, dominee. All I can tell you is that a month ago I returned from Kaffraria and, in my opinion, the people are in no state to fight.'

'I'm glad to hear it,' said the dominee. 'But this time they tell me they've got the Russians to help them.'

'The Russians?'

'Well, Mr Thompson, they're as black as the Kaffirs. Natural allies!' They shook hands and parted, and Michael ran to catch up his parents in-law who had just entered van Rensberg's tavern. Because women were not allowed in the public bar, they repaired to the upstairs room, unchanged over the years, except for one chair, which was set apart and placed against the wall; on it, rested a hand-printed card with the words: 'Piet Retief, the great Boer leader, sat upon this chair. Do not use.'

It was Miss van Rensberg, tall and taciturn as her father had been, who ushered the three mourners into the upstairs room. (Rumour had it that she wanted to join Retief's party, but the leader would not take unmarried women and, since no one volunteered to wed her, she remained to help her father and inherit the Tavern.) While she was taking their orders—tea and sandwiches for Mrs Filmore, brandy for the men—a servant entered. 'Madam,' he said, addressing Miss van Rensberg, 'it's that boy Gwali. He is wishing to know if he can put that wagon in the yard, and sleep there tonight!'

Miss van Rensberg glanced enquiringly at Michael, who shrugged.

After a moment's consideration, she said, 'Yes, tell him it's all right.'

'He has no money, madam.'

'I'll take care of that,' said Filmore.

'I can afford to let a Kaffir sleep in my yard without payment,' she responded grimly, dismissed the servant, and followed him out.

An after-funeral gloom settled over the three mourners. 'Dreadful!' declared Filmore, covering his face with his hands.

'What is it John?' demanded Mrs Filmore, alarmed; she half-rose in her chair, imagining he was ill.

'Dreadful,' he repeated, 'to think of that poor woman wandering all over the place with just that Kaffir for company.' Michael murmured his agreement, and wandered over to the tall window which overlooked the back yard. There, he saw Gwali removing the heavy wooden yoke from the ox. Her words suddenly flooded his mind, the answer to his question, 'Are the warriors ready?'—'Yes, to die,' she had said. He repeated the warning to the Filmores and told them, too, of dominee Burger's concern about the Russians. He meant to cheer them up, implying the story was ridiculous nonsense, but neither husband nor wife laughed; if possible, it was as if a heavier gloom descended.

'Three times in my life, I've beat the Kaffirs back,' said Filmore with some passion. 'And I'll do it again, Russians or no!' He made it sound as though he had had no help from anyone.

'There cannot be any truth in it,' Michael said. 'I've seen the people in the last month. They're in no mood to fight, I can tell you.

Their last beating put paid to them altogether.' He liked to pontificate on these questions; it fed his self-esteem.

'Yes, but those of us who are a little older remember only too well what those savages are capable of,' said Mrs Filmore, munching on a sandwich.

'Nevertheless,' argued her husband, 'we ought to take precautions. The Russians are black, after all!'

'White,' said Michael.

'I thought yellow,' observed Mrs Filmore.

'Black,' repeated Filmore in a way that prevented argument and further conversation; but Michael persevered. 'Well, all I can say is the Russians will have to be dashed clever to beat England in the Crimea *and* land an army at the Cape! I tell you it's all ridiculous nonsense!' The Filmores chose to ignore his words, which they viewed with a good deal of suspicion, for he worked and lived among the Kaffirs, and what was much more alarming, spoke their language. But Filmore could not ignore what his son-in-law said next. 'We must stop this hatred of the Kaffirs. It is not worthy of us. We must raise them up, bring them out of darkness, shed the light of Christianity upon them—' the platitudes were endless, and meaningless, but he enjoyed saying them, and playing the humanitarian. It had become a part of him, this playing of parts, an involuntary adjustment of personality: to his father-in-law, he presented a benign man of the world; it was one of many masks.

Filmore, whether he knew Michael's words were humbug or not, was determined to have his say. 'Bring 'em out of darkness? They're murdering barbarians, no more, no less! I've lost more than a dozen friends at their 'ands and so 'as your father—so it doesn't become you, young fellow-me-lad, to play Wilberforce with me!'

Mrs Filmore picked up the tail end of the conversation, and brought her mind to bear on Michael's father, speculating whether he would remain in England or return to the Cape. Michael ceased to listen or take part; Sybille's dying words still haunted him, and he made a mental note to question Gwali further.

Gwali intruded once more into what had become a kind of wake. Much later, long after Mrs Filmore had retired, when her husband was holding forth on how he had the foresight to stick to wheat when others had given up the crop, Michael chanced once more to cross to the window, this time in order to breathe some fresh air. He had drunk more than was usual for him, and his mind was a little

266

clouded so that what he saw startled him inordinately. Down in the yard, Gwali had lit a lantern inside the wagon and it shone like a luminous star; within, Michael could discern silhouettes animated as in a shadow-play; one he recognised as Gwali, it appeared cross-legged, listening to another man who gestured wildly, pointing with a forefinger which, by the curious arrangement of the light, seemed disproportionately elongated. Michael watched the strange charade for some minutes, and then heard a Xhosa chant, and saw the two shadows begin to sway to and fro. In his befuddled state, Michael tried to identify the words, and came to the conclusion that the two men were offering up a prayer to the Xhosa shades, the spirits of the departed, but this puzzled him, for he knew Gwali to be a Christian. Later still, he did not, at once, connect this event with Miss van Rensberg's unexpected appearance, and the news she brought; shortly after midnight, she burst into the room, wearing her dressing gown and nightcap, deeply agitated.

'Oh, Mr Filmore,' she cried. 'Something terrible's happened—the Kaffirs—the Kaffirs have all run away!'

The two men, a good deal the worse for wear, hauled themselves to their feet. Michael was the first to speak. 'Run away?' he repeated foolishly. 'Why should they run away?'

'I don't know!' replied Miss van Rensberg. 'It must be another invasion, but all the servants have gone!'

Instinctively, Michael returned to the window and looked down at the yard: the wagon was no longer there; Gwali had disappeared, too. Suddenly, Michael understood the scene in the wagon, and it explained Miss van Rensberg's news: the Kaffirs had been summoned by messengers to join the legions who were, presumably, preparing to invade the Colony, yet again.

'This is it,' Filmore announced. 'This will be Armageddon!'

'I must get back to Alice,' Michael said, searching for his hat.

'They never give any warning.' Filmore continued. 'Murdering bastards!'

Miss van Rensberg helped herself to the last of the brandy. 'Do you think they'll attack Grahamstown again?' she asked.

'Not if I can 'elp it,' said Filmore. 'Now, don't you worry, mejuvrou, I'm 'ere to protect you.'

By then, Michael, on all fours, had found his hat under the table. Heaving himself up with difficulty, he said, 'Will you be all right?' Filmore lurched at him viciously. 'Raise them out of darkness?' he bellowed. 'Christ man, we'll all soon be dead, and you'll be to blame!'

3

Michael emerged into the empty street; the night was hollow and starless, and the fresh air caused him to reel: like an acrobat his knees buckled and he cavorted into the middle of the street where he managed to regain his balance. He looked about: an ominous emptiness greeted him. As he turned for home, a lone horseman galloped past and Michael called, 'Have they invaded?' but the rider could not have heard and was quickly out of sight.

Walking unsteadily, his fears increased, fed by the disturbing sequence of events of which he could not, as yet, make sense: he recalled Gwali using the word *uthixo*, and not Christ when Miss Henning died; and the man gesticulating in the back of the wagon; and the chant to the departed Xhosa souls. Now, all the Kaffir servants, according to Miss van Rensberg, had deserted, and the sight of the horseman galloping fast down the empty street somehow added to his unease. But most worrying of all, Sybille's warning, 'The warriors prepare to die. Tell Brownlee.'

More puzzles: the town crier was not about warning the inhabitants, and when Michael passed the barracks there was the reassuring sight of the sentry asleep: he could make no sense of it, 'They can't attack,' he said aloud. 'They can't. They're in no state to fight.'

Although it was not on his route, he found himself passing the graveyard of the Reformed Church. There he paused, leaning up against the iron railings, and gazed at Sybille's grave: the flowers he had placed on the mound of freshly dug earth were no longer there, blown away by the wind, he supposed. For a brief moment, thoughts of the imminent danger vanished; his heart was with Sybille now, Gwali beside her, scouring the countryside for a shadow. But the image of Gwali rekindled his feelings of apprehension: he could not free his mind from the picture of the wagon canopy aflame, and the dark shadows inside which returned to disturb him. Without being really aware of what he was doing, he opened the catch on the iron gate, and stumbled forward, down the avenue of marble memorials until he came to Sybille's grave.

He tried to recall her as she was when he first knew her, but all he saw was himself, as though in a mirror, a child again, and he was assailed by a sharp, jealous reminder of Gwali and it frightened him.

How, he wondered, could he still feel this envy, resent, at this distance of time, a dead woman's love for a little Kaffir? Then, with alarming clarity, he had a sudden insight: she judged what was *in* us, he realised, and the burden of her judgement was too painful for him to bear. But for that brief moment he saw her resolute and immovable, true to her God, to her fellow-men and to her own being, which embraced one goodness, one creation, one Godhead, strong and weak, masters and servants.

He turned to leave the churchyard, but paused, looked back and called, as though a triumphant taunt, 'Among the people I am God.'

4

His life was to undergo further unaccustomed turbulence and, though trivial, it was nonetheless disturbing: when he entered his house in the early hours of that morning, turning the key as quietly as he could, he was confronted by Alice standing on the narrow stairs, convulsively rocking the baby, Victoria, and screaming hysterically, 'Where have you been? How could you leave me all night alone? You're cruel, cruel, *cruel*!'

He was not yet fully sober, and found it difficult to focus properly. Swaying a little, he said, 'What's the matter, is something wrong with Victoria?'

'*Where have you been?*' Alice cried. 'Don't you know I've been alone all night, where were you?'

'Quietly, quietly, sweetheart, I'm here now.'

'Now, yes, now! But I've been alone all night!'

'Well, you're not alone now!'

'You don't care about me at all!'

'We've been mourning Miss Henning!'

'But what about me? I've been all alone!'

'You've said that before!'

'It's true!'

'I know it's true!'

'Well you could apologise, you could say sorry, at least you could comfort me!'

'Stop shouting!'

'I *won't* stop shouting!'

'I'm not going to listen to you shouting all night—'

'I've been all alone—'

269

'I can hear you—'

'I hope you can, all alone, all night—'

'Oh shut up!'

'You shut up!'

'Oh shut up!'

'Shut up, shut up, shut up!'

He pushed past her and mounted the stairs, their repetitions accompanying them all the way up to the bedroom. The baby began to cry and Alice's complaints were interspersed with 'There-there' and 'Hush, baby' which infuriated her husband even further. 'Put the baby to bed, for God's sake!' he bellowed.

'You don't care, you just don't care, you don't care about me or the baby or anything! My mother said I should never have married you. She said you were a self-satisfied, self-opinionated ass!'

'Your mother?' Michael repeated, falling on to the bed. 'She pleaded with me to marry you!'

'You just don't care!' Alice hissed.

'She pleaded with me, your father pleaded with me, everyone pleaded with me to marry you, so don't you come here with—'

'Pleaded with you? May God strike you dead for those lies! There-there, baby!'

'Pleaded with me!'

'Lies!'

'I don't care what your mother said,' Michael muttered. 'I'll tell you what my father said, that's more to the point. He said never marry a woman on the rebound, that's what he said!'

'I wouldn't have married you if I wasn't! Hush, hush my little angel!'

'No, you'd have married Logan Stanley, that's who you'd have married!'

'Logan Stanley's worth ten of you!'

'Logan Stanley,' Michael said again, screwing up his face as though he had just sucked a lemon. 'Logan Stanley!'

'Logan was clever and considerate!'

'Clever not to marry you, that's for sure!'

'Logan was a gentleman!'

'Logan put his hands up his patients' skirts, that's what Logan Stanley did!'

'Michael!'

'Rapist! That's what Logan Stanley was, that's why he left so suddenly, because they don't care for doctors who rape married women!'

Alice ran from the room, cradling Victoria as though to protect her from Michael's language. Michael continued to shout, 'I saved you from a fate worse than Logan Stanley!' and then he subsided, grumbling to himself, until a drowsiness began to envelop him. When he woke, it was to see Alice, with her back to him, in the bed; she was crying.

Roughly, he put his hand under the bedclothes and found her thigh. She squeezed her legs tightly together; he tried to get at her breasts, but her arms prevented him. 'Come on! You're not unwell, are you?' he said accusingly.

'You're horrible!' she cried into her pillow.

Disconsolately, he moved away. Then, he noticed that he had not undressed for bed, and he began to unbutton his coat; but his fingers soon wearied of the task, and Michael decided that, as he would have to rise in an hour or two, there was little point in putting on his nightgown. Fully dressed then, he lay on his back, hands tucked under his head, gazing at the ceiling.

Unasked-for, a memory of long ago sprung to mind: the return from Fort Wiltshire, and Fathma's breasts suddenly appeared and provoked him. He twisted and turned, unable to suppress the picture of Captain Jones' fingers on her nipples, turning and twisting them as though they were delicate screws. Once more, he put out a hand towards Alice, but her whole body stiffened and he knew it was hopeless to persist. As sleep finally dashed his hopes, he heard again, like a doom-laden echo, Sybille's garbled warning and, in the last moment of consciousness, a confusion of images in which all the phantoms he so scrupulously censored from his waking life vied for supremacy, and a sense of foreboding poisoned even his sleep.

20

Messengers

The invasion did not materialise, but the puzzles remained unsolved. For several days after Sybille's funeral, Michael's unsettled state lingered: it was presaged by an excruciating headache, the result of too much brandy and too little sleep. But even when that lifted and the nausea which supplanted it passed, there remained a nagging discomfort, as though something he had promised to do had been left undone. In the grip of this uncertainty, he wrote to his father the news of Sybille's death, but it did little to help. Alice forgave him, but not in a direct way, not by apologising: she merely carried on as though nothing had happened, and the incident was never mentioned again. But, as is the way with these things, the name Logan Stanley, which had not been spoken in her presence for three years until Michael's outburst, was mentioned again to her, the very next day. While shopping in the market, she found herself beside Logan's mother, an elderly, elegant woman who had borne her son's disgrace with fortitude.

'Miss Filmore,' said Mrs Stanley with not a little malice.

'Mrs Thompson,' said Alice, correcting her. The old woman smiled politely, discussed the rising price of bread—another sly dig, since Alice's father, with his huge supplies of wheat and grain, was thought to be directly responsible for the increased cost. The two women passed on to the next stall, and, while examining a jar of pickled peaches, the elder woman said, 'Logan's stationed in Cape Town now, you know.'

Alice's heart quickened hearing the name again in so short a space of time. 'No,' she replied. 'I did not know.'

'Oh, yes, he's done very well. *Major* Stanley he is now. There's some talk of him becoming personal physician to the Governor.' And then, looking directly at Alice, 'We are very proud of him.'

Nervous and fluttering, Alice answered with a meandering résumé of her life with Michael, when they were interrupted by a horseman galloping round the perimeter of the square, shouting, 'The Kaffirs! The Kaffirs! To your homes! To your homes!' and the women separated without a word and the market was suddenly deserted.

Alice ran all the way home, locked and barred the doors, and told Michael of the warning. She did not, however, recount her meeting with Logan's mother and if her husband had had less pressing matters to concern him, he might have noticed that, in the days that followed, his wife was unusually quiet and preoccupied. Fresh rumours of a Kaffir attack swept the frontier. When Michael was well enough to return to work, he was immediately aware of the strained atmosphere that pervaded the whole town. Men went about their business armed; women and children kept to their houses, the doors locked. Rumours of an invasion were commonplace, but, from long experience, the colonists did not relax their vigilance. The savagery of previous Kaffir Wars had left deep scars. Each time the people had been led to believe that the full force of Kaffir aggression had been spent, and each time the claim was disproved by more killing, more atrocities, more terror. Fear and hatred walked hand in hand. 'Just give us the chance,' one colonist said, 'and we'll wipe the murdering bastards off the face of the earth.'

And so, the people of Grahamstown, in the first week of June 1856, fell back, as they always did in time of need, on their faith to fortify them. In churches, Dutch and English, the ministers called on God to strengthen the people, protect their homesteads, and help them to triumph over their enemies. 'God is our weapon,' preached the Anglican bishop, John Armstrong. 'He will not desert us. To the north, our brothers the Boers, hopelessly outnumbered, beat back the murdering Zulu. Was it their military skill *alone* which supported them, a few hundred against many thousands? Was it, you may ask, David's skill with the sling *alone* that gave him victory over Goliath and the Philistines? No, dear brethren, God was their weapon, as He is ours. The knowledge that He is our armourer allays all fear. So let us say with the psalmist, "I will call upon the Lord, who is worthy to be praised: so shall I be saved from mine enemies." ' (The Bishop was, incidentally, severely rebuked by the

Government for praising the Boers in this sermon: '... it is not fitting, my lord Bishop, to extol men who are presently engaged ... in founding republics in order to escape the jurisdiction of Her Majesty's Government.')

But those few who had access to the facts, and were trained to assess them, judged the latest rumours to be false. One of these was Michael's immediate superior, Charles Brownlee, the Gaika Commissioner, but he was equally convinced that across the Great Fish River the people in their red blankets were indeed stirring; but not, he was certain, to make war.

2

Over the years, Charles Brownlee had developed an unfailing instinct in regard to the complex political manoeuvrings of the Xhosa chiefs as they jockeyed for power, superiority and greater influence. It was as if he knew their minds better than they did themselves. So that, when the first whispers of war-like preparations filtered through to him, his immediate reaction was not to dismiss them out of hand. As the whispers persisted and mushroomed into rumours supported by apparently incontrovertible evidence, the more Brownlee was inclined to believe that they had some foundation in fact. He had lived too long on the frontier, had moved too freely between white and black, not to be convinced that there was a mystery which, when solved, would explain the recent disquiet.

To begin with, he investigated the stories of the desertion by Kaffir servants. Here he was able to prove that the tales were grossly exaggerated, for the theory was that they had run off to join their brothers to make war. What Brownlee discovered was that either the servants returned, or that other reasons, such as fear of punishment for thieving and drunkenness, accounted for those who did not. But he was not altogether satisfied: two of the deserters who had voluntarily returned would give him no explanations for their sudden departure. To his question, 'Do you train with the spear?' they replied, 'No.' In his notes, Brownlee recorded: 'They are frightened of something. I am certain of it.'

Military intelligence appeared to confirm Brownlee's conclusions. In despatches from British Kaffraria no mention was made of any preparations among the Kaffirs, and the expected massing of warriors on the frontier did not materialise, but, here again, there was cause for a pin-prick of doubt: one report made mention of unusual activity by messengers speeding from village to village. Why, Brownlee wondered? What were the chiefs saying to each other?

The Governor of British Kaffraria, Colonel Maclean, took neither Brownlee's view, nor that of the colonists. He considered that there was absolutely no cause for alarm. He dismissed the story of the Russian alliance as 'lunacy of the highest order'; the frontier posts were not reinforced, and troops were not placed on the alert.

So it was, that when Michael was well enough to return to work, he entered an office where the atmosphere reflected his own troubled mood. He was given the task of sifting through reports, both military and civilian, and, after intensive reading, Michael discovered a clue.

'There is something puzzling, sir, in one of the despatches from Fort Wiltshire.' He wore the mask of efficiency for Brownlee.

'Yes, yes, dear boy, come along, come along,' said the Commissioner. Michael had the effect of making him impatient, especially as he took such time to page through the documents, find the place—'I am very busy this morning, Thompson.'

'Here we are, sir. It seems that a patrol apprehended a man, not named, in British Kaffraria.'

'Well?'

'This fellow speaks of great activity in two of the villages he visited.'

'What sort of activity?'

'Messengers, that's all he says.'

'But we know about the messengers!' Brownlee said, pushing a hand through his unruly hair and making it more unruly.

'No, sir, that's not my point.'

'Well, come to it, come to it, there's a good boy.'

'This man who was apprehended, sir, was asked what he was doing in British Kaffraria, since he had no permit and was therefore in the territory illegally—'

'Yes, yes, I have understood—'

'When questioned in this fashion, he answered, according to the despatch, that he was interested in purchasing land.'

'Impossible,' Brownlee said.

'That's what I thought, sir, but I assure you it is so.'

'Thompson, dear boy,' Brownlee began, oozing indulgence. 'How can a chappie buy land in British Kaffraria? It is not permitted, and even if he did cog the dice of some poor unsuspecting chief, he wouldn't be allowed to live there. There must be a mistake.'

'No mistake, sir, I assure you. Look,' and Michael placed the page before the Commissioner.

'Yes . . .' Brownlee murmured. 'I see . . .'

'It does seem odd, sir.'

'Decidedly puzzling.'

'My question, sir, is why should a fellow want to buy land somewhere it is of no use to him and where, in any case, it is forbidden by law.'

The matter was not resolved then, for they were interrupted by a clerk informing them that a messenger had arrived from Sandile, Chief of all the Gaika. Brownlee rose in great excitement. 'This may be what we've been waiting for. Show him in.'

The messenger, wearing nothing but a loincloth, entered and bowed low, but seeing Michael refused to speak. 'My words are for the Chief alone,' he said, meaning Brownlee.

Michael retired, curiosity rampant. He found it impossible to concentrate on any further reading. Twice, he found a reason to pass the Commissioner's door. On the first occasion he heard nothing, but the second time the messenger's words were clear : 'There will be war! War!' Alarmed, Michael returned to his own room, and noticed that it was already five o'clock, the time he would normally leave for home. He was now plunged into a paroxysm of indecision, for he wanted to do nothing that would cause Alice a second bout of re-crimination. Half an hour passed : Sandile's messenger was still closeted with Brownlee. Michael summoned a Hottentot servant and scribbled a note to Alice :

Dearest,
    Urgent business keeps me. I do not know when I shall be home. Do not wait supper. Michael.

One by one, the clerks and servants said goodnight, until only Michael and the night-watchman were left. There was no sound except for the voices from the Commissioner's office. By eight o'clock, Michael decided he, too, would leave, but as he reached the front door, Brownlee burst from his room, calling, 'Thompson! Thompson!' and then strode into the hall to see his assistant in the act of pulling on his gloves.

'Good boy,' called Brownlee, marching straight past Michael out into the street. 'Come along, come along, dear boy, we're off to see

276

the Governor. You'd better come with me, because I don't want to have to repeat myself.' Then, in the *taal*, he ordered the Hottentot watchman to give Sandile's messenger food and a bed. 'He's been travelling for ten days,' he confided to Michael as they walked briskly in the direction of the military barracks. 'They have more wind than a bagpipe.' At the Reformed Church Dominee Burger saluted them. 'Have the Russians landed?' he called.

'Ignore him,' hissed Brownlee.

Michael waved as reassuringly as he could, and trotted to keep up with his superior, who was striding purposefully across the street, hair and cloak flowing.

When they sailed past Mr Filmore's office, Michael saw his father-in-law still at work and hoped he would notice him with the Commissioner but the merchant was too engrossed in his accounts. It was then that Michael chose to tell Brownlee of Sybille Henning's warning.

'She said that? The warriors prepare to die?' Brownlee repeated, but without slackening his pace.

'And that I should tell you, sir.'

'Rum!' said Brownlee.

'I beg your pardon, sir?'

'Nothing makes sense,' Brownlee replied, but not to anything Michael had said. The remark had only significance for himself.

'Is there—is there going to be war?' Michael asked.

'Let's see what the Governor has to say, shall we?'

3

The Governor was at dinner. His young aide-de-camp, Lieutenant Droxford, fresh from England, sought to persuade the Commissioner and his assistant to wait at least until the Loyal Toast was drunk.

'Wait, my dear boy?' said Brownlee. 'I don't think Her Majesty would thank you for asking me to wait. What I have to say may affect Her Majesty's health rather more acutely than His Excellency's wine.'

The young officer was not easily persuaded. 'I don't really think that H.E. will take to being disturbed,' he said. 'You won't have to wait long, Commissioner. They're on the savoury now.'

The Governor's house was modest in size, yet it had the air of a grand country house. The hall, where Brownlee and Michael now disputed with the young lieutenant, was deliberately left bare of furniture to give an impression of greater size. A circular table stood in the centre and was covered with military headwear of varying brilliance: two of the hats were decorated with large plumes, another with fur, and a fourth with an elaborate network of gold braid. Upon an elegant gilt chair lay, incongruously, four dress swords. A set of prints depicting cavalry officers, either on parade or at full charge, lined the walls. Three doors, prettily panelled in the style of Fragonard, completed the area, and, over the middle door, there hung a portrait of Queen Victoria in her coronation robes.

A burst of laughter erupted from the room to the right, and it served to increase Brownlee's impatience. 'Dear boy,' he said, 'please inform His Excellency that I am here on a matter of some urgency.'

'Tell you what,' said Lieutenant Droxford as though he were about to suggest a game. 'I'll go in and let H.E. know that you're here, and tell him that you're quite prepared to wait until he's ready to see you.'

'Just tell him I'm here!' Brownlee cried, his voice losing some of its more mellow notes.

At that moment, the dining-room doors opened and a galliard of imposing women, led by Mrs Maclean, processed across the hall. The three men bowed courteously, and the ladies inclined their heads and fluttered their fans as though they were minor royalty. When they had disappeared, Droxford said, 'There you are! Perfect! I'll tell H.E. you want to see him.' With that, he marched smartly into the dining room and, seconds later, reappeared. 'H.E. says you're to wait in here.'

'You told him it was urgent?' asked Brownlee crossly.

'Rather.'

They passed under the portrait of the young Queen and into a sombre room which was the Governor's study. Once more, Droxford left the two visitors alone but promised to return shortly with the Governor. Brownlee paced up and down, occasionally pausing to study a large map of the British Isles that covered almost an entire wall. 'Extraordinary,' he would mutter after each inspection and then continue his tour of the room. Michael sat on the edge of a cavernous armchair, awed by the occasion, for it was the first time in his career that he had set foot in the Governor's residence.

They waited for almost half an hour. Then, to a chorus of 'Hurry back old boy,' and 'Can't guarantee there'll be any port left,' the door opened to admit Colonel Maclean, the Governor of British Kaffraria.

He was a gigantic figure, almost seven feet tall, broad, with a head as round as a cannon ball, and he was extraordinarily impressive in his dress uniform, like a glittering red and white obelisk. 'My dear Brownlee,' said Maclean. 'How very nice of you to call. Please forgive me for keeping you waiting so long.'

Michael was disarmed: the giant exuded charm to match his size; all tension vanished, and the Cape Colony suddenly seemed secure and protected. When Brownlee presented his assistant, the Governor said, 'I'm very pleased to meet you, Mr Thompson. I hear you're doing a first-class job. Pray be seated.'

Port was offered, and cigars; Michael accepted both, Brownlee neither. When all were settled in the grey haze of cigar smoke, Maclean began by stating that, in his opinion, there was no cause for alarm; Brownlee countered by saying he was not so certain. The Governor then declared that he wished there was a way of convincing the colonists that there was no need for further vigilance, and that he could put an end to all the rumours. Michael became aware of a disconcerting mannerism displayed by his host: Maclean always repeated the last few words of the previous speaker's remarks so that Michael found himself waiting for this reaction, rather than concentrating on the more important points of the discussion, as when Brownlee stated the purpose of this visit:

'I received today, sir,' the Commissioner said, 'a message from Sandile.'

'Message from Sandile. Now, wait a moment, I get very confused with these Kaffir names. Do take it slowly, won't you? Sandile. Which one's he?'

'Sandile, sir, is the Chief of all the Gaika.'

'All the Gaika. Now I'm right in saying, am I not, that these are the chaps who are resident in British Kaffraria.'

'Precisely.'

'Precisely. In fact, they're the chaps under my control.'

'That is correct, sir. Sandile is second only to his brother Kreli, Chief of the Gcaleka and Paramount Chief of the Xhosa nation, who lives outside your territory, sir, to the north.'

'To the north. Tight rein now, Mr Brownlee, must get this straight. Sandile: chief of the Gaika. Kreli: chief of the Gcaleka, but being the elder brother, also chief of the whole damn lot.' The Governor was only really interested in the population under his authority from the standpoint of a military strategist. Names, tribes, rivalries, he maintained, only confused the issue.

279

'It appears that Sandile would have us believe that he has intercepted various exchanges between his brother Kreli, and Mosheshwe, Chief of the Sotho.'

'Of the Sotho. Ah! Know him: Mosheshwe. He's the chap who gave us a damn good hiding at Berea.'

'That's the one, sir. Evidently, Kreli has been urging a military alliance between the Xhosa and the Sotho. A military alliance, I need hardly add, to defeat the British. According to the messenger, Mosheshwe has been reluctant to entertain such an alliance since he considers Kreli's warriors less than first-rate.'

'Less than first-rate. So they are! We routed them three years ago.'

'Mosheshwe, it seems, has accused the Xhosa warriors of being more interested in their cattle than in fighting. Kreli has made various offers to Mosheshwe pledging, in the event of victory, all the land from the sea to the Kei River.'

'The Kei River. Damn cheek, not his to give. It's mine!' He chuckled, and looked at the others to join him; Michael dutifully smiled.

'Mosheshwe, so the intelligence insists, is not to be tempted,' Brownlee continued. 'His response to Kreli's offer was to ask for, in the messenger's words, "proof of your people's will to fight and an assurance that they will not immediately sue for peace the moment their cattle is captured".'

'Cattle is captured. We've heard nothing of this. What d'you make of it, Mr Brownlee?'

'I think we must take it seriously, sir. That is why I am here. Kreli was humiliated by our victory in '53, and I've no doubt he's looking for revenge.'

'For revenge.' Maclean frowned. 'What d'you want me to do? Send a force in?'

'No, sir. That is precisely what I do not want.'

'Do not want. I don't think I follow your line of thought.'

'In the first place, sir, I suspect that this may be an exercise by Sandile to discredit his brother in our eyes. If it is not, then, of course, it must be taken seriously as a threat to our security.'

'To our security, precisely. What do you propose?'

'I intend to visit Sandile and investigate the matter thoroughly. At the same time, Mr Thompson will visit one of the lesser chiefs to see if they have received embassies from Kreli, so that we may get a more detailed picture of what is going on.'

This was news to Michael but he did not in the least mind the idea of an additional tour of inspection. He sat, sipping his port, and puffing on his cigar, feeling that he was at the very centre of events.

Brownlee said, 'What I want from you, sir, is your agreement to my plan: that you will not send troops in to British Kaffraria unless you have proof positive that the Xhosa are going to invade the Colony.'

'Invade the Colony. But that may be too late.'

'I think not, with respect. I will only obtain the truth from Sandile if he does not feel threatened by your soldiers. Kreli, on the other hand, resides far to the north. If he and Mosheshwe are to join forces then they will have to move their armies a long way before they invade the Colony. What I am asking, sir, is this: you will hold back your forces unless Kreli and Mosheshwe march south.'

'March south.' Without warning, Maclean turned sharply to Michael and asked, 'What about the Gaika themselves, aren't they in a position to attack us? What happens if this is a trick by Sandile to make us think that his brother's active, while all the time he himself is spoiling for a fight?'

For a moment, a look of panic crossed Michael's face, but he quickly recovered. 'Your Excellency, I have recently returned from Kaffraria and, in my opinion, the Gaika are in a very depressed and despondent state. They did not seem to me to be a people preparing for war.'

'For war. Well said. I'll believe that. My reports contain exactly the same assessment. There's no evidence of military training, or troop movements, nothing but damned messengers haring about the place. All right, Mr Brownlee, you and your Mr Thompson go out and investigate. I'll hold back my lads unless I'm forced to act. Does that suit you?'

'It does indeed. Thank you very much, sir.'

Maclean rose, signifying that the meeting was at an end. On his way to the door, he paused, and for a long moment, looked intently at Brownlee. 'I'll tell you what puzzles me, Mr Brownlee: how do you give a prospective ally proof of your people's will to fight? Not an easy one. Well! Goodnight, gentlemen, thank you for calling on me.'

Michael returned to his home that evening bubbling with excitement after his conference with the Governor, and with the prospect of his impending journey. But when he entered the door and called, as was his custom, 'I'm home!' no sound greeted him. Again he called, 'Alice! Alice!' Silence. Then, on the hall table, he saw a note propped up against the oil lamp:

> I cannot stay another night alone. I am going to Ma and Pa. A letter came. It is on your desk.
>
> Alice.

Excitement gave way to depression: an awful loneliness consumed him and he sat down on the bottom stair and re-read the note. He stared at the emptiness surrounding him, craned his neck to look up the shadowy stair-well, as if to make sure there was really no one about. Then, remembering he had sent his wife a message to say he would be late, anger transformed his mood yet again. 'Selfish!' he said aloud and, taking the lamp, trudged up the stairs to his study.

On his desk was a letter with a London postmark. His heart quickened, and he tore open the envelope:

> My dear dear boy,
>
> Well, here I am in dear old London town. Not half big, I can tell you. And the heat! Somehow worse than Albany. I have a touch of the bronkials.
>
> I have been round my old haunts, but of course I know nobody any more, everyone is either dead or gone away. Funny to walk down the streets and not to hear a fellow say hello. I can't go a yard down any road in Grahamstown without stopping for a chat.
>
> You remember me telling you about your Uncle Charlie, your mother's brother who first mentioned the Cape of Good Hope to me? Well, he's in Newgate prison for selling a house that wasn't his. God is just.
>
> I cannot yet say I have made up my mind to stay, but will let you know soon as.
>
> Kind regards to your family, the Filmores and all my friends. Write soon. I remain, your loving
>
> Father.

Soothed by the letter, Michael returned downstairs to the kitchen. He found a leg of cold chicken in the larder, and sat at the table to eat it. Both letters, he soon discovered, served to enlarge the loneliness which enveloped him. He missed his wife and father, for different reasons but with the same intensity. And then, realising the need to dispel the gloom, he decided that no purpose would be served by staying in Grahamstown a moment longer: he would leave at once for British Kaffraria.

He packed his bags, saddled his horse and rode off into the night and, this time, left no message for his wife.

21

Uthixo

I

Michael forded the Keiskama River near its mouth where it flows into the tranquil Indian Ocean; once he had gained the northern bank, and the sea slowly disappeared behind the hills to his right, he was within the territory of British Kaffraria. The peace he had always experienced inside these borders returned, and with it a sense of purpose. The transformation was clear to see even from the way he sat on his horse, more upright, more confident. He surveyed the flat, monotonous landscape as though he had created it with his own hands.

But he had not gone very far before his peace of mind was disturbed. He was wending his way through a dense and shadowy copse when his horse reared, and whinnied with fright. Michael peered through the close-growing bushes but could see nothing. At first, he thought perhaps that a wild animal was prowling nearby but there was no sound or any sign of life. He dug his spurs into the horse, but the animal would not go forward. Uneasy, Michael took out his pistol, dismounted, and led the horse through the copse out into the open.

Returning to the saddle, he looked back and thought he saw movement in the bushes. For many minutes, he sat watching the copse, but all appeared peaceful and still. The horse jogged on at walking pace.

The feeling that he was being watched and followed persisted, but there seemed to be nowhere for anyone to hide, except for the sporadic crop of rocks or tree clumps. He saw no shadow, heard no footsteps, yet he was convinced that there was someone keeping close.

By mid-morning he arrived at the first village which was ruled by the chief, Umhala. It was not a large village, some thirty huts, grouped in a traditional semi-circle and, in the opening of the arc, stood the cattle byre made of brushwood. In all such villages the cattle was kept in the very centre, in pride of place, for cattle was the people's wealth and livelihood. The huts were built on a low ridge and faced eastwards to catch the early sun.

Almost at once, Michael became suspicious. No one came out to greet him, which was unique in his experience. The Xhosa were a friendly people: civil, polite, talkative, hospitable. He had always been welcomed before, always asked whence he had come and whither he was going. This day, no one appeared; it was as if the village was deserted. Then he saw another unusual sight: never before had he observed so few cattle in the byre, and never had he seen the byre guarded, but here, two young warriors stood on opposite sides of the brushwood fence, their spears at the ready. Yet Michael had seen cattle left unattended in open country, sometimes for two or three days; the Xhosa respected the property of their brothers, why now, suddenly, should they find it necessary to mount guard?

As he dismounted, he received the first acknowledgement of his presence: in silence, people emerged from their huts, crawling, for the doorways were low, sometimes no higher than three feet; once outside, they sat in groups and stared at him, alert, watchful. And Michael noticed that there were few men among the villagers, mostly young girls and old women. At last, from the largest hut, Umhala himself emerged. Michael approached him and, as was the custom, the two sat on their haunches, facing each other.

'You are welcome,' Umhala said, but his eyes were cold and distant.

'I am pleased to be here,' replied Michael. 'Do you not ask me whence I come and wither I am going?' The chief remained silent. 'Am I to ask you whether you have learned any new dances or tunes?' which was a question demanded by the Xhosa love of formality.

'We have learned nothing,' Umhala replied sullenly.

Michael realised for the first time that Umhala was unattended by his advisers and councillors, something he could not recall ever having seen before. For, in their delicate and complex political structure, the chiefs were not autocrats. Even Kreli, the Paramount Chief, was subject to a council. It was the method the people employed to participate in their own affairs: councillors informed the chiefs, both at local and national level, of the people's sentiments, and they were free to admonish any chief with great freedom and truth. And if the chief abused his authority or treated his council's admonition with contempt, then the people showed their displeasure, not by taking up arms against him but, more effectively, by gradual emigration, leaving the domain of the chief, and thus robbing him of his power. It occurred to Michael that perhaps Umhala had been the object of such a demonstration, although he knew the man to be a good and just chief, and well loved.

'Where is the *ilizwe*?' Michael asked, which was the name for the local council.

'They hunt,' replied Umhala.

'*All* the men hunt?' asked Michael, looking round at the women who surrounded them.

'All the men hunt.'

A long pause ensued, in which Michael considered the best way to deal with this unaccustomed recalcitrance. He said, 'Where is the ambassador from Kreli?'

Umhala showed no reaction whatsoever. He continued to stare at Michael. 'There is no ambassador from the Great Chief,' he replied.

'And from Sandile?'

'There is no embassy from Sandile either.'

'Why are the cattle guarded?' Michael asked, hoping to catch the chief off guard.

'Why is your money guarded?' the chief replied.

'Have people been stealing your cattle?'

'It is better to guard before people steal than after.'

Michael's patience evaporated. 'Listen, Umhala, you want me to send the soldiers in and give you a bloody good hiding? You watch how you speak to me, you understand? There's something going on and I want to know what it is! Now you make up your mind to tell me, otherwise you'll be in trouble. Come on, boy, let me hear what you have to say.' He wore no mask now.

'I have nothing to say!' Umhala replied angrily.

'Watch your tone, you Kaffir bastard. I'm the boss here. You give me some respect otherwise you'll get it good and strong from the soldiers. Just remember who I am.'

'I remember who you are,' Umhala said as though it were a threat.

Then Umhala's dog appeared from a hut and in his mouth he was carrying a large piece of raw meat, devouring it hungrily. Michael was more astonished by this sight than anything else he had seen that morning.

'You feed your dog on meat now?' he asked.

'I feed my dog,' Umhala said.

'On best beef?'

'On food.'

Michael held up a threatening finger. 'You're in trouble, Umhala. I'm not putting up with your insolence.' He took out his notebook. 'You're going to be punished: thirty strokes. I'm writing it down for the soldiers to see. They'll come and they'll give you thirty strokes, you understand?'

Umhala rose first, which was another act of insolence, for by doing so, he had failed to acknowledge Michael's superiority. When Michael stood, he said, 'I can make it forty, you know,' but he knew nothing was to be gained by persisting. He turned sharply, strode towards his horse, and mounted. As he turned to leave, he heard the distant sound of singing, and, far beyond the crescent of huts, saw the hunting party returning, a long line of men, carrying on poles their game. But when they drew closer, Michael realised that it was not game they were carrying, but oxen: two huge carcasses.

He called to Umhala, 'Do you hunt your own cattle now?' but received no reply. Instead, Umhala turned and crawled into his hut. Pale with anger, Michael dug his spurs into the horse, and galloped from the village.

Michael encountered the same insolence from three other chiefs. With each successive interview, he became more and more desperate, for he was not a man of natural authority, and robbed of respect for his official position, he was rendered impotent. A kind of panic rose in him, and he felt again what he had felt the night of the wake, at Sybille's graveside, a confusion of remorse and self-assertion. 'Among the people I am God!' he had said, and now that no longer appeared to be so. It was as simple as this: in the Colony he was a nonentity; but, here, he was a man of importance. Or had been: it was as though his entire world was in danger of disintegrating.

He rode for some miles and eventually his anger and panic subsided; in their place came determination. He had convinced himself that Umhala would not have behaved in that fashion without encouragement; nor would the others: he was beginning to suspect a conspiracy, for the Xhosa always acted in concert, almost never autonomously. Michael wished he could discuss his concerns with Brownlee: why had they hunted their own oxen? and why guard the byre? and the dog gorged on prime beef . . .

By evening, he sheltered near a solitary rock that rose out of the earth like a gigantic fist. While he sat chewing biltong, the dried sinew of the springbok, he again had the strongest impression that he was being watched. Once more he drew his pistol and walked slowly round the base of the rock, but saw nothing. He scanned the ground for footprints, but the earth was too dry and hard for a man to leave any impression. From a height, he decided, he would be able to survey the area, and so he began to climb the rock, until he reached a ledge half-way up. He gazed out at the desolate landscape, but there was no sign of life. He rested for a while, and was about to descend when he saw, a mile or so to the north, a covered wagon approaching, and he watched it come nearer and nearer. It was not long before he could identify it as Sybille Henning's, but he could not see anyone at the reins.

2

In the evening light, the wagon looked like a spectre trundling over the scrub, and when Michael, at last, reached it and could still see no driver, he was possessed by an irrational fear, as though he were confronted by an apparition.

He grabbed hold of the reins which were hanging loose over the ox's rump, and pulled the beast towards a cluster of bushes. Then he circled the wagon and saw immediately the bloodstains on the canopy. Raising the rear flap, he peered into the back: there lay Gwali, his left side soaked in blood, his pallor ominously grey. By edging his horse nearer, Michael was able to scramble aboard.

The blood flowed from a wound in Gwali's shoulder, but Michael could not easily tell how deep it was. He leaned close to the stricken man's chest and listened: the heartbeat was still strong. And, as Michael crouched there, his eye caught sight of the gold cross round Gwali's neck, and he was seized by jealousy again, as though Miss Henning had just that moment given it to her latest convert. Michael was surprised by the intensity of the feeling. He wanted to pull the chain from the man's neck, but Gwali stirred, moaning with pain.

Quickly, Michael searched the back of the wagon, hoping to find medical supplies of one kind or another. He saw a small wooden box, opened it and found inside Sybille's family Bible and her diaries, page after page of it, the handwriting at first neat and orderly, but developing later into a scrawl which punctuated mostly blank pages. He closed the lid of the box, for he felt he must not intrude upon her privacy, yet he longed to read it, for no other reason but to know what she had said about him.

'Jesus, Jesus,' Gwali called in a faint voice and Michael returned his attentions to the injured man, gently slapping his face and saying, 'Come on, Gwali, it's me, master Michael, open your eyes.'

But Gwali continued to mutter deliriously. One word caught Michael's ear: *amagotya*, which means unbeliever. 'No,' Michael said. 'You are not *amagotya*, you are *tamba*,' meaning the opposite. At this, Gwali opened his eyes for the first time and there was no mistaking the terror they expressed. 'No! No!' he shouted. 'I am not *tamba*! I am *amagotya*!'

'You believe in our Lord Jesus Christ?' Michael demanded, but Gwali lapsed once more into semi-consciousness.

It took Michael a little time to make him comfortable. Using the water from his canteen sparingly, he bathed the wound which was not as serious as he had first thought, but Gwali was weak from the loss of blood. In the corner, under a pile of boxes and books, Michael found a bundle of tattered patchwork quilts, stained and faded. One he covered Gwali with, the other he laid across the box that contained Sybille's diary, making it into an improvised pillow. Slowly he trickled water onto Gwali's lips, until the injured man was able to drink.

Night had come, cold and bleak. Low, crimped clouds obscured the stars and the moon, and an icy wind knifed its way across the barren veld. In the back of the wagon, Gwali began to shiver, his teeth chattering uncontrollably, and Michael, chilled too, gathered wood and built a fire near the bushes where the ox was tethered. Carrying Gwali like a child, he laid him near the warmth, covered him with more of the quilts; he wrapped himself in the blanket he had rolled into his pack.

Again Gwali opened his eyes and saw Michael as though for the first time. 'Master, master,' Gwali said, 'there is blood on your hand.'

'You have been hurt, Gwali. It is your blood.'

'No, no, no!' he cried, becoming agitated. 'It is the blood of *uthixo*! Put your hands into the wounds and you will believe!'

'Gwali, you have been wounded!' Michael said sharply. 'Who has done this to you?'

'Tell me, tell me, master, does the Lord Jesus live?'

'He lives,' said Michael.

'Is He risen from the dead?'

'He is risen from the dead.'

'Is He in Heaven with His father?'

'He is with His father.'

'Oh God, oh Lord, oh God, oh Lord,' Gwali sobbed. 'Do all the people rise from the dead?'

'Oh come on, boy, you know better than I do,' answered Michael. 'The people rise on the Day of Judgement, you know that!'

'For my people it is near.'

'It is not near for any of us!' said Michael.

'It is, it is, master, for my people—' he struggled up on to one elbow, but Michael restrained him. 'The people prepare to die!'

Michael, holding the blanket tightly, crawled towards Gwali. 'That's what Miss Henning said. What does it mean?' he asked urgently. 'Today, I saw cattle guarded in villages, and oxen hunted in the field. I saw a dog fed on rich meat, and the chiefs spat on me. What does it mean, Gwali? What does it mean?'

'*Uthixo* stirs!' Gwali answered.

'What?'

'Jesus is strong, and they war on Him.'

'Who wars on Jesus?'

'*Uthixo* is stirring.'

'Tell me, Gwali.'

'They'll kill all the *amagotya*!'

'All the unbelievers? You mean those who do not believe in *uthixo*, but in Jesus, is that what you mean? Is that why you are wounded?'

'They will kill all those who do not believe!'

'Believe what, Gwali?'

And slowly, bit by bit, between bouts of delirium and startling lucidity, Michael pieced together the story Gwali had to tell.

BOOK SIX

22

Nongquase

Across the river Nxuba (which you call the Great Fish, Gwali said), across the river you call Keiskama, beyond the mountains, the beloved Amatolas, lie dull, lifeless plains. Here, the Xhosa, the people, driven from their mountains three years before, now live. The wars that swept them northwards, ever northwards, had been bloody and, so their enemy each time thought or hoped, decisive. True it was, Gwali said, that the people had lost spirit: they turned sad eyes towards the Amatolas and longed for their former homes.

You must know that the Xhosa are a nation, as the English or the Zulus and the French are nations, but they do not reside in a kingdom, nor are they ruled by a king. (It was Gwali's way to explain with pride, as though to a child.) Rather, he said, think of the Xhosa as one large and mighty family, a cluster of chiefdoms, some more important than others, depending on their ties, by blood, to the most powerful chiefdom of all, senior in lineage to the Great House, whose head was the Paramount Chief of all the people, Kreli, Chief of the Gcaleka, to whom all owed allegiance.

In one of the lesser chiefdoms, whose dominion extended along the banks of the Gxara river, there was a village, not large, twenty or thirty huts. (From this village, Gwali said, my parents came, and many of my family still live there.) In one of the huts, lived a girl, thirteen years old; her name was Nongquase. She was small for her years, but beautiful: her face delicately shaped by pronounced cheekbones that gently curved to her chin. Her eyes were large, but deep set, and she exuded a modesty much admired by her elders. She was an unremarkable little girl—or so everyone thought—obedient, hard-working and placid. Her only distinction was that her uncle, the brother of her dead father, was Mhalakaza, the most renowed of Xhosa seers, an important man, and much feared by some, but not by all. (Mhalakaza is my uncle too, said Gwali, through my dead mother. This girl Nongquase, my cousin, I have never seen, for she was born long after I left the village.)

On a certain morning in May of this year 1856 (the year of Our Lord, Gwali said), Nongquase woke early and suddenly, as though startled by a noise. In the dawn gloom, her eyes traced the circular framework of saplings that formed the roof of her hut: they were tied with bark and covered with woven reed mats and grass and, because she was fatherless and poor, the inside was not mudded over as other huts were. She stared at the low doorway under which even she had to crouch in order to pass. The moment she was awake she felt, as she had done for as long as she could remember, the closeness of the place; she sniffed the stifling air, and listened to the peaceful breathing of her sisters, which produced a kind of panic in her. It was apt that they called these places *indlu yempuku*, the mouse's house; it was especially apt for Nongquase who, in many ways, Gwali said, was as timid and as nervous as a mouse.

Careful not to wake the others, Nongquase slipped out of the hut. It was a cool, cloudy morning and she thought no one was about until she saw her mother collecting grain from the flask-shaped pit to the rear of the huts. The two waved, and walked towards each other.

'Are your sisters awake?' asked her mother.

'No.'

'Could you not sleep?' Nongquase did not answer but gazed at her feet tracing patterns in the dusty earth. 'Did you dream again?' for often Nongquase had cried out in the night, and spoken of demons who invaded her sleep.

'No, mother,' she answered truthfully, but refrained from confiding the feeling of alarm experienced on waking.

'You can dress and help me.'

'I—I was going to the river to bathe,' said the girl.

'Very well, But put something on. It is cold.'

Nongquase, without going back into the hut, reached in and withdrew a cowhide cloak belonging to her elder sister. Wrapping it round her slim and fragile body, she waved again to her mother and ran from the village, past the cattle byre, down to the Gxara, dropped her cloak on the steep bank and waded into the icy water. She cried out against the cold and then, holding her breath, plunged full length into the stream and when she emerged, exhilarated and refreshed, she felt that somehow she had shaken off the fears of night and of waking, and with high spirits, she greeted the new day.

Suddenly she became still. Further up, on the far bank, she saw cattle grazing, guarded by men she could not recognise. She was certain they had not been there when she first entered the water and, what frightened her now, was that they seemed to make no noise: the cattle trod silently, and when the men spoke or laughed, as one did on seeing her, she was unable to hear their voices. The man who laughed greeted her, raising his hand in salute, but Nongquase could not find the courage to return his courtesy. And then it occurred to the girl that this man was her father whom she had never known, and somehow there was no doubting the knowledge: her whole being confirmed it with absolute certainty. She took a step forward, the water eddying round her thighs, held out her arms as though to welcome an embrace, but the man turned, rejoined his friends and was gone without looking back at her. For many minutes the girl stared at the place where she had last seen them, mistrusting the evidence of her eyes, blinking repeatedly as if, by doing so, the strangers would reappear. Then she saw, or thought she saw, the horns of the oxen among the rushes, as though the cattle were being driven deep into the river. After that, there was nothing: just the bushes, the reeds, the muddy bank, and the vista of uninterrupted scrub. It was the quiet that frightened her, the dreadful calm of morning. Then a vulture screeched above her head, shattering the silence. Nongquase turned, scrambled up the bank and, grabbing her sister's cloak, ran back towards the village.

The inhabitants were waking, stretching, yawning, greeting each other and the day. Over a score of fires, the women were cooking a mixture of grain and milk, and the men sat in groups discussing their plans for the day's hunting which they regarded not only as a means of procuring the necessities of life, but also as a sport of which they were passionately fond. As a rule, they hunted in large parties, which became animated and active social events. When they found game in open fields, they tried to surround the animals, or to drive them to some narrow pass where the hunters stationed themselves on either side and, as the herd rushed between them, they would pierce the animals with showers of assegais. This day they were planning an especially large hunt and the talk was raucous and lively.

Only the occupant of one hut had not emerged, and he was Nongquase's uncle, the seer, Mhalakaza. His four wives were already at work cooking his breakfast—the Xhosa preferred all activities to be communal—but Mhalakaza himself was still asleep. (He did not go out on the hunt, Gwali explained, for he considered it unsuitable to a man in his position.) He was only just forty, but because he did not have a tooth in his head, he looked a good deal older, and when he spoke he made a sort of hissing sound which could be both frightening and comic. (The young men called him 'The Whistler' and the more impudent, 'Windy'.) The voices of the others, at last, woke him and although he tried to shut out the sound by stuffing his fingers in his ears, it was futile. Irritably, he rose, beginning his day, as was his custom, with a murmured incantation to the shades, the spirits of the dead: his brother, his sister, his parents, and all his ancestors reaching back in time to the source of all power, *uthixo*. Then, he dressed in his wild animal pelts, and his leopard-skin cloak which distinguished him as a man to be reckoned with. Mhalakaza was something of a dandy: he pushed handsome ivory bracelets on to his arms, fixed his copper ear-rings and, round his neck, he hung an elaborate collar of iron beads interspersed with buttons traded at the Kaffir Fair in Fort Wiltshire. Thus, satisfied with his appearance, he crawled out of the hut.

The bad temper caused by being woken earlier than he had wished, still pricked him: he looked about for someone to vent it on, saw his wives and, at once, scolded them for not stirring his breakfast dish often enough. Cross-legged, he sat before his hut, trying to look enigmatic as though he alone possessed a great secret, and wanted nothing better than to confide it to someone. (They laughed at him, Gwali told Michael, because Kreli, the Paramount Chief, had once described him as a buffoon, which gave the people licence to mock him.)

Then Nongquase returned, shivering, from the river. 'Here is some food,' said her mother, but the young girl did not listen, and ran straight into her little hut, into the dark, and crouched against the wall, covering herself with animal skins, for she was still gripped by the fear of what she had seen on the banks of the Gxara. Her mother thought of this behaviour as unusual in one so docile and followed the girl into the hut.

Nongquase's teeth were chattering and her skin had pimpled over from the cold and fear. 'What troubles you, Nongquase?' asked her mother.

'I am cold,' replied the girl.

'Did you bathe?'

'I did.'

Her mother felt the girl's brow which was warm to the touch. 'But you are not cold,' she said.

'I am, mother, I am, I am cold!' insisted the girl.

'Are you sure, Nongquase, that something did not happen by the river?'

'No, mother, nothing happened.'

'Nongquase, look at me—'

And then it burst from her: 'Oh, mother! I am frightened!' The story tumbled out: how she had seen the silent cattle and the silent men, how one had greeted her whom she knew to be her father.

It was this last piece of information that disturbed the older woman. A young girl dreaming of the shades was one thing, but actually seeing them in waking moments was another. She said, 'I will fetch your uncle Mhalakaza. He will know what to do.'

At this, Nongquase sat up and took hold of her mother's arms. 'Oh please, mother, do not send my uncle to me! Please!'

'If you have seen your father, you must tell Mhalakaza!' and she left Nongquase alone.

Nongquase feared her uncle not because of his knowledge of the shadow world, but because of his predilections here on earth. She dreaded being alone with him, for, several times in the past, he had sat beside her allowing his hands to creep beneath her cloak, finding her new and promising breasts, pinching, between thumb and forefinger, her untried nipples; or tightly gripping her thighs; or resting his hand on her buttocks. And when she had complained, he threatened her with terrifying eternity after death.

Presently, the girl's mother returned with Mhalakaza. 'Tell your uncle what you told me,' said the woman, and Nongquase, her legs tucked under her, eyes modestly downcast, once more recounted the story. When she had finished, she chanced to look up and saw on her uncle's face an expression of intense excitement; he was staring, but at nothing in particular, and he snapped his toothless gums up and down as though gnawing an invisible bone. Mhalakaza turned to the girl's mother. 'Leave us!' he ordered. A stifled cry of protest escaped from Nongquase but it was not heeded: her mother crawled through the low opening, and Nongquase was alone with the seer.

'Girl,' he began, 'have you told me the truth?'

For a long while, Nongquase did not answer. Pale sunlight had filtered into the hut, and strange shadows played across her uncle's face, accentuating his pinched cheeks and his bulging forehead; he appeared more terrifying than ever, and his jaws were never still. 'Answer me, Nongquase,' he commanded.

'I am telling you the truth, my uncle,' she said at last.

'How did the cattle appear?'

'I saw the horns of beautiful oxen peeping from beneath the rushes.'

'And you saw your father?'

'Yes, my uncle.'

'Your father died when you were a babe, how did you know it was he?'

'I knew, my uncle.'

'How did he look?' asked Mhalakaza, but the girl could not find the words; she shrugged uncomfortably. 'Was he tall?' he asked.

'Not very tall, my uncle.'

'Taller than me?'

'Yes, my uncle, taller than you.'

'How were his eyes, round or long?'

'Long, my uncle.'

'Was he fat or thin?'

'Thin, my uncle.'

'And did you not hear his voice?'

'No, my uncle. I heard no sound from him, or from the others, or from the cattle.'

'These other men you saw, were they of our people?'

'I could not say, my uncle.'

'Think, girl.' Mhalakaza said fiercely. 'Were they dressed like your father, were they of our colour, or were they white like those across the Nxuba?'

'Of our colour,' the girl replied.

'And wore our clothes?' Nongquase hesitated; Mhalakaza persisted. 'Well,' he demanded, 'were they dressed like your father or in some other way?'

'Some other way.'

'Girl, take care what you say. These others were of our colour, yes or no?'

'Yes, my uncle.'

'But they were not dressed like us?'

'No, my uncle.'

'How were they dressed then?'

Again Nongquase paused; she said, 'Like soldiers.'

Mhalakaza shuddered, and then nodded many, many times. 'Yes, yes,' he said but not really to Nongquase, 'yes, it is good.' He rose. 'You are to stay here in this hut. You must talk to no one, not even your mother. Only to me must you talk.'

'Yes, my uncle,' she said and watched him crawl from the hut, his leopard-skin cloak catching in the narrow opening. When he had gone, Nongquase lay down and almost cried with relief, for Mhalakaza had not touched her; he had been too preoccupied with her story, and she was grateful. But, as she lay there, rejoicing in what she thought of as an escape, a shadow passed across the entrance of the hut and she saw a young man with an assegai place himself outside on guard. All at once, panic returned, the panic of a mouse in *indlu yempuku*, trapped.

After Mhalakaza had ordered the guard, he visited the chief, an ageing, ineffectual man, and recounted Nongquase's experience.

'What does it mean?' asked the chief.

'It means that the hunt must be cancelled this day,' said Mhalakaza. 'I am going down to the banks of the river to discover the truth of this matter. When I return, you must hold the *ilizwe*,' which meant a council of the elders.

The chief had no alternative but to agree. Mhalakaza strode through the groups of disappointed hunters and made his way down to the river bank. (Two or three boys tried to follow him, Gwali said, but the seer noticed and said he would punish them on his return if they continued to disturb his secret and private deliberations.)

The village waited for his return. The men had not altogether given up hope of a hunt that day, for most of them judged Mhalakaza to be a self-assertive man who had, for many years, been looking for a way to increase his importance throughout the Xhosa nation. 'Nothing will come of it,' they said. 'Mhalakaza is up to his tricks again.' One or two were less certain; whispers of Nongquase's story had reached their ears and the fact that she had claimed to see a dead man, her father, was not something that could be easily brushed aside.

In due course, Mhalakaza returned from the river. (Many, Gwali said, noticed a difference in his bearing, more upright, more determined and yet, unusually subdued.) The chief called the *ilizwe*, and Mhalakaza stood in the centre of the gathering and addressed them. (All the people of the village, Gwali said, came to listen.)

He told them of what Nongquase had seen. 'I questioned her closely,' he said, 'and from the way she described her dead father, my brother, I was convinced she had seen him. She also told me that these strangers were of our colour but dressed like soldiers. So, I went down to the river to see for myself.' He paused dramatically. (One of the young boys called out, 'We know all that!' but, fortunately, Mhalakaza did not hear.)

'I must tell you, my chief, that when I reached the banks of the Gxara, I saw no one.' A sigh of disappointment, mocking from the men, genuine from the women, greeted the news. 'But—' Mhalakaza said, raising a forefinger. 'But, I looked along the bank where Nongquase said she had seen them, and what did I discover? Freshly-made cattle tracks in the earth, the print of soldiers' boots and, even more wondrous, the outline of a naked foot! And so, while I was thus engaged, upon my knees, examining these signs, a shadow fell across the earth. I looked up, and there, there before my eyes, stood my dead brother!' (Now, even the men gasped in wonder.) ' "Do you know me, Mhalakaza?" my brother asked. "I know you, my brother," I replied. "Go back to the village, Mhalakaza, purify yourself for three days, and on the fourth day, sacrifice an ox. Then, and only then, may you return to the river." I thanked my brother for these words and he had one more thing to say. "Tell Nongquase, my daughter, that I could not speak to her, because I can only speak to those who have ears to listen." And with that he was gone. I saw no others, no soldiers of our colour, no one but my brother.'

The silence he had hoped for gripped the assembly. He alone stood, proud and straight, all eyes on him, everyone waiting for his next pronouncement. 'Now,' he said in a solemn voice that many at the back could not hear, 'I will go into my hut and purify my body and mind for three days as my brother ordered.' He turned and marched majestically towards his hut.

For three days and nights they heard him chanting, crying out, purging himself of evil spirits. (The man from whom Gwali had this story said he happened to look into the hut on the second day, and saw Mhalakaza stiff as an assegai, eyes wide but sightless, spittle running down his chin.) On the fourth day, he emerged and before the whole village sacrificed an ox. Then, the people formed themselves into two lines, and between them Mhalakaza walked, once more returning to the river.

Now the people waited in silence. Gone were the doubts, for they all knew that it was death to a seer who mocked the shades. Patiently, fearfully, they waited. Towards sunset, Mhalakaza returned. He walked with a new determination, confident and proud, and approached the chief, but his message was for the old man's ears alone. (Those who watched, Gwali said, could see the terror on the chief's face.) Mhalakaza did not address the people. Instead, a messenger was despatched at once to Kreli, the Paramount Chief. All Mhalakaza said was, 'I saw my brother again, and the soldiers also this time. They told me many things. Great sacrifices are demanded of us.'

'Who are they,' asked someone, 'these soldiers?'

'They are the Russians,' replied Mhalakaza, 'black like ourselves. And they have come to drive the English back into the sea.' And with that, he disappeared once more into his hut while his messenger sped to Kreli.

2

The distance it would take you thirty days to travel, Gwali said, one of my people can cover in ten. Like a deer, Mhalakaza's messenger ran, north across the flat country, leaving behind village after village, through the vast tract of unfriendly land between the Keiskama and the Great Kei Rivers, which you call British Kaffraria, and some call Kaffirland. And the people who saw the messenger pass were filled with expectation: what did the seer Mhalakaza have to say to the Paramount Chief?

The messenger had never seen a village as large as the village of Kreli. More than a hundred huts, arranged in a crescent moon, on a high, commanding ridge, facing east and the rising sun. The messenger first beheld the great *kraal* from a distance in the early light of an autumn dawn, when the earth was as still as on the day of Creation. And there, before his eyes, like a string of shining beads, was the centre of all earthly power, the palace of the Great Chief.

When he entered the gates, the messenger's eyes grew large at the sight of so many cattle, and the man trembled with fear at the noise of the royal village wakening, of the shouts and cries, of the bustle and the movement. He trembled too, knowing in whose presence he would soon speak the dreadful message of his master, Mhalakaza.

Two warriors, tall and strong, wearing the feathers of the crane in their headbands, held their spears to the messenger's throat. 'I come from Mhalakaza,' he said, 'with a message for the Great Chief.' One ran off and disappeared inside the largest hut. The sun rose higher; perhaps it was noon when the warrior returned and beckoned the messenger to join him.

'You will wait here,' he said, and the messenger sat, with many others, in a large covered area through which one must pass to reach the Chief. Men came and went, chiefs, warriors, ambassadors, a constant, shifting procession of men each more gorgeously attired than the last. Once he heard laughter, and the four guards who stood at the door laughed too, and the messenger guessed that he had heard the voice of Kreli himself.

An old man was seated beside the messenger, knowledgeable and wise; he took it upon himself to inform the stranger of the comings and goings until the newcomer's head burst with the wonder of such activity: 'That is the ambassador of Mosheshwe, chief of the Sothos. Now Kreli receives the legates of the Mfengu, the Pondo and the Thembu. For you must know that we are surrounded on all sides by other nations and it is the Great Chief's wish to unite all in one mighty alliance.'

'*Hau!*' exclaimed the messenger, which is the sound of astonishment and admiration.

'Here is the ambassador of Sandile, chief of the Gaika, the second in our nation, younger brother of Kreli.'

'*Hau!*'

Towards evening, when the torches were lit, and the shadows doubled the number who waited, a young man passed through, for whom all stood. 'That is Dema,' explained the old man. 'He, too, is brother of the Chief. He has a wise head even though he is young and to him above all, the great Kreli listens.'

At last, a guard called, 'The messenger from Mhalakaza,' and the man, his heart thumping, stood and raised his hand. 'Come,' said the guard.

Through one doorway he passed, then a second, and a third until he found himself in an enormous hut, where the roof seemed as large as the sky. Men stood in groups talking animatedly and none paid attention to the messenger who followed the guard. Then, the messenger recognised Dema leaning over, talking to a man who sat on a throne which was bathed in leopard skin. The messenger fell to his knees, for he was in the presence of the Chief of Chiefs, Kreli, chief of the Gcaleka, chief of the Xhosa.

The messenger dared not look up, but from under his brows he could just see the royal hands playing with the leopard's tail. The guard said, 'The messenger from Mhalakaza,' and prodded the man, who raised his head and found himself looking into the eyes of the Chief. (I have seen him once, Gwali said, he was short and square and handsome, but now he is fat because for three years he has not waged war.)

'You have come a great distance,' Kreli said. 'You passed through many villages?'

'I did, Great Chief,' replied the messenger but his voice sounded as though it belonged to another.

'You travelled the length of British Kaffraria?' He spat out the words and showed his teeth.

'I did, Great Chief.'

'And is it true that the villages cannot breathe because they herd them together like cattle?'

'It is so, Great Chief. I did not run more than an hour without seeing a village.'

The reply caused Kreli to look up at Dema and to shake his head, but there was also danger in his eyes. 'And the people sit and stare at the sun, and the young men do nothing but hunt, and the women gossip, is that not so?' But he did not give time for the messenger to answer. Turning again to Dema, he said, 'I have this from a hundred mouths. The people sit and die. They wait for old age.' Dema said nothing, and his face did not betray his thoughts. Kreli continued, restless and yet thoughtful. 'I will see Sandile's messenger again. We will have something to say to him. I will not be lied to! It is a matter for the *isizwe*!' which is the name of the highest council of the nation.

Dema, bony and sinewy, said, 'Perhaps, my brother, we should hear the message of Mhalakaza.' But Kreli was not ready yet to be diverted. He beckoned his brother closer and talked at speed into his ear, and Dema, in reply, said, loud enough for all to hear, 'What we seek is the hope of victory. The people know what they would gain!'

With a dismissing gesture, Kreli silenced him. In the hall, the others fell silent, too. 'Come now,' said Kreli, still angry, 'the message from Mhalakaza.'

'Great Chief, Kreli of the Gcaleka and the Xhosa, greetings from your servant Mhalakaza.'

'Yes, yes,' said Kreli, fidgeting with the leopard skin. 'The message.'

'My master's message, Great Chief, is for your ears alone.'

Kreli scratched his head. 'Your master Mhalakaza gives me nothing but trouble!' he cried. 'Speak!'

The messenger's mouth was dry, and his tongue swollen. 'My master's message,' he whispered, 'is from the shades, Great Chief.'

A look of weariness passed over Kreli's face, and Dema's, too, who said, without lowering his voice, 'Are we to be troubled by the gibberings of a madman?'

Kreli addressed the messenger. 'This is the eighth message from the shades Mhalakaza has delivered in three years. You expect me to put these important persons to the trouble of going out and coming in? You speak now.'

Fear made speech almost impossible. 'I cannot, Great Chief, upon my death, I cannot.'

Such anger the messenger had never seen. Kreli clapped his hands, like thunder it sounded, and the hall was suddenly empty; but Dema remained and Kreli, seeing the look of doubt on the messenger's face, said, 'You will speak in front of my brother. Come now, your message.'

Nervously, the messenger began with the things the girl Nongquase had seen; gaining courage, he recounted Mhalakaza's meeting with his dead brother; confidently, he embarked on the seer's self-purification, and the sacrifice of the ox. Sensing his audience's interest, he told of Mhalakaza's return to the Gxara river.

'When he reached the bank he again saw his brother and the strangers. They were of our colour, Great Chief, but they told Mhalakaza they were Russians who are presently fighting the English in a war far across the seas. They have now come, they told Mhalakaza, together with the dead heroes of the Xhosa, to aid us in our struggle against the English.

'But before this may come to pass the Xhosa must lay aside witch-

craft, and they must sacrifice some cattle. Only then will their ancestors arise and with the help of these Russians drive out and destroy our enemies. When this day comes to pass, fresh cattle will
appear and, if no crops are planted, a great abundance of food will
also be ours.

'My master Mhalakaza has been appointed to speak for these de-
liverers, and he has been ordered, Great Chief, to acquaint you of
their words.'

Kreli was thoughtful and looked quizzically at the messenger
who was frightened of those searching, questioning eyes that
were never still. But Dema said, 'We have heard all this before. Mhalakaza's prophecies are never fulfilled. Tell your master
that the Great Chief thanks him for his courtesy and for making
known—'

But Kreli interrupted him. 'Did you say some of their cattle must
be sacrificed, or all their cattle?'

'Some of their cattle, Great Chief,' replied the messenger.

'Hmmm,' Kreli murmured thoughtfully, like a leopard purring,
and Dema, sensing his brother's mood, dismissed the messenger, telling him to wait.

Once more the messenger stood in the outer room, but this time
near the door and he could hear the voices of the chief and his
brother, and sometimes the words they spoke.

'When prophets speak, I listen!' Kreli said, but there was laughter
in his voice.

'Prophets, yes,' answered Dema, 'but not Mhalakaza.' Both
laughed at this.

Then the two men talked of the past, and the messenger heard the
names of the seers of former days: of Mankanna who was said to be
immortal but drowned trying to escape from Robben Island; and
Mlanjeni, too, who also commanded the people to abandon witchcraft, and who ordered them to slay all the cream-coloured cattle,
and who promised to make the warriors invulnerable to the English
bullets. 'Yet,' Dema was heard to say, 'our father, the great chief
Hintsa, died of an English bullet in his heart!'

Then, the messenger heard nothing but the rumble of their voices
and out of their confusion came Dema's indignant question, 'I? Visit
Mhalakaza? I?' and after some minutes, he appeared, wearing his
anger for all to see, and as he strode from the hall, he said, 'Come!
Take me to your master, Mhalakaza, the prophet!'

(From whom do you have this, Michael asked. From the messenger, replied Gwali, who listened at the door.)

3

Dema was gone many days before he sent news to his brother. 'I myself did not see the strangers, the shades of whom we have heard so much. Mhalakaza assured me they were on an expedition in the Cape Colony. The man is mad. I will return after visiting our brother, Sandile.' To which Kreli replied, 'Stay with Mhalakaza. I myself am coming.'

The royal journey was conducted in secret, for Kreli did not want the purpose of his mission known, nor did he dare to let it reach English ears that he had entered the territory over which they ruled. From village to village he passed; only the chiefs knew of his coming, and he travelled simply, astride an ox, without ceremony or retinue. But when he came to the outskirts of Mhalakaza's village, to the banks of the Gxara, Kreli paused and was robed in a leopard's skin, and on his head were placed the feathers of the blue crane which are the sign of a great warrior. Thus adorned, he entered the village. There was much jubilation, and much ceremony. Dema was the first to greet him, though somewhat sourly, for he placed no reliance whatsoever on such wild talk as Mhalakaza's. Alighting from his ox, Kreli ordered the prophet brought before him.

'That is impossible,' Dema replied politely. 'The prophet is in constant communication with the spirits and cannot be disturbed.'

'Then take me to him,' Kreli said, ignoring his brother's slightly impudent manner.

Once Kreli was inside Mhalakaza's hut, his warriors cleared a space so that no one could approach or hear what was said. But the presence of the Paramount Chief in their village greatly impressed the people. 'If Kreli has come,' said one old woman, 'then you can know that Mhalakaza speaks the truth.'

The day wore on and still the two men were closeted together. They did not call for food, nor was there any sign of life from the hut. Then, just as the sun was setting, Kreli emerged on all fours, followed by Mhalakaza. They stood, and all noticed the Great Chief's eyes, wide and excited.

Without formality, Kreli cried out, 'I have seen Mhalakaza's horse, dead many years and now returned to life!'

A triumphant shout went up from the people. Kreli continued:

306

'Send messengers to all the chiefs of the Xhosa, of all the Gcaleka, to my brother Sandile of the Gaika, to each and every one, this message: *kill all your cattle*, plant no crops and the white man will disappear into the sea from whence he came. On the great day, herds of cattle will rise from the ground, and all the dead warriors will rise, too, the crops will grow before your eyes, on that day, the white man will be no more!' Raising his eyes to the sky, he called in a high-pitched voice, '*Uthixo*, you are stirring!'

(And in her hut, Nongquase, who had not spoken for three weeks, not even to her mother or to her uncle, lay in the dark, a guard at her door, afraid and alone. She, too, listened to the chief's voice calling on *uthixo* and, in that moment, she cried out, 'Frogs! Mice! The ants!' but no one heard her.)

4

Miss Henning, Gwali said, heard news of the prophecy from a frightened man who had left the *kraal* of Kreli to show his displeasure. This was near the Kat River where the Hottentots had been settled. All the missionaries scoffed at the news, but not Miss Henning. She knew the danger and, Gwali said, she knew the prophecy would be believed. Aged and frail, she set off. 'My boy Michael will do something,' she said. 'We must warn.' (And Michael, hearing this, smiled.)

On the way south they saw, from a distance, the procession of Kreli returning to his royal village, and the further they travelled, the more they became aware of the messengers speeding with the news, delivering the commands of the chief: destroy your cattle, destroy your wheat, and the English will be driven into the sea.

Three days from Grahamstown, she was taken ill, and never recovered. After her funeral, Gwali told how the messenger of his uncle Mhalakaza sought him out and ordered him to return to the village. That night, all over the Colony, the messengers came and ordered the Xhosa back into their homeland.

But when Gwali heard what would be done, he raised his voice against Mhalakaza, against Kreli, calling on Jesus Christ to save his people. '*Amagotya*', unbeliever, they had called him, and Mhalakaza banished him from the village. But he had not gone far, when warriors attacked him and pierced his shoulder with their assegais. 'This is the warning from Mhalakaza to those who do not believe,' and they left him to die.

And all over the land the wheat is destroyed, and the cattle slain. The dogs grow fat, and even the vultures are sated.

5

While it was still dark, Michael laid Gwali in the back of the wagon and set off on the return to Grahamstown. Shortly after sunrise, he turned to the wounded man and asked, 'Are you awake?'

'Yes, master.'

'Do you think you could fire a gun?'

'With my good hand I could fire a pistol,' Gwali replied.

'Good. Take this,' Michael said, handing Gwali his own pistol. 'There is someone following us. I can smell it!'

Gwali struggled up on his knees and crouched behind Michael who sat on the driver's bench. 'Push my rifle near to my left hand,' Michael said, 'and be ready.'

The certainty that they were being watched every inch of the way remained with Michael, though he saw no evidence to support the feeling. Gwali, whose eyes were sharper than Michael's, confirmed it: 'There is just one man, I think, master. Just one.'

They came to a narrow gorge, formed by two huge boulders which had fallen aslant a dried-up river bed. The ox lumbered down the steep bank, the wagon bouncing on the rocks and trampling the bushes, and just as Michael was pulling tight on the reins to slow the beast, an assegai thrown from on high landed directly in their path. The ox came to an untroubled stop. Michael, off-balance, tried to grab his rifle and while he was fumbling for it, Gwali cried, 'Look!' and before them stood a young man, tall and proud, naked but for his loincloth. Michael managed to raise the rifle and aimed at him.

'I come in peace,' said the young man, holding up his hand in salute.

'What do you want?' Michael asked.

'To talk.'

'Yes, well talk, boy, I can hear you.'

'My name is Dema. I am brother to Kreli, chief of the Gcaleka, also I am brother to Sandile—'

'Yes, boy, I know who you are. Come over here and say what you have to say.'

Dema walked slowly up to the wagon. When he was level with Michael, he asked, 'Are you Brownlee?'

'No. I am Thompson. I am to Brownlee what you are to Kreli.'

'Will you see Brownlee?'

'Perhaps.'

'I have a message for Brownlee.'

'Tell it to me, boy, I will see that he receives it.'

'Who is that man?' Dema asked, pointing at Gwali.

'He is my servant,' answered Michael.

'*Amagotya* or *tamba*?' he asked, and before Michael could reply on his behalf, Gwali said, '*Amagotya*.' 'That is well,' said Dema, then he turned and walked into the shade of the boulders. 'I do not talk in the sun,' he said, and Michael knew, from his manner, that he was indeed the brother of the Chief.

'Stay here, Gwali,' Michael said. 'And keep the pistol ready.' He hopped down and joined Dema in the shadows. 'What is your message for Brownlee, boy?'

Dema said, 'Tell Brownlee that Mhalakaza is mad, and that my brother Kreli is mad. Tell him the dead will not rise, nor the cattle, nor the wheat. Tell him these things.'

'But the people kill their cattle, and they destroy their wheat.'

'That is only on the orders of my brother Kreli. The shades do not speak to Mhalakaza. They do not speak to my brother. Those two want the people thin and hungry so they will fight. Then the great Mosheshwe will join us, and you and yours will be driven into the sea.'

'If these things come to pass,' said Michael, 'why should you seek to prevent them?'

'Because I have seen your shrines, and they are built of stone, and ours are built of grass and reeds.'

'Where have you seen our shrines?' Michael asked, narrowing his eyes.

Dema looked away. 'In Theopolis I saw them.'

'What were you doing in Theopolis?'

'I was at school there in the mission station.'

Michael did not conceal his surprise. 'Are you Christian?' he asked.

'I am a believer in Jesus Christ of Nazareth. I know Jesus and I know *uthixo*. You give Brownlee my message. You tell him to stop my brother, tell him to save my people. Only Jesus has the victory.' And like an antelope, he ran to his assegai, retrieved it from the earth, and disappeared into the bushes.

23

Napakade

The Colony heaved a sigh of relief: there was to be no war, no invasion. People talked knowledgeably about witch-doctors and witchcraft, confusing both with prophets and prophecies. They smiled indulgently at the fanciful tales of Russians and dead horses restored to life. They entered their churches, knelt before their resurrected God nailed to a cross, and thanked Him for preventing war. The Bishop of Grahamstown preached a sermon, taking as his text Chapter 21 of Revelations: 'And I saw a new heaven and a new earth: for the first heaven and the first earth were passed away; and there was no more sea,' but he did not perceive the connection. To all, to the ministers of religion and their devout congregations, the prophecies of Mhalakaza and the beliefs of the Xhosa belonged in another world, not just across the river, but in another universe. 'Hell, those Kaffirs'll believe anything,' Dominee Burger said.

In a matter of days things had returned to normal. Grahamstown woke as if from a bad dream and resumed its daily life. Alice, full of contrition, left her parents' farm and rejoined her husband, chattering away as she always did, caring for the baby, Victoria, and trying not to complain when Michael spent unusually long hours away from her, for Michael was one of the few who was not able to relax. His position demanded concern. The welfare of the Xhosa was a part of his work, and the present crisis brought, in an unexpected way, urgency to his life, and he welcomed it. It was also his way of restoring the world in which he was god.

When Charles Brownlee returned from his visit to Sandile, he and Michael shared their information. The words of Mhalakaza and

Kreli, it seemed, had produced a divisive reaction. Among the Gcaleka, Kreli's own tribe, the response had been swift and immediate: vast numbers of cattle were killed, and the people devoured the sacrifices in expectation of the day of deliverance. But, among the Gaika, Sandile's tribe, the reception was more mixed. Brownlee reported that Sandile himself hesitated, and had not issued orders for the slaughter of cattle, and many of the Gaika chiefs opposed the commands of Kreli. (But others, like Umhala, as Michael could confirm, had obeyed without question.) Brownlee was determined to widen the divisions that already existed. He was intent on splitting the Xhosa into two camps. 'That way, dear boy,' he said to Michael, 'half may be saved.'

Accurate information was an essential factor in his reckoning. To this end, he enlisted spies and sent them forth into Kaffraria: Gwali was one. And Michael's task was to collate the intelligence and keep the Commissioner briefed. Brownlee himself journeyed back and forth, pleading with the people not to sacrifice their cattle. He won to his side the chiefs Tyala, Soga, Nxowana and Go; and to those who opposed him, and claimed the day of deliverance was near, he uttered one word by which he became known throughout the land: 'Napakade', which means never.

2

And these whispers from the spies:

The people hesitate, pause between life and the life to come. Kill our cattle? Sacrifice our pride, our wealth, the meaning of our existence? Are we to believe the promise of death conquered? Shall we see the herds of cattle rising from the ground? Shall we see new crops appear out of parched, infertile earth? Shall the white man drown in the bottomless sea? Death *and* our enemy vanquished? Dare we hope this much?

The contagion of rumour heralds the Millennium:

A child of the prophet Mhalakaza has risen from the dead!

Sutu, the mother of Sandile, has pleaded with her son to obey the shades. 'It is all very well for you, Sandile,' she said. 'You have your wives and your children, but I am all alone, I long to see my husband again. You are keeping him from rising by your disobedience to the commands of the shades.'

The people have seen warriors fly through the heavens pursuing celestial deer. Armies, crane-plumed and battle-ready, march in their ranks across the night sky.

Our ancient heroes, preserved and perfect, pierce the rough sea, march in legions across the restless waves, some on foot, some on horse, and then, beckoning us, sink once more into silent watery splendour.

Horns of oxen, white among the reeds that grow in dark and murky pools, are seen, and in subterranean caves, bellowing can be heard, the clashing of horns and the stamping of hoofs, cattle impatient for their release on the day that is to come.

Dead men, aeons buried, rise and cry out for the cattle slaughter. The longer you delay, the longer we must wait for our resurrection.

The Millennium is near.

3

Danger to Brownlee's plans appeared from an unexpected source:

Dear Brownlee,

I must inform you of my decision to summon reinforcements from Cape Town. The present mood of the Kaffirs constitutes a danger of the highest order to the Colony. All the 'prophecies' are directed against the English, and it would be foolhardy not to take their possible effect seriously. I have also strengthened all border posts. I suggest that when you travel into British Kaffraria, you do so in the company of a military patrol.

My Intelligence Reports all point to a deep-laid plot dreamed up by the Paramount Chief. There is even mention of white men being involved. If any of your people confirm or deny these theories, I would be pleased to receive the information.

Yours sincerely,
Colonel Maclean
Govr. Brit. Kaffraria.

To which Brownlee replied:

Dear sir,

Thank you for your letter informing me of your decision. I cannot conceal my disappointment. No doubt Your Excellency has acted on the best advice available, and will, of course, have considered the possibility that a military response from our side may be precisely what Kreli and his allies most desire.

I note your advice regarding any visits I may make into British Kaffraria.

Yours sincerely,
Chas. Brownlee
Gaika Commissioner.

'God preserve me from the military,' Brownlee said to Michael.

'How do you think Kreli will react, sir?'

'He will say that we are looking for war. It can only strengthen his hand. Still, dear boy, we mustn't despair. There is hope yet.'

The Commissioner had instituted a conference at noon each day. Here the reports were discussed, and the appropriate course of action decided. Brownlee remained optimistic: so long as he could keep the pressure up on Sandile to resist Kreli's commands, the better were his chances of success in preventing the cattle slaughter.

It was Michael who reacted more strongly to Colonel Maclean's communication. 'Sir ...' he said like a schoolboy with a problem, studying the Governor's letter.

'Well, what is it, dear boy?' Brownlee demanded.

'This mention H.E. makes about whites being involved ...'

'Bunkum!' declared the Commissioner.

'Yes, but, do you remember, sir, the report about white men purchasing land in the territory. I wonder if there's any connection.'

Vaguely, Brownlee recalled the information. 'Oh yes,' he said. 'We discussed it. We decided that was bunkum, too.'

'There may just be something,' Michael replied.

'Well, investigate, dear boy, investigate.' Michael gathered up his papers and marched to the door. 'You're coming along very well, Thompson, dear boy,' said Brownlee. 'Perhaps crisis brings out the best in you.'

Michael did not see the double-edged nature of the Commissioner's parting words: he glowed with a new fervour in the light of what he considered to be an unreserved compliment. With increased vigour he set to work following up his suggested line of enquiry.

It did not prove difficult: Lieutenant Droxford, Maclean's aide-de-camp, was helpfulness itself. He remembered the case well, for it was the first Intelligence Report he had dealt with on his appointment to the Governor's staff. The man had been arrested inside British Kaffraria and was accused of illegally buying land from two or three Xhosa chiefs.

313

'Where is he now?' Michael asked.

'He was held in Fort Wiltshire originally,' said Droxford. 'I'll see what I can find out.'

Two days later, Michael received a note from Droxford:

Our man is in detention at the military barracks here in Grahamstown. He rejoices in the name of John Smith. I enclose a pass for you to visit him.

That same day, Michael presented the pass at the barracks and requested an interview with the prisoner.

'John Smith, hey?' said the sergeant-of-the-guard. 'You can take it from me that's not his name. This way, please, Mr Thompson.'

The sergeant led Michael into a small area which was divided into three cells reserved for civilian prisoners. Only one was occupied.

John Smith was lying face down on his bunk, apparently asleep. 'Hey, Smithy?' called the sergeant. 'Here's a visitor for you,' and he unlocked the door to admit Michael. 'Just give us a shout when you're ready to go.'

Michael took a little time to adjust to the dim light; by then, the prisoner was sitting on the edge of his bed, rubbing sleep from his eyes. Smith was short and sat very straight, but Michael gasped involuntarily, for he recognised him at once: the prisoner's fingers playing with a woman's nipples had haunted Michael's dreams for more than two decades. 'Captain Jones,' he said.

'Oh God! You know me, do you?'

'We have met,' said Michael.

'When?'

'Oh, a long time ago. It doesn't matter. I won't tell them who you are.'

'I say, that's damn decent of you, Mr — ?'

'Thompson.'

'Thompson. Thompson. No, can't say I remember you.'

He did not seem a day older: his hair was a little grey, and a good deal untidier than Michael remembered, but there was no mistaking the clipped accent or the jutting chin; he bore himself proudly as though he were astride a charger.

Michael sat next to him on the bed. 'I had no idea you had left the service, Captain,' he said, taking a file from his attaché case.

'That's a damned polite way of putting it. Drummed out. In '48. Trumped-up charges, of course. I ran things by the book. Made a lot

314

of enemies. Well, that's water under the bridge, what?' Jones paused, and putting his head to one side, looked at Michael quizzically. 'Won't you tell me where we've met?'

'At Fort Wiltshire.'

Jones became alarmed. 'Oh. You're too young to have traded up there, aren't you?'

'Yes, and it really is of no importance. I was just a boy then.'

Jones was relieved. 'Oh well, what can I do for you?'

'I wonder if you'd mind answering some questions relating to the offences with which you are presently charged.'

'Ask away.'

'When were you arrested, Captain?'

'Don't call me Captain, there's a good chap. Don't want these fellows to know who I am. They can be damned hard on old soldiers. Just call me Smith.'

'When were you arrested, Mr Smith?' Michael asked.

'End of May.'

'And you were charged with buying land from Kaffir chiefs, is that correct?'

'That is what I was charged with,' Jones replied pointedly.

'Was there any truth in the accusations?'

'Absolutely none,' the prisoner replied vehemently.

'I want to assure you, Mr Smith, that anything you say will go no further than these four walls. I give you my word. I am not seeking information on behalf of the army, please believe me.'

Jones hesitated, then lowered his voice. 'Actually,' he said, 'I was on to rather a good wheeze. As a matter of fact, I purchased almost two hundred square miles!' He laughed delightedly.

'But what for?' Michael asked. 'You know very well that white men are not allowed to reside in British Kaffraria. What possible advantage could there be in owning land there?'

'I'd rather not answer that question.'

'Very well,' said Michael. 'I'll come on to something else. At about the time you were purchasing this land, was there talk of a Russian alliance with the Kaffirs?'

'I believe there was,' Jones answered airily.

'Can you remember where you heard this?'

'Oh, it was common gossip at the time, wasn't it?'

'I suppose so. You don't remember hearing it from anyone specifically?'

'No.'

'Had you heard about the Kaffir prophecies?'

'Vague rumours. You know, I've spent my life among the savages. I put in a good deal of service in Fort Wiltshire. After my little contretemps with Her Majesty's Government, I traded among the people. Arranged transactions of various kinds, you know the sort of thing. One heard all kinds of wild talk.'

'Do you know a Kaffir called Mhalakaza?'

'By Jove! I do indeed. Witch-doctor, isn't he?'

'You could call him that.'

'Toothless old devil, I know him, yes.' Jones leaned forward and winked repeatedly. 'Between you and me, the gentleman in question has rather a sharp taste for young girls, what? You're a man of the world, aren't you, Mr Thompson?'

Michael smiled non-committally.

'Look, keep this to yourself, but this Mhalakaza chap, fairly lusty old beast, you know, had one ambition. Can you guess what it was?' Michael shook his head. 'Wanted a white girl! Anything under the age of fifteen, don't you know. Well, difficult to arrange, old boy, I can tell you. But I—well—just as a favour, d'you see—I arranged for a little Ceylonese to cajole him. He wouldn't have known the difference, she was really rather pale.'

Michael blushed, studied his notes, and then asked, 'Did you ever discuss the Russian alliance with Mhalakaza?'

Jones burst out laughing. 'We may have done, but we mostly discussed alliances of another kind!'

'Did you ever visit his village near the Gxara river?'

'No.'

'Are you sure?'

'I said no.'

'Do you know a girl called Nongquase?'

'Never heard of her.'

'I have given you my word that this conversation will go no further. I beg you to tell me the truth, for, by so doing, you may save the lives of a great many people.'

'Look, old boy, I know what you're getting at!' Jones said, rising. He was angry now. 'You're trying to get me on a treason charge, aren't you? You're trying to tie me in with the Russians, you think I'm a spy, don't you? Well, I'm loyal to the Queen, boyo, make no mistake about it. I was purchasing land, that's all I was doing!

Listen, I'd seen documents—' but he did not continue; it was apparent that he thought he had already said too much.

'What documents?' Michael asked.

'I'm not saying any more.'

'Captain Jones, I will ask you directly what is in my mind: did you, or anyone known to you, conspire with Mhalakaza to deceive the girl called Nongquase into believing she had seen visions on the banks of the Gxara River?'

'Why the hell should I do that?'

'If, by so doing, the Kaffirs were to kill their cattle and destroy their wheat, a great famine may result. Then there might be some point in purchasing land.'

'I say, boyo, have you got rats in the upper storey? Look, I don't give a tinker's cuss whether those Kaffirs live or die. All right, you want to know why I purchased the land, so I'll tell you. I saw secret documents that stated categorically that we were going to occupy British Kaffraria and drive the black bastards further north. I'm a businessman and a businessman is as good as his information. I'm entitled to a profit, am I not?'

'*I* have never seen such documents,' Michael replied, as though he were privy to all Government secrets.

'That's your bad luck, boyo, I'm telling you the truth.'

Michael rose. 'Thank you, Captain Jones, I will not trouble you further. Sergeant!'

Before Michael left the cell, Jones said, 'I'd be grateful if you could use any influence to have me released, Mr Thompson. This isn't really what I'd call suitable accommodation.'

'If the opportunity arises—' Michael said.

'Yes, yes, yes, don't go out of your way. One other thing. There's a girl comes here every day, tries to visit me, but they won't allow it. An exquisite Siamese child, well, I would like to see her, if you know what I mean, perhaps you could tell her the right chap in authority to smile at, what?'

'I am not permitted to carry messages from prisoners.'

'Pompous ass!' said Jones and threw himself on to the bed.

4

Nongquase, too, had a visitor.

Ever since the visit of Kreli to the village, the girl had been subject to intermittent and terrible fits, crying, screaming, struggling, lashing out at demons only she could see. Many times her mother pleaded with Mhalakaza to visit the girl, but the seer had sealed himself off from the world outside: guards surrounded his hut and anyone approaching that sacred place was ordered to crawl on their knees in obeisance to the prophet and the shades whose spokesman he was.

But the girl's cries continued night and day, shattering sleep and meditation. Mhalakaza was forced to abandon his self-enforced solitude, and to visit his niece.

(Some said that, on seeing the prophet for the first time in many days, they noticed how thin he had grown, so that his eyes bulged in his skull.)

Nongquase writhed on the mud floor of her hut, legs stretched wide, her tongue, like a thirsty dog's, stabbing her lips.

'Be still, Nongquase!' Mhalakaza barked.

'The ants!' she cried, pulling at her flesh as though she were being consumed by the insects.

Savagely, Mhalakaza kicked her in the ribs so that she spun on to her stomach. Again he lashed out, and again, and again. Then, still with his foot, he turned her once more on to her back and urinated over her face. 'From now on you be still!' he screeched. But twice more she called out, and twice more he struck her.

'The mice, the frogs!' and later, 'Shelter from the wind!' Then she became quiet, her jaw half open, locked.

The people were impressed with the silence that settled inside the girl's hut. And when Mhalakaza emerged, Nongquase's mother asked, 'May I see her?'

'You may not!' answered the prophet. 'The shades embrace her.'

'Why does she cry out to the frogs and to the mice and to the ants? What did she mean to shelter from the wind?'

Mhalakaza reached the entrance of his own hut, and turning to the people, said, 'Nongquase has seen the daylight dreams for which I have waited. The day when the cattle will rise will be preceded by a terrible whirlwind that will sweep away all who do not obey the orders of the shades. White men will be turned into frogs, into mice and into ants. Nongquase has seen these things.'

The Millennium is near.

24

Amagotya

The sickness of the blind eye produces a paralysing complication: it is called optimism, and the English colonists were particularly susceptible to it; with the coming of spring, Michael suffered a savage attack. 'All will be well,' he told Alice. 'We are winning.'

True it was that Brownlee seemed to be succeeding in dissuading the Gaika from slaughtering cattle and wantonly destroying their wheat. Xhosa politics—'the Congress of Vienna, dear boy, has the air of a Sunday-school picnic in comparison'—was a game the commissioner played well. His powers of persuasion had been directed at Sandile who, by nature weak and vacillating, saw only personal advantages in not obeying the commands of his brother, Kreli: by allowing Kreli and the Gcaleka to destroy themselves, Sandile and the Gaika would emerge as the most numerous, the most powerful tribe among the nation. On these frail susceptibilities Brownlee played, believing the prophecies to be a plot hatched by Kreli and Mhalakaza, and therefore to be answered by similar intrigues. Ignoring the possibility that there were spiritual forces at work, Brownlee offered rewards of position and prestige to those who opposed the Paramount Chief. 'Napakade!' he cried. 'The prophecies will never come true and you will never drive the British into the sea.'

In his office in Grahamstown, Michael kept a wall-chart of the progress Brownlee was making. Like his map at home, it was brightly coloured: those chiefs who had pledged not to take part in the slaughter were named in red; those who could not be persuaded were shown in green, and the column of red was growing steadily. It was a vivid display, an encouraging tally of the *amagotya* and the *tamba*, the non-believers and the believers. Like Michael, the Xhosa chiefs placed their faith in what was most convenient and encouraging.

There was much to feed Michael's euphoria: Mhalakaza had named the Day of the Millennium as the full moon of July. When the full moon waned, he promised the August moon instead, and when that came and went Mhalakaza decreed that the dead had not risen because not all the people had slain their cattle. Disappointment swept the Xhosa, and raised the spirits of those who sought to save them.

Then, in September, Captain Jones was brought to trial charged with illegal entry into British Kaffraria, and with fraud. Since his interview, Michael and Lieutenant Droxford had tried to discover whether or not the document to which Jones had referred really existed. Neither man could believe that the Government intended to annex portions of British Kaffraria in order to expand the Colony, for only war with Kaffirs could result from such an action. When their search proved fruitless, Michael brought the Captain's accusation to the attention of Mr Quentin, an advocate from Cape Town who appeared for the prosecution. Under a brutal cross-examination, Jones was forced to admit that he had invented the existence of the document. He further confessed that he, together with others —'a gentleman does not name names'—had deliberately spread the rumours of the prophecies in order to foment war. 'We looked at it this way,' he said. 'If the Kaffir invaded yet again, for whatever reason, the British would be forced to drive him back further north. That would mean there'd be land for the picking. Our intention was to stake our claim before anyone else.'

'What price did you give for the land which you had no right to purchase?' demanded Quentin.

'Oh, the Kaffirs are easy game. In one instance, I purchased a thousand acres for two strings of beads.'

The trial lasted three days. On being found guilty, the Judge sentenced Jones—'a scoundrel whose exploits rank with Attila the Hun'—to nine years imprisonment. After one month, the little Captain hanged himself, leaving no letter of regret or farewell. To Brownlee, Michael said, 'I cannot help feeling sorry for the poor fellow. I believe half his sentence was for being an ex-army officer. Still, it does prove that there were evil forces at work on both sides. May he rest in peace.'

And Gwali, returning briefly from Kaffraria, said, 'The *amagotya* grow, master. The Lord Jesus loves all men, even my people. He has caused the sun to shine and the shades cannot live in the sun. The dead will only rise when Jesus commands.'

Summer, brazen and irresistible, smothered all in a voluptuous heat; optimism flourished but it, too, like the seasons, is subject to the laws of change.

2

The first hint Michael received that his optimism was being cured occurred not in his office, but in his home; the mixture of well-being and hopefulness he had so carefully nurtured first soured, and soon began to curdle.

Early one November evening, Michael arrived home sweaty and tired. It was stifling indoors, and Alice, chirping with concern, suggested they should get some air and take Victoria for a walk in the new perambulator Mrs Filmore had given them. Reluctantly, Michael agreed.

Arm in arm, they strolled, Michael pushing the baroque carriage proudly. Then, as they were turning for home, they heard drums and trumpets, and marching feet.

'Soldiers!' cried Alice excitedly. 'Oh do let's go and see.'

'I don't think so, dear,' said Michael. 'I am rather tired.'

'Oh please, let's. Victoria would love to see the soldiers, wouldn't you, Victoria?'

'Very well, dear.'

They pushed their way through the gathering crowd. Either side of the main street, people lined the route, cheering wildly, as the first horsemen appeared, leading a military band, followed by the marching soldiers.

'These are the reinforcements,' said Michael knowledgeably. 'In case of an attack.'

An elderly man beside them heard the remark and said, 'We'll destroy the Kaffirs once and for all! Look at 'em, look at 'em, such fine fellows.'

It was as the horsemen drew level that Alice gasped, and involuntarily gripped Michael's arm tight. He was about to ask her the cause when he saw, in the second rank, an officer, handsome and erect, smiling in their direction.

'It's Logan Stanley!' Michael cried, but the drums and trumpets were close enough to be deafening, and Alice did not hear him. She took hold of the perambulator and backed out of the crowd; Michael quickly followed, running to catch up with her.

They walked towards their home without a word being said. Dinner was equally silent. And only when they settled into bed, the heat suffocating and oppressive, did Michael find the courage to broach the subject. In the dark he said, 'Why did you run away like that?'

'You know why,' she replied, turning away from him.

'If you want to see Logan again, do so.'

She did not reply, but reaching backwards, she found his hand and squeezed it. He moved closer to her, his hands on her thighs, but she said, 'No. I'm—I'm—upset.'

That night neither husband nor wife slept well. And the very next morning, Dema appeared in Grahamstown and sought an interview with the Gaika Commissioner and his assistant.

3

'There is a new prophet,' Dema said. 'Another girl, in Umhala's territory. She is called Nonkosi, and her words have spread through the Gaika.' The young Christian chief, with the eyes of a fanatic, faced Brownlee and Michael in the Commissioner's office. 'Even the names are similar,' he said. 'Deliberately!'

'What is her prophecy?' Brownlee asked.

'She tells that she was playing near the Impongo river, bathing like the other girl, when a man, calling himself Umlanjeni, rose out of the water. She was afraid but even so she visited him again the next day. He spoke to her, saying he had come to waken the dead, and that she was to tell this to all the chiefs. He showed her six cows floating in the water, their heads just breaking the surface. Then, taking her by the hand, Umlanjeni led her to the land of the spirits where she saw pigs and goats and cattle and corn, and even huts waiting in readiness for the day that is to come. And Umlanjeni would not give her food in the land of the spirits, for, he said, it would kill her as long as all the cattle above were not slaughtered.'

'She has actually visited the land of the spirits,' said Brownlee. 'This goes further than Nongquase.'

'Do you not see,' said Dema passionately, 'that my brother Kreli is desperate. He has ordered Umhala to make this girl say these

322

things, otherwise the chiefs do not kill. My brother wants the people hungry so they will fight!'

Michael said, 'It'll all blow over, just as it did with Nongquase.'

Dema thumped the desk with his fist. 'It will *not* blow over!' he shouted. 'The Gaika are killing their oxen. They are burning the wheat fields. I have seen these things with my own eyes.'

'We've had no new reports—' Michael began, but Dema interrupted. 'I am telling you what I have *seen*! Already, my people, the Gcaleka, are starving! Now the Gaika will follow also,' and then he covered his face with his hands and cried, 'I have prayed to Jesus but He will not listen. Please, please, help my people!'

In the days that followed all reports confirmed Dema's story. The words of the new prophetess swayed the doubters. Even Sandile had given orders to kill. From one end of the frontier to the other, the army was placed on the alert. Gwali reported that already hungry tribesmen from the north were entering British Kaffraria in search of food. The carcasses of dead animals were strewn across the countryside; the grain pits were empty and the wheat fields burnt to stubble. There were rumours that the *tamba* were murdering the *amagotya*. By the weekend, many who had bravely refused to obey the orders of their chiefs streamed into the Colony. Some surrounded the office of the Commission, and mission stations and military outposts reported a steady flow of refugees seeking protection.

Panic, optimism's cure, also besieged the Commission. Brownlee, the marionette strings slipping from his fingers, abandoned political in-fighting, and took defensive measures. 'If the slaughter continues on this scale,' he said, 'we will have a hundred thousand starving people on our hands, dear boy. Food, that is what they need, food!'

And Michael, eager to allay his own fears, said, 'I think I know where I can lay my hands on enough grain to alleviate much suffering.'

4

At five o'clock on the first Monday in December, a day of unrelenting heat, Michael hurried out of his office, and rushed across the main street to *J. Filmore—Provision Merchant*.

Filmore and his two clerks were, as usual, hard at work. Being early in the month, he was balancing the books for November, and estimated that he had made the largest profit for a single month he had ever recorded. Thus, he was especially well-disposed towards the world in general and to Michael in particular.

'Very nice to see you,' he said. 'Hope Victoria likes her perambulator. Cost a fair bit, you know. But there's no stopping Mrs Filmore when she's money in her purse.'

'I'm here on business, sir,' Michael said.

'What sort of business?' Filmore asked, intrigued.

'I want to buy some grain,' Michael said.

'You want to buy some grain?' repeated Filmore. 'What the hell would you be wanting with grain?'

'I need a thousand bags,' Michael answered.

'Are you going into business on your own? Or maybe you're setting up in competition! For Heaven's sake, what would you be doing with a thousand bags of grain?'

Michael explained the situation, and that relief supplies might be urgently needed. Filmore scratched his head, and peered at his unlikely customer. 'Let me see if I understand you, m'boy. Are you asking to buy a thousand bags to save the Kaffirs?'

'That's right, sir.'

'Who's to pay for it?' asked Filmore sharply.

'The Commission,' Michael replied. 'The money's good.'

'I should damn well hope the money's good!' cried Filmore, all benignity vanishing. 'It's mine, that's how good it is!'

'There may be more than a hundred thousand starving people pouring into the Colony. Someone's got to feed them,' Michael argued.

'Why?' Filmore asked, but did not let Michael answer. Furious, the older man continued, 'Are you trying to tell me that the Government is going to use my hard-earned money that I pay in taxes to buy grain to feed the Kaffirs?'

'Mr Brownlee has every right, under the law—'

'To hell with Brownlee, and to hell with the law, too! You've taken leave of your senses! Are you saying we're to pay ourselves with our own money for grain to save the Kaffirs?'

'It's not *all* your money!' Michael responded loudly.

Filmore's rage exploded. 'I'd like to know who pays as much taxes as I do! By God, I've never been so insulted in all my life. They've caused enough suffering! I wouldn't give an ear of corn to prolong the life of one Kaffir one minute on this earth, by God, I would not! Even if it was your own money that you were wanting to buy with, I would sell you nothing! D'ye understand? This is a scandal! Using public money to save those murdering bastards! God help you and your kind if that's what this Colony's coming to. You haven't heard the end of this! I'll take this up with Maclean and, if necessary, the Governor himself! Get out of my sight! Save those Kaffirs? *Let the bastards die!'* He had driven Michael back towards the door; the clerks watched wide-eyed. *'Get out of my sight!'* he shouted and Michael could not find the words to stem the violent outburst. *'Get out!'* screamed Filmore. *'I'll have you stopped from helping them!'*

Michael ran from the office. When he was gone, Filmore turned to his clerks and, still raging, said, 'I'm going straight to the Governor. I'm not going to have Kaffirs fed on my money, or my grain! *Let them all die!'*

25

Tamba

From Mhalakaza, the spokesman of the shades, these words spread among the people:

The *amagotya* shall be destroyed.

From the land where the dead wait, where the warriors prepare for the great battle that is to come when the English shall be driven into the sea, the word has come that the *amagotya* have delayed the Day of Deliverance because they keep their cattle. The last full moon of the year was the appointed time, but now the heroes have dispersed. They will return for the first full moon of the New Year, and if not then, by the new moon.

Before the Dead rise, you will see the sun ascend the sky from the west. In mid-heaven the burning eye will unite with the pale moon and all the earth will be covered in darkness. Then will the heavens rain powder, and all who have not obeyed the orders of the shades will be consumed by fire.

The *amagotya* shall be destroyed.

2

Despair was now Michael's constant companion. It was as though he had been caught up, almost against his will, in the inevitable climax that was rapidly approaching. From the prophecies, the day appointed for the Xhosa Resurrection was 10 January 1857, the day of the first full moon of the new year; failing that, on 14 January, the day of the new moon. It was now December and time was short.

Surreptitiously, using agents and subterfuge, Brownlee and Michael accumulated bags of grain. The attitude that Filmore had so vehemently expressed was, they discovered, widely held. But by buying a bag or two at a time over a wide area, they approached the pitiful target of one thousand which Brownlee had set. In Stutterheim, near the frontier, they met with the one and only act of unconditional generosity: an old Boer, du Plessis, gave them two hundred bags and refused payment. He had lived, it transpired, with a Xhosa woman for more than thirty years and when she deserted him in the expectation of being reunited with her ancestors, it broke his heart. 'If you can save her,' he said, 'you will always have my prayers.'

On Christmas Day, the Colonists gave thanks for the birth of their Saviour. In not one church were prayers offered up for the salvation of the Xhosa who were in danger of starving to death across the frontier. The old year gave way to the new. 10 January came and went and the sun did not meet the moon. Four days later, the two heavenly bodies again failed to unite.

The Millennium is near.

3

And again from Gwali:

When the January moon died, Mhalakaza sent word that if the next moon rose blood-red, Kreli the Paramount Chief must visit him once more; and the next moon rose blood-red, like an overripe orange.

From the north Kreli came, attended by a vast retinue of followers, five thousand warriors and eighteen councillors. The great column of men, like a monstrous snake, thundered its way down the length of the land until, on 8 February 1857, the Paramount Chief arrived at Mhalakaza's village. Once again, Kreli alone was admitted to the seer's presence and after many hours, reappeared, trembling. Before the vast gathering he stood, with Mhalakaza, like a skeleton, beside him, and even Nongquase was brought forth and made to kneel before the Chief. (Her bones started from her flesh, Gwali said, and her face was the face of two eyes. She could not speak and she knew neither Kreli nor Mhalakaza.)

In a voice that some claimed was not his, Kreli addressed the multitude. 'The day is at hand!' he cried, in a hoarse whisper. 'One cow and one goat may be kept by each family. The rest are to be slain in eight days. On the eighth day from this day, the dead will rise. Warriors prepare! Your ancestors are at hand. The English will be slain and their gods destroyed forever! The shades have spoken! *Uthixo* has spoken!'

4

On 12 February 1857, a week before the day of reckoning appointed by Kreli, Michael and Gwali set forth in Sybille Henning's wagon, loaded with sacks of grain.

Michael took Alice in his arms and kissed her. 'I don't know how long I will be this time. Pray for me, Alice, and for the people I serve,' he said, with the smile of an unctuous priest.

She answered, 'Michael, whatever happens know that I love you.'

'What do you mean whatever happens?' he asked.

But she shook her head, covered his lips with her fingers and said, 'Just know that I love you.' With that, he kissed the baby Victoria on her mouth, and climbed aboard the wagon.

Some days later, they reached Fort Wiltshire, and there they waited for the 18 February to dawn.

Across the border, the people, dressed in their finest animal skins, sat on the dry earth and they too waited for the dawn, and for their ancestors to join them.

5

It was a Wednesday. The sun rose as it always did in the east, and began its slow, stately progress across a cloudless sky. At noon, it seemed to pause, and the people looked up and waited for the moon to appear. But the sun moved on until it reached the western horizon; there, in summer splendour, it sank, and darkness descended on the land.

6

A wagonful of grain will not feed a starving nation. The *tamba* made their way to the new cattle pens and freshly-dug grain pits, but they remained empty. One hundred and fifty thousand head of cattle had been destroyed, and where, where was the fulfilment? From Mhalakaza came the message that the ancestors had risen but their entrance into this world had been delayed because of an argument between two great dead chiefs as to which one should take precedence. With day succeeding day, the *tamba* waited for the argument to be settled, and their cattle byres and the grain pits remained empty.

328

On the third day after crossing the frontier, Michael and Gwali, escorted by a small detachment of soldiers, saw the dead bodies of those who had earliest obeyed the prophecies; they had been starving longest. The vultures, fattened on cattle, now fed on human flesh. To those survivors who still had strength to walk, Michael said, 'Go to the frontier, you will be fed there!' The grain he carried was for those further inland who would not be able to reach the border.

Even at night, Michael could not shut his ears to the sound of crying. Men, women and children, desolated by their shattered faith, howled recriminations at the bright stars, like neutral spectators in a black and balmy sky. By day, he saw the sufferers, so emaciated they resembled apes. In ditches, and in river beds, lay the corpses of the faithful.

On the first day of March, the wagon reached the village of Umhala, the chief whose insolence had so offended Michael. As on the previous occasion, no one came out to welcome the visitors; not out of defiance this time, but because they were dead. Umhala himself lay in his hut with his favourite wife snug in his arms; the stench of their rotting flesh caused Michael to stagger out into the fresh air, and he vomited by the doorway to the hut.

'Gwali,' he called. 'Set fire to the huts. We're too late.'

But Gwali was on his knees by the empty cattle pen, his face turned towards the cruel noon sun. His lips moved constantly in prayer, and he did not hear the command. The soldiers poked around the huts; even they, accustomed to destruction, were sickened. Michael, weak and dispirited, walked slowly across the open ground, along the gentle curve of the huts. Now and then he paused, and looked inside: in each, the dead lay: babes at the breasts of their mothers, children so wizened they appeared prematurely aged. He reached the wagon and held on to the tailboard for support. The sweet, cloying odour of decay clung to his nostrils; he gazed at the desolation, helpless and empty.

He was beyond remorse or regret. He felt nothing, except revulsion. And then, slowly, he too sank to his knees. 'Oh God,' he murmured, 'Oh God, God, God.' It was an accusation not a prayer.

The attack came without warning: like screaming birds of prey twenty emaciated men and women descended on them. They had been hiding in a copse nearby, watching and waiting. Immobilised by shock, Michael saw their approach and then, forcing himself to act, scrambled on to the wagon, found his pistol and fired into the mob. A woman fell, but still they came. By then, Gwali had stood and held up his arms as if to embrace his attackers. Michael reloaded and fired again, and the soldiers made for their horses, loaded their rifles and fired, too.

Gwali cried, 'We have food for you, my children!'

But they did not stop. Avoiding the wagon, they fell on Gwali and tore at his flesh. Again Michael fired, and again, and now some of them turned on him, rushing the wagon. One of the soldiers, a young corporal, climbed into the rear of the wagon, and taking his bayonet slit open a sack of grain, spilling the contents over the ground, then another and another, and in so doing halted the advance of the desperate men and women who now fell upon the grain and stuffed it into their mouths.

Pointing to those who still surrounded Gwali, Michael cried, 'Stop them! Stop them! They're tearing him to pieces.' The soldiers fired repeatedly: they fired on Gwali's attackers, and on the ones who fought over the grain, and they did not stop until all were dead.

Michael watched the massacre as though he were witnessing a charade, unreal and shadowy. Seeing the bodies of the scavengers fall across Gwali whose face, ruptured, bloodstained, unrecognisable, was, for a moment, visible in the melee, Michael was seized by an overwhelming sense of relief, somehow satisfied that Gwali was lying there, his flesh torn and raw; yet the conscious part of Michael rejected the sensation. 'I don't want him dead!' he cried, the soldiers' bullets exploding all around. 'I don't!' But even he, in the confusion of noise and movement, of screams and violent death, was aware that he was experiencing an uncontrollable pleasure seeing the man dead, even though his mind recoiled from it. It was not until the last shot had been fired that a terrible and familiar constricting pain assailed his chest as if he were being crushed by enormous pincers; when he breathed the noise was like the cries of the dying. In the hollow of his ears he heard Sybille Henning's voice, 'There is always a cure,' but the pain continued and the pressure increased until the sunlight burst his eyes and all was dark.

When he regained consciousness it was as if someone was dragging the left side of his face and body downwards. At first he thought that the hungry were tearing at his flesh, too, but he soon realised that he was in the back of Sybille's wagon, and he was aware of a young corporal looking down at him, and of something gold and shiny in the man's hand.

'How are you feeling, Mr Thompson?' the corporal asked.

Michael tried to answer but discovered he could not move his mouth; one side of it was numb and lifeless.

'Is this yours?' the corporal asked, showing the gold object to Michael, a little cross, which swung to and fro. Michael managed to shake his head. He wanted to say, 'It's Gwali's,' but no sound came.

The corporal said, 'Well, finder's keepers,' and pocketed the cross. 'You sleep now, Mr Thompson. We'll be in Fort Wiltshire by morning.'

7

The Colonists did not pause to question or to mourn. Life, many said, must go on, and John Filmore summed up the feelings of all frontiersmen in a letter to Michael's father, Richard, in England:

There is good in all things. Just think, my old friend, that we never have to fear the Kaffirs again. They're finished. Those of us who have been here from the beginning know what that means. It's almost unbelievable and I for one cannot get used to the fact: the Kaffirs will never invade again.

Estimates of the Xhosa losses were wild and various, but the Government guessed at over fifty thousand dead; some said more than that. The participants in the drama became the subject of gossip and rumour: Kreli, it was whispered, escaped; Mhalakaza was among the dead, but with his last breath accused the Paramount Chief of instigating the prophecies; Nongquase and Nonkosi had also fled the Colony; of Dema, no more was ever heard. Colonel Maclean gave a ball, not, of course, to celebrate the death of so many thousands but to commemorate the thirty-seventh anniversary of the 1820 Settlers; the timing was unfortunate. Charles Brownlee did not attend. For many months he laboured to alleviate the suffering of the starving. Indefatigable to the end, he said, 'They brought it on themselves. We did what we could.'

At Easter, Christ alone rose from the dead.

8

When Michael was returned to Grahamstown in the last week of March 1857, his wife, Alice, was not there to receive him, for news of his collapse had not preceded him. These letters tell the story. The first is dated before his departure from British Kaffraria:

2nd Feb. '57

Dear Alice,

I am now stationed to Grahamstown where I shall be for several months during the present Kaffir emergency. I know I have caused you unforgivable suffering. Please, please permit me to pay my respects and to offer you my humble and heartfelt apologies.

Sincerely yrs.
Logan Stanley (Major).

4th February

Dear Major Stanley,

Nothing will be served by our meeting.

Yours faithfully,
Alice Thompson (Mrs).

8th Feb. '57

Dear Alice,

I want no more than to apologise for the suffering I must have inflicted. It is a little thing to ask. Grant me the opportunity, I beg you.

Sincerely yrs.
Logan.

The day after Michael's departure:

Friday 13th February

Dear Major Stanley,

If you would care to call on Monday next, the 16th February, at noon, I shall be pleased to receive you.

Yours sincerely,
Alice Thompson.

They did not correspond again for more than a month; clearly there was no need:

14th Mar. '57

Beloved,

I cannot see you tomorrow as planned. I am obliged to take the night duty at the hospital, since we are being imposed upon by so many Kaffirs who are in need of treatment. I apologise, dearest girl. Will Monday be convenient?

Ever,
Logan.

And, some days later:

19th March

My own one,
    I should love an outing in the country on Sunday. Mother is to take Victoria for the day to the farm. I have told her I must see a *doctor*! ! ! !

Eternally,
A.

On that Sunday, 22 March, Michael returned to Grahamstown lying in the back of Sybille's wagon, attended by a medical orderly from Fort Wiltshire. Apart from feeding the patient, and attending to his general needs, there was little the orderly could do: Michael was paralysed down his left side. The wagon came to a halt in the narrow yard at the rear of the house, and when the orderly knocked loudly on the door, there was, of course, no reply.

'I expect she's at church,' he said to Michael. 'We'll wait. She won't be long.'

Continuum:
The family historian

Continuum:
The family historian

The prisoner knows that from a great distance of time and with ever-increasing knowledge it is possible to deny the part played by the gods in the affairs of men, and, in so doing, answer inadequately the question why, which is the question history repeatedly asks of events. Why do civilised people allow themselves to be possessed and corrupted by madmen? Why are the few able to triumph over the many? Why does a proud and virile nation condemn itself to a cruel and ignominious death? Believing all his life that he was a rational being, and yet something more than a reed that thinks, the prisoner concluded reluctantly that the answers lie in forces outside individual consciousness. For whether man created the gods, or the gods man, seemed to make little difference: in either case, for those who believed in the gods, or for those in whom the gods believed, those forces existed, were an ultimate omnipotent reality, and directed not only the lives of individuals but also the lives of nations.

In his solitude he has come himself to rely on these external powers. He does not pray to them, nor does he commune or meditate; but he is aware of their existence nevertheless. At this moment in time, even though incarcerated and forbidden the fellowship of other men, and knowing he has no part to play in shaping his own destiny, he is aware that events arrange themselves around him, that he, too, is part and parcel of a pattern not of his design. (In this, he feels the bond between Johannes Henning and Michael Thompson.)

The pattern begins to take shape when the young pimply guard is dismissed by the burly sergeant.

'There's a visitor for you,' says the sergeant.

'My uncle? Is the minister here?' the prisoner asks.

'No. Not the minister. A friend.'

'Who is it? I may not want to see him.'

'He said to say Oom Erik,' the sergeant answers and goes.

Despite the memory of Oom Erik, the family lawyer, waiting for him on the first day of his imprisonment, handing the keys to the officer-in-charge, avoiding the prisoner's eyes, flustered and embarrassed, the prisoner cannot help feeling a surge of elation. Oom Erik will be the first friend he has seen for almost six months.

They meet in the hall, and embrace. Oom Erik, old and bent, has tears in his eyes. He holds the prisoner's face, and gazes on him lovingly. Then, with a fierce and deliberate effort at cheerfulness, says, 'You know what I fancy? A game of snooker!'

In the mausoleum they call the billiard-room, the prisoner throws off the cover from the neglected table, while Oom Erik finds the balls and the wooden triangle. The prisoner is aware that Oom Erik has come for a purpose, but also knows that he has not yet found the courage to explain it. Instead, Oom Erik says, 'Hey, have you heard the van der Merwe story about him meeting the Prime Minister?'

'I've heard it,' replies the prisoner.

'What, the one about we've got a Kaffir doing that job?'

'Yes, that one.'

'Oh, you've heard it.' He is clearly disappointed.

'You break,' says the prisoner.

Oom Erik leans across the table and the white ball disperses the triangle of reds. He says, 'By the way, have you received a letter recently?' His tone is too careless to be really casual.

'No.'

'Are you sure?'

'Sure.'

'Not an official letter, even? I mean, you know, Government business?'

'One from Uncle Jacobus. I tore it up without reading it.'

'Agh man, you should never tear up letters. You never know, you might have been getting a rebate on your taxes!'

The game continues; both are inexpert and all the reds still litter the table.

'And you never even read it, hey?' says Oom Erik.

'No.'

'That's a pity.'

'Why?'

'Well, it was a personal letter, not from the minister to a prisoner, but from an uncle to his nephew who's in trouble.' He pots the first red.

'I don't want his sympathy.'

'It was a perfectly harmless letter I believe,' says Oom Erik, chalking the cue. 'All he wants is to come and see you.'

'I don't want to see him.'

'He's coming nevertheless.'

'When?'

'Well, you know, he's a busy man. He's got to speak at one or two bye-elections, sign a few deportation orders, refuse to reprieve a couple of condemned men, he's a busy man.' He chuckles.

'When is he coming?'

'In about a month. He asked me to tell you.'

'Why?'

Oom Erik shrugs. 'I don't know. When he didn't receive a reply to his letter, I think he was genuinely concerned. He asked me to see if you were all right.'

'Oom Erik, there are tears in my eyes.'

The lawyer laughs. 'Agh, man, don't be so otherwise.'

'Tell him I won't see him.'

Oom Erik does not reply, but lines up his next shot. 'So tell me,' he says, changing the subject, 'how do you pass your time?'

The prisoner tells him of the family history.

'Your family!' Oom Erik says. 'Man, it's like a bad joke! Hey, by the way, have you heard the one about the fellow who dies and they don't know what religion he is?'

'No.'

'Ah well, this man dies you see, and they don't know how to bury him. So they send for the predikant and he says, "No, he's not Dutch Reformed." "How do you know?" they ask. "No Bible by his bed," replies the dominee. Okay, so they send for the R.C. Padre. "No," he says, "not ours either, he's got no holy pictures or crucifix on the wall." So they send for the Rabbi and at once he says, "Yes, he's ours." "How do you know that, Rabbi?" "Fitted carpets," says the Rabbi!' He laughs and pots the black. 'That's your family all over. If you died, they wouldn't know how to bury you, that's for sure!'

'They could try lime,' says the prisoner.

Oom Erik pauses. 'Agh man, don't be so touchy, I only meant it as a joke. Your grandfather was just the same, he was touchy about your family. Man, we used to tease him and your grandmother. We used to say he must be the only chap in the world who advertised for a wife!'

'Advertised?'

'It was only a joke.'

'Tell me,' says the prisoner, his senses suddenly alert.

'Don't you know the story?' Oom Erik asks.

'No.'

'Haven't you ever seen your grandfather's scrapbook?'

'I can't remember.'

'It's in the library, I'll show you,' and before the prisoner can stop him, Oom Erik leads the way into the library, stepping over books, maps, papers that are strewn across the floor. 'Man, you have been busy,' he says, going to a shelf. 'Here they are.'

'I never even noticed them,' says the prisoner.

'Yes, he kept all the cuttings about his career and so on, from the time he was a young advocate, then a K.C. and then when he became a judge. All his cases are here. No, this isn't the one,' he says, replacing the book. 'It must be an earlier one.' At last, he finds what he is looking for. 'Yes! Here we are! Man, we used to tease him about this!'

The prisoner comes to the old lawyer's side, and peers over his shoulder. A cutting from the Grahamstown News and a letter are pasted on the same page. The date is 1886:

HENNING. Family historian seeks any documents, letters, diaries, etc. which contain a reference to the aforementioned name. Reply PO Box 14, Cape Town.

And the letter:

> Safehaven
> nr. Grahamstown
> 4 September 1886

Dear Sir,

With reference to your advertisement which appeared in to-day's newspaper.

My father, Mr Michael Thompson, was a pupil of a Miss Sybille Henning some time in the 1830s. Among my father's belongings there was a wooden box containing diaries, letters and a family Bible bearing the name Henning. Almost all the documents are in Dutch with which I am not familiar. If these should be of any interest to you, I should be happy to let you examine them. I look forward to hearing from you.

Yours faithfully,
V. Thompson (Miss).

'Man,' says Oom Erik, 'we used to tease him about that.'

'Victoria,' says the prisoner.

'Yes, a fine woman your grandmother. She and Dawid were the happiest couple I knew until—until—your mother . . . poor Anna . . . Man, the stories I could tell.'

'Tell,' says the prisoner.

And Mpobe knows he stands at the very gates of *Kuzimu*, the kingdom of the dead.

BOOK SEVEN

26

The official historian

If I may state the obvious, Oom Erik said, there are two strands to your birth, as with all children. First, there is your mother Anna, the eldest child of Dawid and Victoria Henning, *née* Thompson, a couple ideally suited despite the differences of their backgrounds and upbringing, good Boer stock on the one hand, 1820 English on the other. If there were such a thing as the *Almanach de Gotha* in South Africa, then the Hennings would hold a golden place. (Although I, being the family lawyer, know where the skeletons are hidden; but all great families are entitled to their skeletons.)

Ostensibly, the Hennings and the Thompsons, as I have explained, were brought together by a newspaper advert, but the truth is more subtle than that, for you must ask yourself what led Dawid to place adverts in newspapers in the first place? The answer is, of course, his love of the family, his pride in the Hennings. I do not know when he first became interested in genealogy, but certain it is by the time he had qualified as an advocate, he was already obsessed—I do not put it too strongly—with the history of his illustrious name. And so, in reply to the letter from V. Thompson (Miss) and in the hope of gaining more information, he set off for Grahamstown in late September, 1886. History, is the invisible cord that bound them together.

He saw Safehaven for the first time, as Sybille did, from afar. As his hired horse and cart crested the hill he caught a brief glimpse of the long, narrow farmhouse nestling in the valley. Dawid was twenty-seven years old but, like most lawyers, middle-aged the day he was called to the bar.

Dawid Daniel de Villiers Henning, the paragon of respectability, proudly traced his ancestry to that Daniel who slaughtered Bushmen on Lion's Head; that Daniel who disappeared from history on the death of his mother Agatha; that Daniel who, like the illusionist's assistant, magically reappears in 1835 with enough money to buy a large farm in Paarl, acquired how? By selling slaves. When the trade was abolished in 1807, Daniel made his fortune in smuggling human cargo north, beyond the boundary of the Cape Colony. Dawid's attitude to him is exquisitely expressed in the official history: 'The old scallywag, it seems, had engaged in some nefarious activities concerning slaves, but he put his fortune to good use in later years, donating large sums to the church of which presently he became an Elder; it is to him that we Hennings owe a debt of gratitude that can never be fully repaid.'

And so the serious young advocate, the scion of Cape aristocracy, guided his horse and cart down the well-worn paths that led to the English farmhouse near Grahamstown. He had only been working on his family history intermittently for about three or four years. At the time of his visit to Safehaven he knew nothing of Johannes Henning's secret trial and his daughter Sybille's quest; as far as he was concerned, their lives were lost under the dead leaves of time.

He did not know what to expect as he approached the house. The letter from V. Thompson (Miss) conjured up thoughts of a formidable English spinster, repressed and severe. (The countryside, too, put him in mind of England although he had never been there, but the green hills, the neatly ploughed fields, the comfortable scale of the landscape, all suggested that island for which he felt envy, admiration and suspicion.)

He was in for a surprise. When he neared the house he was aware of activity: rugs were hung over the verandah-rail, and furniture was clumsily piled on the verandah itself; it looked as though someone was either moving in or moving out. He was greeted by a woman, two or three years older than himself, carrying a paint-pot and brush, her face streaked with sky-blue, vermilion and turquoise, but even so, he was aware of a handsome face beneath and of a glowing, exuberant spirit.

'I'm looking for Miss Victoria Thompson,' he said in his heavy Dutch accent. 'This is Safehaven, is it not?'

'It is,' the woman replied. 'And I am she.'

'I seem to have come at a bad time. But I did say in my letter that

I should be here before lunch.' (A professional trait : he hated to be wrong.)

'It's always a bad time. You must be Mr Henning. To tell you the truth, I had forgotten all about you. We're redecorating. Do come in. You'll have to sit on the floor.'

The work was being carried out by Miss Thompson herself, and two servants, Katie and Benjamin, both Xhosa, who were quite as speckled with paint as their mistress. Dawid found himself in a long, empty room, the walls stripped ready for an undercoat, the ceiling a shining blue. One wall was painted in two colours : half vermilion, half turquoise. Miss Thompson saw Dawid's look of astonishment and laughed. 'I'm trying to decide which is the better colour for the room. It's always been such a gloomy place. I'm hoping to brighten it up a little. Which do you think, Mr Henning? Red or green?' He hesitated, played with his hat, sniffed. She said, 'Not forgetting the blue ceiling. Do take into account the blue. That must be a vital factor in any decision you may make.'

'Well, I suppose, if one has to choose, I would say the red.'

'Red it shall be!' she declared, then, turning to the servants, said 'Katie, make coffee. Benjamin, go to my father's room and fetch the box.'

That was their first of several meetings. The contents of the box, Sybille's box, were impossible to assess in a short space of time, so Dawid remained all that day at Safehaven, ate a picnic lunch seated on the floor and by late afternoon had removed his jacket, rolled up his shirt sleeves and was busily and happily applying the first coat of vermilion to the living-room wall.

For three days thereafter he visited the farm. All morning he would study the diaries and documents. In the afternoons, encouraged by Miss Thompson, he helped with the decorating. On the evening of the third day, which was the last Friday in September, Miss Thompson invited the young, serious lawyer to dinner; it provided the first opportunity for the couple to speak in a relaxed, intimate way, without the constant interruptions occasioned by painting and papering.

'That was excellent, Miss Thompson, I have never eaten Yorkshire pudding before, but I trust this will not be the last occasion.' He dabbed his lips with the napkin which he then folded carefully and neatly. He was, by nature, upbringing and profession an extremely formal man. Good manners, politeness the strict observance of etiquette, were to him the lubricant of social intercourse, be it between man and woman, families, or friends. The law, with its quasi-religious ceremonial borrowed almost intact from the British, provided the perfect background for such a man: the courts, the judges, the advocates, the attorneys, the whole glittering paraphernalia, provided a buffer against a more harsh and complex reality. In his world, there were rules and customs which moulded a man's speech, dress and behaviour; you knew where you were; all that mattered was position. So it was somewhat strange and novel for him to be seated across the table from Miss Thompson, complimenting her on the food, and conversing on topics outside his professional competence. It was, he decided, because she made him feel important for his own sake.

'Tell me, Mr Henning, are the diaries of any interest to you?'

'At first cursory glance, they seem to lie beyond the scope of the history I am writing,' he replied.

'Why is that?'

'Because I am chiefly concerned with the main branch of my family. This girl Sybille would appear to have been a little unbalanced. Nowadays, she would certainly be committed to an asylum. Besides which, since she produced no offspring, she is, as it were, a cul-de-sac. Women, if you will forgive me, are only interesting to genealogists for the fruit they bear.' He flushed, and knew immediately that he had made a tactless remark in the presence of a spinster. Trying to retrieve the situation, he only managed to make it worse. 'By that I mean to say that, in any walk of life, a woman's natural function . . .' His voice trailed off, but when he glanced at his hostess, he saw that she was smiling, momentarily enjoying his discomfort; she rose to pour coffee and, as she did so, came to his rescue. 'From the little I know of your ancestor, Mr Henning, she seemed a remarkable woman. Think of her: travelling all over the place in those days. Think of the danger! Just looking for someone!'

'The reason for her journey is certainly a puzzle I should love to solve,' he answered, relieved that the conversation had once again come to life. 'It is certainly not possible to understand her motives from the diaries.'

'My father's private theory was that she was looking for a brother,' Miss Thompson said, and led the way to the other half of the room where she removed a paint-stained dust-cover from the sofa.

'That cannot be so,' said Dawid. 'She had but one brother, my grandfather, Daniel Henning.' He paused before seating himself. 'Am I permitted to smoke a cigar, Miss Thompson?' he asked.

'Please do. There were many theories regarding her search. My grandfather, John Filmore, who also knew her, was convinced she was out to seek revenge on a lover. On the other hand, my grandmother believed she was looking for her own long-lost child. And, I must say, that seems to me the most likely. I cannot conceive of a woman devoting all her life for revenge, or for the sake of a brother. But a child, that would be utterly believable.'

'If it is not an impertinent question, Miss Thompson, how is it that you are even familiar with the life of this woman? In your letter to me, you said you couldn't read Dutch. Is there some other source for this story of which, perhaps, I am unaware?' and he sat beside her while she poured the coffee.

'Oh, Sybille was often talked of in this house,' she replied airily, but Dawid was not a lawyer for nothing: he was quick to spot her evasiveness, eager to discover the reason for it. 'But you are obviously interested in history, are you not?' he asked.

She burst out laughing with such gusto that he thought he had again committed a *faux pas*. 'History!' she exclaimed at last. 'History? I'm sick of it, Mr Henning.'

'It is difficult to believe that anyone with a lively mind can tire of history.'

She seemed about to tell him something, for she studied his face, eyes narrowed, as though she had lost track of the conversation for a moment, but Dawid had the impression that she was summing him up, debating whether or not to confide in him. Artlessly, she changed the subject. 'You've been an enormous assistance to us these last few days, Mr Henning, I do not think we would ever have finished this room if you had not been so helpful. It was most kind of you.'

'All I can say is that whenever I see red again, I shall think of you.'

She smiled politely, though the joke did not impress her. Yet, she believed there was more to the man than his dull, dry, formal manner allowed her to perceive. She had a clear impression of his strength and reliability.

'I must confess, Miss Thompson,' Dawid said, 'that it has also puzzled me, I do not put it stronger than that, it has puzzled me why a lady with your vitality, if I may say so, of your intelligence, should live alone here on this farm. If I did not know your circumstances and, let us say, you happened to come up in a witness box, I should at once decide you were a town sort of person. I would say that this woman needs life around her, activities, society, charities. Yet, I would be wrong. Won't you solve the puzzle for me?'

For a moment, she was at a loss for words, not out of embarrassment, but because she genuinely found it difficult to explain: she shrugged, smiled, made a gesture of helplessness with both hands and then said, 'I do like the town. And when my father died two years ago, I could easily have sold up and moved. But I did not. I am used to this place.'

'Do you actually run the farm yourself?'

'Oh no. Although originally the farm did belong to my grandfather Thompson, it was bought some thirty years ago by my maternal grandfather Filmore. He was one of the largest landowners in the district and for many years a manager was employed here. I simply allowed that arrangement to stand. Of course, it has problems and one has to be lucky to find the right person, but at the moment I have an excellent man, a Mr Naude, who has twelve children and is not afraid of hard work.'

There was again a pause in the conversation; both stared out of the window at a night sky brilliantly illuminated by the full moon: they could even see the apples on the trees in the orchard, like gigantic pearls.

'Do you ever visit Cape Town?' Dawid asked.

'Very rarely. Is that where you live?'

'I have a small house there, in Tamboers Kloof. But, I, too, am a farmer's son. We have a place in Paarl.'

They talked freely again, talks of crops and cattle, of wool and sheep, fruit and wheat and weather. Then, he told her something of the history he intended to write, enquired about her family and was again answered by evasions. 'Our family is quite ordinary,' she said. 'I want to hear more about *you*.' Dawid glowed; her interest made him talkative and expansive. She learned he was the elder of two brothers; the younger, Balthazar, was also interested in history but in a more practical way: he had studied archaeology and was now lecturing on the subject at Victoria College, Stellenbosch. Between them they supervised the running of the farm since their father,

Hendrik, was old and infirm. Then Miss Thompson said, 'But you must work very hard, Mr Henning, what with the farm and your legal practice and writing your family history—'

'Ah, but that is only a hobby. I am not a great one for society. I do not like parties, and my brother I account my closest friend. So my little history is very important to me. Some people think I'm a trifle mad. I will go to any lengths to run down a document, or answer a reply such as yours. I was sorry when you said you were sick of history. It plays a very important part in my life.'

Once more the searching look came over her eyes, once more she seemed to be assessing him. 'And you are not only interested in your own family, it seems.'

'The past in general fascinates me. Our country's a young country and its history is still manageable so to speak. Goodness knows what I would do if I were an English historian.' He chuckled, but when he looked at her, he became still, for it was obvious that she was troubled. 'Have I said something to offend you?'

'No, no,' she replied but still did not give him her full attention. 'It's so strange . . .' she murmured.

'What is?'

'My father was swamped by history, overwhelmed by events. His life was ruined, devasted by being in the wrong place at the wrong time.'

'Ah, but now you touch on something that really concerns me and to which I have devoted some thought.' His whole face came alive and expressive as he warmed to his subject. 'It is my experience, Miss Thompson, that the past is very like a tidal wave. You may see it form and swirl and shape itself out in the ocean and pray to God that it does not come your way. But if it does, there is nowhere you can hide. Think, for example, of being Huguenot in August 1572, slaughtered on the whim of Catherine de Medici, just because you happened to be born a Protestant. In some ways, I suppose, you could say that we are all in the wrong place at the wrong time. Who knows what *we* will have to face? Who knows what events are forming now that will irrevocably affect our lives? But this, as I say, is what it means to be alive at any time, in any place. That is why, in my own church, based on the doctrine of Calvin, we believe in two wills, the Divine which is perfect, and man's which is corrupt. History swamps us when the two wills clash.'

For the first time he had become truly animated, and she regarded him with new interest. There was some passion in his words and she had rarely been spoken to as an equal by a man. It was as though he made no allowances for her sex; he did not talk down to her or explain that which was unnecessary. The experience flustered her a little, for his sudden display of energy, which she interpreted as masculinity, took her by surprise. Dawid, for his part, feared that he had been too aggressive, not in words, but in manner, and because both of them had retreated momentarily into themselves the evening came to an abrupt end. Dawid, carrying Sybille's wooden box under his arm, thanked her for an enjoyable dinner, and Miss Thompson watched him from the verandah as he rode off, the moon lighting his way. Both must have thought they would never meet again. But, that night, in a Grahamstown hotel, Dawid, perhaps with future historians in mind, confided to his diary:

She is a remarkable woman in every way. I cannot ever recall being so relaxed in the company of a female. There is something loving in her personality, something hospitable and caring. She should be a nurse, for she has that in her which cures. I fear I offended her several times, being my usual clumsy self, but even my clumsiness diminished during the course of the evening. Though, at the end, when I got hopelessly swept away by the sound of my own voice, I did say 'now you touch on something that really concerns me' as though everything else she had said was totally boring. She must regard me as a typical Boer. I do not know why but I feel it important that she should think well of me.

The following morning he returned to Cape Town and, with that last sentence of the diary entry in mind, he wrote Miss Thompson a formal letter of thanks. To his surprise and delight, a week later he received a reply:

Dear Mr Henning,

It was most kind of you to write and I am indeed pleased to learn that you enjoyed your visit, and that the papers in Sybille's box were of some interest to you.

I shall be visiting Cape Town next month and, if it is not an imposition, I would appreciate seeing you as I wish to consult you on a personal matter. Perhaps you could arrange an appointment.

Yours sincerely,
Victoria Thompson.

352

The meeting took place in October. Dawid, since receiving her letter, had been debating endlessly with himself as to which was the best way to entertain her. Should he preserve the formality of her request and see her in chambers? or should he invite her to lunch? or dinner? or would a casual, relaxed walk in the Botanical Gardens be best? was it legal advice she was seeking? what did she mean by a personal matter? In the end, he decided he would be more comfortable with her one side of his desk, and he the other. The weeks passed slowly for him, and he discovered that, as the day approached, he was unaccustomedly nervous and ill-at-ease. On the day itself, he cut himself while shaving and all that morning he could concentrate on nothing but his impending visitor.

Dressed for town, she looked dazzling. 'She was like summer itself,' he wrote that night. 'Her dress, her parasol, her hat were of the lightest materials and she seemed to float as she entered. Her smile, of course, is the sun, her eyes December blue; she radiates goodness and she warms me.' Thus the young advocate, who would have squirmed if anyone else had used such language, described the woman with whom he was by now hopelessly in love.

'I have come,' she said, 'for some advice. It is not strictly speaking a legal matter, but I expect you to charge me as you would any other client.'

'Miss Thompson, it would be a great honour for me to advise you . . . as a friend,' he replied, continuing to maintain his austere manner. 'You must understand I cannot advise you professionally on any other basis, since my clients usually come to me only through an attorney.'

'How unlike you are to my lawyer at home!' she said gaily. 'I believe he charges me if I greet him in the street!' She reached into her large handbag and produced a bundle of papers, rolled like a baton, and held with black ribbon. 'To business,' she said, placing the papers on the desk. 'Mr Henning, I come here with a sense of outrage and indignation.'

'I'm sorry to hear it.'

'Neither are emotions I entertain often, I assure you. But in this, I believe I am fully justified.'

'May I ask the cause?'

'This!' she announced and once more delved into her bag and produced a book which she handed to Dawid. He opened to the title page: *Reminiscences of Kaffir Life and History* by Charles Brown-

lee. 'Do you know it?' she asked. 'It has only recently been published.'

'I have heard of it, but not yet read it.'

'That book, Mr Henning, contains a terrible libel.'

'On whom?'

'On my late father, Michael Thompson.'

'Would you refer me to the pertinent passages?'

'That's just the point,' she said. 'He isn't mentioned. It is a libel by
omission!'

Dawid could not refrain from smiling. 'I don't believe I have ever
heard of a libel by omission.'

'Please don't laugh, Mr Henning. I have not come here to make
mischief. I regard this interview with the utmost seriousness.' She
lowered her eyes and sat quite still. 'I did have it in mind to consult
you when we first met at Safehaven, for I had already read that
dreadful book. But I had not yet decided what action to take, chiefly
because I did not feel I knew you well enough. You see, asking of
you this favour requires that you become acquainted with some details of my parents' marriage which are not the sort of thing one
wants bandied about. That is why I have brought you these documents,' and she handed Dawid the bundle of rolled papers.

'What are these papers?' he asked, delicately untying the black
ribbon.

'They contain among other things what I believe to be a true account of the incidents touched on by Mr Brownlee in his book. They
are in my handwriting and were dictated to me by my father,' and
she began to relate the events concerning the last years of Michael
Thompson.

2

Victoria could not remember her mother, Alice. ('She was hardly
ever mentioned in my presence. She committed a great wrong and I
believe was utterly selfish.')

On the day Michael returned from British Kaffraria, his left side
paralysed, his mind contorted and confused by the events he had
witnessed, Alice was not there to greet him, and she did not set foot
again in their house. She had, that morning, visited her doctor who
informed her she was pregnant. In the afternoon, she kept an as-
signment with Logan Stanley and the two were last seen at Faure's

Livery Stables where they hired a horse and cart. Some days later she wrote a letter not to Michael, but to her mother, Margaret Filmore. The contents were never revealed; the letter was burned and no more was said.

It was left to the Filmores to pick up the pieces. On their farm, Michael partially recovered, but was unable ever to walk with ease again: his left leg dragged behind him, and his arm hung limply at his side. He tired quickly, and his speech was slurred and often confused; on their farm, too, Victoria spent her childhood.

When Richard Thompson, away in England, received the news of Michael's stroke, he booked his return passage at once, and four months later gazed with heavy heart at the drawn, distorted face of his son. It seemed as though he were re-living an earlier period of his life, when Michael was a child and confined for all those years to bed. After lengthy discussions and much heart-searching, Thompson insisted that he remove Michael to Safehaven where the old man wanted more than anything to care for him. With uncharacteristic generosity, but doubtless out of a feeling of guilt prompted by his daughter's behaviour, John Filmore arranged for his friend to resume the management of Safehaven, exacting a token rent and allowing the former owner to run the place as he thought best, and to benefit from whatever profit he could obtain. Thus, for the first sixteen years of her life, Victoria saw her father but once a week, on Sundays, when the two families met in church and, afterwards, would repair to Safehaven for a traditional English dinner.

The child grew up in exciting times. In 1867, another small girl, playing half-way across the country on the banks of the Orange River near Hopetown, was attracted by a bright, shining stone; two years later, between the rivers Vaal and Modder, another diamond was discovered, valued at £25,000; men rushed to make their fortunes and began to work the mines that were to prove the richest source of diamonds in the world. The Colony achieved a fame and importance that it had never previously enjoyed. The British, attracted by the glittering light as the Three Kings were to the Holy Star, pushed north, annexing the diamond fields and any other territory they could lay hands on, and stared across the Orange River and the Vaal, where those men who insisted on a proper relationship between master and servant without interference from outside, had established an inviolate claim to the land; the inevitable tidal wave was gathering far out at sea.

Then, in August 1870, three months after Victoria's fourteenth birthday, Mrs Filmore complained of stomach pains; in a matter of weeks she grew haggard and thin; by Christmas she was dead. Eighteen months later, in February 1872, her husband collapsed in his office, in the presence of his two clerks, and never recovered consciousness. Richard Thompson was appointed Executor in his will, and Victoria inherited a large fortune; Safehaven became her home, an old dispirited man and an invalid her constant companions.

('Looking back,' she said, 'I must have appeared so heartless, for nothing could depress me or dampen my spirits. To poor old grandfather Thompson, my cheerfulness was doubtless a terrible trial. And I suppose there was nothing much in my life to be happy about, since I was virtually housekeeper and nurse to father and son. Grandfather Thompson became very eccentric in his old age and suffered long bouts of melancholy. He believed that the Cape was cursed and nothing but catastrophe could come from living there. He made me promise that, when he died, I would see to it he was buried at sea. Which I did. He slipped away quite peacefully in his sleep and I arranged for his body to be committed to the deep of the Indian Ocean. And so, my father and I were left alone.')

It was not so much her cheerfulness, but her indomitable spirit which sustained Victoria. The shining quality that attracted Dawid was compounded of compassion and faith, but chiefly of hopefulness. In some ways, it was a decidedly English attribute, an inner conviction that could not conceive of defeat. 'And now,' she said, 'I come to these papers, Mr Henning. I will tell you why and how they happened to be written.'

About five years before her present interview with Dawid, in 1881, her father had received a visitor, an old friend, Charles Brownlee, the former Gaika Commissioner, a saddened, disappointed man who had never recovered from the terrible destruction the Xhosa had brought upon themselves. At first, there was nothing unusual about the meeting. The two men talked of old times, discussed Michael's health, and Brownlee made the usual encouraging noises about the excellent prospects for the invalid's recovery. Towards the end of the visit, however, the real reason for Brownlee's call was revealed: he had embarked on a book about his experience as Gaika Commissioner, which would deal, in the main, with the events of the Xhosa suicide; he wanted to check some facts. He began to question Michael, who became more and more agitated and confused, one word running into the next, creating a world of jumbled identities and disordered chronology. At one moment, he insisted that Sandile was Governor of British Kaffraria, at another that Colonel Maclean was uncle to Nongquase. Seeing the effect that reviving these memories had on the invalid, Brownlee apologised and offered to leave. But, as he reached the door, Michael, with sudden, chilling lucidity, asked, 'You'll do me justice, won't you sir? I did try, I did try.'

Brownlee, without thinking, said, 'Oh, no, my dear chap, my book isn't to be about personalities. It's to be a serious history,' and left.

That night, and all the following day, Michael ran a high fever and was, from time to time, delirious. He shouted out, called on *uthixo*, murmured the name of Gwali over and over again. For long periods he talked only in Xhosa and, when he recovered, he had but one burning thought in his brain: to justify his own part in the events, to set the record straight.

Paper was bought, and a dozen quill pens. For two days, he tried to write but the physical effort was too much, and he was forced to bed once more. 'It's no good, Vicky,' he said, 'I can't do it. I can't read my own writing even when I do get it down.'

'There, there, papa,' Victoria said, gently laying him back on his pillows. 'Mr Brownlee will make it all clear. There's nothing to fret about.'

'Brownlee! *He* wasn't there! *I* was there! I saw things he never even dreamed of! Terrible things! You can do so much and no more. I swear I did all I could . . .'

In the end, it was decided that he should dictate his memoirs to Victoria. Each day, from ten until noon, she sat by his bed and took down his words; each evening she would read back what had been said. After a while, she hardly listened to his voice, but recorded his words more or less automatically.

But he never finished the self-justification. He reached that point where he witnessed Gwali's death, but the memory tormented him so that he could not collect his thoughts for several days. 'I want to explain why I acted as I did,' he said. Those were the last words he ever uttered. During the night, he suffered a second and more massive stroke. By morning, he was dead.

'I have not deleted one word,' Victoria said to Dawid. 'There are references to my mother which are frank and embarrassing, but I have not removed them. I want you to read it, Mr Henning, and then advise me. My own opinion is that, with judicious editing, I should make every effort to have it published, to show that people did not behave as heartlessly as Mr Brownlee would like us to think.'

'I will read it and give you an honest opinion.'

'My father has been dead four years. I must confess that the document has caused me some anguish. Then, when you came to examine the records left him by Sybille, you seemed to me the ideal person to ask, being both lawyer and historian. And even though there are those indelicate passages to which I have referred, it does not seem so awful to confide them to an advocate. I feel sure you must have heard worse in your career.'

Because Victoria was to remain in Cape Town for a further week, Dawid agreed to read the pages and pronounce before she left. They arranged to meet the day before her intended departure.

In the quiet of his house in Tamboers Kloof, where from his study window he could look out on the sheltered town and the bay beyond, Dawid set to work. He read speedily but carefully and made just one reference to the document in his diary:

The English are extraordinary. They do not accept power gracefully. They have to condone the use of it on every sort of shabby pretext except the true one. If it is land they are after, then it is because they wish to convert the inhabitants. If it is a market they want, then it is to bring good government to the conquered. The only exception to this rule is their love of justice which is their saving grace. But why, why, regret the defeat of one's enemies? One cannot judge the past. Men react *because* of the time, not in spite of it. And, in any event, the English have always reacted too late. Thompson was like an ant in an earthquake. The Xhosa chose death because there was no joy to be found in life. The English were superior in every way, just as the white man, in general, is superior in every way. Only a fool would argue otherwise. History proves it. The Kaffirs collapsed in the face of a morally superior enemy.

With these thoughts in mind, the two met again in his chambers a week later. Dawid confided little of his private thoughts to her. But he did advise her that the work was historically valueless, not nearly objective enough for his taste. He tried to convince her that to publish could only bring harm; best to let sleeping dogs lie.

They argued a little while longer and, as it was already past noon, he suggested they lunch together to discuss the matter further. In the bright October sun, they strolled down Adderley Street, formerly the Heeregeracht, the mountains behind them, protective and comforting. In both their memories, the sequence of events was confused. She remembered he talked continuously and was clearly nervous, wiping his brow from time to time with a spotless white handkerchief. His own recollections were more inward. 'I am not usually an impulsive person,' he wrote, 'but I knew as we stepped out into the sunshine that I would propose. I talked a good deal of nonsense which was strange, for I had only one thought in mind, one question: "Will you marry me?"' Neither were certain whether he asked the question or whether they first heard the newspaper seller crying the headlines of a special edition. In either case, to her profound astonishment Dawid Henning proposed marriage and, perhaps, simultaneously, the little Malay boy came running by, calling, 'Gold! Gold strike in Transvaal!' And Dawid turned to her, his eyes glowing, and said, 'You see? It's prophetic!'

27

The difficult daughter

I

History did not swamp Dawid and Victoria Henning, Oom Erik said, nor did tidal waves break upon their shore. Their lives proceeded as though they were following a well-rehearsed, impeccably choreographed formation dance. Not that their relationship was entirely without complications, but these were of a trivial nature, and to be expected.

Victoria did not at first accept her ardent and surprising suitor. She asked for time to think, and he willingly granted it. The upheaval that marriage would mean mortified her; Safehaven was the centre of her life and Dawid would doubtless insist on her living in Paarl or Cape Town; it would mean giving up everything she had known and cultivated. Could she reconcile herself to being the wife of an up-and-coming advocate? On his side, Dawid, too, had difficulties, but not of his own making. His aged parents opposed the match, for Victoria was English and the 'watering down of our blood', as Dawid's father put it, was to be resisted. For six months following the proposal, the couple did not meet, though Dawid wrote passionately persuasive letters once a week, to which Victoria replied, less frequently, cataloguing her doubts. In the summer of 1887, he had argued her into accepting him: on 7 December their engagement was announced; two years later, they were married. By that time, Oom Erik said, the danger of history devouring them had passed, for, in fact, the enemy had been beaten.

The enemy: the Xhosa and the Zulu, the two great black nations, had, by the time of Dawid's marriage to Victoria, been defeated. New territories were created to house them, vast tracts of impoverished land, reserves on the grand scale. No longer were they called by their ancient and proud names; from then on, they were known, unwisely it might be thought, as Natives, and the Hottentots were now Coloureds, Cape Coloureds, and already they outnumbered their fathers who sired them. And the whites? European, if you please, Briton and Boer. The lines of demarcation had been drawn. From that moment, the proper relationship between master and servants was frozen. The savages had been tamed and were now consigned to the zoo. No statesmen, no leader, no political party would allow the balance to be altered by one single gram. The history that followed was simply a hardening of that which was already hard. The Europeans might fight wars, politic for power, enter the world arena or confine themselves to the sub-continent; it was of no importance to the inhabitants of the zoo. For the most part, they were forgotten or ignored and, if and when remembered, it was only to add to their suffering, to remind them that they had best remain behind the bars. The Europeans pledged themselves to this motto: 'Nothing must change,' and from the moment the first white man set foot on the sands of Table Bay, and saw the grease-covered Bushman, nothing had changed.

The events to which Europeans now addressed themselves were peripheral to their *raison d'être*. Gold, upon which a nation's wealth is valued, was found to lie in lavish abundance on the Witwatersrand, the reef of white water, and with it came the Industrial Revolution a hundred years late. The diamond companies, already rich, reached out and grasped the goldfields, greater in extent than any other. In their hundreds of thousands, the Zulus flocked to work welcomed by the seductive slogan above the gates of the depot: *'Abathanda imali, abathanda izinkhomo indhela elula eya eGoli; nanti iHovisi!* Lovers of money, lovers of cattle, the road is easy to the City of Gold; here is the office!'

The British, like King Midas, reached out too: they annexed Zululand, the principal source of cheap labour, and thus enslaved a people they had already defeated in a long and bloody war. The first tycoon, Cecil John Rhodes, the son of an English parson, with unequalled ruthlessness, energy and ambition, amassed a vast fortune, hungered for power and dreamed his Imperial dream. In 1890 he became Prime Minister of the Cape: with a hand over his eyes to shield them from the sun, he gazed into the future and saw a shimmering road leading north, and, beside it, a railway that would stretch across the Vaal, across the Limpopo, beyond Lake Victoria and the reaches of the Upper Nile to Cairo; anyone who obstructed that highway must be swept aside.

The Boers obstructed the highway and possessed the gold. In the Orange Free State and in the Transvaal they flourished, independent of Britain and Cecil John Rhodes. A thick-set, bearded man who, as a boy, had joined the great trek north, now presided over the South African Republic: Paul Kruger, as determined, as aggressive, but more principled than the Premier of the Cape Colony. A head-on collision was inevitable and, in 1899, it occurred with dreadful ferocity. Kruger, courageous, untutored, a founder of an extreme fundamentalist faith who refused to believe until his dying day that the world was round, versus Cecil John Rhodes, Bishop Stortford's Grammar School and Oriel College, Oxford; Boer against Briton; isolationists in conflict with empire builders. The British may speak of expansion or of justice or of good government for all but, at the heart of the conflict, was the Boer's age-old doctrine: to resist any interference from outside. The Boers lost a battle, but they would never cease to fight the war. Peace, or more accurately a truce, was signed at Vereeniging in 1902 and eight years later, with Kruger and Rhodes in their graves, other names captured the public imagination, Jan Christian Smuts, Louis Botha, James Barry Munnik Hertzog, distinguished veterans of the recent conflict, all Boer generals, who now sought to reconstruct a new country: in 1910 the Cape, the Orange Free State, Natal and the Transvaal were bonded together to form the Union of South Africa, a nation with two flags and two anthems, and the majority of its people enslaved. The words of Smuts, the statesman, the friend of the British, the arch-betrayer:

'All ... are agreed ... except those who are quite mad ... that it is a fixed policy to maintain white supremacy in South Africa.'

In the lunatic asylum the inmates are always convinced of their own sanity.

2

What can I tell you about Anna, your mother, Oom Erik asked, that will not pain you? What can I tell you that you do not already know? Remember her as I remember her: think of her beauty, of her kindness, of her gaiety. Do not think of her as ill.

Her childhood could not have been more idyllic. Born a year before the war, she was too young to be affected by the conflict of loyalties within the family circle, although Dawid and Victoria managed to remain respectably detached. Predictably, Victoria sided with the British, Dawid with the Boers, but neither voiced their sentiments; it was something tacitly understood between them which did not, at first, necessitate discussion or argument: both pledged themselves to the Union, sang *God Save the King* and *Die Stem van Suid Afrika* with equal gusto.

In the beginning, Dawid and Victoria supported Smuts, the reconciler, the eternal optimist who told people only what they wanted to hear. ('Instead of mixing up blacks and whites in the old haphazard way, we are trying now to lay down a policy of keeping them apart as much as possible.') The Hennings were South Africans; their marriage, Dawid said, symbolised the new hope, their daughter, Anna, the new citizens; the time for national differences was past. He disapproved of Hertzog and his Nationalist Party; he disapproved of the *Afrikaner Bond* with its fierce allegiance to a so-called Afrikaner culture; they might call the *taal* Afrikaans but it did not stop it from being a language without a literature, without a true and tried tradition. No, it was best, Dawid decided, to work for one nation, one people, united and strong. And into this reckoning, Dawid taught his daughter, come only men of white skin; one nation has no other meaning.

Was she neglected, you ask? Well, both Dawid and Victoria led busy lives. His career was all-important to him, and his devotion to duty paid off: in 1911 he was appointed King's Counsel and, ten years later, realising his life's ambition, a judge. Victoria, too, was busy, what with the wounded, and orphans; she even risked influenza in the epidemic of 1914 to nurse the sick; she was a loyal and faithful wife. And don't forget, she'd given your grandfather a son as well, Jacobus the Illustrious.

The first symptom that anything was amiss with Anna occurred in her fifteenth year: suddenly, she was missing, missing from home, from school. Imagine, Oom Erik said, the panic of an eminent K.C., imagine the frantic searching; imagine the police, the hospitals, the morgues. In the end, they found her in Worcester of all places, in bed with her English master, a man named Norris; he was arrested, she was below the age of consent, but Dawid managed to have the charges dropped. We, who did not know enough or care enough in those days, used all sorts of euphemisms from 'man-mad' to 'over-sexed', tried to simplify, explain, excuse, but failed hopelessly to understand. Someone—it may have been Victoria—called her an 'exhibitionist' which was thought then to be vaguely obscene. True it was Anna thirsted for attention; equally true that she was indiscriminately attracted to men and, more disastrous, they to her. No amount of counselling or reasoning could restrain her. Adolescence was said to be a phase that would certainly pass; but adolescence stained the rest of her life, wild, uncontrollable, painful. Make of it what you will.

Beside beauty, she had an intellect of masculine vigour, which promised an outstanding academic career. But universities have male students, and male lecturers, and Anna devoured both uncritically, and with a lack of fondness or satisfaction that magnified her concupiscence in the eyes of those who cared, or said they cared.

Now, Dawid Henning avoided scandal as some men avoid the plague: both fear death if contaminated. Did he not, in the nightmare hours, call into his mind the faces of Sybille Henning and Alice Thompson? Did he not secretly acknowledge his daughter's shameful inheritance, knowing that she displayed the imbalance of the one, and the instability of the other? Anna must be watched, he decided, and who better than his younger brother, Balthazar, the archaeologist? Dry, dusty Balthazar with his passion for ruins. Research assistant, they called her and, miraculously, it seemed to work: for months she was demure, calm, and studious. Then, the note: 'I am pregnant, forgive me, Anna.'; the empty aspirin bottle, the stomach pump and the vomiting. It was Balthazar who confessed to Dawid: 'I am the father,' he said.

Silence: the shock of severed lives recovering: uncle and niece; brother and brother. A gynaecologist summoned in secret at the dead of night could not detect any sign of pregnancy. Anna convalesced as though her own life had avoided detection; a child stillborn would have been better than no child at all.

And always the misery of the happiness that might have been: John Ferguson, whom she said she loved, killed in Flanders; Willem Botha, whom she said she loved, already married; Paul O'Connell, whom she said she loved, ordained a priest. Hers was a frantic, unpredictable world, lived on the knife-edge of hysteria.

Difficult for a judge; distressing for a mother. Employment must be found to exhaust the fragmented vitality. But what? In the end, with customary inadequacy, David placed her as a secretary in the

364

office of the Attorney-General of the Cape Province, under the watchful gaze of a Mr Konradie, a senior prosecutor and an old family friend, a man of the highest integrity, a man he could trust.

Which, Oom Erik said, brings us to the second strain, your father, the Jew, Leonard Levine. His first application for a post at the Attorney-General's office was dated 4 June 1928, and it was unsuccessful. His second on 8 January 1929 was formally acknowledged by return, and three weeks later he received a letter of appointment. It is the curious circumstances that are sandwiched between rejection and acceptance which brought the young Jewish advocate to the door of the House of Henning.

28

Leonard ben Julius

They came from worlds apart, and the circumstances which brought the two together span more than seven months or even seven years or seven centuries. The events have their origins in the mystery of times past, in Babylon and Egypt, in Alexandria and Rome, in the enforced restlessness of a people compelled to wander the earth, a people chosen to survive.

Where, where have they not set foot, the children of Abraham, Isaac and Jacob? In Babylon four thousand years ago, and in Egypt half a millennium later, they chant their mystic words to a jealous god who cannot be seen. From Babylon it was that Nebuchadnezzar carried off the elite of Judah to Mesopotamia which, for ten centuries, became the most populous and wealthy cradle of Jewry, and, six hundred years before the birth of Christ, when Lao-Tse and Confucius were emitting their stately wisdom on which China flourished, when Buddha was pointing out the Way in the Deer Park at Benares, and Ionian Greeks were making a beginning of all that is known as science and philosophy, then the Judaeans dispersed throughout the civilised world, became Jews, the People of the Book, held together by the far-reaching tentacles of the Law, the record of their past history, and the hope of a glorious resurrection. And the longing to return to the homeland, preached with priestly fervour by Ezekiel and set down by him in immortal prose, fulfilled by Cyrus the Persian who sent back those who volunteered to rebuild the Holy City, Jerusalem. Did not the poets say that in the history of the Jews a thousand years are but as yesterday? Persia fell, the Macedonians conquered; the centre of Jewry shifted to Alexandria. In that bustling, brash Hellenistic city of the ancient world, the Jews developed their talent for business and theology, their twin spurs, the aspiration to comprehend both the senses and the spirit. A fateful moment in their history had arrived, for the Jews had discovered their unique gift: the ability to ponder and worship the mystery of God's nature without for a single moment neglecting the ways of man. The understanding, the belief that the body housed the soul, and was therefore one and indivisible, gave birth to a glorious vitality that was to prove both triumphant and tragic: for the Jewish talent to straddle heaven and earth, to balance with such apparent ease on the tightrope between Jehovah and Mammon, was to cause them as much sorrow as it did joy. To those who were not Jews this mystery, this duality was a constant source of wonder, envy and resentment of unreasoning magnitude. Of all the peoples on this earth, the Jews alone appeared to have fashioned a key that unlocked a terrible and powerful source of human energy to be resisted, their enemies said, at all costs. The Jewish insight into the oneness of things was to be the greatest single cause not only of their survival, but also of their persecution and suffering.

Rome destroyed Jerusalem and strengthened the Jews' reliance on Law and Scripture, and thus prepared the civilised world to receive the birth of Jesus of Nazareth, the prophecies made Man and God. From Babylon to Arabia where Mahomet came under their spell and acknowledged a common father in Abraham; and thence, to Spain and Portugal, to Italy and Sicily, one foot in the civilised world of Islam, the other in the half-barbaric kingdom of Western Christendom, but carrying with them enough of the learning that was now Arabian but had once been Greek, to help attend at the true Renaissance which, at the close of the 11th century, began to raise the West out of the blood of the Dark Ages into the light of mediaeval Europe.

In that new Europe, the Jews found powerful patrons, Kings and princes, championing their cause against indignant Guilds and Estates of the Realm who regarded the newcomers' presence as a threat. But monarchs are only all-powerful when their subjects wish it so: by the 13th century, the Jews were forced to move once more and found their way across the Danube to Poland, their refuge for seven hundred years. And then the tide flowed back again, buffeting the Jews into the Age of Discovery. The world was convulsed as never before: in 1492, when Columbus believed he had discovered the Indies, countless Jews from Spain and Portugal, most of the

Italian states and nearly all the south German cities were expelled, causing yet another revolution, for, in the cities of the Mediterranean, so long the market-places of civilisation, trade languished while men sought untold riches across the North Atlantic. But in Marseilles, Leghorn and Levant, the exiled Jews found refuge and their commerce flourished. In the north, Hamburg and Frankfurt gathered to their profit what Augsburg and Nuremberg had tossed away; in London and Paris money clinked as never before, and Amsterdam, the centre of the United Provinces in their Golden Age, was maliciously nicknamed the New Jerusalem. And already, Jews had found their way to the Americas, there to develop 'Jew commerce', the new and risky trades in sugar, tobacco, indigo and cotton. And so, at the Cape, the first Jew to land on the southern tip of Africa was Fernão Martins; not one who professed his faith, but a 'new Christian', fluent in Portuguese, Arabic and Hebrew, he acted as mariner-interpreter to Vasco da Gama and sailed on his Admiral's ship the *San Gabriel* from whose decks the Portuguese first saw the land they called Natal.

The Jews spawned a new breed of celebrity: the international financier, the government adviser. The descendents of Joseph in Egypt served a dozen masters. There was Cromwell's 'Great Jew' Carvajal, and Robert Walpole's Gideon; in Frankfurt, Rothschild the money-lender rose from the ghetto to see five sons ennobled by five European monarchs and, in England, Disraeli flattered Victoria. There were musicians, writers, philosophers, doctors: 'the old and powerful yeast of mankind,' they were called. Confine them to a ghetto and they will escape; persecute them and they will survive; banish them and they will return. In Russia, the Tsar's power stretched from the Sea of Okhotsk to the Gulf of Bothnia. Alexander III, upon whom all Jews spit, added the word *pogrom* to the language of persecution: from 1882 onwards, the Jews fled from the Cossacks. In a thousand *shtetl*, the small townlets of eastern Europe, the Jews packed their belongings, poor and rich, dull and clever, eminent and anonymous. To America the land of the free, to England the land of the just, and to South Africa not yet a land of anything.

For a Jew it is not such a gigantic step from the streets of Riga to the streets of Cape Town. Their clothes may suit the burning sun and their accents assume the guttural overtones of Dutch, they may play havoc with English syntax, but they are Jews, their faces and their spirit proclaim it, the self-same Jews who may be seen in

Brooklyn, or Whitechapel, upholders of religion and pure breeding, the twin bands of iron that have held them together throughout the ages. And do they not all hope that their sojourn in each new resting-place shall be brief and uneventful? Do they not in their synagogues, their *shuls*, face east and pray 'Next year may we meet in Jerusalem?'

Brief and uneventful are forlorn hopes. In the streets of Cape Town they bustle to and fro, chattering in their own tongue, Yiddish, rich and expressive, a treacle of a language, interesting themselves in commerce, finance, art, literature, politics, life. Energetic and restless, discouraged from being otherwise, the Jew has not ministered to what Carlyle called 'the pot-bellied equanimity' of his neighbours or his hosts. Naïve to believe it possible of a people who produced Moses and the Prophets, Jesus of Nazareth, Karl Marx, Sigmund Freud and Albert Einstein and to whose number one Julius Levine, a second-hand furniture dealer and a descendant of the priests of Solomon, fervently believed would be added the name of his youngest child, Leonard.

2

Immigrants, and Jews are the most practised immigrants in history, know that false pride is the greatest handicap to survival. A man has only one obligation—his family; and to house, feed, and educate his family, he must work with all his heart and soul and body; the nature of the work may fortunately in some instances prove to be what the man likes and does best, but, if not, no great matter. Survival is all.

So it was that Julius Levine, a man without obvious skills or talent, had, after his arrival on these shores in 1899, aged seventeen, fallen by accident and necessity into the second-hand furniture business. It was not a trade for which he was ideally suited, but then Julius belonged to that unfortunate class who never learn for what they are ideally suited. He was not a self-assertive man by nature; he would have been happier owning a shop, selling things to people who made a conscious decision to come in and buy. But in the second-hand furniture trade it was the dealer's obligation to sniff out likely customers and then to force them into puchasing articles they did not really want: that was the difficult part and Julius avoided it as much as possible; so it was that he accumulated more than he disposed of. Yet, despite these drawbacks, Julius had married Freda Kanterowich, managed somehow to rent a house in Mount Street, fed and educated three children. In his children, Julius had achieved his most remarkable success, for the elder son Emanuel was now a doctor in Port Elizabeth, and the younger, Leonard, had earned the magical letters B.A., LL.B. behind his name which meant he could practise law and appear in the Supreme Court of the Union of South Africa. (The daughter, Lilian, who came between the two boys, was married to a pharmacist in Johannesburg, which was more than could be expected of a dutiful daughter.) And when Julius allowed his mind to dwell on his children, which he often did, he discovered that, invariably, his thoughts turned to Lennie.

Lennie: clever, handsome, golden Lennie. Julius knew it was wrong for a father to have a favourite child but try as he might not to indulge his younger son openly, he could not help but adore him. His two other children, Emmanuel, the doctor, and Lilian, seemed to understand and appeared not to mind. In fact, they teased Julius about it in front of Lennie and no ill-feeling resulted. Freda, Julius' wife, was more just; she loved all three children equally and well, and Julius envied her for that. He could not explain why Lennie should hold such a special place in his heart, but he had only to look at his son to feel a hopeless tenderness, a massive sense of pride. Was there anything he would not do for Lennie?

But such love, such opulent love, bred anxieties and anguish in rival abundance. The past year had been harder to bear for Julius than for Lennie. To watch his son, night after night, return home forlorn and weary, not from working but from unwanted idleness. Julius had thought, foolishly now he realised, that when B.A., LL.B. were appended to his son's name, the future would be bright and glorious. Not so; three briefs had come Lennie's way in the first half of the year, one in the second. And had Julius not tried to drum up more work for his son? Had he not bullied and badgered every attorney of his aquaintance in the hope of a brief? They had been kind but, in the end, unhelpful. And worse, in recent weeks, was to hear Lennie lying, pretending for his father's sake that work was beginning to come in, but Julius noticed that the attorneys Lennie said briefed him were invariably from out of town, men Julius had never heard of and could not possibly interrogate; he noticed too that the briefs were never for court appearances, but consultations in chambers. If Julius were rich there would be no problem: he would work till his last breath to keep Lennie, because he believed with every fibre of his being that his son would be important some day, perhaps a Judge, Prime Minister, or even *more* important, why not? But Julius could give only so much and no more; there was a limit not to his generosity, but to his supply.

Lennie: caring, kind, compassionate Lennie. Julius had but to think of the boy for his mind to be flooded with memories: Lennie, learning to walk and talk and count and sing; Lennie, top of the class in Latin, English, History; Lennie, Chairman of the junior debating society at twelve; Lennie, singing his *Bar Mitzvah* in the clearest treble the Rabbi said he had ever heard; and Lennie, accompanying his father in the van, going the rounds, loading the furniture into the back and seeing, it must have been for the first time, Hanover Street and District Six where the Coloureds lived, twenty to a house—a house? a hovel: the horror on Lennie's face, looking up at Julius, asking: 'But papa, how can we let them live like this?' And Julius, pricked by shame and guilt, answering in the only way he knew: 'All you can do, Lennie, is thank God it isn't us.'

And now Lennie was twenty-five, an advocate who could not make a living. When he had been turned down for the post in the Attorney-General's office, Julius had wept as if the disappointment was his own. Well, everything happens for the best: that was Julius Levine's motto. Optimism is another requisite for survival.

It was optimism of the 'you-never-know-what-you'll-find' variety that caused Julius Levine to make a purchase, seemingly routine, but with important consequences, on his way home one warm, balmy evening, 7 January 1929. He was seated at the wheel of his battered Ford van when he happened to pass near the Castle and saw one of the older town houses in the process of demolition. By force of habit, Julius braked and pulled into a side-road, then went to make a brief inspection of the building just in case there was anything of interest left inside.

Three Coloured workmen were packing up for the day. 'Which one of you's the foreman?' Julius asked.

'I am, master,' said one of them, a Malay.

'You pulling down this place?'

'Yes, master, we just stripped everything bare. Tomorrow we start properly.'

'Any bits and pieces?'

'How you mean, master?'

'Any furniture, it don't matter to me if it's broken. I'm willing to pay you boys something.'

371

The three exchanged interested glances. 'There's some stuff in the cellar,' the foreman said hopefully.

'Okey-dokey, we'll take a look,' replied Julius.

The cellar was reached by steps that ran down the outside of the house. One of the workmen lit a candle to light their way, and Julius took it from him to examine the shadowy, unidentifiable shapes that littered the cramped space below ground. There were empty tea chests mostly, a rusted bed ('Who needs beds?' said Julius), several broken chairs past repair. The only object of any interest to the dealer was an old wardrobe, with a mirrored front, in remarkably fine condition. When he opened the door, an avalanche of empty boxes struck him and the smell was appalling. But he liked the look of it and instructed the workmen to load it into the back of his van. For the wardrobe, and the two or three mysterious packages left inside, he paid five shillings.

When he entered his house in Mount Street which was quite as cluttered as the cellar from which he had just emerged, he greeted his wife Freda in Yiddish, and then asked, 'Where's Lennie?'

'At a meeting, where else?' Freda replied. She was gruff and practical, with fierce standards, and anyone who did not conform to those standards risked ostracism and damnation. She held respectability and gentility above all else; she talked of 'good breeding' and worse, 'bad blood', but she was the rock upon which Julius built his house and upon whom all her children, of which she counted her husband the eldest, relied. Breadwinning apart, she was both mother and father to all the Levines. 'I'm not waiting supper for him,' she warned. 'So—did you have a good day?'

'Fair. I bought you a wardrobe.'

'But I don't need a wardrobe. I got no clothes, what for do I need a wardrobe?'

'We'll think of something.'

'Dinner's on the table,' she said. 'Go and wash your hands, Julius, you and your wardrobe, and then come and eat.' She was no *nudzh* as they say in Yiddish, no nag; but children you treat like children.

Obediently, Julius washed his hands, and before tasting Freda's meat stew and *tzimmis*, the latter a delicious sweet carrot dish, the aroma already invading his nostrils, he stole into Lennie's bedroom, found a piece of paper and quickly scrawled, 'Had a good day.' And into an envelope he slipped a pound note as a present for his son.

'You're sure Lennie's at a meeting?' Julius asked seating himself across from Freda.

'That's what he told me,' she replied, serving her husband.

'Those meetings,' Julius grunted regretfully. ('Thank God it isn't us,' he had told Lennie, but in his heart he rejoiced, and loved his son the more for not being able to utter that prayer.)

3

But Leonard was not at a meeting; at the time his mother and father were sitting down to their evening meal, he was knocking on the door of his uncle's house in the hope of borrowing fifty pounds. Uncle Marcus was Julius's brother—the Jews' penchant for Roman names has never been satisfactorily explained—older by four years and richer by many thousands of pounds. He had made his money out of selling wines and spirits to the Coloureds, and lived now in Oranjezicht, a suburb of modest villas where Jews were wont to move once they prospered. Leonard was on his uncle's doorstep out of desperation, for the truth was that the brothers had not spoken for almost twenty years; the reason was never known, perhaps not even to them, but the feud was deep and intense, and both brothers unforgiving and apt to make vicious innuendoes, whose full meaning was more often than not lost on the listener. But there were good reasons, family reasons, why Leonard had decided to seek his uncle's help: Marcus had held him at his circumcision and was, in effect, his godfather, and therefore, someone to whom you could turn in time of trouble.

'Lenshki!' Marcus cried, seeing his nephew, and tears immediately sprang into his eyes.

'Hello, Uncle Marcus, may I come in?'

'May you come in? What kind of a question is that? May you come in? The house is yours, come in, come in.'

Once inside the well-lit hall, Marcus said, 'Let me look at you,' and took Leonard's face in both his hands, tears running freely now. 'No, I can't look at you. All I can see is my own father, God rest his soul.' Tall and thin and serious, that was Leonard: with a shock of unruly black hair forever in need of a comb. 'Agh! You could be a film star!' Marcus said with a dismissive gesture and led the way into the living-room. 'Auntie Greta's out,' he said. 'She's playing poker. Poker? Highway robbery she plays. She'll come home and I'll be a poor man, you mark my words. She can't see the cards any more. "Get glasses," I said. But will she? Never. She's too vain. So for her vanity I could go broke. So, Lenshki, don't stand—the chairs won't break.'

The room was furnished in a three-piece suite covered in uncut moquette, with anti-macassars on the backs of the chairs and sofa; nests of polished teak tables blossomed at every corner and on the floor lay a luxurious Persian carpet: there was no style, no taste, and yet you knew you were in a room that was lived in, and part of a house that was cared for.

'So,' said Marcus when the two were seated. 'You'll have something to eat?'

'I'm not hungry, thank you.'

'Have you ever been hungry? I don't think I've ever known you to have a meal. Eat, for God's sake. You'll end up looking like Gandhi and you know what trouble *he* caused.' Lennie shook his head. 'All right, look like Gandhi, who cares?' Marcus smiled, his eyes glowing with warmth. 'Lenshki, Lenshki, this is nice. Out of the blue like this, oh, you don't know how happy you make me. So. Tell me. Come on. Give. How's the advocate? You had some juicy cases? Divorce, that's where the money is, Lenshki. Concentrate on divorce, you'll end up an Oppenheimer. *Nu?* Tell.'

Lennie sat with his hands clasped between his legs, as though in pain; he never once looked up at his uncle. 'That's—that's what I've come to see you about, Uncle Marcus. Things—things aren't going too well.'

'All right, so you'll wait a year before you take silk,' Marcus continued, jocularly, insensitive to Lennie's predicament.

'No, it's bad, Uncle Marcus. Things are going badly. I—I can't seem to get started, I don't seem to attract any work—I've had two or three briefs but—don't tell my father, don't tell my father—' Lennie broke off and winced inwardly; he knew he had given offence.

'There's no danger of me telling your father,' Marcus said bitterly.

Lennie decided to plunge. 'I've come to see you, Uncle Marcus, because I'm desperate. I'm at my wits' end. I just don't know who to turn to. I owe for my office, for my furniture, for the telephone, I had to talk to someone.'

'How much do you need, Lenshki?' Marcus asked, but his tone was serious, cautious.

'I need—I need fifty pounds.'

Marcus sighed and ran a hand over his shiny, bald pate. 'Fifty pounds,' he repeated, sighing again.

'I have to be honest with you. I couldn't possibly promise to pay it back in any given time. But things have got to get better, Uncle Marcus, simply because they can't get any worse. But this I can promise: as soon as I've got the money you can have it back.'

Marcus nodded. 'I know that, I know that,' he said. 'It's not a question of paying back. From relations I don't take IOUs,' and then added one of his innuendoes, 'You ask your father about me and IOUs, he'll tell you.'

'I have to be honest with you—'

'Naturally—'

'I don't want you to think I'm about to be deluged with briefs—'

'I understand—'

'Can you help me, Uncle Marcus? Fifty pounds, that's all I'm asking. If you can't manage fifty, twenty would be fine, can you?'

Marcus stood and reached into his back trouser-pocket from which he took a fat bundle of notes. 'Will fifty be enough?' he asked, counting the money with his thumb.

Lennie rose, too. 'Plenty, plenty, just fifty, that's wonderful,' and he felt his knees weaken with relief.

Marcus held up the loan as if to hand it to his nephew, then pulled it back, keeping it close to his chest. 'Lennie, I have to make a condition.'

'You mean interest? Whatever you say.'

'Interest, what d'you take me for? You think I'd charge interest to my own nephew? Are you mad?' he was genuinely angry. 'Ask your father if I charge interest!'

'I'm sorry—'

'I should think so.'

'Well, what condition—'

'Lenshki, if I lend you this money, you'll have to make me a promise.'

'What?'

'You have to promise me, on your mother's life,' Marcus said with funereal solemnity, 'you have to promise that you'll give up your meetings, give up politics.'

Lennie did not reply; he gazed expressionless at his uncle who shrugged apologetically as if it hurt him to say those words. Both men faced each other allowing the silence to make it more difficult for either to speak. At last, Marcus found his voice. 'You're surprised you get no work. You're surprised you owe left, right and centre. Well, I'm not. Who's going to give you work? Hmm?

Who'll give a Communist work? Only other Communists, and how many you got? Twenty? Thirty? Enough to keep a young advocate? Don't make me laugh, Lennie, believe me, it's damaging your career. You'll end up in the gutter. Promise me, now, here, in my house, man to man, on your mother's life.'

'I can't do that,' Lennie replied dully, without emotion, just a statement of fact.

'Think about it. Come back tomorrow. The money'll be here—'

'I couldn't do it, Uncle Marcus.'

'It's for your own good, Lennie, you want a career? I'm telling you how to have a career.'

'I'd rather starve—'

'Don't be so quick to offer, you may have to! What are you trying to do, Lennie? You want us thrown out of here as well? You want them to say the Jews aren't here ten minutes and they want a revolution, is that what you want? You want us all thrown out? Where will we go this time? Hmm? Tell me, where? Peru? Borneo? Where d'you want us to go? Because that's what'll happen, Lennie—'

'Thank you, Uncle Marcus. It's best we don't say any more. Please. I'm sorry I troubled you. Good night. Give my love to Auntie Greta. Good night.' He turned to go.

'Ah!' cried Marcus fiercely. 'Take the money!' and he threw the bundle of notes down on the floor, scattering them over the Persian carpet.

'No,' said Lennie and continued to walk down the hall to the front door. 'Good night.'

Marcus pursued him. 'Oh? So now you've got pride. Since when do Communists have pride? Take the money, you need it, for God's sake take it, I don't want it—'

'Good night,' he said again, opening the door.

'Pride like your father, you've got pride! And you'll end up just like him! You'll end up a second-hand advocate, you mark my words!' But by then Lennie was out on the front path, and had closed the door behind him.

4

Lennie half-walked, half-ran down Upper Orange Street back towards town, hands thrust deep into his trousers, shoulders hunched as though a cold wind were biting through him, his uncle's words resounding in his head.

Of course, the old man was right, there was no denying it, he had diagnosed the reasons for Lennie's failure accurately, which were, as Marcus had said, political affiliations that the staid established attorneys would prefer the young advocate not to have. But Lennie's convictions were heartfelt, they were not a pose, they could not be shrugged off or, worse, sold for fifty pounds. He believed, both intellectually and emotionally, in a new social order, a re-structuring of the society in which he lived, he wanted to sweep away the corrupt dung-heap under which men hid their greed and aggression. The Communist Party provided him with all the answers, which was a measure of the limit to Lennie's intellect.

When Lennie first joined he learned, with sorrow but not despair, that the Party was preoccupied only with the interests of the white working class, and although it repudiated the Colour Bar entrenched in the Mines and Works Act of 1926, it remained ambiguous in its true attitudes. Gradually, however, with the influx of younger men, the intelligentsia like Lennie, the members began to work more and more with non-Europeans, starting a night school where reading and writing were taught as a means to understanding Marxist doctrine. But, like all South African institutions which appear radical, its public utterances, Lennie discovered, in no way reflected the members' privately held beliefs. The vast majority secretly subscribed to a system that enshrined the master–servant relationship; publicly they attacked old established patterns of thought and behaviour, but in the main were more obsessed with labour relations, trades unions, economic theory, Marxist dogma and ways of satisfying the Party's thirst for power. The daily, hourly hurt to ten million fellow citizens touched them hardly at all.

But Lennie was touched; he felt genuine concern for the plight of his 'Coloured comrades' as he liked to call them. Following the lead of the Central Committee, he had opened a small night class above a clothes shop in Hanover Street, teaching illiterate coloured adults to read and write. No other task in his young life had brought him more satisfaction. The night when Ahmed Roopi had read with such difficulty to Lennie and to his half-dozen fellow students, the passage beginning, 'The wealth of those societies in which the capitalist mode of production prevails . . .' was a moment of excitement never to be equalled. It was the same Ahmed Roopi who had been instrumental in urging Lennie to apply for a post in the Attorney-General's office. The previous October, Ahmed's father had been arrested and charged with the theft of cigarettes from a warehouse where he worked as caretaker. The man swore that a gang of white youths were guilty. Lennie agreed to defend Roopi senior. The case lasted an hour; Roopi was found guilty and sentenced to a year's imprisonment. What horrified Lennie most was the way the prosecution had been conducted: the blatant connivance with the police, a desire not to put the facts before the court, but to obtain a conviction, against which Lennie had been powerless. Two days after the verdict, he applied for a position, but was unsuccessful. His father Julius accused the Attorney-General of being an anti-semite of towering proportions, 'a Tsar in wolf's clothing', and certainly anti-semitism played a part in Lennie's rejection.

Thoughts of the Roopi case turned Lennie's attention once more to his present desperate financial plight and to that uncomfortable, striving part of his own nature which he despised in himself, but seemed unable to control. There was no denying that he cared for his fellow-men and wanted to serve them; there was also no denying that he hungered for society's approval for what he did and for what he was. Lennie was not a man like Michael Thompson, who wanted to be accepted or who wanted to feel superior; at the centre of his being was an unshakeable belief that he *was* superior; what he desired was other people to believe it. The duality of his actions was born out of his sense of service and his social conscience on the one hand, and a need for the outward trappings of success on the other. Had he been of a calmer, less embattled temperament, he might have realised that the first could have fed the second, that service and reward are not necessarily mutually exclusive or incompatible, but that would have meant rewriting the dogma to which he so passionately subscribed to 'the means justify the end.'

But Lennie, youthful and aspiring, was not the man to reconcile the divisions within himself. He could only admire one half, and condemn the other. Here he was, a communist, who believed man needed only that which was useful, and yet he had rented an office, hired a desk, a chair, a hat-stand, a waiting-room sofa, telephone and secretary (who admittedly he had sacked without paying her salary), to furnish a practice that did not exist Julius had offered him second-hand stuff, but Lennie refused. No, it had to be new, comfortable, impressive. Why? Lennie shuddered, unable to answer.

He tried to examine the other important circumstances which surrounded him: his Jewishness, his family, his place in society. Shortly after his *bar mitzvah* he rejected belief in God, yet he was at pains to justify the mystic attachment he felt for his fellow-Jews. Suffering, history, shared experience bound them to him, not religious mumbo-jumbo. Lennie knew that his position in the world was conditioned by race, not class. He had written once, when he was fourteen, an essay on 'Assimilation: the Jewish destiny', but his mother had found it in his desk and had forbade him to allow anyone to see it. Yet, he still believed that anti-semitism would only disappear when the semite disappeared. The Jew must take on the responsibility himself, for no one else would. 'Lennie,' his mother had said, 'the trouble with you is, you're an idealist,' and Julius had replied, 'Don't say it as though it were a curse.'

Julius: Lennie could not bear any more the questioning, hopeful look in the old man's eyes each evening; could not accept his indiscriminate love and charity another day. And it was this train of thought that led Lennie towards the decision to apply again to the Attorney-General, although he could think of no rational reason why his second attempt should be any more successful than the first. But he reasoned it thus, and the convolutions reveal the conflict within him: he needed money and a public platform from which to flaunt his ideals; he needed to remove the cloying pressure of his family and he needed a way to express his individuality outside the stifling confines of racial barriers. An official position answered all the requirements. He would try again.

He walked for many hours that night and the resolution brought new confidence; just before midnight, he arrived home, and heard his father's hoarse whisper from the bedroom, 'Is that you, Lenshki?' 'Yes, papa, it's me.' He heard the bed creak as Julius turned over, for the old man could not sleep until he knew his son was safely home.

When he entered his bedroom and found the message and the money, Lennie's spirits plummeted. He sat on the edge of the bed gazing at the pound note as though it represented all that he despaired of in his own nature. Quickly, as if he did not want to see himself do it, he stuffed the money into his wallet, took pad and pen from his bedside cupboard, and wrote to the Attorney-General. The next morning, 8 January, he dropped the letter in by hand and hoped against hope for success.

29

The second-hand advocate

The three weeks that followed this second application of Lennie's took on the nightmarish quality of the unexpected, the frightening and the unlikely, although there was one encouraging incident: arriving at his office he found a letter which contained a five pound note and scrap of paper on which was written in Uncle Marcus's unmistakable handwriting: 'From an anonymous giver.' For the rest of the time, however, the nightmare took control.

Most of Lennie's day was spent swivelling round and round in his hired chair. Occasionally, he summoned the energy to read or write —he was working on an article entitled 'A Trade Union for All?'— but found difficulty in concentrating. The office was gloomy and depressing; the one window looked out on a small garage with a corrugated iron roof and, beyond, the fire escape of an office block. He received little mail, and his appointment diary was blank. He did not eat lunch, but walked in the Botanical Gardens each day and he advanced the time of this outing first by five minutes, then ten, until he was leaving the office at half-past eleven and returning at three. It was on returning from his walk one day that he trotted up the creaking wooden stairs and found his former secretary, Golda Schaskolsky, waiting for him on the landing, nervously twisting the strap of her handbag. Once inside his office, Lennie said. 'And what can I do for you, Golda?' knowing well enough what the answer would be.

Golda was a timid creature, and pitifully unattractive with a bulbous nose, close-set myopic eyes and a perpetual cold. 'Lennie,' she whined, 'I'm sorry, but you've got to pay me.'

'Golda, I told you next month, I promised!' Lennie explained impatiently.

'I can't wait till then, Lennie.'

'You're going to have to.'

'My brother Morrie says you've got to pay me or else.'

'Or else what?'

'He didn't say or else what, he just said or else. You know Morrie.'

'You tell Morrie it's a criminal offence to make threats.'

'I'll tell him, Lennie, but it won't make any difference.'

'Look, Golda, you think I want to keep you waiting? You think it gives me pleasure to owe you eight weeks' salary? You know me. If I had it, I'd give it to you. But you'll have to wait. Tell Morrie he's not to worry. You'll get every penny next month.'

'He won't like it,' Golda said, sniffing.

'Just tell him. What's he going to do, sue me?'

'I'll tell him,' she answered, turned and forlornly shuffled down the stairs that led to the street.

Lennie returned to his desk and dismissed Golda from his thoughts knowing that he could have kept her and her brother quiet with a couple of pounds out of Uncle Marcus's gift, but Lennie wanted the money for a more serious emergency. That, too, was not long in coming.

At five o'clock, just as he was about to leave for home, four Coloured men entered the office and began to remove the furniture. Lennie bullied, pleaded, cajoled.

'It's not up to us, master. You better talk to the boss. He's downstairs on the lorry.'

Lennie ran full pelt into the street; there, supervising the loading of the repossessed furniture, stood Sammy Lurie, a former classmate of Lennie's who had, while Lennie was at university, built up a thriving furniture business.

'Sammy!' Lennie cried. 'How can you do this to me?'

'Watch and you'll see,' said Sammy, ticking off each item as it was loaded.

'Sammy, look, put it all back, please, I—I can pay you.'

'I'll put it back *when* you pay me.'

Lennie showed him the five pound note. 'I mean it! Look, I've got the money!'

Like an owl swooping on its prey, Sammy snatched the note.

'That's for five weeks. You owe me for ten.'

'But Sammy!' Lennie yelled, outraged. 'At least put the stuff back. I'll pay you the rest.'

At that moment, one of the coloured men reported that the office was clear. Sammy said, 'Sign here!'

'But Sammy, Sammy, please give me a chance!'

'If I had a penny for every chance I've given you, Lennie, I wouldn't have to do this for a living.'

Desperately Lennie followed Sammy round to the driver's cabin. 'But Sammy, we've been friends for years, our parents are practically related, haven't you got any fellow feeling?'

'Only for solvent people I've got fellow feeling,' and he started up the engine and drove off.

Some days later, Lennie had another visitor, at home this time, and one whose words and actions disturbed him more than his creditors could ever do. The visitor's name was Oskar Blatt, and he was, amongst other things, a member of the Central Committee and the secretary of the Cape Town cell of the Communist Party.

2

The purpose and eventual outcome of Oskar Blatt's visit, though unimportant in the history of the Communist Party, was to prove a crucial factor in the life and subsequent career of Leonard Levine.

Lennie did not take the political in-fighting of the party seriously; he involved himself as little as possible with the groups and factions that inevitably form in such organisations. And so it was that when his mother announced that Oskar Blatt was waiting at the front door, Lennie was puzzled and faintly disquieted, for he was not accustomed to visits from members of the Central Committee.

If the impossible had happened and the Communists had come to power in South Africa, then, unquestionably, Oskar Blatt would have been given the Ministry of the Interior. A Jew born in Odessa, Oskar was one of nature's secret policemen: he thrived on secrets, he grew fat—enormously fat—on secrets, he wallowed in secrets as a hippopotamus wallows in mud. Obese, sallow and bald, he was constantly nervous and on edge, as though he expected at any moment either to be arrested or to be summoned to assume the reins of government. He liked people to underestimate him, for it helped him to survive; as an ideologist, his creed was power; had he remained in Russia he could have served Lenin, Trotsky or Stalin with equal loyalty.

Freda, who disapproved of Oskar—'has he ever seen a bar of soap?' she asked—kept him waiting in the narrow hallway while she went to fetch Lennie. There the fat man stood, filling the door frame, hopping from one foot to the other, picking his blackened finger-nails to the quick, and puffing a Turkish cigarette which dangled from his sensual mouth. The moment Lennie appeared, Oskar trundled towards him and talked in a toneless whisper, his accent impossible to place accurately, for upon Odessa had been laminated Athens, Cairo, Marseilles and Buenos Aires. 'Lennie, Lennie, I'm glad you're in. Where can we talk?'

'What's the trouble, comrade?'

'Ssh! Drop the comrade. Call me Oskar for God's sake. Where can we talk?'

'Come into the lounge,' Lennie said, holding open the door that led off the passage. Oskar squeezed past him into a room that bore witness to Julius Levine's weakness for buying more than he sold. The four walls were tightly and neatly crammed with chairs, tables, chests of drawers, rolled-up rugs, pictures and lamps. But, in the centre of the room, beneath an ornate crystal chandelier a small, square space had been cleared and here stood a black upright piano —Blüthner, Leipzig—a duet stool, a standard lamp and two cavernous armchairs. 'What's all this about?' Lennie asked.

'I've a message from Shura Shanban,' Oskar explained urgently. 'He asks: will you support him?'

'For what?' Lennie asked.

Oskar shook his head violently. 'That's all I can say. Just answer yes or no. Do you support Shura?'

'But I have to know more, Oskar.'

Agitated, Oskar looked for a place to stub out his cigarette, then thought better of it and continued to puff the stunted butt. 'All right,' he said. 'I can't go into detail, it's not possible, you mustn't ask me. But last month, did you or did you not make a speech to the Foreign Affairs committee?'

'Yes . . .'

'Did you or did you not say that we must stand on our own feet here in South Africa, without interference from Moscow.'

'Yes, I did.'

'Then, you're with Shura.'

'I don't understand, Oskar—'

'Lennie,' croaked Oskar earnestly, 'Do you trust me?'

'Yes . . .' Lennie answered but not wholeheartedly.

'Then come with me now. There's a meeting at Shura's, absolutely vital, get your jacket, we'll go now and not a word to a living soul!'

'You have to tell me more, Oskar!'

'Will you keep your voice down? More? All right I'll tell you more,' and he put his face close to Lennie's. 'It's about the leadership.'

A curious, unaccustomed thrill passed through Lennie's body. Having been nothing more than an active rank-and-file member, he felt suddenly sucked in to the very centre of the Party. To his ever-lasting good fortune, he agreed to accompany Oskar Blatt. They said little on the walk to Shura Shanban's house but just as they reached the front door, Oskar turned to Lennie. 'I *know* we're doing the right thing,' he said, and rang the bell.

They were admitted by Miss Arenstein, a bird-like spinster from Kiev. No one knew her first name and she rarely talked, except to voice her favourite cry of despair, 'Black! Things are black!' A life-long Party member—both her parents had been executed in the cause—she was used as a slave by the men, performing all the menial, unwanted tasks from making tea to licking envelopes. She led Oskar and Lennie down a corridor into a dimly-lit bedroom.

When Lennie's eyes grew accustomed to the pale, sickly light, he recognised three other men. The host, Shura Shanban, his son-in-law Max Teitelbaum, and a Scot, George McPherson. Shura was a prince of the Party with an irreproachable pedigree: twice exiled to Siberia by the Tsar, he was someone who (and this was his chief claim to fame) had actually shaken hands with Karl Marx in London in 1880. Now in his seventies, suffering from emphysema, he hardly ever moved from his bed. Propped up against pillows, sipping lemon tea from a glass he held in both hands as though to warm them against the Siberian winter, he played the role of arch-intriguer, his illness contributing a sepulchral overtone to everything he said.

Max Teitelbaum, who was married to Shura's daughter Fanny, was a taut, slender man of fifty; he had grown his beard to resemble Lenin's but that was his only distinction; he lived in the shadow of his father-in-law and deferred to him on all issues. The third man, George McPherson, was an immigrant from Clydeside who had settled in Cape Town in 1919. Tough and wiry, it was said he could crush a walnut in one hand. He claimed that the sinking of the *Titanic* had converted him to Communism, for he believed, though he could not exactly explain why, that the tragedy was caused not by the iceberg, but by the capitalist system. A man of little guile, and even less intellect, his standard response to the inevitable question, 'But what *is* Communism?' was 'Read the Sermon on the Mount, laddie, it's aw' in thair!'

Once Lennie and Oskar had taken their places at the foot of Shura's bed, the meeting began in earnest. From time to time, Shura swigged from a large bottle of sickly-red cough mixture and wheezed alarmingly. Between spasms, he managed to issue the solemn injunction that secrecy was of the utmost importance since lives may depend on what was decided that night.

One of the recurring fantasies of Communists, especially those who belong to the weaker and more ineffectual parties around the world, is to enact, at regular intervals, a struggle for leadership, thus mirroring the deadlier charades performed in Moscow and elsewhere. Such a fantasy was being indulged that night in January 1929 in Shura Shanban's bedroom. The reasons for these flights of fancy are plain and understandable: the conspirators, whose political energies were daily frustrated by the denial of real power, found an outlet in *coups* and counter-*coups* within their own party. It was an outlet, too, for their private frustrations, for all bore the mark of personal failure: Shura, the former bookkeeper, Teitelbaum, the door-to-door jewellery salesman, McPherson, the riveter turned bicycle mechanic and Oskar Blatt, the liftman who ferried people up and down a department store, reeling off in his nervous whisper the goods sold on each floor. Lennie, albeit unsuccessful, at least had youth and a university degree on his side, but even he was possessed of vast reserves of unused vitality.

Round the bed they gathered, their faces lit by the solitary light above, as though they were models for Rembrandt's 'Anatomy Lesson'. First, they heard a diagnosis of the present situation from Oskar who, as a member of the Central Committee, knew in intimate detail the strengths and weaknesses of the entrenched leadership; next, it was Shura's turn to cough and splutter the vaguest outline of a plan that would, he hoped, place at the head of the Party his beloved, dutiful son-in-law, Max Teitelbaum. Lennie learned that he himself was to be appointed, along with McPherson, to the new Central Committee; Oskar would become General Secretary. Miss Arenstein's role, it seemed, would remain unchanged. Shura modestly declined an official post because of his age, but there was no doubting his real intention, which was to use Teitelbaum as a puppet. They were not concerned that night with details: it was the overall strategy that mattered, and the unqualified loyalty of all those present. Their political pretext was that they were acting to disavow Moscow in favour of internationalism. Ideology was reduced to slogans, bandying about meaningless and tarnished jargons: Trotskyists, Mensheviks, deviationists and the rest; they even talked of *kulaks* and collectivisation. But these were side-issues: what mattered most was that they were plotting and intriguing, for that is what they understood and loved best. And Lennie, though he would not realise it for many years, could count himself blessed to be among their number.

The discussion ended with the unanimous resolve to act as soon as possible, but the exact methods were yet to be finalised. While Miss Arenstein puffed up Shura's pillows for the umpteenth time, each man, in turn, shook hands with their self-appointed leader. 'Tomorrow,' he wheezed, 'I will take more soundings. Oskar, can you get the lunch hour off?'

'Certainly, Shura—'

'Good, good. Gentlemen, think of yourselves as the tip of a pyramid. Tomorrow, Oskar and I will set about constructing a solid and indestructible base. And now, Miss Arenstein, be so good as to turn off the light.'

Out in the street, the five walked some way together before parting for their respective homes. They were in high spirits, all except Miss Arenstein who remained silent as usual. None had second thoughts about the course of action to which they had committed themselves. Lennie revelled in the secret comradeship, his agile mind delighted in the elaborate tactical manoeuvres the power struggle demanded. He was young and he was clever and he was *involved*. Temporarily, all his pressing personal worries were forgotten.

When they finally parted, Max Teitelbaum said, 'Well, we stand on the eve of great events. Of such meetings history is made.' Again, they all shook hands. The last words were left to Miss Arenstein. Holding Lennie's hands and looking deep into his eyes, she said, 'It's black. Black.'

The day after the secret meeting, a Friday, Lennie was barred from entering his office. The caretaker of the building stood at Lennie's door, arms folded across his chest, as though he were guarding The Treasures of Pharoah. 'Unless you pay all the rent you owe, Mr Levine . . .'; Lennie knew it was pointless to argue. He handed over his keys and walked home.

'Why aren't you at the office?' Freda asked.

'I've got a headache,' he replied, avoiding explanation at all costs.

'Find yourself a girl friend and stop going to so many meetings, you won't have so many headaches.'

He lay down on his bed and dozed fitfully, putting from his mind the latest set-back to his career. His thoughts were of the Party, of Shura Shanban and the Central Committee. Contented, he dreamed of success and fame and power. In mid-afternoon, Julius returned. Friday, the eve of Sabbath, the *Shabas*, was a short working-day for all Jews. They would go back to their homes to wash and dress in readiness for the weekly service at the synagogue. Julius was particularly early this day and he looked in on Lennie. 'Mama tells me you're not well.'

'I'll be all right.'

'I'm going to unpack and give a look-over some of the rubbish I bought this last month. You'll help?'

'No, papa, I want to think.'

'You can think while you help. I've got there a big wardrobe I can't lift myself.'

'Later, papa.'

With a shrug, Julius left him. Half an hour later the old man burst into Lennie's bedroom once more, this time bubbling with excitement. 'Lennie, come quick. I've found me a portrait, it's may be a Rubens, come quick!'

In the yard at the rear of the house lay the wardrobe on its back, the doors open, and Lennie could see that not all the contents had been unpacked. Stretched out on the ground, a stone at each corner to keep it flat, was an unframed oil-painting, dirty and stained, but unmistakably a portrait of a dwarf.

'What do you think?' Julius asked.

'Have you got some white spirit? Let's clean away a little bit.'

'Here,' said Julius, handing his son a small bottle. 'You do it, I'm too nervous.'

Kneeling down before the portrait, Lennie carefully wiped away some of the grime on the bottom edge until a richer texture of colour showed through. 'It looks good, Papa,' Lennie said catching some of his father's excitement. 'He's an ugly little bugger, I'll say that for him.'

'A dwarf, certainly. Wasn't Rubens always painting dwarfs? He paused and clapped a hand to his forehead. 'Oh God! Or was it van Dyck? One of them, I'm sure—'

'There's some writing here,' Lennie said, working away gently at the canvas. 'B—E—Z—'

'Careful, careful, don't do too much. On Monday I'll take it to Abe Shapiro. He'll do it proper. He knows what's what.'

For some minutes, father and son gazed at the painting of the ugly, deformed creature. Then, Lennie asked, 'Where did you find it, papa?' and Julius told him of the house near the Castle where he had discovered the wardrobe.

'Perhaps there's some other things in there—' and he turned his attention to the cardboard boxes that were stuffed inside. Together, they pulled them out. It was the second one that yielded the discovery: inside a box that had once contained Lipton's Tea, they found a large pile of parchment, each page filled with intricate handwriting in High Dutch. Although Lennie had studied the language at school he was not proficient enough in it to decipher the complex hand, but he did recognise a name, repeated over and over again throughout the document. 'Henning,' he said.

'Who?'

'Henning. He's a judge.'

'Is that the name on the paper?'

Lennie pointed to several places where it appeared. 'This could be valuable,' Lennie said.

'What, for lavatory paper?'

'No, papa! The Judge'll buy, I bet you! He collects stuff to do with his family, it's well known. You can try—'

'What, me sell to a Judge?'

'Why not?'

'Listen, Lennie, I get nervous selling to *schwarze*, how would I be with a Judge?'

Lennie was about to argue when his mother interrupted. 'There's someone to see you, Lennie,' she called from the kitchen window which overlooked the yard.

'Who is it?' Lennie asked.

'Who knows?'

Julius said, 'You go and find out. I'm going to take the painting to Abe Shapiro *now*! He'll give a quick look and tell me what he thinks before he goes to *shul*. And if it's a Rubens, I'll go to *shul* with him!'

Lennie saw a stranger standing at the front door: he looked like a weight-lifter or a Japanese wrestler, and his arms hung like a gorilla's, as though to parenthesise his vast bulk. He was dressed for the synagogue in a dark blue suit and a snap-brimmed hat. He introduced himself as Morris Schaskolsky, the brother of Golda, Lennie's unpaid former secretary.

'How d'you do,' Lennie said nervously, but smiling with all the warmth he could muster.

'I want to talk with you,' Morrie said. 'We'll take a little walk.'

'We can talk here,' said Lennie.

'We'll walk!' growled Morrie.

The two men went out into the street. With a jerk of his head, Morrie beckoned Lennie to follow him round the side of the house. The moment they had turned the corner, Morrie suddenly thudded into Lennie, pushed him up against the brick wall and held him tightly by the throat. 'Send messages like that and I'll kill you!'

'What messages?' Lennie gasped.

'Golda said you'd have me arrested!'

'I never! I never!'

'Don't shout! She said you told her it was illegal to make threats! Golda wouldn't make that up! She hasn't the brains!'

'Let go of my throat!'

'Pay your debts!'

'I will, I will!'

'When?' Lennie choked. 'When?' Morrie again demanded, tightening his grip. Just then, Julius appeared at the corner, the painting of the dwarf tucked under his arm. Alarmed at the scene, he stumbled forward. 'Hey!' he shouted, 'let go my boy! Let go of him! I'll call the police!'

At once Morrie let Lennie go and when Julius drew level, he tipped his hat politely to the older man. 'I'm sorry, Mr Levine, but your son owes my sister money—'

Lennie sank down on the pavement and started to sob. Julius knelt beside him. 'Lennie, Lennie, are you all right?' but his son could not answer for the pain in his throat.

'I want my sister's money, Mr Levine!'

'Shut up!' yelled Julius. 'Get away from here, you Peruvian!' Peruvian was a synonym for barbarian, but used only by South African Jews to describe other South African Jews. Morrie stood his ground, 'I'm not going from here until I get some money!'

Angrily Julius reached into his pocket, withdrew two pound notes and tossed them on the ground. Morrie scrambled to retrieve them. 'I'll be back for some more next Friday, and the Friday after that and the Friday after that until the whole debt is paid! At five o'clock before I go to *shul* I'll be here. And if I don't get the money, I'll break every bone in your son's body!' He walked off, but had only gone a few steps when he paused, turned back, tipped his hat once more and said, 'Oh, and good *shabas* to you both.'

Julius helped Lennie back into the house, and managed to get him into the bedroom without Freda hearing. But, once inside, Lennie fell on the bed and sobbed until Julius thought his own heart would break. The whole story tumbled out. Patiently, Julius tried to understand the extent of his son's liabilities and soon realised just how large they were. The money would have to be borrowed. Perhaps Uncle Marcus—but Lennie confessed he had already tried and been turned down. 'My only hope,' cried Lennie, 'is to get a job with the Attorney-General and there's not much chance of that!'

'Well, God is good,' said Julius. 'Everything happens for the best. Perhaps the painting's a Rubens, who knows?' And after a little while he added, 'I think I'll go to *shul* tonight. You'll come?'

But Julius went alone. He prayed as he had never prayed before. That night, he tossed and turned on his bed, with Freda asleep beside him. His brain was weary and confused with thinking of ways to help his son. And then, like a flash of lightning, the idea occurred to him. 'My God!' he said aloud, 'of course! The Judge!'

30

Second-hand dealers

Two days passed before Julius Levine could summon enough courage to visit Dawid Henning. He told no one of his intentions. To Lennie he would say, 'Don't fret, don't fret, we'll think of something,' and, of course, 'Everything happens for the best,' but that was mostly to bolster his own lack of confidence. The more he tried to reason away his terror—'A Judge is only a man, a man like any other man'—the more terrified he became. From bitter experience Julius knew just how clumsy he could be when confronted by people in authority, especially those who were not Jewish, although he had to admit that even the prospect of meeting, say, the Chief Rabbi made his knees tremble. A Judge! A *goyisher* Judge! Julius would be ill-at-ease, garrulous, he was certain of it, bound to say the wrong thing, bound to offend, bound to do Lennie more harm than good. Hourly, he put off the dread moment of decision. From superstition rather than religious fervour he did not dare make a business call on the Saturday, since Jews are forbidden to handle money on their sabbath and it would not do to risk the ire of the Almighty; Sunday, being the Judge's sabbath, was also excluded, but on Monday he could find no excuse at all: at five o'clock in the afternoon he parked his van on the steep hill, directly opposite the Henning house in Tamboers Kloof, and kept watch, but his anxiety was constant because he did not know what to expect: would the Judge arrive in a limousine? would he be escorted by soldiers? would he be wearing his scarlet robes? how, how, would he look? Half-an-hour after his vigil had begun, he saw an elderly man turn the corner and come slowly towards him, and then, to Julius's surprise, the man fumbled for a latchkey and disappeared into the Henning house. Could this be the Judge? True, he wore a stern, intent expression, walked gravely and carried himself with unmistakable dignity, but would a Judge wear such a shabby overcoat, and carry his own briefcase? There was only one way to find out.

With a tremendous effort of will ('for Lennie, for Lennie' he kept telling himself), Julius stepped out on to the pavement, cast his eyes briefly towards the sky and, in Hebrew, muttered, 'Who is like unto Thee, O Lord? Who is like unto Thee, glorious in holiness, awe-inspiring, working wonders?' He had taken some care in selecting the prayer, for he did not think it fitting to make a direct plea for help, but the form he settled on contained all his hopes for, what seemed to him, the infinitely more difficult request he had now to make of the earthly judge.

Slowly he crossed the street, his legs heavy as lead. Half-way, his courage momentarily failed him—'what will I say to him, what will I say?'—and he stood dead still, staring at the house as though it were a spectre he hoped would soon disappear. On he walked, opened the garden gate, shuffled up the steps towards the front door. Suddenly, panic again seized him; every thought flew from his head and yet his finger continued to reach out and pressed the bell. Once more he gazed heavenwards and, in a terse and desperate whisper, called, 'We beseech Thee, O Lord, save *now*! We beseech Thee, O Lord, make us *now* to prosper!' Then a Coloured servant opened the door.

2

Dawid was in his bedroom when the doorbell rang. He had just removed his overcoat and jacket, loosened his bow-tie when the servant, Janey, announced there was someone to see him.

'Who is it?' Dawid asked.

'I don't know him, master,' she replied.

'Has he visited me before?'

'I never seen him, master. He's a Jew-boy.'

Puzzled, and a little irritated, he re-made his polka-dot bow-tie and slipped on a charcoal-grey alpaca jacket. 'You better come with me, Janey,' Dawid said, as a precaution, for Judges cannot be too careful with strangers, and led the way down the corridor to the front door where he came face to face with Julius Levine.

Dawid could think of no obvious reason why Janey should at

once have known that the caller was a Jew: the man had not the usual features of his race, for the nose was not particularly hooked, or the ears abnormally large, or even the lips especially sensual. Yet, at first sight, Dawid was certain the girl was right. What was it, he wondered? The sallow complexion? the soulful, heavy-lidded eyes? the stained, black Homburg hat? the slightly servile inclination of the man's head?

'Mr Justice Henning?' Julius said.

Yes, a Jew, Dawid thought: the accent confirmed it, the intonation had the lilting mixture of hopefulness and pleasure. Dawid nodded curtly, and remained wary and on guard.

Julius told the Judge his name. 'I'm a second-hand dealer,' he added. 'Forgive me, but I don't have a card.'

'A second-hand dealer?' Dawid repeated incredulously, and somewhat amused. 'But I have nothing to sell.'

Julius also feigned amusement. 'And I'm not here to buy,' he replied, and shrugged as though to apologise. 'It's the other way round as a matter of fact: I'm the one who wants to sell.'

'You want to sell *me* something?' Dawid's astonishment was largely assumed and overdone, but it assuaged his unease to treat the Jew as a figure of fun.

'Certainly I want to sell you something. A social call, sir, this is not,' and Julius glanced up hopefully to see if the Judge had understood his little joke which, apparently, Dawid did, for he snorted at the preposterousness of such a suggestion. 'But I don't want to buy anything either!' he responded, using both hands in an exaggerated way, as he believed Jews were in the habit of doing.

The gesture of mockery stung Julius, and, strangely, relaxed him. It was easier to deal with a man for whom you had lost respect. 'If you'll forgive me saying so to a learned man like yourself,' Julius said not altogether able to conceal the scorn in his voice, 'how can you say you don't want to buy anything when you don't know what it is?'

'I cannot imagine anything you have that I would want to buy. Good evening to you,' said Dawid, and made to close the door.

'Not even with your name on it?' Julius asked hurriedly.

'My name?' Dawid repeated, peering round the crack. 'You have something with my name on it?'

'Correct.'

'Something that belongs to me?'

'Not yet, but I'm hoping it will,' replied Julius, grinning.

'What is it?'

'Papers.'

'What sort of papers?'

Julius looked beyond the Judge at the servant hovering in the background, and lowered his voice. 'I would rather talk to you privately,' he said.

Dawid hesitated, but dismissed the girl and turned his attention once more to the Jew. 'I'd like to know more about these papers,' he said, 'before I go any further.'

'You're entitled,' replied Julius expansively. 'It's parchment, maybe two hundred sheets, unbound.'

'Where does my name come into it?'

'All over the place, every page almost. It's the only thing I could read because the rest is all in Dutch, you follow me, and I'm no scholar. But, as I live and breathe, on the very first page of all was your name: Johannes Henning.'

Dawid caught his breath, but did not dare show the excitement he felt. 'Be so kind, Mr . . .?'

'Levine.'

'Mr Levine, be so kind as to bring the papers into my study. I should like to examine them.'

Julius quickly trotted down the steep path and across the road to his van. Reaching into the back, he withdrew the Lipton's Tea carton and returned to Dawid who led him into the study, a small room and, it appeared to Julius, unnaturally tidy, all polished surfaces gleaming; there was, too, the rich, heady scent of stinkwood, furniture wax and old leather-bound books. On the walls, in those few spaces where shelving was absent, hung drab and pale watercolours of the Cape landscape. While Julius admired the contents of the room, Dawid sat at his desk and began to examine the parchment.

A long time elapsed before anything was said, but in that strained, elongated silence the Judge had read enough to understand the significance of the words on the first page: *Report on the conduct of the Reverend Johannes Henning, Minister of the Reformed Church of the Netherlands and the events at Henningsdorp completed at the Cape of Good Hope, 10 February 1794.* He had read enough of van Haarten and Muller and the rest of the rebels with their Khoikhoi concubines, of his ancestor and Alala, and of their lost child, Adam; he understood Sybille's journey now. This was the moment the Past turned bitter in his mouth; the moment when Dawid Henning felt himself assaulted by a savage and terrible violence. And, for the first time in his long, protected life, he was suddenly exposed and brought face to face with his own image. He who had cultivated, encouraged and enshrined the family history was now ensnared by its very roots. He had thirsted for the past as long as he could remember and now, drinking of it, tasted too late the poison. Panic and revulsion spreading from the root, nurtured by the poison, rose and suffused him. The crime of which he had just read burdened the Judge as though it were his own. And in his confusion, the first coherent thoughts to surface were ones of self-protection: he, the Judge, the heir of respectability and righteousness, the pride of family pride, the inheritor of a hitherto unblemished name, could not, must not ever let it be known that the founding father was a renegade predikant who had bred a half-caste. He was now paying the penalty for a past which had never been absolved or transformed; he was being made to suffer for all the diseases of the soul which cripple his fellows. He was being punished for believing that tomorrow is made in the perfect image of yesterday: what was, is, and shall be forever more, the lie upon which his life now foundered.

He looked up from the pages and was brought sharply back to the present: there stood the Jew, hands behind back, his hat still upon his head. Now Dawid's thoughts raced: how much had the man understood of these pages? how much did he know of the contents? how much was he able to read? who else had he told or shown? And those questions sired others: would the Jew understand Dawid's fear of discovery and, if so, manipulate it? was Dawid now to be pressured and blackmailed and compromised? Desperately the Judge pleaded with himself for calm, reasoning that, so far, the danger was only in his own mind, but nevertheless he was determined to discover the extent of the Jew's knowledge. At last, with a great effort to control his unsteady voice, Dawid said, 'I apologise for keeping you waiting, Mr Levine.'

'Please!' said Julius, holding up both hands as though to surrender. 'I have all the time in the world. Read as much as you like!' The man's ill, Julius thought. How pale he is, and his hands tremble.

'I have read enough, thank you,' Dawid said, trying to sound as cheerful as possible.

Julius took a step towards the desk. 'Are you all right, sir?' he asked solicitously.

'Yes, thank you,' Dawid answered hoarsely, but thought at once that the Jew was mocking him. He knows, he knows! He's gloating over my discomfort!

Julius was indeed chuckling. 'Forgive me,' he said, 'but I'm going to give you a piece of advice, because I can tell you're no business man. You don't have to be a Houdini to see that what you've just read is hot stuff, am I right? So, take advice: what you should've done is to give a quick glance at the papers, tell me it's not exactly what you wanted, but you'll buy to do me a favour. So—now you get rid of me for ten bob. Then, *after* I'm gone, that's the time you should read. But already the price goes up, and why? Because I can see you're interested!' Julius had thought the Judge would laugh at this, but he did not. He stared blankly as though he had not quite heard. Julius, less certain of himself, said, 'You don't mind me saying such things, huh? It's only a little joke, you follow me?' He had known all along he would become garrulous.

The Judge's panic flared again: the phrases the Jew used—'hot stuff' and 'the price goes up'—convinced Dawid that the trap was about to be sprung. How should he react now? Should he become indignant? Should he throw the man out? call the police? what? No. Be calm, Dawid decided, obtain proof before you act. You are not in court now, he told himself. You cannot charge the Jew with contempt. 'How did you come by this document?' Dawid asked, placing both hands under the desk so that the Jew could not see he was trembling.

Julius, disconcerted by the Judge's nervousness, finding it infectious, launched into a long, detailed and often irrelevant account of how he found the wardrobe with the cardboard tea chests inside. He disclosed how Lennie had been the one to suggest a visit to the Judge. And when he mentioned his son, Julius tried, but failed, to tell the Judge more about Lennie's plight, his application to the Attorney-General's office, but the conversation seemed to slip from him. All the while he was talking, his thoughts tumbled ahead: tell him about Lennie, tell him about Lennie, tell him about Lennie—

'And you don't read Dutch?' Dawid asked impatiently.

'Not a word.'

'And your son, does he read the language?'

'He studied at school, certainly, but for this stuff you need to be an expert. Thank God, though, Henning's the same in any language.' Tell him about Lennie, tell him about Lennie—

'And how much would you want for these papers?'

'I'll tell you the truth, historical documents are not in my line. I'm a furniture man myself. Certainly, I've sold old maps, navigation charts, who knows what people wrap their rubbish in? But old parchment, that sort of thing, I don't get much call for it. So—perhaps you'll make me an offer?'

Dawid searched his mind to find the right sum: it must not be too low to be derisory, nor must it be ridiculously high as to give away the value of the merchandise to the buyer. 'I'm not a rich man,' Dawid said, 'but—but would ten guineas seem a fair price?' he asked tentatively.

Julius, even though he was an experienced dealer, could not conceal his surprise and delight. 'Ten guineas?' he repeated. 'You want to buy my van as well?' Wonderful, thought Julius, I can cut the offer in half, appear generous and, perhaps, in return—

'I don't understand,' Dawid said, but he knew he had gone too far; if the Jew did not previously know the value of the contents, now he'll suspect—

'Sir,' Julius began solemnly, both hands held before him as though they supported imaginary melons. 'These papers I found by chance. To tell you the truth, I was more interested in the wardrobe. Now, I'll take a quick profit as fast as the next man, but I'm not here to make my fortune out of you. And I'll tell you something, if you make offers like that it's no wonder you're not a rich man. I'll take a fiver and trouble you no more.'

Hastily—too hastily, he wondered—Dawid removed a five pound note from his wallet and handed it over and, in doing so, manoeuvred the Jew towards the door. All he could think of was the dealer's last words, 'I'll trouble you no more,' and the relief they brought.

Julius saw the danger: he realised he would be out in the street before he had said what he really came for. He must delay. Now: 'I'll give you a receipt,' Julius said, pocketing the money and searching for a pencil.

'Really, there's no need,' said Dawid. Relief had made him incautious. He wanted only to get the man out of his house as quickly as possible; he wanted to preserve the secrecy of the transaction and he wanted no proof to exist that he had ever met Julius Levine. 'There's no need for a receipt,' Dawid repeated, holding open the study door.

Julius turned to him in surprise. 'What? You a Judge, you're telling me to break the law?' His voice curled into the nasal register. 'You want we should both end up in prison?' Julius chuckled.

'Yes, yes, of course, a receipt,' Dawid said. And then, as though he comprehended the texture of the situation for the first time, thought: this man is a danger to me.

Meanwhile, Julius had placed his invoice book on the Judge's desk. He licked his thumb to turn the pages and juggled with a piece of bright blue carbon-paper. How could he get round to Lennie, Julius wondered? Lennie, Lennie, Lennie, screamed in his head. 'How shall I describe the goods?' Julius asked. 'What shall I put? Historical documents?'

'No,' Dawid answered at once. 'Call them—call them—just—papers.'

'Whatever you say,' agreed Julius, scribbling in the book and tearing out the page. 'Here we are. It's been a pleasure to do business with you.'

'I'll show you out.'

It's now or never, thought Julius. Now: 'Sir,' he said and watched the Judge turn to face him, frowning, displeased. 'Me, I'm thinking now, could I ask from you a—a—favour?'

Dawid studied the Jew: eyes downcast, shoulders stooped, the very picture of supplication. Now it comes, thought Dawid, regretting he had not called the police. The man has waited for proof to exist that I paid him and now comes the demand, the blackmail. 'What sort of favour?'

'My son,' Julius muttered.

The Judge caught his breath and backed away. 'If he's on a criminal charge, you mustn't speak to me about it. You will do him more harm than good, and I shall be forced to call the police.'

Julius slowly raised his eyes. The astonishment he had experienced at Dawid's generous offer for the documents was mild in comparison to what he now felt. 'A criminal? My Lennie?' he said, and then he laughed, deep and rich and baffled.

Disconcerted by the reaction, but quick to put things right, Dawid said, 'I did not mean to offend you, Mr Levine.'

'When I tell you what he does for a living, you'll also laugh, believe me,' Julius said, still spluttering. 'He's in the same business as you: he's a lawyer!'

Dawid smiled involuntarily. 'I see,' he said.

398

'Believe me,' Julius said, suddenly earnest, and taking a step towards the Judge. 'I would never have mentioned it, but since this short acquaintance, I know you to be a kind man, and I wondered, I—' but his voice dried up, and he stood gazing at the polished floor.

'Go on,' said Dawid.

'It's—it's difficult for me—and whatever you do, for God's sake don't ever say a word to Lennie that I mentioned him to you, oh God, he'd never forgive me—but you see, my son, sir, he's the youngest, bless him. I got two older ones, Emanuel, he's a doctor, and Lilian, she's married to a chemist, so they're well taken care of, thank God. But Lennie . . . Lennie, he's twenty-five, an advocate, a B.A. LL.B., a clever boy, but a little wild, a little impatient, like any youngster. You got children you know what I'm talking about. For a whole year now my Lennie's been sitting in his chambers—chambers? a hovel—waiting for briefs. I'll tell you in confidence, if he earned fifty pounds last year, I'd let him retire. Nothing. Not a penny. So help me. I would never mention this to you otherwise, but who else can help an advocate if it's not a Judge?'

'I can't put work in the way of advocates, Mr Levine. Everyone knows that the first years are the most difficult. Tell him to have patience—'

'Sir, am I asking you you should tout for business for my son! God forbid! Me, I'm a fool, but not such a fool! I don't explain myself well, Lennie's right, I'm too—too—I don't get to the point! You got to forgive me, sir. I'm not here to sound like a beggar. But, I'll explain: last October, my Lennie applied for a post in the Attorney-General's department. A fortune he won't make, I told him, but at least it's living. But—they turned him down, who knows why? Now, he's applied again, and this time, if he don't get it . . .

'All I'm asking is, a man in your position, you happen to be sitting next to the Attorney-General, it's not impossible you should mention my son's name. Leonard. Leonard Levine, it's an easy name to remember. Leonard Levine, B.A., LL.B., it's got a tune.' The two men stared uneasily at each other. 'Have I done such a terrible thing?' Julius continued. 'Have I asked such an impossible favour? But in this world, am I right, it's not *what* you know, but *who* you know?'

Can any man be so naïve, so crude, Dawid wondered? Only knowledge of what was in those documents could give a man such brash confidence and allow him to insinuate so blatantly, the Judge concluded. And yet, he would never be absolutely certain whether or not the Jew had read the report of Johannes Henning's trial, and he could not find the answer by scrutinising Levine's serious face. At last, he said, 'I would find it very difficult to recommend someone I had never met. I'm sorry I cannot be more helpful.'

Julius nodded, then shrugged apologetically. 'No adventures, no gains,' he said. 'But you didn't mind my asking, did you?' Dawid made no reply, and Julius closed his eyes briefly as though to acknowledge that the Judge's silence contained a rebuke. When they reached the front door, Julius said with a sad smile, 'Next time, I won't bother to ask for money first, I'll ask the favour straight out!' and before Dawid could stop him he had trotted down the steep steps and crossed the road to his van.

Dawid did not sleep well that night, nor any night for almost two weeks. The words he and the Jew exchanged echoed over and over again in his mind. The more he tried to convince himself that the Jew was harmless, representing no threat at all, the more did an irrational terror rise to mortify him. *This man is a danger to me.* In these dark moments, he would do his best to put from his thoughts the consequences that would follow if he ignored the blackmailer, but always the bleak and terrible prospect of discovery vanquished concealment and optimism. Visions of the Jew, distorted and vile, haunted him: 'So . . .' the spectre crooned, 'perhaps you've got Coloured blood, sir, who could say?' and no amount of protest could defeat the slur. Nightly, Dawid wrestled with the problem. At times, he saw the Jew a prisoner in the dock, accused of slander; at others, it was the Judge himself who stood accursed, surrounded by his fellow lawyers, hostile and merciless, by the press, by the public, every man and woman until he stood condemned and discredited. And it occurred to Dawid that one could not remain a pillar of society once the foundations were found to be rotten.

After some days of this inner struggle, Dawid, at last, decided it would be best to play safe and recommend Levine's son to the Attorney-General. After all, he argued, eyebrows may be raised at a Henning showing favour to a Jew but at least there, he believed, the matter would rest. Calmly resolved then, he instructed his Clerk, Mr Nel, upon whose discretion he could absolutely rely, to discover why Leonard Levine had been rejected by the Attorney-General in October last.

'Levine?' repeated Nel with just the faintest hint of disapproval. 'Yes, he's a young advocate whose abilities have been brought to my attention. Oh, and Nel, the enquiries should be discreet. Go through the back door, you understand?'

In due course, Nel reported back: Leonard Levine was a member of the Communist Party who made speeches from a soap-box at the bottom of Adderley Street, and who taught Coloured illiterates to read and write. At first, Dawid was alarmed, for it was now out of the question for him to recommend the Jew. And gradually, the knowledge that Levine's son was a Communist dispelled his anguish, and peace of mind slowly returned to the troubled Judge. He reasoned thus: let them threaten me, let them accuse, for who will believe Jewish Communists? Is it not well known that they will go to any lengths to overthrow the established order? Is it not possible to construe an attack on the integrity of Mr Justice Henning as part of a world-wide conspiracy? Of course: they were discredited before they opened their mouths! Revolutionaries, anarchists, destroyers of society, what care they for the honour of one of His Majesty's Judges?

Confident that the danger had passed, Dawid was one day climbing the steep hill homewards when he saw the second-hand dealer's van. Quickening his pace, he darted up a side road to avoid any possibility of again coming face to face with the Jew; but too late: he heard the oily voice calling, 'Sir! Judge! Sir! A moment—' but Dawid hurried on, fear and physical exertion causing him to breathe hard and painfully. 'Sir, don't run!' the voice called again. 'Maybe I've got something more to sell—'

The Judge's nightly terror returned: it was obvious that the Jew had lain in wait for him. (Which was true, but all Julius had wanted was to remind the Judge of his son's existence.) Dawid had never known such despair. What *more* did the Jew have on him? what *more* could there be? His cloistered tranquillity was, it seemed, forever shattered. In his search for a way out, he even felt his sanity threatened. Then, gloriously, the clouds lifted: one morning, at breakfast, he read a report in the *Cape Times* concerning some reorganisation of the South African Communist Party, and he thanked God for intervening on his behalf: miraculously—there could be no other explanation as far as the Judge was concerned—the solution to his problem appeared as if it were a revelation from on high.

What had happened was that Lennie more or less forgot about his application: other matters captured his imagination and preoccupied him. The treasures of the wardrobe were only once more discussed between father and son. On returning home three or four days after his first meeting with the Judge, which he kept secret, Julius announced that he had sold the painting of the dwarf to the Groote Kerk in Adderley Street. It transpired, after cleaning and repairing, that the deformed sitter had been a Church Commissioner in the late 18th century, one Bezuidenhout. The portrait, Julius was told, was to be displayed in the office of the Moderator himself. 'And did you sell those papers to the Judge?' Lennie asked. 'No,' answered Julius, feeling compelled to lie lest Lennie discover the substance of the interview. 'What've you done with them?' his son asked. 'I'll use them for wrapping glass and china,' replied Julius with a shrug that expressed indifference. And there the matter rested.

One of Lennie's real gifts was his ability to put from his mind unpleasantness. He regarded his outstanding debts and the closure of his office as nothing more than temporary set-backs. Had he once taken an objective view of his situation he would soon have realised that he had no career, and no prospects. The practical problems would sort themselves out, he told himself, but in what precise manner was not, for the present, his chief concern. After all, he had a roof over his head, albeit his parents' roof, he was fed, his father slipped him the occasional fiver (and kept Morrie Schaskolsky quiet on Fridays), so he had enough for all his needs. Letters from his other creditors he tore up without opening. 'Something will turn up,' he said confidently. No; Lennie had more exciting problems to exercise his mind.

The conspirators, who now referred to themselves as Shanbanists, met on two further occasions in their leader's bedroom. Several schemes for accomplishing their *coup* were put forward, the most ruthless and impractical coming from the rotund Oskar Blatt: it involved physically restraining the incumbent Committee from attending a crucial meeting by placing them under a form of house arrest. George McPherson was the only one to support him, since he offered to supervise the operation in person and to supply the necessary bully-boys to assist. But they were argued out of the plan by

Lennie, who insisted on a more legal approach to the problem. His own plan, which he formulated at the second meeting, depended on putting before the membership a resolution which would require a decision by secret ballot; this, in turn, would be supervised by Oskar Blatt who would appoint Lennie, Teitelbaum and Miss Arenstein as scrutineers. It would be no great difficulty then to rig the ballot and thus force the Committee's resignation. (It was not an original scheme; he had simply followed a similar tactic which a Party colleague informed him had been employed by Lazar Kaganovich in the Ukraine.) Lennie's proposal was carried by three votes to two, Miss Arenstein abstaining. It was now decided that Lennie should draft the all-important resolution and present it to the conspirators as soon as possible. When they parted, Shura Shanban urged them all to behave normally, to go about their everyday business and to carry on with any activities concerning the Party in which they might be involved. 'Fellow Shanbanists,' he said, 'trust no one.'

Apart from attending meetings of sub-committees and study groups, Lennie had but one serious activity on behalf of the Party which he felt obliged to continue, and that was his monthly class for Coloured illiterates who met above a clothes shop in Hanover Street, the main thoroughfare of District Six, the poorest and grimiest section of Cape Town where only Coloured people lived.

Amidst row upon row of cheap cotton dresses and blue serge suits which hung on moveable black enamel racks, a dozen or so Coloured men and women, their ages ranging from six to sixty, sat in a semi-circle round Lennie, copies of *The Story of An African Farm* and *Capital* upon their laps. Communist missionaries, unlike their Christian counterparts, did not believe in sugaring the pill. Once the rudiments of reading and writing had been learned—in the case of Lennie's class over a period of eighteen months—then the mouth was forced open and down the gullet was thrust, undiluted, Commodities and Money, Production, Absolute Surplus Value and not even a sweet to take away the taste. No gentle Karl Marx meek and mild; no shepherds, no stars, no stables and no Kings. And did the converts understand any more of one dogma than another? did they not, both now and in the past, feel swamped by the excreta of European culture, and did they not, like their ancestors before them, nod to the Word without believing it, for the sake of—what? In the case of the former, a morsel of bread, and for their descendants a chance to learn to read and write. But Communists and Christians alike did not relay *all* the message to their converts; for, as with savages made Christian, the profound socialist belief in man's brotherhood was withheld. Black Christians were excluded from the true fellowship of white Christianity; non-European Marxists were never informed that the proletariat have nothing to lose but their chains. They were not told they had a world to win. Workers of the world—perhaps; but not workers of all colours.

And so, with fixed frowns and dazed eyes, the class of twelve struggled to understand. Each in turn read from the massive tome and Lennie listened, corrected and explained. The pupils regarded their teacher as a friend, called him by his first name and, for the duration of the lesson, all imagined that their colours had been watered to the selfsame hue, all believed that what they were doing was worthwhile and important and contributing to a new world order that would be infinitely better than the old.

They had been working for almost two hours, oblivious to the dress racks, to extraneous noise, to the haze of smoke from their cigarettes, when suddenly the solitary naked electric light went out. At once, there were mumbled expressions of regret, mild and light-hearted curses, flaring of matches and embarrassed laughter, but then, without warning, heavy, booted footsteps sounded on the wooden stairs. 'Who's there?' Lennie asked, too late: he felt some-one take hold of him by the neck, he heard a woman scream, and then a reverberating pain exploded in his head. He reeled back-wards, reached out to save himself but grabbed at cotton dresses which ripped from their hangers. All now was confusion: screams, shouts, crashing bodies, agonised cries; and then the beams of two or three torches played like spotlights over the melee, until one settled on Lennie, groaning and writhing on the floor, his body en-twined in bright, incongruous patterns of a dozen cotton prints now stained with blood from a gash above his eye.

'There he is,' said a gruff male voice from behind the torch and Lennie, instinctively shielding his face, tried to escape the powerful, stabbing beam which slowly advanced, blinding him. He felt again pain as he was kicked in the groin and in the stomach, but he heard the voice: 'Levine: you're finished, you understand? You're ex-pelled!' Somewhere far off police whistles sounded and the torch went out. Lennie tried to get up but nausea overcame him; he fell back, retched, and rolled over in his own vomit.

The next thing he remembered was the street lamp dancing, and someone calling, 'Run, Lennie, run!' Nearby, he heard a woman wailing and the tinkle of broken glass. Only then did he realise he was lying on his back in the gutter, and again, 'Go on, Lennie! The police are here! Run!' By holding on to the lamp-post, he managed to haul himself to his feet and, dimly sensing the imminent danger, stumbled forward faster than he intended until he reached the next lamp-post, the pain in his thigh almost unbearable. But the night air was beginning to clear his mind and the determination to escape took command. He lurched forward once more, turned into a narrow darkened alley and, hugging the wall, eased himself slowly along; he found another alley and another until he could barely hear the shouts and the police whistles any longer.

More than an hour later, he came upon a bus shelter not far from the City Hall. There he rested and, fighting the unceasing pain and recurring nausea, wiping the blood from his face, tried to understand what had happened with such alarming, devastating speed. Vaguely, his instinct told him the attack had been perpetrated by some anti-Communist group, rabid Afrikaners or the like. Then, he remembered the phrase, 'Lennie, you're finished, you understand? You're expelled!' but he could not, to begin with, fathom its meaning simply because he did not want to. Gradually, though in turn baffled and sceptical, the explanation that seemed to him too bizarre to be credible insisted itself: *you are expelled* the voice had said and Lennie, battered as he was, knew there could be only one meaning.

The City Hall clock struck ten, and it was as though a note of urgency had sounded, a call to confirm with utmost speed his conclusions. Once more, keeping to the shadows of the back streets, running, stumbling, falling, he made his way to the house of Shura Shanban. He did not notice that the front door was wide open, or the table in the hall upturned and the vase broken; but when he entered Shura's bedroom, he paused in the doorway and gazed with disbelief at the savagely disordered room. Then he heard coughing and the familiar grating wheeze, but he could not see Shura.

'Shura?' Lennie called. 'Where the hell are you?' A thin reedy voice answered him and Lennie staggered forward to the bed, almost collapsing on it, and crawled over the rumpled bedclothes to see the old man lying on the floor covered, as though dead, by blankets. 'I can't breathe!' cried Shura, and Lennie uncovered him: his face was a terrible grey-green colour, and his pyjamas had been ripped and mutilated.

'My medicine! My medicine!' Shura gasped, and pointed to the bottle that lay just out of reach; clumsily, Lennie retrieved it by lowering himself to the floor beside Shura. The old man gulped down the medicine but still did not fully regain his breath.

'What's happened?' Lennie asked, clutching his groin and rocking to and fro in an effort to ease the excruciating pain. 'What's happened?' and he began to cry, uncontrollably, bloated sobs of self-pity and helplessness.

'Oskar—' the old man wheezed.

'What—?'

'—Oskar and Miss Arenstein—'

'Are they here? Are they hurt?' Senselessly he called out, 'Oskar! Miss Arenstein! Where are you?' like a little boy frightened by the dark.

'No,' rasped Shura, and the effort was paid for by another coughing spasm. 'No—they—they—betrayed us—'

'What—?'

'—betrayed us—'

'Who betrayed us—?'

'Oskar and that skinny bitch!'

A sense of loss engulfed Lennie and for want of comfort he took the old man's hand and held it tightly, continuing to cry while Shura swigged once more from the bottle. 'The bastards,' Lennie said at last.

'I've been expelled,' Shura said. 'I've been expelled!' as though by saying it often enough he would come to believe it.

'Oh God!' Lennie cried.

'Me! Expelled! Me!'

'Me too, Shura, me too!'

'After all I've given to the Party!'

Lennie let go of the man's hand with a violent jerk. 'Given to what?' he asked, spitting out the words.

'The Party, the Party!' Shura cried.

'Oh, fuck the Party! I'm bleeding!'

4

The cogs rotate; wheels, and wheels within wheels slowly and jerkily begin to move, back and forth, back and forth; the inexorable machine rumbles forward: Leonard Levine was being taken care of.

Two days after the brawl in the clothes shop, the following paragraph appeared in the *Cape Times*:

> Recent reports from usually reliable sources indicate that a serious split has occurred in Cape Town Communist Party ranks, leaving the Party severely weakened. Officials of the Party would neither confirm nor deny rumours that Mr Alexander "Shura" Shanban, Mr George McPherson, Mr Max Teitelbaum and Mr Leonard Levine had resigned in protest against Russian influence in the Union's affairs.

The next day, Mr Justice Henning's diary reveals a luncheon with a Mr Hans Konradie, a senior prosecutor in the Attorney-General's Department. No record exists of what was said, but there is no doubt that Leonard Levine's name was mentioned. None are more expert at nudging and winking, at making vague detached suggestions, than lawyers. A word here, an emphasis there, a reminder of past favours shown or sought, the subtle innuendoes of influence. And how did the meeting end? With Dawid nervous and apprehensive lest the bait had not been taken? frightened, in succeeding days, that every knock upon his door would readmit the Jew?

And so the ridiculous fantasy of the Shanbanist plot, the pathetic dream which had ended in a nightmare, had also worked to Lennie's advantage, though at some cost. Shura was removed to hospital where he spent the ensuing six months; Max Teitelbaum was badly cut about the face when his attackers shaved off his Lenin beard and moustache; George McPherson, the bicycle mechanic, had both his hands broken, which prevented him from earning a living for many weeks. Oskar Blatt and Miss Arenstein moved rapidly up the Party hierarchy. And Lennie, suffering from internal bruises and contusions, and bearing a scar above his left eye that would always be visible, lay inert and dejected, cared for by his loving, anguished parents. His world had been shattered; during many long hours of convalescence he cursed his stupidity: why, why, he asked, had he allowed himself to become involved in the childish games of sick and feeble men? why hadn't he *thought* before acting? And yet, somewhere in his heart he held the fault to go deeper than that. It was the recurring schism within him: the need to serve others and the need to serve himself, as though the balance between the two was impossible to achieve. Did his life, he wondered, have to be committed to one thing or the other? Was it not possible to serve and be served? Could altruism not be bought with personal ambition? Communism, which for so long had seemed the answer, was now denied him. He could no longer appease his need for advancement with night classes for illiterates, with speech-making at the bottom of Adderley Street. When his spirits were at their lowest, a dreadful temptation obsessed him: to set aside his lofty ideals for the moment and concentrate on building a career which would then give him position, power and the means to be useful to his fellow men. But, in his half-waking moments, he would see himself once more a social missionary, bringing food to the hungry, succour to those in need, living as the poor live. And while he thus tormented himself, struggling to subdue his strident nature, the cogs rotated and the wheels within wheels turned.

The letter was brought by the caretaker of Lennie's former office. The man said he knew it was important because in the top left hand corner were the words 'From the Attorney-General of the Province of the Cape of Good Hope'. Lennie was summoned to an interview.

Bandaged, and leaning heavily on a stout walking stick, he set off. Hobbling up St George's Street, the young, failed advocate, the ex-Communist, the ambitious, humane Jew, was still making bargains with himself. Even as he entered the building and knocked on the door he was planning the future over which already he had little control. If he was offered a position, he said to himself, he would only take it up as a temporary measure, use it as a stepping-stone to make his name, a stepping-stone . . . but to what exactly he did not know.

The interviewer, the seedy, pale Hans Konradie, with nicotine-stained hands, a perpetual cigarette between his lips and ash, like a veil, covering his lapels, said, 'Now Mr Levine, just one thing more. It's a little difficult for me to understand. You see, I've got here a note that says you make speeches of a political nature, on behalf of the Communist Party, against the Government. But here, on the other hand, is a report in the *Cape Times* . . .'

Lennie interrupted. 'The report is correct,' he said. 'I am no longer a member of the Communist Party. I won't be making any more speeches.'

'I see,' said Konradie. 'Your friends were right. They said you'd turned over a new leaf.'

'What friends?' asked Lennie, genuinely puzzled.

Konradie smiled and winked. 'You'll be hearing from us,' he said.
A week later he was sent a second letter inviting him to join the
Attorney-General's staff. Julius Levine smiled and the next Friday
evening offered up special prayers for the health and well-being of
Dawid Henning and his family. Uncle Marcus, reading of his
nephew's resignation, sent him a cheque for forty-five pounds. At
the end of January, during a blistering heatwave, Lennie sat for the
first time at his desk; he shared a room with two young English-
speaking advocates, Maynard and Bell, and next door, beyond a thin
wooden partition, in a small and ill-lit office, worked Mr Konradie's
secretary, the Judge's daughter, Anna Henning.

BOOK EIGHT

31

'A case for the Jew-boy'

It is an old saying that when non-Jews take a job their first question is, 'What is the pay?'; when a Jew takes a job his first question is, 'What are the prospects?' In the beginning Lennie was too busy, too stimulated by his new and bustling environment to worry about the answer, but as he grew more familiar with his routine duties, dissatisfaction set in which, in turn, produced Lennie's automatic reflex, a burning desire to succeed. To this end, Oom Erik said, he made good use of his opportunities.

Lennie's first contact with Anna Henning was curt and inauspicious. On the day he began work, Lennie was still wearing a plaster over his left eye, the only visible reminder of his beating. On passing through the office on that Monday morning, Anna glanced at him and said, 'You look as if you belong in the dock, not at the Bar.'

'Who's she?' Lennie asked Konradie when she had disappeared into her own office.

'My secretary,' replied Konradie sternly. 'Her father is Mr Justice Henning, and a friend of mine.'

Later, when he was left alone with his two young colleagues, Brian Maynard and James Bell, he enquired after Konradie's secretary again. 'She's the laziest bitch that ever drew breath,' said Maynard, a thin-lipped, studious man.

'I call her the office bike,' said Bell who was red-faced and pompous. 'Because everybody rides her,' and he winked.

There, for the moment, Lennie's interest in Anna rested, for he had now to learn the ins and outs of his new post, assimilate the office atmosphere and, in general, find his bearings. It transpired that Konradie had been given permission by the Attorney-General himself to conduct an experiment in office organisation. Konradie, a dry, disappointed man, believed that greater efficiency could be achieved by the department if it was run on similar lines to an advocate's chambers in private practice. Thus, his own position and power was greatly enhanced, for Konradie took the plums and threw the stones to the youngsters; it was the master–pupil relationship: if a man was to advance in the department hierarchy, Konradie's influence and favour were vital factors.

Lennie discovered there was much to be learned, not so much about law, but about form. Every criminal case was first heard in the Magistrate's Court at a preliminary hearing. It was then up to the Magistrate to decide, having heard the evidence, whether or not to commit the accused to trial in the Supreme Court. Concealed behind that relatively simple process was a procession of Sheriffs and Deputy-Sheriffs, of Chief Clerks and Assistant Chief Clerks, summaries of evidence, warrants, charge sheets, subpoenas, summonses, statements by witnesses and, of course, court appearances. Lennie's first case was a trivial affair, he thought: *Rex* versus Louisa Dickens, on a charge of keeping what was known as a gaming house. He obtained a conviction. Twice, in his third week, he appeared before Mr Justice Henning. (Dawid stared at him with solemn interest and on both occasions summed up against him.)

But Lennie had not been very long in Konradie's office before he realised that being a Jew proved a disadvantage. Hardly a day went by without some snide remark being passed about his antecedents. Konradie was particularly agile at slipping in a sly little dig. ('I've a nice tasty little rape for you, Maynard, and an embezzlement for you, Levine—oh no, the defendant's name is Cohen, so that won't do. We don't want you to become unpopular with your co-religionists, do we? Maynard, you take the embezzlement. Levine, you can manage the rape. I expect you know all about rape, hey, Levine?') The lugubrious Bell was if possible even less subtle. He insisted on telling the oldest anti-Jewish jokes in a lisping voice and using his hands as though he were a juggler in a circus. ('Abie thaith, "Dat's vy a thynagogue ith round: you can't hide in the cornerth ven dey come vit de collecthion!"') The Instruction Conference, which was called the I.C. and took place to brief the prosecutor before a case was to be tried, was renamed by Bell the 'I-key' in Lennie's honour.

But Lennie suffered all with that particular look of patience and pity Jews learn to assume at an early age; and in truth, it did not really hurt or upset him too deeply, for he knew he was by far the ablest of the three, a fact even Konradie would not have attempted to deny. But that very self-confidence, however justified it may have been, was what eventually charged Lennie's ambition with restlessness, for he soon began to believe that he was deliberately being held back and not being given the most interesting work. While he was plied mostly with petty cases, assaults, burglary and 'guilty pleas', Maynard and Bell were chewing on the juicier meat of financial swindles, criminal libels and the like, and able to display their knowledge of the law which galled Lennie, for in the kind of criminal cases he was being given to prosecute, the clear presentation of the facts was the only talent required.

Among his own community, too, he was regarded with a certain suspicion. The Jews did not regard the Civil Service as a means to success and riches: the prospects were *never* good enough, no matter how high a man rose. It took Lennie several hours to explain to his father what some acquaintance had meant by saying to the old man, 'Well, Mr Levine, what's it feel like to have a son who's the only Yiddisher Scotchman in the Irish Fusiliers?' ('What's it mean?' asked Julius. 'You're not in the army!') But no one could really dent Julius's pride in his youngest child. 'One day, you'll see, never mind Attorney-General, he'll be Governor-General!' he would say to the scoffers.

Apart from Anna's brief and acid comment on his cut eye, she and Lennie barely exchanged another dozen words in his first month. She kept aloof from the daily office activity, and remained mostly in her own room which she called her 'cubby-hole.' The accusation of laziness Lennie understood, but her moral reputation which Bell had imputed puzzled the newcomer since he saw no sign of flirtatiousness, let alone the wantonness his colleague had so crudely suggested. On the contrary, she armed herself with a remote and icy manner, as though a permanent sign hung round her neck: 'Keep off—trespassers will be prosecuted.' In the eyes of the young recruit, the reality of Anna Henning was a strikingly attractive woman, obviously experienced and knowing, but quite unaware of his presence even when she sometimes deposited briefs on his desk; she left the office early on Fridays in the latest model of a glamorous La Salle convertible: she was clearly out of his class and out of his reach. And yet Bell's insinuation lingered, and on occasion, Lennie met Anna in his fantasies and dreams.

2

Lennie was a virgin. At school they had called him 'Tosser' because he was forever standing about with his hands in his pockets, a far-away look in his eyes. Freda used to scold him openly for it to the point of making him blush, and Julius, with a lighter touch, would say, 'Confucius says, "Boy who stands with hands in pocket, feels cocky!"' which would make the old man chuckle but embarrassed Lennie quite as much as his mother's forthright approach. In adolescence, he played the usual party games, kissed Corinne Cohen who, first to his horror then delight, pushed her tongue into his mouth, rubbed himself like a little puppy against Sylvia Myerson on the beach at Muizenberg and, as a result, experienced his first orgasm in his bathing trunks and had to run into the sea before anyone would notice. But he had never gone much further than that. Jewish girls, he discovered, were aggressively moral in their teens, determined to keep themselves pure for their prospective husbands. And he was not one to loiter at the entrance to the nurses' home in the hope of picking up a *shikseh* which means, in Yiddish, a non-Jewish woman, especially a young one, and when used aptly can imply loose morals, too.

And so Lennie became furtive about matters sexual. He would spend hours looking in the dictionary for words that would excite him: vagina, clitoris and even masturbation, the meaning of which he knew only too well. He took to writing short stories of indescribable obscenity and perversion; one was discovered by his elder brother, Emanuel, who was about to report the author to Freda but, on reading the story, decided against it and asked Lennie for a second instalment.

As Lennie grew into early manhood, both at university and later, women undoubtedly found him attractive. He exuded a wiry, un-settling energy, and had a way of looking at girls that implied a greater experience of life than could be supported by the facts. Politics captured his imagination early. He spent most of his free time reading. Bernard Shaw was his great hero—after Marx, of course—and it was Shaw who introduced him to Ibsen, whom Lennie believed to be a socialist dramatist. He once said in a speech that if a man wanted to be a good socialist he should read Marx, Shaw's Pre-

416

faces and Ibsen's plays. And yet it seemed he had more energy than most of his contemporaries, and more than he was able to utilise. Membership of the Communist Party, which incidentally was a decidedly infertile hunting ground for attractive women, consumed a good deal of that surplus energy, but after his expulsion, he found the evenings long and hot and disturbing. After a busy, active life, he was suddenly lonely again. He had grown away from his school friends; he saw many of them, of course, at the synagogue which he attended occasionally to please Julius but more often in the hope of meeting someone new; he went to parties rarely, for he did not dance well, had little small-talk and invariably began to discuss politics and social problems with an intensity at odds with the occasion; people said Lennie Levine was heavy-going.

He developed a passion for walking; not along the mountain paths or country lanes, but up and down the busy Cape Town streets, the busier the better. The promenade, 'the street-walking' of an earlier time, still flourished: Plein Street, Darling Street, Adderley Street, looking in shop windows, meeting friends, gossiping, arguing, laughing, that was how Capetonians passed their evening hours. And on Sundays they walked as far as the Pier which jutted out into Table Bay from the foot of Adderley Street to hear the band—the orchestra they called it—play Strauss and Offenbach and Franz Lehar. And it was there that Lennie saw Anna with the elderly gentleman.

He had walked that evening with a purpose, for he wanted to see the photographs outside the Alhambra Theatre in van Riebeek Street. The Alhambra, which was mostly used as a cinema or bioscope as the locals called it, had an interior modelled on the palace in Granada, and a ceiling to represent the Spanish night sky with floating clouds and little lights that twinkled like stars. It was much too expensive a place of entertainment for Lennie, but he liked to study the display cases whenever he could. On this particular Sunday there were photographs of Sybil Thorndike and Lewis Casson. ('If they come to Cape Town, they're good old has-beens,' Lennie had heard a woman say with customary Colonial self-deprecation.) Miss Thorndike as St Joan and Jane Clegg, Mr Casson as himself. He wished he could see the Shaw play, hear the words spoken by good, clear English voices, for Lennie was something of a snob regarding accents and deplored the local dialect. He gazed longingly at the actors' faces, and the scenes from the plays, sighed and turned towards the Pier.

417

To an accompaniment of a selection from *The Tales of Hoffmann*, Lennie strolled along, watching the young men row their girl friends in small boats below in Table Bay. It was a beautifully calm late summer's evening, and the mountains seemed nearer then usual, more protective. Lights from the Pier flashed on the waters of the Bay, and from the tea-room came the busy hubbub of Sunday pleasure.

When Lennie first saw Anna and the man they had their backs to him, and he thought she was walking with her father. But when they turned he was surprised to see that her companion was about sixty, bearded Voortrekker fashion and powerfully built. He was doing most of the talking and there was something about his manner that made Lennie think he was pleading with Anna. Once he took hold of her hands but she snatched them away and, as she did so, turned and saw Lennie. Embarrassed, he stood frozen to the spot, staring at her, knowing he should walk away but unable to. That moment seemed endless: Anna looking at him, the orchestra playing the *Barcarole*, people passing to and fro but without disturbing the intensity of their locked gaze. Then Anna whispered to her companion and together they hurried off; still Lennie watched them, though she never once glanced back at him and soon they were blotted from sight by van Riebeek's statue.

Lennie thought little more about the incident but he experienced an unaccountable sense of disappointment, as if his image of Anna as someone mysterious and sophisticated and sensual had been disturbed by the sight of her with a man old enough to be her father.

The next day, Monday, he was in court and did not see Anna; but on Tuesday morning, he arrived at the office early, made himself a cup of tea and settled down at his desk to read the *Cape Times*. The front page was filled with news of the General Election campaign. Smuts, the leader of the Opposition, had made a speech advocating one African state from Cape to Cairo. Hertzog, the Prime Minister, warned of the 'Black Peril' that would engulf the white man as a result. Lennie turned to an inside page and, to his astonishment, saw a photograph of Anna's Sunday escort. Beneath a headline— PROFESSOR HENNING'S CLAIM—was a picture of Professor Balthazar Henning, 'the distinguished archaeologist', as the caption explained. Her uncle, evidently.

Professor Balthazar Henning, one of the Union's leading archaeologists, who has for many years claimed that the European arrived in the Cape long before any of the Native tribes, told an audience at the University of Cape Town yesterday that he may soon be able to prove his theory. The Professor is at present engaged on a 'dig' near Tulbagh in the Cape Province and is on one of his rare visits to the City. He said early findings indicate that he and his assistants may be working on the site of one of the earliest and most primitive Christian settlements so far discovered. The Professor, in response to the spirited questions, was not prepared to put a date on his new finds. A lively exchange took place between the Professor and Dr Franklin Smith, the visiting American historian. Dr Smith asked the lecturer whether he was meaning to imply that Europeans had ventured into the interior prior to 1652, the year of van Riebeek's arrival. In answer, Professor Henning said, 'Some of you may be in for quite a surprise.'

Lennie reflected on the scene he had witnessed and was again intrigued by the passionate look of supplication he remembered on the old man's face. When Anna herself arrived she paused at the door of Lennie's office and there passed an unspoken understanding between them: Lennie was reading his newspaper, and she had a copy tucked under her arm. He felt obliged to say something but there was a dangerous, warning expression in her eyes which he did not fully comprehend, but he knew instinctively that she did not want him to mention what he had seen. She smiled nervously, a slight twitch of the lips, and then hurried into her cubby-hole. And Lennie, leaning back in his chair, hands clasped behind his head, wondered what it was all about and contemplated the motives that induced an uncle to plead with a niece.

A week or two later, there was an office party to celebrate one of the typists' twenty-first birthday. Everyone stayed to drink her health in champagne which she provided and, when that ran out as it quickly did, to continue with pilsener beer. Many were sick as a result and Konradie passed through all the stages of intoxication from benignity to belligerence. Anna kept to herself as usual, sipping beer from a chipped enamel tea-mug, but somehow endowing the action with a kind of disdainful elegance, although it was plain to see she had difficulty in focusing.

Lennie, to avoid dancing to the music that blared forth from the wind-up gramophone, appointed himself barman, and stood behind one of the desks dispensing refreshment; thus he had drunk hardly anything at all when, out of the general chatter and laughter, and the jaunty strains of Billy Mayerl and the Savoy Orpheans playing 'Don't Bring Lulu' in the background, the voices of Konradie and Anna exploded in a harsh and noisy argument. 'You're nothing but a lousy, bloody policeman!' shouted Anna, her feet planted firmly astride to maintain balance. 'A lousy policeman that's what you are—'

'I happen to know the old reprobate was here because I read it in the newspaper!'

'How could you? You can't bloody well read!'

'I've got your father to think of,' Konradie whined like a school-girl prude, 'he's my friend—'

'—you leave my father to me—'

'—won't have you drag him into the gutter—'

'Lousy policeman!'

It was Bell who came to the rescue. 'Now then.' he bellowed, 'don't let's spoil the party. Hey! We haven't sung "I'm Twenty-One Today!" Come on, folks—' and like a bandmaster he began to conduct the guests in the song. Temporarily, the row subsided, but Lennie kept his eye on Anna and Konradie, and saw that soon they were once more sniping at each other, sharp, short exchanges, like angry cats, clawing. The moment the song was over Bell called for a speech, and the others joined in until the birthday girl was persuaded to stand on a chair and address the gathering. She had hardly begun when Anna suddenly screamed, 'Well, ask Mr Levine then!'

Lennie's head shot round to see Anna leading Konradie towards the improvised bar. 'What's Levine got to do with it?' Konradie demanded, his upper set of dentures unexpectedly popping out of his mouth and causing a general splutter of laughter from everyone except the birthday girl who burst into tears. 'Ask Mr Levine!' Anna cried again, pushing Konradie forward while he covered his mouth to rearrange his false teeth.

'Ask him what?' he hissed.

'Ask him about Sunday!' Anna said.

'To hell with it!' answered Konradie, trying to back away.

'All right, I'll ask him,' said Anna and she turned to Lennie, her eyes glazed but angry, and Lennie thought how ugly she was drunk. 'Where was I last Sunday?' she demanded.

'Last Sunday?' Lennie repeated with an inane smile, pretending to be slightly tipsy which was a way of covering his embarrassment.

'Tell him!' Anna ordered while poking Konradie in the ribs with her forefinger.

'Last Sunday . . .' Lennie began carefully as though he were expecting to be prompted, 'Last Sunday . . . you were on the Pier . . .'

'*Right!*' she said, pummelling Konradie's arm. 'Bloody right! And who was I with?'

Lennie affected to giggle helplessly which made Anna laugh too. 'What's he laughing at?' she asked of no one in particular. But just then, Konradie lunged forward across the desk as though he were cross-examining a hostile witness. 'And how would you know who she was with, Mr Levine?'

'Well—I know—' said Lennie, 'I know—'

'Yes, Mr Levine?'

'I know—because she was with me,' Lennie blurted out.

'*Right!*' said Anna joyfully.

A look of bewilderment crossed Konradie's face. 'With *you?*' he repeated.

'Yes—on the pier—the orchestra was playing Offenbach—' and he sang the first few notes of the *Barcarole* which Bell took up in a throbbing baritone and encouraged the others to join in.

'You see?' said Anna to Konradie beneath the din, but loud enough for Lennie to hear. 'You see?' she repeated triumphantly. 'Go swing your truncheon somewhere else!' and setting her sights on the door, tottered out.

Shortly afterwards, the party broke up and Lennie found himself the recipient of winks, nudges and, in one or two cases, congratulations. 'Dark horse, hey, Levine?' said Maynard enviously. And from Bell, in a loud whisper, 'Whose pricks are bigger? The Jews or the Kaffirs, hey?'

But Lennie did not mind. His assumed drunkenness had now taken hold of him, and he felt truly elated by what had taken place. He staggered home singing the *Barcarole* and fell on to his bed laughing uncontrollably. Julius looked in. 'So—what's funny?'

'Everything. I've been to a wonderful party. I'm twenty-one today, twenty-one today . . .'

With sudden concern Julius asked, 'Are you *shikker?*' which means drunk.

'Yes!' cried Lennie, unable to let go of the pretence. 'Very, very *shikker!*'

'Don't let your mother see you like this, God forbid. Keep your voice down.'

'Papa,' Lennie said, 'I'm going to go to the very top!'

'Certainly,' said Julius. 'Only if you speak so loud and your mother finds out, it'll take a little longer because you're going to have to find some other place to live first.'

'To the very top!' Lennie said again, kicking his legs in the air.

'Okey-dokey,' said Julius, smiling at his son's antics; then he shook his head sadly. 'When *goyim* give a party, all they do is drink.'

And when he was left alone Lennie stopped giggling but continued to feel elated: was he already planning to use the situation Anna and Konradie had created? Had he some definite scheme worked out that was certain to advance him up the ladder? Or, like Iago, could he say, '"Tis here, but yet confused; Knavery's plain face is never seen till used'? In the event, Lennie, ever the pragmatist, capitalised on the fears and weakness of others; but for now, he lay on his back thinking of Anna and her uncle, of Konradie, of his own future, and wondered what tomorrow would bring.

3

A note on his desk:

Dear Mr Levine,

I am extremely embarrassed about last night and filled with remorse. Please forgive me for involving you, but thank you for what you did. I know you will understand my reluctance to give you any explanations for what happened, but even so I hope you will forgive me.

Anna Henning.

Shortly after the lunch break, Konradie stormed into the office, still wearing his gown and tabs from his morning court appearance, and said, 'Levine, I want to see you.' When Lennie, bristling with anticipation, passed through Anna's office on the way through to her chief, she smiled sympathetically as though to give him confidence.

'Levine,' said Konradie when the two were alone in his office. 'I've got something very serious to say to you.'

'Yes, and I've something very serious to say to you, sir,' said Lennie quickly. 'I'm glad to have this opportunity of talking to you.'

This direct attack flustered Konradie. 'You've got something to say to me?' Konradie asked, closing an eye and cocking his head to the side as he did when he thought a witness was lying.

Lennie launched forth, and although Konradie tried on several occasions to interrupt him, the young advocate was not to be stopped. He catalogued his grievances as though he were presenting a case to the jury. 'I don't want advancement at the expense of others, Mr Konradie,' said Lennie, 'but Maynard has twice acted Junior to you and Bell once to the Attorney-General himself. I've had more guilty-pleas than they've had hot dinners. And that's not all. I've never been up into the District Courts. Maynard's done Port Elizabeth, and Bell—'

Konradie at last managed to intervene. 'What are you saying, that I'm deliberately—?'

'No, sir, I'm not saying that—'

'—because these things happen—'

'It does seem strange, sir, that I haven't had a fair crack of the whip—'

'There's no conspiracy against you, Levine—'

'I never said there was—'

'—the work is allocated—'

'All I'm saying is that perhaps in future—'

'All right, all right, all right,' said Konradie. 'You fellows, I don't know what you expect. You haven't been here three months and already you expect—'

'No, sir, I don't expect anything except to be treated fairly—'

'Will you let me finish when I'm speaking, man? All right. You've made your point. But I asked *you* in here. I have something to say to *you*!'

'I know that, sir, and all I ask is that you bear in mind what I've said—'

'Yes, yes, yes!' Konradie hissed, slapping the desk. 'But I'm not finished with you yet, Levine. I've got to talk sharply to you.'

'Oh? About what, sir?'

'About Miss Henning.'

'She was a little bit tipsy last night, that's all—'

'Never mind that. I'm going to ask you a question now, and you better tell me the truth. Was she with you on Sunday as you said?'

'Yes, sir,' Lennie answered.

'Now look here, man, I'm going to give you a piece of advice. Your career matters to you, hey?'

'Yes, sir—'

'Okay then, you keep away from her or you'll make so many enemies you won't be able to appear on a tennis court never mind a District Court.'

'Well, sir, she's an adult, she has a right to go out with whom she pleases—'

'And I'm telling you different, Levine, you understand—'

'I understand, sir, but—'

'Never mind the buts! Listen, Levine, I'll do a deal with you, okay?'

'A deal, sir?'

'You keep away from Miss Henning and I'll put something tasty in your way. You understand what I'm saying?'

'I don't see what the one thing's got to do with the other—'

'I'm talking about a deal—'

'I know that, sir—'

'—don't play the bloody fool with me, Levine—'

'I'm not, sir—'

'You heard what I said, hey? You keep off her and you won't regret it!'

'I understand, sir.'

'Is it a deal?'

'It's going to be difficult, sir, after all, Miss Henning—'

'Never mind Miss Henning, it's up to you—'

'Yes, sir.'

'Is it a deal, then?'

After a discreet pause, Lennie nodded, and was curtly dismissed.

It took a month for the conversation to bear fruit. One evening, just as the office was closing, Anna dropped a file on Lennie's desk. 'With the personal compliments of Mr Konradie,' she said, and then lowered her voice. 'Take my advice, Mr Levine, give this case to one of the others.' She did not allow him the opportunity to reply. Intrigued, he untied the file which contained the commital proceedings from the Magistrate's Court in Graaff-Reinet: *Rex* versus François Pietrus van Heerden. He was about to read the Summary of Evidence when Konradie looked in on him. 'You've been a good boy, Levine, now there's something to get your teeth into. And if you can't get a conviction on that, don't come crying to me!' He chuckled as he called his goodnights and left.

Briefly, the facts of the case were these: a manager of the Boulter

424

farm near Graaff-Reinet, the accused, van Heerden, on returning from watching a rugby match with a friend, Benjamin Louw, had stopped off for a drink, as was their custom, at the Commercial Hotel, Geldspoort, a small village or *dorp* some six or seven miles from the Boulter farm. After consuming a large quantity of beer the accused, holding an empty bottle, had wandered out into the back yard to the lavatory. Some minutes later, he returned, his jacket and shirt soaked in blood. He said, 'I've just killed a Kaffir. He tried to hit me, so I did him with the bottle.' The police were called, and van Heerden made a statement in which he alleged that the dead man, Nathan Zimbali, had for no apparent reason tried to hit the accused; a short scuffle ensued in which Zimbali managed to get his fingers round van Heerden's neck. Van Heerden had no alternative, he explained, but to hit the man hard with the empty beer bottle. But, after the post-mortem on the deceased, it was discovered that Zimbali had been hit from behind with the bottle, and that once stunned, the accused had lifted a large stone and crushed the man's head. Clearly, the medical evidence and the accused's statement were in conflict. The police charged van Heerden with murder and he was, in due course, committed for trial at the forthcoming session of the District Court.

And while Lennie read, imagining he was alone in the office, on the other side of the wooden partition, Anna Henning was waiting for him.

4

Anna sat at her desk very still and alert as though she were about to take dictation and, although she appeared controlled and aloof, this attitude of cool awareness in fact camouflaged a nervous expectancy, an inner excitement of a deeply unsettling magnitude.

She wanted to repay the young Jewish advocate who had so innocently rescued her the night of the party, and she was determined to repeat her warning not to prosecute the case Konradie had given him. Konradie: her anger flared when she thought of him. Seedy, ashen little Konradie who reported back to her father if she so much as looked at a man. Why did she put up with it? why, at the age of thirty, did she allow herself to be treated like a wayward schoolgirl? She could not readily find the answer, for the truth was that she welcomed a watchdog, needed to be spied on and kept in line. The last few years, ever since she had been Konradie's secretary, had been calmer, more tranquil than she had known for some time, and secretly she recognised, though she would never easily admit it, that Konradie's loyalty to her father had contributed to her stability. Superficially, she would tell herself that the large allowance her parents made available to her was too comfortable to lose; but more profoundly, the mystery of parental authority haunted her and she required in some urgent but ingenuous way Dawid and Victoria's approval.

Maturity, or what passed for maturity, had come late to Anna. Even now, in appearance, none but the cruel or envious would put her age as high as thirty. Slim and athletic, she exuded physical health as though sun and sea and country air were stored within her. Yet, it did not do to look too closely at her eyes, for, despite her glowing complexion and the wonderful elegance of her unlined face, her eyes were unnaturally bright and often fidgety, as if she were making a conscious effort to display a youthful, unflagging vitality.

Anna would have flourished in cities like London or New York. Cape Town was too small, too provincial for her, and she despised it. Anonymity was what she craved for, and in her mind anonymity was synonymous with freedom: she longed to be swallowed up by a great metropolis where no one knew or watched or censured her. Cape Town was suffocating and cloying: she had only to nod to an acquaintance in Adderley Street at noon, for her parents to know of it by midnight.

Those who disapproved of Anna, and they were many, could not deny her one virtue, which was kindness. 'She would give you the shirt off her back,' her brother Jacobus had once said, critically, but not without affection. Many thought that generosity was partly the cause of her troubled adolescence and youth. 'She is *too* giving,' Victoria had said. When Anna herself looked back on those confused, confusing years, she could not explain why she acted as she did, but she knew then, as she did now, that her behaviour was wild and unpredictable even to herself. She could not account for the long periods of tranquillity being followed by extravagance and hysteria. Yet, she regretted little of her past; she accepted joy and despair as she did the colour of her eyes, or the shape of her mouth. She bore no grudge against the men she had known, and had Anna been able to control the savage, self-destructive misery which unaccountably assailed her from time to time, had she been able to rely on her kindness, her relationships would have endured and given pleasure instead of ending, as they always did, in pain.

Now, sitting in the cubby-hole, waiting for Leonard Levine, she felt a familiar excitement. She had told herself she was acting out of the best motives, to repay a debt to the young man. But even so, and this had nothing to do with Leonard Levine, somewhere within her she sensed danger, and out of danger grew excitement.

She heard him closing his brief-case and the scraping of his chair as he stood. She heard him whistling now, tuneless but happy, and she heard him walk towards the door. With a last nervous jab at her hair, she stepped out of her office and they met in the corridor.

'I thought everyone had gone,' Lennie said.

'You're late tonight, Mr Levine.'

'I was reading *Rex* versus van Heerden.'

'You're going to take it?'

'Of course. It's a big chance for me.' An uncomfortable silence followed, he standing at his door, she at hers. He said, 'Miss Henning, why did you say I should let one of the others prosecute?'

Her eyes danced and she smiled. 'Take me to tea and I'll tell you.'

'Well, I—' he stammered glancing at his wristwatch. 'It's late—I—'

'Don't worry,' she said, 'I know about your promise to Mr Konradie. I know other things as well, things to your advantage. Don't worry about Konradie.'

'I'm not. Where d'you want to go?'

'Oh, Stuttafords, of course.'

'That's okay by me,' Lennie replied but at once he slipped his hand into his pocket to ascertain whether or not he had enough money; but there was no note, just two coins. That particular discomfort of not knowing whether you can afford what you order set in, and gave Lennie a feeling of unreality about everything he did or said.

Stuttafords was the smart place for tea. On the first floor of the department store there was a tea-room and an extension to it called the Balcony which overlooked Adderley Street. There, on any evening, gathered the matrons exhausted after a day's shopping; there young men took their girl friends, businessmen their colleagues and customers, and there Anna took Lennie. Tea, toasted buns and cream cakes, that was what people ordered without even looking at the menu. Lennie had never treated anyone at Stuttafords before, so he did not know the price of things; he kept his hand in his pocket desperately trying to make up his mind whether either or both of the two coins was a penny, a florin or a half-crown.

They were fortunate to get a table by the window but almost as soon as they sat down it began to drizzle, although the sun still shone.

'Monkeys' wedding,' said Anna.

'What?'

'Rain in sunshine.'

'Oh.'

Anna studied faces: she stared frankly and disconcertingly as though she were an artist about to paint a portrait. 'You're an ambitious boy, aren't you, Mr Levine?'

'Is that bad?' Lennie responded defensively.

'No, but you shouldn't let it show.'

The waitress placed their order on the table. Because the tea-pot was silverplate, the handle was too hot to grip: Lennie offered his handkerchief and Anna poured tea. Just then, Lennie saw at a table behind her back his uncle Marcus talking animatedly to another man. Lennie looked quickly away but Uncle Marcus saw him and hurried over.

'Lennie! *Mazel tov* on all your news! Well, aren't you going to introduce me?'

Lennie winced; the Hebrew good luck wish embarrassed him; Uncle Marcus embarrassed him; being with Anna Henning embarrassed him; not having enough money embarrassed him. 'Hello Uncle Marcus. This is Miss Henning. This is my uncle, Marcus Levine.'

Uncle Marcus with all the goodwill in the world offered his hand which Anna took a little reluctantly. Lennie could see the disapproval in his uncle's face. (He knew what the older man was thinking: 'My nephew out with a *shikseh! Oi!'*.)

'You got from me a letter?' Uncle Marcus asked.

'Oh! Yes! I did. And thank you. I've been meaning to write, I should've thanked you—'

'What thank-you!' Uncle Marcus said with a huge gesture of revulsion. 'Who wants thanks? I only want to know if you received the money, that's all.'

Lennie wished the ground would open and swallow him; he wished his uncle would lower his voice; most of all he wished he could make his uncle understand he had too little money to pay the bill.

'So! Well! I won't keep you,' said Uncle Marcus. 'It's nice making your acquaintance, Miss—and Lennie, I should get in trouble with the police, God forbid, you'll fix it for me, please God!' and chuckling, he squeezed Lennie's cheek affectionately and left. Out of the corner of his eye, Lennie saw him recounting to his friend the tragic news that his nephew was having tea out of the faith.

'So, Miss Henning,' Lennie began without really knowing what he was going to say next.

'So, Mr Levine,' said Anna.

'Tell me why I shouldn't take the case.'

'Can't you guess?'

'No. It seems straightforward enough to me.'

'Straightforward?' She was genuinely surprised.

'Have you read the details?'

'I typed the Summary,' she said.

'Then you know all about it,' he said, pushing his cup towards the tea-pot. She poured him another cup of tea.

'What makes you say it's so straightforward?' she asked.

'A man kills another man, the medical evidence supports the facts—'

'Motive?' she asked.

'Van Heerden was drunk.'

'And do all drunks murder their fellow-men?'

'The victim was a non-European, Miss Henning.'

'Right.' She lit a cigarette without offering him one, but almost at once stubbed it out again.

'So?'

'Are you really stupid or just naïve?'

'How d'you mean?'

'You're going to ask for the death penalty, I suppose,' she said in a flat, matter-of-fact tone.

'Of course.'

'You think you'll get it?'

'I'll ask for it—'

'You're avoiding the answer, Mr Levine. Think about it: you're going up-country to prosecute a European for murdering a Kaffir. You're going to ask for the death penalty. What's your forecast as to the outcome, Mr Levine, speaking professionally?'

Lennie passed a hand through his unruly hair. 'I'll get a conviction, Miss Henning. The medical evidence is irrefutable.'

'You're stupid *and* naïve,' she said. 'Why do you think Konradie gave you the case? To do you a good turn?'

'He owed it to me.'

'I'm going to do you a good turn, Mr Levine, because I really do owe you something. You know what Konradie said when he asked me to hand you the brief? He said, "Anna, I think we've got a case for the Jew-boy." '

Lennie looked away, down at the busy street, at the flower-sellers opposite, the colours of their blooms blurred by the rain-streaked window as in an impressionist painting. Lennie gazed at his own reflection and Anna's. 'Telling me that,' he said, 'just makes me more determined.'

'You'll never get a conviction in a million years, Mr Levine. They're setting you up for a failure. "He wanted a nice juicy case," they'll say, "and he couldn't handle it." '

'I'll handle it.'

'Don't be childish. Just think: local jury, local man, European, the victim non-European, come on, think.'

Lennie turned to look at her. 'Did Konradie honestly say that? I mean about a case for the Jew-boy?' She nodded. 'I'll show them then, Miss Henning. I'll get a conviction if it's the last thing I do.'

'I came here to warn you,' she said, 'not to make you more determined. You realise what'll happen if you don't get a conviction.'

'No—'

'You won't get the juicy cases any more, Mr Levine. You can complain once in this office and they may listen. But if, after you've complained, you don't deliver the goods, that's it. You take what you get and no arguments. This is important for you.'

'I know that.'

'Then don't be a fool, Mr Levine. Give the case to Bell or Maynard. Let them fall on their faces.'

'I'm grateful to you, Miss Henning—'

'Anna—' she said abruptly.

'I'm Lennie—'

The conversation was suddenly suspended and both regretted it. Clumsily, Lennie said, 'You see, I believe that I've got a duty to perform, European, non-European, it doesn't much matter to me—'

430

'I thought you'd resigned from the Communists,' she said but without malice.

'I have.'

'And who do you support now, Smuts and the S.A.P.?'

'No, I voted Labour at the last election—'

'Oh? So you support my brother?' she said, laughing.

'He's not Labour. He's a Nationalist—'

'Right, but there was a convenient coalition between the two—'

'*Was*,' said Lennie. 'And it fell apart as I always knew it would. I knew Hertzog would have to call an Election, I knew it—'

'All right, you knew it. I'm not going to have a political argument with you. Politics were forbidden in my home. My father's Dutch and my mother English, so there was bound to be conflict. We weren't allowed to discuss the pros and cons. How did we get on to all this?'

'You were warning me off—'

'Right. I remember now: you have a look at the Nationalists' Manifesto. Think how the Afrikaners will vote up-country in Graaff-Reinet. Think of that jury of yours. Think of the European in the dock.'

'Miss Henning—'

'Anna.'

'Anna, I'm grateful to you, I really am. But this is just the sort of case I think I ought to be prosecuting. It not only smacks of justice, it smacks of social justice and that's to my liking.'

'So you won't let me repay the favour?' she said.

'What favour?' he answered as if to disparage her kindness. 'All I did was to see you with your uncle and say I hadn't. It's nothing that needs repayment.'

She laughed nervously, and talked rather faster than before. 'My uncle, oh yes, he's an archaeologist, you know, his wife recently died and he's very lonely. My father and he don't get on but he wanted to see me—'

'Funnily enough,' Lennie said, 'my father and Uncle Marcus don't get on either—'

She cut him short with an impatient wave. 'Please,' she said sharply, 'I don't wish to discuss my uncle any more. He bores me.' She reached into her handbag for another cigarette. 'Well, light it for me, light it for me—'

'I don't have a match—'

'Oh God!' she said and searched for her lighter, which she handed to Lennie. 'Go on, be a gentleman—'

He lit the cigarette and his hand was trembling, for he was disturbed by her sudden change of manner. She had been so gentle the moment before, and now she was strident and edgy. Lennie said, 'I'm sorry, I didn't mean to be rude—'

'If you haven't got matches, you haven't got matches—'

'No, I meant about going on with the case—'

'That bores me, too. If you want to make a fool of yourself, make a fool of yourself. I don't know why I even bothered with you. I should've known you'd be stupid.'

It was Lennie's turn to become excited. 'Do you think it's stupid of me to prosecute a murderer? Or are you warning me on behalf of your Nationalist brother? Does he not want a good prosecutor up there, or perhaps he wants all the European murderers to go scot-free, does he? Are you here on his behalf?'

'I'd rather you kept your voice down just at the moment—'

'Are you?'

'Please, we're not in court. I'm not in the witness-box, we're not making our reputations now!'

'All I did was apologise for not taking your advice—'

'My advice?' she repeated as though he had said something obscene.

Was it his imagination, or had the other customers gone quiet? The whole tea-room seemed to have plunged into silence. He glanced round, again saw Uncle Marcus, who winked suggestively. When he looked once more at Anna, she was leaning back in her chair, eyes closed, puffing on her cigarette. She looked peaceful and very beautiful, he thought. 'Anna,' he said. 'I'm sorry if I was rude or—'

She opened her eyes as though she was astonished to see him. 'I wish I knew why we were sitting here,' she said.

'We're sitting here,' said Lennie, 'because you were kind enough or interested enough—'

Again she interrupted. 'Are you married?' she asked.

'No.'

'Nor am I.'

Lennie sniggered uncomfortably. 'Well, we're both young. Plenty of time.'

'I suppose you've got lots of girl friends, have you?'

'No.'

'What, just one steady?'

'No. Not even one steady.'

'Oh dear, what seems to be the trouble? Bad breath?'

He laughed. 'I hope not. No, I've been more interested in other things, important things, that is, to me.'

'Perhaps it's your hair: it's very untidy, you know. Perhaps if you combed it more often . . .'

And so the conversation meandered into the personal and trivial. Soon, they were discussing the personalities of their colleagues at the office, and laughing at them. Anna was doing a cruel impersonation of Konradie and Lennie was giggling helplessly when the waitress interrupted them with the bill. With sinking heart, Lennie reached into his pocket. Anna said, 'I invited you. I'll pay.'

'No—no—' said Lennie, continuing to fumble, but now with relief.

Anna handed the waitress the money. 'You can leave the tip,' she said, rising.

Like a conjuror, Lennie palmed the coins and quickly glanced at them: he slid the two pennies under a saucer. As they neared the exit, he said, 'Anna, thank you—'

'My pleasure—'

'And thank you for telling me what Konradie said—'

'I wish you'd take my advice, Lennie,' she said, gripping his arm as though to stress the gravity of what she was saying.

'I can't. I'm going to see van Heerden hanged.' She shook her head sadly just as Uncle Marcus came up and drew Lennie aside. 'Excuse me, miss—' then, in a hushed whisper to Lennie, 'My friend and me we're having a bet. The *shikseh*, she's your secretary, am I right?'

'No,' said Lennie innocently and left Uncle Marcus anxious and alarmed.

Anna and Lennie walked towards her La Salle which was parked up a side street. She said, 'If I were to give you a glimpse of what's in store for you, I wonder if you'd change your mind then?'

'I'm too obstinate,' he said. 'Besides, I like you looking at me as though *I* were the condemned man.'

'But you are,' she said without a trace of humour. When they reached the car, she turned to him with a quizzical look. 'I'm going to take you out again in a week or two,' she said.

'Oh?'

433

'Yes, and don't worry about Konradie.'

'I'm not.'

'He won't find out—'

'Where will you take me?' he asked, smiling.

'Oh ... to an election meeting, I think—'

'An election meeting?'

'For my brother, Jacobus. Hear what he has to say. It might make you change your mind. Goodnight.'

32

The faithful

The General Election campaign of 1929 was in full swing, and the background to it was this: the Prime Minister, General Hertzog, had presided over a coalition of his own Nationalist Party and the Labour Party. The marriage was not so unsuitable as it might appear at first glance. Back in 1911 Hertzog had advocated territorial segregation of white and black as the only viable solution to the country's problems. The Labour Party held similar views: European civilisation, they said, the permanent maintenance of the White community in a position of political and economic supremacy, could only be preserved by the reduction of 'race contacts'. The five-year tenure of the coalition, or Pact as it was called, had seen the introduction of legislation to implement the Parties' shared views: The Mines and Works Amendment Act of 1926 became known as the Colour Bar Act; there were attempts to segregate the Indians in Natal and even to repatriate them, because it was learned they were buying properties in European residential areas in Durban. Smuts, the Leader of the Opposition and the South African Party, opposed these measures, not on humanitarian grounds, but because he believed that legislation was not the wisest method of entrenching European civilisation in the sub-continent. Hertzog persisted with his policy and tried to remove the Cape Africans from the Common roll but he failed to get the necessary two-thirds majority of both Houses in joint session. Yet, curiously, as if to assuage the guilt of his forefathers, he tried to introduce the Coloured Persons Rights Bill which would confirm the voting rights of the Coloured people in the Cape and extend the franchise to Coloured people elsewhere, thus acknowledging the half-caste race his ancestors had created as socially subsidiary to Whites, but socially superior to Blacks; this Bill also failed to get the two-thirds majority of both Houses. Meanwhile, he had steamrollered through the House a trade agreement with Germany which brought forth a howl of protest from Smuts.

Then, a serious schism between Left and Right occurred in the Labour movement which resulted in Walter Madeley, a leader of the Left, being appointed Minister of Posts and Telegraphs. One of his first acts was to meet representatives of the Industrial and Commercial Workers Union, against the Prime Minister's wishes, to discuss the wages and conditions of postal workers, and non-European postal workers in particular and, obstinately, the Minister decided to raise their wages. The Coalition disintegrated: Madeley refused to resign so, since a General Election was due, Hertzog himself resigned. The stage was now set.

While the Labour Party performed its dance of death, the leading actors stepped into the spotlight: Hertzog, the Prince of Isolation and Segregation, Smuts, Rhodes' understudy, the Prince Imperial, playing the part in a moustache and beard not quite as full as King George V's. Smuts it was who entered first: 'Let us cultivate feelings of friendship over this African continent so that one day we may have a British Confederation of African States ... a great African Dominion stretching unbroken throughout Africa!' Enter Hertzog, a man of mild appearance with gold-rimmed spectacles to give himself the scholarly look. 'Smuts,' he cried in a surprisingly passionate voice, 'is the apostle of a black Kaffir state ... extending from the Cape to Egypt ... and he foretells the day when even the name of South Africa will vanish in smoke on the altar of the Kaffir state he so ardently desires!' The plot of the piece was unfolded in the first scene; the play was as old as the land itself.

But if the stars seemed suitably remote and high-sounding, the crowd scenes took on a terrifying reality. Hertzog had played on his supporters' fears and age-old prejudices so that gangs of young Afrikaners stormed their way in to S.A.P. meetings to destroy the prophets of Kaffirdom. In a growing atmosphere of deep emotion and increasing violence, the Election campaign reached its climax.

Because the number of constituencies was to be increased, Jacobus Henning was standing for the first time as candidate for one of the new districts, north of Stellenbosch, the heartland of Afrikaner nationalism. This was his public initiation into politics although he had, since university days, been active behind the scenes. An attorney by profession, he was an upholder of the Afrikaner culture which was not yet three hundred years old, and many of the old hands in the party said he was a man to be watched.

2

In the first week in June, Lennie and Anna attended her brother's final election meeting. It was decided, for the sake of appearances, to journey separately which would not arouse Konradie's suspicions. (Cheating the policeman was also something that excited Anna.)

They met at the entrance to a small hall which stood behind the Dutch Reformed church in barren countryside. It was a chill winter's evening, but the meeting was well attended. In their scores the faithful came, on foot, by horse, in old jalopies, cartloads of them and, on guard outside, stood the young élite, great-coated military fashion, Boer commando hats at rakish angles, scanning the faces of the audience as they shuffled into the hall.

Anna said, 'It's best we don't sit together,' and they found seats one behind the other near the back. Lennie gazed at the assembly, feeling strange and foreign. An usher was arranging papers on a baize-covered table that stood on the narrow platform and, near the front, small groups had gathered talking raucously and confidently, speculating on the prospects of the party or breaking off to greet friends and family as the hall slowly filled. Not all were so animated : here and there sat men and women who did not speak, but stared, eyes fixed, jaws set; to look at them one might have thought they were in church, such intensity did they bring to these proceedings.

Anna sat just in front and to the right of Lennie, so he could see the slender line of her neck and, if she turned a little, her profile. She seemed to know several people, for she waved or nodded regally from time to time, and it was difficult for Lennie to realise the honoured place she and her family held in this society, for the respect and deference she was shown were strangely at odds with the woman he knew as Konradie's secretary. A young couple approached her and they chattered away in Afrikaans; Lennie felt suddenly excluded and neglected, as though she had forgotten all about him and the reason for bringing him here. What, he wondered, did she hope he would learn ? What could he be taught, what could

437

anyone who was born in this land be taught about the hatreds and fears these people nursed? (And Lennie, persistent as ever, saw the chance for those hopes and wishes men keep secret: he knew what he could make of the case he had been given; he knew he could strike a blow for the underdog and for Leonard Levine, at one and the same time. His presence here, he concluded, was academic; nothing would deflect him from the course he had chosen.)

Men started filing on to the platform to scattered applause; one of them, white-haired and illustrious, leaned forward and shook hands with people in the front row, obviously someone of importance but too old to be Jacobus Henning. Then, just as they were taking up their seats behind the baize-covered table, a voice whispered into Lennie's ear, 'Joined the other side, have you, Lennie?' Lennie recognised the whisperer: Oskar Blatt. 'Henning's your man, I hear,' said Oskar.

Lennie turned: Oskar sat there, an incongruous figure among the lean, sinewy Nationalist supporters surrounding him. He wore dark glasses which made him look like a comic spy and, either side of him, sat two heavily-built men, arms folded across their chests, with dead, deadly expressions. One of them said, 'How's your eye, Levine?' and Lennie recognised the voice at once as belonging to the man who had kicked him that night in the clothes shop. Suddenly, Lennie was frightened; he wanted to escape, and he would have done had not the cheering broken out which greeted the entrance on to the platform of Jacobus Henning.

The resemblance between brother and sister was unmistakable, but Jacobus was heavier-set and his nose was sharper, like a beak. He smiled all the time the applause lasted, and chuckled so that his whole body shook. Yet, there was something prissy about him as though the elegance of his sister had, in the male, become fussy and fastidious. A supporter on one side of Lennie said with great enthusiasm, 'Agh, you can't help liking Jacobus.'

The meeting was called to order by the white-haired man who acted as chairman. He was barely audible but raised his voice just enough to give some theatrical effect to the name of the candidate. Jacobus stood to renewed cheers and much stamping of feet. He began by welcoming his supporters and thanking them for turning up in such large numbers. He had a pleasant tenor voice and used his hands well, pointing to give emphasis, clenching his fist to denote strength, and spreading his arms wide to embrace all those present.

Almost at once he launched an attack on Smuts. 'This detribalised Boer,' he said to laughter, 'this so-called genius from Cambridge, what's his plan? To invite the Kaffirs, and I'm talking about millions of Kaffirs, tens of millions of black-skinned savages, he's inviting them from Cape to Cairo to come in and run our affairs—'

'Nonsense!' cried one of the men with Oskar Blatt.

'Oh?' crooned Jacobus. 'I see we have friends here tonight. Well, friends, how about standing up and making yourself known?'

'No, thanks!'

'Yes, I thought as much. Right, now we know where we are. I'm grateful to you fellows for speaking up so early. Otherwise I might have made my whole speech without knowing you were in the audience, and what a chance I would have missed!' And, with a flourish, he tore up his notes, a gesture which received the desired vociferous response from his supporters. Lennie kept his eyes firmly fixed on the platform. His unease had grown and he knew that the present good-humour must inevitably give way to intolerance.

'Now, my friends, and I mean my real friends, I want you to re-lax. I'm not now about to address you, I'm addressing my remarks to these little fellows from outside. If you talk among yourselves, friends, talk quietly, hey? Now those of you who shout nonsense when I talk about the Black Peril, I know why you shout out like that: it's what you're paid to do by Jan Jewis—er—Christian Smuts. He pays for chaps like you to disturb these meetings because he hasn't got the wit to answer our arguments with facts!'

'Pot calling the kettle black!' cried Oskar.

'I call blacks black not pots!' Jacobus responded and this gibber-ish brought forth the loudest laughter and cheers so far. But Lennie became more seriously alarmed when Jacobus turned his talents to defending the Trade agreement with Germany. 'Smuts, the British Kaffir,' he said, 'condemns us for concluding a treaty with our German brothers, our kith and kin. And why? Because he says it weakens the Commonwealth. Well, I say good, let's weaken the Commonwealth! Let us stand on our own two feet! Do we not call ourselves Nationalists? Does that not mean South Africa for the South Africans? Smuts has only one idea for the Commonwealth and that is one Kaffir State of which we are to be members, a black hegemony on which we are all to be on an *equal* footing! Yes, brother, equal with the black man, that's what Smuts suggests! Equality with the black? Never!'

'NEVER!' cried the audience as one. 'NEVER!' And then a woman at the back shouted loud, *'Stem wit vir 'n witmansland!'*—'Vote white for a white man's land!' and the cry was taken up in all parts of the hall.

'Let me read you something, my brothers—'

'If you can read!' called one of Oskar's friends.

'You'll see soon enough,' said Jacobus taking a book from the platform and opening it. 'This book,' he said, 'is written by a German, a Nationalist for his country, as we are for ours. And what do we find? In a chapter entitled "Nation and Race" he too advocates segregation in his country. Segregation between the Aryans and the Jews. Now, this author says in this book—which is about his struggle to make the German people see the truth why they were defeated in the past, and how to avoid it in the future—he says, "The Jew addresses himself to the workers, pretends to have pity for their lot in order to gain their confidence." And what does the Jew do, then? "He founds the doctrine"—I'm quoting—"He founds the doctrine of Marxism" or Communism as we call it now.'

'RUBBISH!'

'Rubbish, is it? Rubbish when I tell you that the Jews believe in fomenting unrest among the blacks in order to destroy Christian culture. Now, we haven't yet turned our attention to you Communists, but that'll come. I just want you, my friends, to know who exactly supports Jan Jew-Christian Smuts. My friends, as our beloved leader General Hertzog said, South Africa must be governed by pure Afrikaners—'

'Are there any?' called Oskar, and this was too much for the faithful to endure. The scuffle broke out behind Lennie and he was tipped forward out of his chair. Someone shouted, 'Show them what the white man's made of!' as several of the great-coated youths waded in, fists swinging. Oskar's friends were waiting for them and, in the confusion of arms and legs and sprawling bodies, Oskar tried to extract himself and slip away, but he was caught and dragged from the hall.

Meanwhile, Lennie had regained his balance only to be grabbed by one of the youths who took hold of his lapels and started to slap him hard across the face. Anna screamed in Afrikaans, 'He's not with them! He's not with them! Leave him alone!' and pummelled the boy with both fists on the back. It had some effect: the startled youth let go of Lennie and said, 'Sorry—' before climbing over the

440

seats to join in the main fracas. Anna said, 'Come on, let's get away,' and taking Lennie by the hand she pulled him towards a side exit.

Lennie's last impression of the meeting was of Jacobus Henning chuckling as he watched the fight develop. He stood, hands on hips, his face wreathed in sweat, his whole body shaking with pleasure. But once outside, there was another sight to distract Lennie: Oskar Blatt was lying on the ground being kicked by a trio of heavy-booted youths. The fat man, crying hysterically, rolled this way and that like a rubber ball and Lennie paused, half-inclined to go and help him but was too frightened. He chased after Anna, though he could still hear Oskar's cries for help long after they had driven off in her La Salle.

3

Nothing was said as they sped through the night. Anna drove fiercely, sitting on the edge of the seat, clutching the steering-wheel as though it were a life buoy. And then, unexpectedly, she swerved off the dirt road and came to a halt under a canopy of fir trees. There, she leaned back and panted as if she had been running all the way. The sky was overcast, and all around was dark, shadowy and oppressive.

The silence persisted. There was no need for either of them to speak, for both knew each other's thoughts. Anna could not have made her point more thoroughly if she had deliberately staged her brother's meeting. Lennie stared out at the night through the wind-screen which had begun to mist up. For the moment, he felt noth-ing, no shock, no revulsion, nothing. Not one word Jacobus Henning uttered had surprised him. The Nationalists' prejudices and the depth of their passion were well-known; the confusion of terror and abhorrence for the black man was now endemic, a disease that had festered for almost three hundred years without treatment. It went beyond argument, beyond intellect, into the realms of nightmare where all the blasphemies of the soul are spoken and where men may acknowledge as whole and sound the abortions of their inherit-ance.

Anna was the first to speak. 'Did they hurt you?' she asked gently.

'No.'

'Did he hit you hard?—'

441

'No—'

'Let me see—'

'I'm all right!'

'It's not too late to give up the case,' she said.

He did not answer but with his forefinger traced the word 'No' in the vapour on the windscreen. 'You'll achieve nothing,' she said. 'You, a Jew, prosecuting a European for the murder of a Kaffir. They could kill you, Lennie. You saw what happened tonight. For God's sake, don't be a fool. For my sake—'

'I wish I knew what you were up to,' he said.

'Me? If there was a way of explaining, I would. You know,' she said, half-turning to him, 'when you come from a family like mine ... My parents are really the most gentle people, moderate, nauseated by the extremes. My father's a Judge, fair, honest, a man of unshakable integrity. My mother, too—she's English, you know—but all the best qualities: honesty, forthrightness ... and yet, they give birth to Jacobus. A throwback. And I tell you this for nothing, Lennie, he can do no wrong in their eyes. You know what my father says? "A man's political convictions are not something you can criticise if they are sincerely held." You know what that means? It means that secretly my father cheers every time Jacobus opens his mouth.'

'And you?' Lennie asked. 'Where do you stand?'

'I'm with Smuts.'

'And where does Smuts stand?'

'Lennie, don't talk like a child. It's not my fault the white man was born superior. If the Kaffirs were so bloody wonderful why don't they throw us out? There are more of them than us. But what I say is this: they're our children, we have to love and care for them, teach them, show them and who knows? In a hundred years we may not notice the difference. But now there *is* a difference! And I don't say keep it that way now and for evermore like Jacobus does. I say we've got to work to make the differences disappear. We've got to believe they're something that *can* disappear—'

'In a hundred years, yes—'

'It can't be done overnight!' she screamed.

'It never can!'

'Well? Can it? Tomorrow morning can we wake up and find Kaffirs living next to us, men and women who don't know how to wash and clean themselves? Is it possible? You saw what happened

442

tonight. You know what the Nats are fighting for. Don't be a fool! Grow up!'

'"Men and women who don't know how to wash and clean themselves..."' Lennie repeated. 'God, Anna, *men and women*!' And then, almost without knowing he was doing it, Lennie started to cry, to blubber like a despairing child.

'Don't, oh don't cry—' she murmured, taking his hand.

But he pulled away, opened the door of the car and stepped outside. Again she called, 'Don't, Lennie—' but he was walking away from her now, trotting, snivelling. And she came after him, catching him by the sleeve and tugging.

'Lennie, I'm frightened, it's so dark—' and as she said it, she stumbled, grabbing hold in her fall of his leg, pulling him down. Together they lay on a bed of gorse, he crying, and she feeling her way to him. When she was close he reached out for her and held her so tightly she thought she would be crushed. And out of fear and compassion, and the overwhelming dissolution of their private loneliness, Anna Henning and Leonard Levine took refuge, one with the other, mutual and inviolate.

4

It was unfortunate for Lennie that the ecstasy experienced after his initiation was at once interrupted two days later by his enforced journey to Graaff-Reinet. He thought of little else but Anna, and the glorious pleasure of her. At the office the following morning she was her remote, chilly self but she wrote three passionate notes that day, and two the next, and when she handed him his rail warrant, she pursed her lips as if to kiss him.

Now he sat on the train travelling north, watching the monotonous Karoo rolling by, the vast, infinite landscape broken by a solitary tree or by a miniature table mountain; and he saw the native women with pots upon their heads, and he recognised the red blankets of the Xhosa who waved as the train sped by. He found it difficult, almost impossible to concentrate on the case he was to prosecute. *Rex* versus van Heerden, he kept saying to himself as though repetition would spark his energy. From time to time, he paged through the statements and the depositions, the subpoenas and summonses but could not muster his enthusiasm. And yet he was confident, a confidence not directly related to the case, but one that was euphoric and born out of Anna Henning. He told himself that as far as a conviction was concerned, the only thing that mattered was the medical evidence. The victim was hit from behind, and then his skull crushed by the deliberate dropping of a heavy stone. The plea of self-defence was meaningless in the face of that, and Lennie felt a brief burst of excitement at the thought of cross-examining the accused who must, he knew, go into the witness box.

The trial was expected to last two days. At Julius's insistence, the Rabbi in Cape Town had asked his colleague in Graaff-Reinet to find Lennie 'suitable accommodation', which meant a room in a Jewish home, and arrangements had been made for the visiting advocate to stay with Mrs Katz, an elderly widow whose house was near the Court; shortly after his arrival in the town Lennie presented himself at her door and was shown into a spotlessly clean bedroom which would have done credit to any hospital.

Mrs Katz stood at the door and watched him unpack. She was obviously an Orthodox Jewess, for she wore a *sheitel*, the traditional wig, in accordance with the rabbis' decree that once married, a woman's hair should not be visible lest it distract the men from prayer or study. Since Mrs Katz was well into her seventies and of a mournful disposition, the adornment seemed superfluous.

'So—what Levine are you?'

'Julius Levine's son.'

'I don't know him,' she said as if that conferred social disgrace. 'You knew your grandfather?'

'No. He died before I was born. In Russia.'

'Was he from Riga or Tallinn?'

'I'm not sure—'

'Your grandmother's maiden name, was it by any chance Rabinowitz?'

'I don't think so—'

'Was her sister Ruth married to a tailor from Kovno?'

'I don't think she had a sister Ruth—'

'The tailor was called Shapiro, not the same?'

'No, I'm sure not—'

'Good. Because those Levines I wouldn't want in the house. Tell me,' she said in a liquid sing-song. 'You've come to hang the *schwarze*?'

'No, no, I'm here to prosecute Mr van Heerden.'

'The more *schwarze* you can hang, the better for all of us.'

'No, Mrs Katz, if anybody gets hanged, it's going to be Mr van Heerden.'

'A-ha,' she said. 'It's a funny name for a *schwarze* van Heerden. A big white family here, you know, van Heerden.'

Lennie decided not to try and explain again. 'Yes, I know,' he said, patiently.

'And who'll win the Election Wednesday?'

'It's hard to say—'

'God help us if Hertzog wins—'

'I agree—'

'Another pogrom there'll be—'

'I doubt it—'

'Hertzog, *oi Gott*, I think he's got *schwarze* blood—'

'Really?'

'Next time you see him, give a look the *hulz*,' and she pointed to her neck. 'You can always tell.'

'I'll remember. Mrs Katz, could you direct me to the Court?'

'You don't want to eat?'

'No, I have work to do.'

He walked slowly behind her as she shuffled to the front door. 'You see the building with the flag?' she said pointing. 'Not that one. Behind.'

'Thank you. I'll be in about six.'

'You like fish?'

'Yes.'

'All right, I'll see if I can get a piece fish.'

'Don't go to any trouble—'

'If I can't get fish, I'll get chicken.'

'That'll be fine.'

'All right.'

He crossed the narrow street towards the Courthouse, and glancing round, decided there was little to be said for Graaff-Reinet. It was small and ugly and complacent. It stood like an oasis in the desert of the Karoo, was famous for its irrigation and its sheep farms which abounded in the surrounding district. Apart from that, Graaff-Reinet was the seat of the District Supreme Court of the northern Cape Province.

The atmosphere surrounding Lennie's arrival was unexpectedly cordial and polite. The senior prosecutor, Coetzee, a tall, elegant man with impeccable manners, behaved as he believed English

445

lawyers did, and presented a front of courtesy, precision and reliability. 'I am extremely sorry you've had to come all this way, Mr
Levine, but in cases such as this I always insist that a local man does
not prosecute. After all, he has to live here after the jury has
reached their verdict, and it would never do, not with present
circumstances prevailing. I have assigned to you the learned Mr
Modder who will give you any assistance you may require.'

Modder, who was a year Lennie's junior, treated the visitor as
though he were a K.C. and called him 'sir'. Together they went
through the case, and the younger man was helpfulness itself. He
could see no problems, he said; Lennie was bound to obtain a conviction.

'I shall ask for the death penalty,' Lennie said, as if to test the
younger man's reaction.

Modder raised his eyebrows. 'Of course. Murder is murder,' and
he smiled charmingly; it was the first hint Lennie had that he was
being toyed with. That night, after a tasteless meal of stewed
chicken and a morbid conversation with Mrs Katz in which she demanded to know all the details of the hanging procedure, Lennie
slept uneasily. Anna was more in his thoughts than the case, but he
could not clear from his mind the expression in Modder's eyes.
'Murder is murder,' he had said, and smiled.

The next morning Lennie appeared before Mr Justice van Niekerk
on behalf of the Attorney-General. The Clerk called the case; the
Judge ordered the accused to be brought into the dock; and nothing
happened. Or rather a great deal happened, but the accused did not
appear. Amidst a flurry of policemen and defence council, Advocate
Smuts, who was no relation to the General, rose.

'My lord,' he said, 'I crave the Court's indulgence—'

'Where is the accused, Mr Smuts?' the Judge asked.

'That is what we are trying to ascertain, my lord.'

'Who appears for the Attorney-General?'

'I do, my lord,' said Lennie, rising.

'Do you have any idea where the accused is?'

'None, my lord. To the best of my knowledge, he was confined to
one of His Majesty's prisons awaiting trial.'

'One would have thought so,' said the Judge impatiently.

Just then, a dock warder handed Advocate Smuts a note. Again.
Smuts rose. 'My lord, I am now in a position to explain. It seems,
my lord, that the accused, François Pietrus van Heerden, has been

446

taken ill in the last hour. I have here in my hand a medical certificate to that effect.'

The document was handed to the Judge, who read it with judicial irritability. 'Very well,' he said, 'we cannot hold a trial without the accused.'

'No, my lord,' said Smuts.

'The case is adjourned until the accused is well enough to appear, Mr Smuts, you will make the necessary arrangements.'

'I will, my lord.'

And the Judge nodded to his Clerk who called the next case. Lennie, hopelessly bewildered, turned to Modder who was seated behind him. Modder smiled his charming smile and shrugged apologetically. Then he whispered, 'Well, that's that, hey?'

Lennie nodded, rose and bowed to the Judge before leaving the Court. Modder followed him and when they stood in the corridor outside, Lennie's feeling of anti-climax suddenly erupted in anger. 'What the hell was all that about?'

'You heard as well as I, sir,' said Modder, but too innocently for Lennie's liking. 'Did you know anything about this before we went into court?' Lennie demanded.

'No, sir—'

'Listen, Modder, I know the tricks these buggers get up to. What are they hoping for? That next time they'll get someone who won't go for the death penalty?'

'Van Heerden's ill, that's all there is to it—'

'You tell Advocate Smuts or whoever else is behind this, that when van Heerden's well, or when they *say* he's well, I'll be here. You tell him that, Modder. This case is mine and no one else is going to prosecute. Understand?'

'I'm sure Advocate Smuts'll be very interested, sir.'

Lennie grunted explosively, and marched off down the corridor out through a side door into the open air. He found himself in a confined alley, and leaned against the wall in an effort to regain his composure. His cheeks were burning, and his mouth dry. Standing there, with a sharp breeze buffeting his gown and tousling his hair, he determined to see the case through to the sweet or bitter end. They're not going to get away with this, he thought. I'll convict this bastard if it's the last thing I do. And with his determination thus redoubled he slipped back into the Courthouse and met Mr Coetzee in the corridor.

447

'I do apologise for this,' said Coetzee. 'Modder has told me all about it. What a nuisance! But there you are, these things happen, hey? I expect you'll be off back to Cape Town. Remember me to Mr Konradie.'

For the moment there was nothing more Lennie could do except to follow Coetzee's suggestion and return home. He crossed the road to Mrs Katz and began to pack his clothes. Like an evil spirit, the old lady suddenly appeared at the door and, once more, watched him.

'You hanged the *schwarze* already?'

'No. I'll be back for that.'

'The Rabbi said you'd stay two nights, perhaps three.'

'I'll pay you for three,' Lennie said curtly.

'They pay you if you hang the man or not?'

'Yes.'

'Some job.'

33

Henningsdorp

On Wednesday 12 June, the country went to the polls. When the results were announced the Nationalists were returned for the first time with an overall majority of eight seats over the other parties. The Afrikaners in factories and on the farms, in *dorps* and in the cities streamed into the churches, fell on their knees and gave thanks to their God. Hertzog had won on an open and unashamed appeal to ancient hatreds and ever-present fears; from now on, the Prime Minister would speak at every opportunity of 'the native menace'. And, throughout the land, his supporters swaggered with a new and virile confidence; none more than Jacobus Henning, who appended M.P. to his name.

Lennie was subjected to a paralysing depression: he felt robbed by the adjournment of the van Heerden trial; the election results prompted throughout the Jewish community nervousness and dejection, both of which were infectious; and, most important of all, the difficulties of meeting Anna were proving insurmountable. (In those days, Oom Erik said, young people did not take flats or live on their own.)

Their problem was two-fold: they had to be especially discreet in the office because of Konradie, and even after office hours caution had to be exercised; but more frustrating was the plain fact that they had nowhere to meet or spend time together. During the week, Anna lived in the house in Tamboers Kloof; most week-ends she spent on the farm at Paarl, for her parents did not favour leaving her alone in Cape Town. Lennie, of course, had his own parents to contend with. Freda noticed some change in her son and said to Julius,

'He's got a girl friend, thank God.' 'How can you be so sure?' asked Julius. 'How? Because he's combing his hair, that's how.' There was little alternative for the couple but to meet on Sundays on the Pier; they would hire a boat and Lennie would row out into Table Bay; if it did not provide the opportunity for love-making, at least they could speak intimately. It provided, too, a chance to discuss the case.

At Lennie's urging Anna, who was privy to Konradie's mail, agreed to try to find out whether or not van Heerden's illness was genuine. Lennie was not surprised by the results of her investigation.

'Of course he wasn't ill,' Anna said, trailing her hand in the water of the Bay as Lennie rowed the boat out from the pier.

'Was it just to get rid of me, then, that they needed an adjournment?'

'Don't flatter yourself, Lennie. They were waiting for after the election.'

'What the hell's the election got to do with van Heerden?'

'Oh, they were gambling on having the right atmosphere for the trial—'

'Who d'you mean by "they"?'

'The Nats.'

'The Nats are interested in the van Heerden case?' Lennie asked incredulously.

'They're interested in Europeans on trial for killing non-Europeans.'

'But what's the election got to do with it?'

'Lennie, you remember at Jacobus's meeting, the man who took the chair, with silky white hair—'

'Yes?'

'Did you recognise him?'

'No.'

'His name's Hanekom, does that ring a bell?'

'Hanekom,' Lennie said, resting the oars. 'The only Hanekom I've ever heard of is the K.C.'

'That's the same one. He practises at the Transvaal Bar. Oswald Hanekom.'

'What about him?'

'He's going to defend van Heerden.'

'Hanekom is?'

'Right. That's why they wanted an adjournment. Hanekom is a big, big noise behind the scenes. They say he's the power behind the throne. He couldn't take on the case during the Election campaign. So they got an adjournment. The case'll come on again about mid-September—'

'Not till then?'

'No. Because Hanekom's busy drawing up one or two bits of legislation.'

'You mean it's not going to be *Rex* versus van Heerden, but Leonard Levine versus the Nationalist Party?'

'Something like that.'

'What's their defence going to be?'

'I don't know. I don't think even Konradie knows that.'

'Is Konradie in on this, too?'

'Everyone's in on it one way or another, Lennie.'

'Well, at least I'll get some publicity.'

'Don't count on it,' she said. 'The Nats like these things kept secret.'

2

It seems, Oom Erik said, that they were fated to make love beneath the stars. (He chuckled at this out of deference to his listener.) But there was nothing they longed for more than to lie, side by side, in a bed, between cold, clean sheets in the comfort and warmth of each other's arms, imagining a sort of domesticity.

A week before Lennie was due in Graaff-Reinet for the second time, he and Anna sat in the back row of a bioscope watching *The Big Parade* with John Gilbert and Renée Adorée; or not watching, but locked uncomfortably across the arm of their seats, kissing and clutching and moaning. And, towards the end of the film, with all passion spent, she whispered, 'I've had an idea.'

'About what?'

'Where we can go.'

'Where?'

'I'll tell you when I've made the arrangements,' she answered, her eyes twinkling with mystery.

The next evening, just as everyone was packing up for the day, Anna slipped Lennie a note:

I've told Konradie you want to go to Graaff-Reinet on Tuesday instead of Thursday. Break your journey at Worcester, and I'll meet you there. Ask no questions!

A.

On the Monday before he was due to carry out these secret arrangements, Anna did not appear in the office. He was told that family business necessitated her being away for a few days, and Lennie guessed this excuse was part of the plan to enable them to meet. On Tuesday, he took the train to Worcester, about a hundred miles to the north-east of Cape Town, but a good deal further south from Graaff-Reinet. Lennie saw the La Salle in the station forecourt long before the train came to a halt, and he knew the moment he saw Anna that she was in one of her high, excitable moods.

'It's only half-worked,' she said. 'We won't be in a bed, but we'll have a sort of roof, canvas, a tent—'

'Anna, tell me what it's about!'

'But I've told you—'

'You haven't!'

'Haven't I? My Uncle Balthazar—'

'What about him?'

'He's going to give us a roof over our heads.'

'He knows about us?'

'He doesn't care, he's very broad-minded. The only trouble is, I thought we could go to his house, but he's not at his house, silly of me, he's on a "dig". Have you ever been on a "dig" before? I've been lots of times, I used to work for him, you know. Oh, remind me, I have something to tell you—'

'What?'

'It'll keep.'

They followed a winding river and came at last to a formation of hills and rocks that was known as Blauwzand Pass. The way was winding, and curled back on itself, the drop to their right was sheer and terrifying and Anna's driving accentuated the danger of the journey. Just before one o'clock, they saw, in the valley below, a camp-site within the shadow of a cluster of tall rocks with spiky peaks that formed a natural fortress. Near the camp ran two parallel ditches and even from this distance they could see men hard at work with spades. And when the car could travel no further, Lennie took their suitcases, and followed Anna down the rocky slope that led to the semi-circle of tents.

A Xhosa woman waved to them from below. 'That's Rosemary,' said Anna. 'She's worked for my uncle many years.' And Lennie saw the woman order a bearer to meet them and carry their luggage.

Anna and Rosemary greeted each other warmly. Lennie was embarrassed by the Xhosa woman who was naked to the waist, with wonderful breasts, dark and inviting. Anna said, 'Where's my uncle?'

'In his tent,' replied Rosemary. 'He has not been out for two days. He is sad.'

'Why?'

Rosemary shrugged. 'I will tell him you have come.'

While they waited, Lennie looked around the site. It was impossible for the untrained eye to discover the focal points of interest, for there was much activity up and down the length of both the deep trenches; there were men with spades digging vigorously, and others with trowels and brushes scratching away at the earth with greater delicacy and precision.

When Balthazar Henning appeared, Lennie was astonished by the impression of strength the man conveyed: he looked as though he were capable of digging both trenches with his bare hands, and his Voortrekker beard enormously enhanced the size of his head. But strangely at odds with his appearance were the tears that glistened in his eyes, and Lennie could see that the hair about his cheekbones was damp.

'Bal,' Anna cried, 'what's the matter? You look terrible, what's the trouble?'

'All in good time,' he said wearily. 'Let me meet your friend.'

Anna made the introductions, and Lennie felt his hand gripped in a steel clamp. 'Are you interested in archaeology?' Balthazar asked.

'Very. But I've never been on the site of a "dig" before.'

'The two of you change into something more suitable and I'll show you round. Mr Levine, you can use the "finds" tent. Anna, Rosemary's made up the office tent for you. And Mr Levine, be careful, hey? Everything's valuable in there.'

'I wish you'd tell me what's upset you, Bal,' Anna said, pouting.

'I will when I show you round.'

Lennie had not brought the right clothes—khaki shorts or a bush jacket—so he simply changed from his suit into Oxford bags and rolled up the sleeves of his shirt. While he changed, he glanced round at the neat rows of discoveries that had been made on the site: fragments of pots, meaningless pieces of wood, spoons, beads and, in what seemed to Lennie to be pride of place, a charred plank on which was written musical notation. And being close to these things, though not daring to touch, gave him a strange sense of the past.

Later he joined Anna and Balthazar, who led them to one end of the far trench. In Xhosa, he told the men to move and he jumped down then turned to help Anna; Lennie was left to fend for himself as best he could.

Balthazar said, 'Now, I'll show you why I'm so depressed. Look at this—' and he pointed to what appeared to be a doorway. 'This,' he continued, 'is the entrance to a hut. See how it makes the lintel? Now, come closer—' and he handed Anna a magnifying glass with which she examined the post. 'What d'you see?'

'Colours, streaks of different colours—'

'Have a look, Mr Levine—'

'Yes,' Lennie said, focusing. 'Paint.'

'You've got it!' said Balthazar. 'That's exactly what it is: paint. Now, step inside, go on, it's quite safe,' and in Xhosa he ordered a workman to bring the hurricane lamp.

They found themselves in a cramped and murky area. Balthazar held the light to a square section that had been meticulously uncovered. 'You see?' he asked. 'You see, the beads?'

'Yes . . .' both Anna and Lennie said with wonderment.

'And here—have you ever seen such a beautiful mask?' And there, rather terrifying, hung suspended from what must once have been a roof, a savagely carved face, primitive and grotesque. 'But this is what really caused the trouble,' and he set the lamp down upon the earth, and kneeled beside it. In the pallid light, they could see what at first looked like a gnarled and petrified tree, some three or four feet high; but when Balthazar outlined for them the shape, they recognised it at once as a charred cross, and at the centre, where the two struts met, were plainly carved the letters 'J—E—'

'But why should this depress you?' asked Anna.

'It didn't. I was elated. I thought I had discovered proof that Christians had been to this place long before the mid-17th century, long before the Kaffirs had ever set foot in these parts. Everything pointed to a primitive Christian culture. I thought perhaps that sailors marooned by Diaz or da Gama had ventured this far into the interior and settled here, perhaps converted Hottentots or Bushmen . . .' He shook his head sadly. 'But a week ago . . .'

He did not finish but led them out into the fast-fading light of afternoon. They followed him down the length of the trench and when they had reached its limit, Balthazar turned right into a short passage which connected the one trench with the other. As they turned, all paused, for, before them stood atop a mound of earth the body of a wooden bird, its wings missing.

'God,' whispered Anna, 'it's beautiful . . .'

'It is meant to be an eagle,' said Balthazar, 'and was once used to hold a Bible, no doubt. I believe we are standing on consecrated ground.'

'But doesn't this support your theory, then?' asked Lennie.

Balthazar beckoned them closer. 'You have to kneel,' he said. 'Look under the body, near the neck, can you read what's written there?'

Anna crouched and squinted, but the light was failing. 'I can't—'

'Here, you try Mr Levine. Use the torch.'

Lennie shone the beam and saw the words. ' "Muller fecit" ' he said.

'That's it,' acknowledged Balthazar, 'And there's worse, near the tail, go on, look . . .'

Again Lennie followed the archaeologist's instructions ' "V. Haarten, 1798" '

'And do all the finds date from the same period?' Anna asked.

'I'm afraid so. I'll tell you the whole story over supper.'

3

They sat round a warming fire, as others had done many years before them, and after they had eaten, they drank brandy from the bottle, passing it one to the other, while Rosemary, without intruding, cleared away and then sat, some distance off, on her haunches, watching the dying flames.

'You see,' Balthazar said, 'I knew when I read that van Haarten had visited this place that my early Christian theories didn't hold water. And even if there'd been no date, I would not have been misled. He's part of the folk-lore here is van Haarten . . . and Muller . . .

'It was like this: they had some trouble with the landdrost of Blauwzand, a rogue called van der Goes, and van Haarten escaped here into the hills to take refuge with half a dozen friends and twice as many Hottentot women. The story goes that, in the course of time, the women deserted them, and out of terrible loneliness they had no choice but to return to Blauwzand and face their punishment. But God was with them, for they had built Him here a church and honoured Him, and not sinned against Him—this is the legend, you understand . . .

'And on the day they returned to Blauwzand, van der Goes was struck dead by lightning, the hand of God, so the people said, and when van Haarten and his friends returned, the people saw that they were bathed in the light of the Lord, and fell on their knees and gave thanks to their Maker. Thereafter, Muller was sent off to convert the heathen, and van Haarten remained to become landdrost of Blauwzand, and he ordered that this place be preserved as a sign of God's love.

'And they returned here with a predikant to consecrate this holy place but when they saw it from afar, they could tell that it was burning, which they took to be a symbol that the past was done with, and the future bright.'

'And how much of that is true, d'you think?' asked Lennie.

'Certainly van Haarten was a rebel and certainly he became landdrost of Blauwzand. As a matter of fact, twenty years ago I started to work in these parts. My brother, Anna's father, had found church records to show that our ancestor Johannes Henning had, for a short time, been the dominee at Blauwzand. That started my interest. But he must have been a most undistinguished fellow, for nothing of him exists at all. Strange, when you work with the past as I do, strange the tricks it plays . . .'

And Lennie, made drowsy and content by the brandy, leaned back and gazed at the night sky, gleaming as though it were polished glass. And he thought that those self-same stars which looked down upon him now, had shone on this place from the moment time began, upon men and women whose individual lives had long since ceased to have any meaning, and yet, he could not free himself from feeling haunted by them. And, into his mind, came these words which Ibsen had written, and he spoke them aloud. ' "What we have inherited from our fathers and mothers is not all that 'walks' in us. There are all sorts of dead ideas and lifeless old beliefs. They have no tangibility but they haunt us all the same and we cannot get rid of them. Whenever I take up a newspaper I seem to see ghosts gliding between the lines. Ghosts must be all over the country, as thick as the sands of the sea." '

When the silence that followed had run its course, Balthazar said it was time to retire, and Anna whispered to Lennie, 'Come to me soon . . .'

And from his tent Lennie watched the Xhosa woman, Rosemary, covering the ashes of the fire with sand and when she had done, she walked slowly into the tent of Anna's uncle, Balthazar.

Lennie darted across the open ground and joined Anna who lay naked, snuggling in a sleeping-bag, and when he had undressed, he slipped in beside her and held her close.

He said, 'Your uncle's all right, then—'

'In what way?'

'That woman, Rosemary, I've just seen her go in to him—'

'Rather her than me—'

'What's that mean?'

She played with the hairs of his chest. 'You remember,' she said, 'that day you saw Bal and me together?'

'Yes—'

'His wife had just died and he wanted me to come and live with him again. He's like van Haarten—he can't be alone—'

'Why "again"?'

'I don't mind you knowing,' she said in an off-hand way. 'Some years ago, I worked for him and we lived together . . .'

'With your uncle?'

'Are you shocked?'

'No . . .'

But he was. And the past had again done its work. 'What was it you had to tell me?' he asked.

'I've forgotten,' she replied.

That night, they neither loved nor fucked.

4

She drove him to the railway station; he leaned out of the window and she stood on the platform; although they held hands both felt an unaccountable distance between them.

Then, she said, as though it were a trivial detail and something quickly to be put aside, 'I remember now what I wanted to tell you, I'm pregnant.'

The whistle blew and the guard waved his red flag.

Lennie said, 'Oh God.'

'We'll talk about it when you come back from Graaff-Reinet. Good luck.'

And Lennie, without thinking, asked, 'Are you sure it's mine?'

If he had struck Anna she could not have looked more despairing. As the train slowly pulled Lennie away from her, she murmured, barely moving her lips, 'Oh, you bloody Jew.'

457

34

The case for the defence

The Court in Graaff-Reinet on Lennie's second appearance had much the same atmosphere as Jacobus Henning's election meeting. Not that it was as crowded—the public gallery, which could accommodate ten, seated half that number—but there was the same friendliness and comradeship between the spectators, the Jury and the Counsel for the Defence, Oswald Hanekom, K.C., white-haired and white-skinned. While the Court waited for the entrance of the Judge, he greeted this one and that one, conferred with his Junior who on this occasion was Advocate Smuts, and, in return, was treated with a good deal of deference and respect.

A few feet away sat Lennie, with the charming and obsequious Mr Modder beside him, watching this preliminary charade with suspicion and not a little resentment. His resentment arose not from the obvious fuss that was being made of his opponent, but from the knowledge that the case was being treated with indifference by the world outside. He had hoped that there would be reporters from the Cape Town newspapers, the *Times* and the *Argus*, but when he asked Modder where the press bench was, he saw only a freckled youth from the local paper. The half-full gallery also annoyed him, but the feeling that the proceedings lacked occasion chiefly emanated from Mr Hanekom himself whose presence instilled such confidence in his supporters that they regarded the verdict as a foregone conclusion. Lennie determined to prove them wrong.

The Defence had requested only one witness to be subpeoenaed on their behalf, a Dr Witte who, it seemed, had lived abroad for many years and about whom Lennie could discover little, but permission had been obtained for the doctor to perform his own post-mortem on the deceased which indicated that, as Lennie had thought all along, Hanekom's only hope was to discredit the medical evidence. In this respect, Lennie was confident he could make the Crown case stick.

At two minutes to ten, the Judge, Mr Justice van Niekerk, entered; he, too, brought a certain indifference with him into Court, but Lennie learned that he did so in all cases he tried. He had a bored, detached way of talking, running one sentence into another as though he were intoning prayers. When he reached his chair, he bowed to left and right, and set in motion the first business of the morning, which was to sentence a prisoner from a case heard the previous day, to three years hard labour for fraud. Then, *Rex* versus François Pietrus van Heerden was called and the accused was put up.

Van Heerden was a tall, gangling man who sweated a great deal although it was cool in the Court. He stood between two dock warders as the charge was read with all the flourish the law allows, invoking the name of His Majesty the King George V, and declaring that upon such-and-such a date, in such-and-such a place, the accused did wrongfully, unlawfully and maliciously kill and murder Nathan Zimbali in his lifetime a servant at the Commercial Hotel in Geldspoort in the aforementioned district of Graaff-Reinet. And when he was asked how he pleaded, he replied in a husky, tremulous voice which gave the impression of harmlessness, 'Not guilty.' It was Lennie's turn to rise and address the Jury.

Lennie scanned their faces before he began. Nine good men and true, and he must convince seven of them that the accused was guilty of a deliberate and cold-blooded murder. He could detect no open antagonism in their ordinary, undistinguished faces, all of them countrymen, all Boers—all, Lennie decided, Hanekom's men. Yet he was certain he could succeed in instilling in their judgement reason, for it is the fate of lawyers to believe in the impartiality of the law.

The facts were not in dispute. On 30 March, the last Saturday in the month, the accused together with Benjamin Louw made the journey by horse and cart from the Boulter farm to Graaff-Reinet, a distance of some thirty miles, in order to watch a rugby match between the Police and the local hospital staff. Van Heerden was the manager of the Boulter farm, Louw a sheep-shearer and his closest friend. As was customary on such outings, the two drank almost incessantly before and during the match. When the game was over, they bought a case of lager beer to quench their thirst on the journey home. There was, it appeared, some urgency about their return, for van Heerden's wife, Geraldine, was pregnant and he did not want to leave her alone too long after dark. In the event, when they reached the village of Geldspoort, ten miles from the Boulter farm, they discovered that they had almost run out of beer. So they parked outside the Commercial Hotel—a rather grandiose name for a small boarding-house—and made straight for the bar. Since it was early, about seven o'clock, there was no one about except the manager, Hans Potgieter, who knew the two friends well. Before having his first drink in the bar, van Heerden excused himself and made his way out to the lavatory in the back yard. He was swigging the last drops from a beer bottle. Minutes later, he returned, empty-handed but covered in blood and said to Potgieter and Louw, 'Christ, I've just killed a Kaffir.' Potgieter and Louw went out into the yard and saw the body of Nathan Zimbali, his skull shattered, lying near the water-pump that stood in the centre of the small yard. A halo of broken glass from the beer bottle encircled the battered head, and beside it stood a large stone, the size of a rugby ball, drenched in blood. Potgieter at once called the local police.

In a statement, van Heerden claimed that Zimbali had tried to attack him without apparent reason. To defend himself, he had struck the man with the beer bottle. (No mention, at this stage, was made by the accused of the blood-stained stone.) The policeman, a young constable, accepted the story and made arrangements for the body to be removed and, in due course, a post-mortem was conducted by Dr Erasmus who, without much difficulty, discovered that the bottle was not the fatal weapon. From the nature of the blows, and the shattering of the dead man's skull, the doctor concluded that the bottle had been used to strike Zimbali from behind, thus stunning him, and when the man had fallen, some heavier object had been dropped on his head. The police returned to Geldspoort, and discovered the stone. They had no alternative but to arrest the accused.

'Gentlemen of the Jury, these are the facts. You will hear from Dr Erasmus, a pathologist of many years experience, how the accused deliberately struck the deceased from behind with the bottle and when the man was lying on the ground, stunned and helpless, he lifted this stone, Exhibit A, and raising it above his head—you can see he is a tall man—dropped it on the head of Nathan Zimbali and, for this heartless, calculated act, François Pietrus van Heerden now stands before you in the dock.

'Gentlemen of the Jury, it is not beholden upon the Crown to prove the existence of motive. But, I put it to you, and you are the sole judges of fact, that it is the very absence of motive which makes this case so horrible. I ask you to imagine the scene. Van Heerden, by then extremely drunk, and you will hear evidence to this effect, staggers out into the back yard of the hotel, sees Zimbali, whose back is towards him, drawing water from the pump. Van Heerden has an empty beer bottle in his hand. In his intoxicated and confused mind, he decides, perhaps as a prank, to smash the bottle on Zimbali's head. This done, he sees the stone, and finishes off his fiendish work. Intoxication is no defence, for the mere act of lifting the stone proves *intent*, which by our law is the difference between murder and culpable homicide. If he had fired a gun, or thrown a knife, it could be argued that he had acted irresponsibly, but the mere fact that he took the trouble to lift that stone and deliberately dropped it from his full height on to the deceased's head, is, Gentlemen of the Jury, proof of intent. It could not have been a mistake. It could have had no other purpose but to cause the death of Nathan Zimbali.'

He had spoken well; the case was clearly put before the Court. A procession of police witnesses now entered the box to give formal evidence. At no time did Hanekom cross-examine; he kept his eyes down on a lined foolscap pad on which he doodled incessantly. No word passed between him and his Junior, and Lennie was disconcerted by the eminent lawyer's continuing indifference.

The first sensation occurred during the examination by Lennie of the accused's companion, Benjamin Louw, a stocky, hairy man, who answered Lennie's questions with unconcealed hostility and with a grim determination to do his best for the man in the dock who was his closest friend. The revelation occurred after Louw had reached the point where van Heerden re-entered the bar of the Commercial Hotel, his shirt and jacket dripping blood. 'Christ,' said van Heerden, 'I've killed a Kaffir.'

'What happened then?' asked Lennie.

'Mr Potgieter and I went out into the yard.'

'For what purpose?'

'What purpose? To see if old Franny van Heerden was telling the truth.'

'Go on.'

'Well, we went out into the yard and saw the body. Of course, I recognised the Kaf—' He stopped himself but too late. The Court erupted in excited chatter. Triumphantly, Lennie glanced at Hanekom, but again received no response. The K.C. merely continued to doodle as though he were taking no part of the proceedings.

'You recognised the murdered man?' Lennie asked, his voice rising to the drama of the moment. Louw did not reply but gazed at his feet, then at the Judge, then at Hanekom, his eyes crying out for help. 'I asked you a question, Mr Louw: did you recognise the murdered man?'

'The witness will answer the question,' murmured the Judge.

'I recognised him,' admitted Louw and then shot a brief, apologetic glance at the accused.

'Why did you recognise him?'

'Because I'd seen him before!' Louw replied as though he were scoring a point.

'Where?' A reluctant pause from the witness. 'Where had you seen him?'

Louw licked his lips. 'He used to work on the farm.'

'On the Boulter farm, d'you mean?'

'Yes.'

'Of which van Heerden was the manager?'

'Yes.'

'And so Mr van Heerden knew him, too?'

Hanekom interrupted for the first time as was to be expected, since Lennie had asked a question which required the witness to make assumptions. But what Defence Counsel had to say was even more bewildering than his former silence. 'If it will save the Court time and trouble,' he mumbled, 'we are quite ready to admit that the deceased knew the accused.' Although Lennie was seated only a few feet away from him, he had to strain forward to catch every word.

'Thank you Mr Hanekom yes Mr Levine?' said the Judge in one bored breath.

Deeply unsettled by this act of generosity on the part of the Defence, Lennie rose once more. Gradually, with new impetus, he pursued the point. Louw was more recalcitrant than ever but Lennie, driving and relentless, managed to extract from the sheep-shearer the admission that van Heerden had, but a week before the crime, sacked Zimbali. Louw described a row, about the substance of which he claimed to know nothing, between the accused and Zimbali.

'How far away from them were you when the row took place?' Lennie asked.

'About a hundred yards.'

'So you couldn't hear everything that was said?'

'No.'

'What *did* you hear?'

'I heard Franny tell the Kaffir to clear off the farm.'

'What happened then?'

'Well, Zimbali bug—er—went off, and we all continued with our work.'

'Did you not discuss the row with the accused?'

Impassive as ever the Judge said, 'The witness has already told the Jury that he doesn't know what the row was about Mr Levine I cannot believe it is of any interest to hear whether or not a discussion took place unless it reveals the cause of the dispute which the witness has said he knows nothing about.'

'I am obliged to your Lordship,' said Lennie and turned once more to Louw. 'But there was a row?'

'*Yes!*'

And Lennie sat, nodding to Hanekom indicating that the examination-in-chief was concluded.

'Yes Mr Hanekom?' said the Judge.

'I have no questions of this witness, my lord,' Hanekom replied, bobbing in his place.

'I beg your pardon Mr Hanekom did you say no questions?'

'That is correct, my lord.'

'All right the witness may step down.'

As Louw stepped out of the witness box he called loud enough for everyone to hear, 'Sorry, Franny,' and then, heavy-footed, stomped from the Court.

Lennie was dumbfounded, and then a terrible panic seized him: had he, by revealing the row, opened the door for Hanekom to pose the probability that Zimbali had attacked van Heerden first, as an act of revenge for losing his job? Had Lennie walked into the trap? He glanced across at Hanekom but the elderly, austere man continued to draw elaborate patterns on his foolscap pad; it was impossible to guess even remotely what he was thinking.

After the lunch recess, Modder examined Hans Potgieter, the manager of the Commercial Hotel, who substantiated much of Louw's evidence. Though, when it came to the background of the deceased, the witness disclaimed any knowledge of previous employment. 'I took him on as a kitchen servant. I didn't ask for references, and I wasn't offered any.'

It was then Dr Erasmus's turn to enter the witness box. When Lennie rose to begin the questioning, he knew the real battle was about to take place, for the pathologist's evidence would be vital in proving that van Heerden struck the deceased from behind, first with the bottle, and then, when the man was down, smashed his skull in with the heavy stone.

Dr Erasmus proved to be a good witness. He did not indulge in too much clinical detail, nor did he employ too many medical terms, which would only have confused the Jury. In plain language, he told the Court that, in the course of the post-mortem examination, he had found the dead man's skull to be shattered, his nose broken and his jaw fractured. Behind the left ear was a wound that had nearly severed it from the head. Above the left temple was a bow-shaped wound, four-and-a-half inches long, through which fragmented edges of bone were visible. Splinters of glass were embedded in the upper neck region. The doctor had no doubt as to the order of events, and stated unequivocally that the empty beer bottle had been used to strike the man from behind—the splinters of glass confirmed this—and that the stone had been used to finish off the victim. The blood of the deceased and the blood on the stone was of the same group: B. The injuries the deceased sustained were compatible with the accused's height and strength. 'He must have raised the stone to the full reach of his arms, and then deliberately smashed it on Zimbali's skull. There can be no other explanation.'

'Thank you, Dr Erasmus,' Lennie said, resuming his seat.

All now turned to look at Mr Hanekom and he played the moment for all the suspense that could be extracted from it. He was greatly assisted by the Judge, who said, tentatively, 'Yes, Mr Hanekom?'

And Hanekom rose. 'Yes, my lord,' he said with some finality. It was as if the whole Court breathed a sigh of relief. At last, Lennie thought, we will get some clue to the defence; alert, he waited.

'I have a very few questions for you, doctor,' said Hanekom in his mumbled off-hand delivery. 'You said that when you conducted

your post-mortem, you ascertained the blood group of the victim?'
'I did.'

'Would you explain to the Jury exactly what a blood group is?'

The doctor, with a clarity that was now expected of him, described how, in 1900, Karl Landsteiner had found that the blood of human beings could, by studying certain reactions, be divided into four groups, A, B, AB, and O.

'This,' said Hanekom, 'is the study of agglutinogens, is it not?'

'That is correct,' replied the doctor, somewhat surprised by Counsel's knowledge.

'And what blood group did the victim belong to?'

'Blood group B.'

'And you drew no other conclusions?'

'None. There are no others to be drawn.'

'Very well,' said Hanekom. 'Did you examine the victim's skull?'

'Of course. It was the principal object of the post-mortem examination.'

'Did you take any measurements of the skull as such?'

'I measured the size of each wound.'

'But no more than that?'

'No.'

Hanekom was about to sit, but just before he did, he asked his last question. 'You've no idea, just as a matter of interest, what the height of the victim was?'

'Five foot six inches.'

'Thank you, Dr Erasmus.'

'Do you wish to re-examine, Mr Levine?' the Judge asked, clearly hoping Lennie would not.

'No, my lord. That represents the case for the Crown,' Lennie looked anxiously at the clock which stood above the Jury box: three o'clock. His heart sank, for he badly needed an adjournment in order to try and discover what Hanekom's interest was in blood groups; but Hanekom had been much too clever: he had timed his opening speech to perfection: the Crown was to be allowed no opportunity to do its homework.

A stillness settled in the courtroom, that particular hush which occurs when a conductor raises his baton. Hanekom, hands on hips, turned to address the Jury.

'Gentlemen of the Jury, I will be brief, because I know you have been sitting here in this stuffy court for two days trying other cases, and now I must ask you to concentrate for a short while longer. You may have noticed that throughout this morning and the early part of this afternoon, I have taken little notice of my learned friend's witnesses. And it may have passed through your mind that old Hanekom is losing his touch—or worse—his mind. But, those of you who know me will admit I rarely do things without a reason, and the reason for my disinterest in these proceedings is quite simple: it is because I know, and you know that François Pietrus van Heerden is not guilty of murder. He may be guilty of doing a fatal injury to this—this—Zimbali, but he is not guilty of *murder*.

'As my learned friend so rightly explained, murder is the killing of one human being by another with intent. You heard my learned friend make great play of the word "intent". And, this may surprise you, we do not contest that there was intent to kill. In fact, we admit it. I mean, you're all reasonable men, if you pick up a stone as heavy as that and drop it down on a skull, there are very few of you here who would not be able to guess what the result would be! No, gentlemen of the jury, "intent" is not the section of the definition of murder with which we disagree. I call my first witness, Dr Karl Witte.'

The horror of what was about to happen did not fully dawn on Lennie; a sense of unreality, greater than he had ever experienced before, began to insist itself. What followed was, to Lennie, a vision of someone else's nightmare.

'Dr Witte, would you state your qualifications, please?' Hanekom asked after his witness had been sworn.

'I am a graduate in medicine of Stellenbosch University, having the degrees M.B., Ch.B., and I am also a Ph.D.—that is, I have my doctorate of Philosophy—from the University of Heidelberg in Germany.' Witte was obviously used to lecturing, for he had a ringing voice and a precise diction, strangely at odds with Hanekom's inaudibility.

'And what academic position do you at present hold?'

'I am presently occupied in conducting anthropological research in Atlanta, Georgia, which is in the United States of America.'

'I am correct in saying, am I not, that the authorities gave you permission to conduct your own post-mortem on the victim?'

'That is correct.'

'Would you tell his lordship and the Jury what the purpose of this examination was?'

466

'I was invited by you, Mr Hanekom, to examine the body in view of the research in which I am presently engaged.'

'And what is the nature of your research?'

'I am studying the theory of evolution in the light of Christian teaching.' (This was received warmly by the few spectators.)

'Now, we have heard Dr Erasmus explain the study of blood groups. Did you make similar tests?'

'Similar, but not the same.'

'Would you explain?'

'I do not, in these cases, employ Dr Landsteiner's classification. Or rather, I do, in part, but I also use my own form of classification. It is called the Witte Table.'

'And using your own method of classification and Dr Landsteiner's, what did you discover?'

'That the victim belonged to blood group B. Witte A.'

'Would you explain?'

'With pleasure,' answered the anthropologist, warming to his subject. 'In Negroid bodies—'

'Forgive me for interrupting you, doctor, but by Negroid, you mean what?'

'Negroid—Negro—it is what Americans call Kaffirs. Negro means black.'

'Thank you. Please continue.'

'In Negroid bodies it has been discovered that there is a greater incidence of Blood Group B than in European bodies, a difference of approximately 18%. It has been further discovered—and this is part of my own research project—that in the Negro who possesses Blood Group B, the agglutinogens bear a greater similarity to the anthropoidal ape than they do to the European.'

Lennie rose to his feet. 'My lord, I must protest at this line of questioning. This is not a defence. This is a study in anthropology.'

The judge nodded. 'I must say Mr Hanekom that I am at a loss to understand the object of this examination it seems to me to have very little to do with the crime with which the accused is charged.'

'With your lordship's permission, if you would allow me to continue, the purpose will soon become clear. I shall not keep the Court long. I fully intend to give your lordship time to sum up this evening—'

'That is very good of you Mr Hanekom,' the Judge observed drily.

'Thank you, my lord,' said Hanekom, also smiling.

'Very well continue Mr Hanekom . . .'

'Doctor Witte, let us put aside these difficult technical words like agglutinogens and anthropoidal. Let us use basic terms like heads and hands and feet. Am I right in saying that, at my request, you also examined the accused, and took certain measurements?'

'That is correct. I measured the accused in exactly the same way as I measured the victim.'

'To make it easier for the Jury, my lord, I wonder if you would permit me to use a blackboard and chalk for this portion of Dr Witte's evidence? It would enable them to see at a glance the table of comparison?'

'Perhaps it would make it easier for me too Mr Hanekom very well.'

Hanekom nodded and the usher opened a side door to admit two Native boys who carried in a blackboard and an easel. They were placed in the well of the Court, within reach of Mr Hanekom who was now handed a box of chalk by Advocate Smuts. 'How would you like me to draw this table?' Hanekom asked his witness.

'In three columns if you please. The first should be headed APES, the second, NEGRO, the third, EUROPEAN.'

'You have no objection if I call the second one KAFFIR for the sake of the Jury?'

'None.'

'Thank you. Pray continue, doctor.'

'Now, the first item I measured, as I have told you was the blood.' Hanekom chalked up BLOOD. 'Under the Ape column would you put B Witte A, the same under column for KAFFIRS, and under EURO-PEAN A Witte E.'

'The European measurement is the accused's blood group?'

'That is correct. In Europeans 45% are blood group A. And under my own system 94% Europeans are Witte E. I have also developed classifications for Jews.'

'Thank you. What next did you measure?'

There followed detailed measurements of the distance between the hairline and the eyebrow, of the cerebral hemispheres and their convolutions. Twice Lennie objected. Twice Hanekom asked him, with disarming courtesy, to be patient until the table was complete. Twice, the Judge allowed the Defence to continue.

'What is the next item?' Hanekom asked.

'The absence of a large globule to the external ear in both the APE and the KAFFIR, but present in Mr van Heerden.'

'Next?'

'The not quite upright stance of the APE and the KAFFIR as opposed to Mr van Heerden's fully upright bearing.'

'Ah,' said Hanekom. 'This is the question of height, is it not?'

'That is correct.'

'What height is Mr van Heerden?'

'Six foot two inches.'

'And the victim?'

'This is the point: fully extended and upright he was five feet six inches, but by the curvature of the spine, I was able to ascertain that, when he walked about, he would stand no taller than five foot. That conforms more or less to the average height of apes.'

And so it continued until the Table was almost complete. Van Heerden had a flattened foot—the ape and Zimbali had none; he had a non-opposable great toe—the ape and Zimbali had none; van Heerden had a wider pelvis, a sigmoid flexure of his spine, smaller canine teeth, a smaller-sized jaw in relation to the greater-sized cranium.

'And last,' said Dr Witte, 'I measured the *penis non erectus*. In the case of Mr van Heerden it measured four and a quarter inches. In the case of the victim, six and two-third inches, and in the case of apes, often longer.'

'Thank you, Doctor Witte.'

The blackboard was moved closer to the Jury box so that they could see more easily Dr Witte's findings which, in all cases, pointed to almost identical measurements in the Ape and the Kaffir. Lennie cross-examined, but Witte held firm. The closing speeches were made and the Judge summed up in favour of the Crown telling the Jury that they had not heard a defence to the charge of Murder. It was to no avail. The Jury retired for ten minutes. At five minutes to five they returned and delivered the verdict of Not Guilty. Not guilty of murder because murder is the killing of one human being by another.

That which had gone before, and that which was to come, is history.

2

There was, Oom Erik said, a strange sequel to the case, for some six months later van Heerden entered the legal history books: he was charged with murder for the second time, and for the second time, acquitted.

What happened was this: after his acquittal for Zimbali's murder, van Heerden's wife, Geraldine she was called, gave birth to a baby. (You may remember she was pregnant during the trial.) The baby was born black. Not difficult now to understand why van Heerden dismissed Zimbali from the farm, not difficult now to understand why he lifted that stone and crushed the black man's head in. He was killing, of course, the father of his wife's black child. And later, much later, he loaded his twin-barrelled shotgun and disposed of Geraldine as well. (The baby he did not harm, but sent away to an orphanage in De Aar.)

Van Heerden was brought to trial a second time; for a second time found not guilty of murder. Reluctantly, the Jury agreed that he was guilty of culpable homicide, which is the killing of another without intent. In these parts they understand the passions which move men to act irrationally.

But I digress, said Oom Erik. You are more concerned with the trials and tribulations of your father, Leonard Levine.

3

The trials and tribulations of Leonard Levine were not yet over. He travelled back by overnight train to Cape Town, but he did not sleep: he lay, as if in a trance, rocked to and fro, to and fro by the speeding train. There had been no cheers in the court, no banner headlines in the press; the decision passed as an everyday occurrence, as an obvious matter of course. Lennie had failed miserably; he had found no arguments against a faith stronger than his, against an impregnable belief. He had witnessed but another ceremony in a tribal rite; he had seen briefly revealed the holy relic of a religious creed which the faithful prefer to keep hidden and secret. Against faith, there is no argument.

Weary, dispirited, he walked as though in a dream from the railway station to the office. When he arrived, Konradie, tight-lipped and white-gilled, was waiting for him.

'Come into my office, Levine,' he barked. Once behind closed doors, Konradie said, 'Mr Levine, you are in serious trouble.'

'What, for losing the case?' Lennie asked, frowning.

'No, Mr Levine, not for losing the case. I have to inform you that your services are no longer required in this office. You are no longer employed here as of *now*!'

'I demand a reason—' said Lennie struggling to collect his confused thoughts.

'I'll give you the reason. You have betrayed my trust,' Konradie said, thumping his desk. 'Last night, it may interest you to know, my secretary, Miss Anne Henning, in the presence of her father, Mr Justice Henning, accused you of fathering her unborn child.'

It was almost as if Lennie had forgotten, but then he had a talent for putting unpleasantness from his mind. He had a talent, too, for survival. He said, 'She's wrong, Mr Konradie.'

'Are you denying paternity?'

'I am.'

'Your denials are of no interest to me. You think I'd accept your word against Miss Henning's. Do you think her father would? Or her brother who is now an M.P. and man of influence? You're career is finished, Mr Levine. We're going to have you struck off, you understand. You won't be able to practise law from Cape to Cairo—'

'The father is her uncle, Balthazar Henning,' he said. (How quickly his mind worked: he was about to touch the nerve of family pride.) 'Miss Henning and I were at his camp near Blauwzand Pass two nights ago. I don't think Uncle Balthazar would deny these allegations because I could accuse him of more serious matters.' (He was thinking of the Xhosa woman, Rosemary. Yes, he had touched the nerve.)

Konradie, brows furrowed, eyes black as thunder, asked him to wait outside, which Lennie did, listening at the door. He heard Konradie say, 'This is urgent, I must speak to Mr Jacobus Henning. I don't care if he's in conference with the Minister, he must be brought to the phone at once. Tell him—' But Lennie heard no more because Bell appeared and, smiling maliciously, affected to sympathise with Lennie for losing the case.

Dazed by the speed and turn of events, Lennie wandered over to his desk and sat unnaturally upright, alert, on guard, his bearing at odds with the confusion of his thoughts. One part of his mind raced, tested over and over again all he had said to Konradie, and he convinced himself that he had robbed the Hennings of their power, snatched from them the initiative, and placed himself safely outside their reach. But, somewhere in his consciousness, this confidence

471

founded on reason did not stretch deeply enough to calm him absolutely. He could not rid himself of a sensation of impending danger, as though he had just been told he was to be the victim of a violent physical attack and could do nothing to escape it: he felt as if at any minute he would snap in two.

Konradie appeared, still smouldering. 'You're to go at once to Parliament. Mr Henning wants to see you. He's waiting now.'

'But I don't want to see him,' Lennie replied limply.

'I advise you to see him if you want to keep your job.'

'I don't. I resign,' Lennie said and he had the impression that someone else had spoken.

Taken by surprise, Konradie was reduced to blustering. 'Mr Henning wants to see you, a Member of Parliament, you can't play fast and loose—'

'Didn't you hear what I said?' Lennie asked. '*I resign!* You tell your Mr Henning from me that he's an infectious disease. I wouldn't want to be in the same room as him!' Lennie stood and began to clear his desk, transferring papers and files to his brief-case.

Konradie grabbed him by the wrist. 'That's a slander!' he cried. 'And who are you to make accusations like that? You've made threats, threats against the Hennings, threats you can't prove—'

'You ask Uncle Balthazar—'

'I've no intention of asking him anything at all. I'm asking you: what do you intend to do?'

'I've told you,' said Lennie, freeing himself from the other's grip. 'I'm walking out of here. I never want to hear the name Henning again. You tell Mr Jacobus Henning M.P. to keep as far away from me as possible, and I'll do the same for him.'

Konradie came suddenly close; Lennie could smell the stale tobacco on his breath. 'You mean if Mr Henning takes no action against you, you'll keep silent?'

Lennie nodded. And when he found himself out in the street, walking homewards, he was convinced that he had somehow vindicated himself, as if he had reversed the verdict of the trial and won a moral victory. It was only later, when Anna Henning's face flooded his mind, that he acknowledged, albeit briefly, the act of betrayal he had perpetrated and try as he might he could not shake free from a sense of guilt, for by then the two sides of his nature had come face to face.

The following morning he was unable to rise from his bed. When

Julius entered his room with the customary early-morning cup of tea, he found his son already awake, or apparently awake, for Lennie lay on his back, eyes open wide, staring at the ceiling. Julius said, 'Ah, so you're awake for a change: that means it'll rain today.' But he received no response; Lennie neither spoke nor moved. Momentarily anxious, Julius peered closely at his son, disturbed by the sightlessness of those staring eyes, trying to detect signs of breathing as he had so often done before when Lennie was a babe-in-arms. 'Lenshki?' he called softly, in a hopeful but nervous tone.

Only then did Lennie turn towards his father: 'I can't move my legs,' he said.

Alarm was instant and overwhelming, for Julius's first thoughts were that his son had contracted poliomyelitis, infantile paralysis as they called it then, the dread of all parents. Doctor Panchansky was summoned and quickly allayed the Levines' fears: it was certainly not polio, but exactly what it was eluded diagnosis. Two consultants were immediately called: Mr Benjamin, whose interest was orthopaedics, and Mr Hurwitz, whose speciality was diseases of the brain.

'Misters?' queried Julius. 'You mean they're not qualified?' The explanation that following British medical protocol specialists were addressed in this fashion did not satisfy him; he remained deeply suspicious of the two men. 'Hmm,' he grunted loud enough for them to hear as they examined his stricken son. 'Hmm. They don't even smell from ether!'

Neither Mr Benjamin nor Mr Hurwitz could discover damage to bone or brain. They departed insisting that Lennie enter hospital for observation and tests. It was left to Dr Panchansky, a brusque but wise general practitioner, to make the most accurate diagnosis: 'It's mind over matter: if he wants to get up, he'll get up.' But both Julius and Freda were mistrustful; that evening they telephoned their son Emanuel, the doctor in Johannesburg, and explained Lennie's condition as best they could.

'We've a man here,' said Emanuel, 'a Professor Sherman, tip-top. It sounds as though he could help.'

'A professor!' repeated Julius, 'that's a little better. They got everything in Joburg.'

It was immediately decided that Lennie should be sent north to the tip-top Professor Sherman, but the problem arose whether Freda or Julius would accompany the invalid. The journey of a thousand miles to Johannesburg took two days and two nights by train, and Lennie would not be able to travel alone.

'A boy needs his mother at a time like this,' Julius said but without conviction.

'And who'll look after the house?' asked Freda, understanding her husband's longing to care for his favourite child. In the end she, the stronger, won as always: Julius would go with Lennie.

'But where will we find the money for two fares?' asked Julius.

'I've got,' said Freda.

'*You've* got?' replied Julius, baffled.

Freda went purposefully towards the door, Julius following like an inquisitive terrier. 'You wait here,' she commanded and, moments later, returned with a bundle of notes.

'My God,' exclaimed Julius, 'but you're a secretive woman!'

'I put it by for a wet day,' said Freda.

Julius eyed the money grudgingly. 'I can't use it,' he said with a flicker of regret.

'And why not?' demanded Freda.

'No. Certainly not. It's your savings. You'll need it maybe in an emergency.'

'But Julius,' Freda said plaintively, 'this *is* an emergency!'

4

Meanwhile, an unaccustomed tranquillity had come to Anna, profound and genuine quietude. (I saw a good deal of her in those days, Oom Erik admitted, and her eyes were still and calm.) But this was not the mood of the other occupants of the house in Paarl: Victoria and Dawid made no attempt to conceal their anguish and their sense of shame. But Anna was buoyant: she drew her contentment from the life within her. The twin prospect of scandal and disgrace provoked no terror; it was as if her pregnancy had liberated her. She thought of Lennie seldom, and felt nothing for him except perhaps a kind of vague affection. But, hearing through Konradie of Lennie's resignation and illness, she wrote the following letter to him in Johannesburg:

Dear Leonard,

I was sorry to hear that you are not well. Though it seems tactless I must tell you that I have never felt better, never felt really as whole as I do now and I have a suspicion that this will be a

474

comfort to you. Do not interpret this as bitterness or resentment. I assure you it is not.

My parents' reaction was predictable and I suppose understandable. Like a Victorian miss, I'm to be sent away to a cousin in the Orange Free State so that I can give birth in secret; this, my mother assures me, is for my own good, but I know that really it is for hers. Also my father does not want me to be a bad moral example to the servants.

As you have probably worked out for yourself, no action is to be taken against you. I could see the look of apprehension on my father's face when he asked if I wished to file a suit for breach of promise, but I assured him I did not and he was obviously greatly relieved because he cannot face, and never could, the thought of our family being publicly humiliated or shamed.

No one seems to understand my feelings at this moment, least of all my parents. I am serene. Can *you* understand? I want this child as I have wanted nothing else. I felt movement for the first time yesterday and I wept unashamedly. I have grown up. And for that I thank you. I know too that having a child will mean that I shall never be alone again, never. And that knowledge is a real source of joy.

And when I dare to think of what the future may hold for him or her, I put aside all thought of pain and suffering, which is everyone's expectation, and hold only to one conviction: that the child may be better than its parents.

Anna.

Some days later she received a package in reply: a copy of Ibsen's plays inscribed 'To Anna, with love, Leonard'. And, in the course of time, she travelled north, through the arid wasteland of the Orange Free State, and in a lonely, secret place gave birth to a boy.

5

And what, the prisoner asked, of my father, Leonard Levine?

Ah well, said Oom Erik, I know a little but not much. I know, for example, that shortly after receiving that letter from your mother he recovered from his illness. Some said he bore the look of a defeated man. I know that Julius returned to Cape Town alone and that Lennie convalesced for some months in Johannesburg, and during that time met and fell in love with one Sharon Blumberg whose father was an attorney. They were married in the winter of 1932 and settled in Johannesburg where Lennie, with his father-in-law's help, set up in private practice, and prospered.

And this curious circumstance: when war was declared in 1939, Lennie volunteered at once. Of course he was in his mid-thirties then and too old for active service, but he rose to the rank of Captain, and was adjutant to the Officer Commanding an Internment Camp near Krugersdorp. And who should he meet among the internees but your uncle, Jacobus, the former Nationalist M.P., placed behind barbed wire for his active support of the Nazi cause. Jacobus told me, Oom Erik said, that Captain Levine was uncommonly kind, and obtained special privileges for him. Captain Levine even asked after Anna's son.

I do not know much more, except the public events. I know that in 1953 Leonard was appointed Queen's Counsel and that when we became a Republic, because those Commonwealth Kaffirs wanted to tell us how to run our affairs, Lennie was prominent in the fight to keep the appendage Q.C. behind his name. And when the authorities suggested that senior counsel should be known as State's Advocate, it was Lennie who pointed out that the abbreviation S.A. to which they would be entitled, stood also for Sex Appeal. In the end, as you know, the authorities, sensitive to ridicule, settled for State's Counsel instead, but the older men, like Lennie, continued to use and still use Q.C. Strange, the concerns of former Communists.

6

Oom Erik has gone and the prisoner is assailed by a terrible and desolate sense of loss. It is as though Mpobe has lost the mole and can go no further. Despair gives way to panic: the welcome darkness is perforated with pin-pricks of abhorrent light: The inevitability of

(*The prisoner is interrupted*)

Epilogue:
The family historian

The prisoner is interrupted. He has worked through the night and into the morning which is sunny and warm and still. Two policemen, the sergeant and the pimply youth, rush into the library.

'Stand up, stand up,' orders the sergeant. 'Come on, come on—'

And, obediently he stands, while the young pimply constable searches him.

'What's all this about?' asks the prisoner.

'You've got a visitor.'

'My uncle, the Minister?'

'No talking!' screams the sergeant.

'He's clean,' says the constable.

'Right. Into the hall with him and don't let him out of your sight!'

Together, the prisoner stands in the hall beside his guard, half his age. They wait for almost an hour. Then, glinting in the sunlight, the prisoner sees a long, sleek Mercedes gliding down the drive, and drawing up at the house. The sergeant opens the rear door.

It is not Jacobus Henning, the Minister. It is a wiry, angular man whom the prisoner has never seen before, but recognises at once by the tuft of untidy grey hair that stands up on his head like a solitary horn. The prisoner, feeling a hollow rushing sensation like being caught at the very centre of a whirlwind, recognises his father, Leonard Levine.

Father and son shake hands as strangers do, for they are strangers.

'Is there somewhere we can talk?' asks Lennie, and the prisoner leads him into the library.

He is older and fuller of face, and he wears the right clothes now:

477

a pale blue safari suit and a striped tie that suggests an English public school. But the Shanbanist scar is still above his eye. 'Are you
comfortable here?' he asks, doing his best never to look at his son.

'I have all I need,' says the prisoner.

Lennie nods, his lips pressed briefly into an apologetic smile. Discomfort hangs about him like an ill-fitting shroud. 'Well, look here,
I'm going to come straight to the point, this isn't easy for me, it isn't
easy for you, but—' he pauses; his eyes flicker nervously around the
room, but never once settle on his son. 'I've come to bring you good
news,' he says, raising his voice and attempting once more to smile.
'All charges are to be dropped.' Now he does look at the prisoner,
watching for a reaction, but his face continues to be masked by apprehension. 'At this very moment the guards are packing up their
things. By lunchtime there won't be a policeman in sight. Now, how
about that? Isn't that good news?'

It is the son's turn to study his father: true, they have never met
before this day, but the prisoner knows too well his visitor, knows
too well the devious mind, the ease with which deals are made and
bargains struck. He mistrusts every word the man utters. 'Why?'
asks the prisoner.

'Why what?'

'Why are the charges to be dropped?'

Lennie passes a hand through the tuft of unruly hair. 'Well, you
know what the Nats are like! They've dropped charges against
whole towns before now! You know what they're like: nothing
must dent the faith.' Another abortive smile, but he quickly senses
that his attempts at flippancy are misplaced; he is too astute not to
realise that only the gravest of tones will match the prisoner's mood
and recent past experience. Nervous, embarrassed, despising the
situation he finds himself in, Lennie seeks to explain the sequence of
events coloured by his own unease. And yet, despite his comfortless
predicament, there is something that happens to him when he
speaks, as though the sound of his own carefully modulated voice is
reassuring, and he launches forth, each word over-enunciated to disguise all that he is and feels. 'Your behaviour,' he begins, 'has caused
a great many people a good deal of trouble.' It is not a reprimand,
but a statement of fact. 'First, let us begin with—with the Coloured
woman whom you slept with, and then wrote a letter to, advertising
your guilt. Didn't you know she was married? Weren't you aware
of the need for discretion? Don't you know that unfaithful wives

478

intend their husbands to find their lovers' letters? Didn't you realise that the letter was tantamount to a confession of guilt? I'm not talking about adultery now, I'm talking about Immorality with a capital I? Good grief, man, to write a depraved letter to some Coloured girl, that's asking for trouble. And quoting Shakespeare sonnets! To a Coloured! Are you mad? Why? That's what I want to know. Why, tell me why, tell me what on earth possessed you to write that letter?'

The prisoner turns away, experiencing a strange and sudden reaction: he is assaulted by a sensation that his tongue is swelling inside his mouth; try as he may to answer his father's question he cannot, physically cannot, and the word 'why, why, *why*?' resounds in his head.

'Very well,' says Lennie, satisfied that he has made his point. 'I will not persist. I think you understand. All I will say is that had you not written in those disgusting terms, then I think your Uncle Jacobus would have had little trouble in hushing up this affair right at the start. He's done it before for members of the Party, and even for their familes and friends, so why not for his own?

'Yes, perhaps none has had more trouble from this affair than your uncle. All politicians have enemies. It is an occupational hazard. There were men, close colleagues, who would have been only too delighted to see him squirm in public. Think, man, your actions could have caused a Government crisis. You must try and understand your uncle's dilemma, if you are to understand your own. Had you come to trial he would have been forced to resign. That's how things are. But, to buy time he detained you here, knowing full well that such a state of affairs could not go on indefinitely. And so the question arose what was to be done with you? How was the matter to be resolved?'

Lennie pauses while he takes out his cigar-case and offers the prisoner one. The prisoner barely notices the gesture; for some minutes past he has been too deeply preoccupied to notice anything. Most of Lennie's words he has heard but not fully comprehended; the unpleasant throbbing in his mouth has increased and his thoughts are burdened with his father's voice asking, 'why, tell me why, tell me what on earth possessed you to write that letter?'

Now the prisoner is aware of his father lighting a cigar, drawing on it pleasurably and then speaking once more. Lennie is rehearsing Uncle Jacobus's conflict, stating this fact: any other form of

479

scandal, financial, political, even charges of bribery or corruption, the Minister could have withstood and weathered, but not the one the prisoner represented, not Immorality with a capital I. And Lennie states his own position with disarming frankness, as though taking pride in being so honest with his son: 'I sympathise with your uncle because I find myself in an exactly similar situation. I too cannot afford scandal. No lawyer can. I am not only talking about the crime you've committed, I'm also talking about your very existence. If you came to court, and your—your parentage was made known—well, I need say no more. When your uncle enlisted my help, I gave it freely, for purely selfish motives of which I am not ashamed.

'And so, a formula had to be worked out concerning the woman who was charged with you, and more particularly with her husband who possessed your stupid letter which we were determined to get hold of. She couldn't be allowed to come to court either and, of course, she could not just be allowed to roam free. That is why your uncle asked for my help. He needed someone he could trust to deal with these delicate matters.'

At last the prisoner finds words: 'What's happened to her?' he asks, his voice catching in his throat.

Lennie waves a reassuring hand. 'There was no real problem with her. I provided both a comfortable and a humane solution. I arranged for a psychiatrist to examine her and he diagnosed a severe nervous breakdown, paranoid schizophrenia to be exact. She is in a hospital. She's being well looked after. And, in time, she will be allowed to leave. No, it was the husband who proved a little more of an obstacle. And that took time. But in the end we came up with a very simple solution: we had him re-classified from Coloured to Bantu and moved him off into the Transkei. That's the best way, all things considered. The main thing was that we got hold of the letter and destroyed it. When that was done your uncle was in a position to drop all the charges.' The last remark is accompanied by the faintest hint of irony which is quickly lost in a cloud of exhaled cigar smoke.

'And me?' asks the prisoner dully. 'Am I to be allowed to walk out of here now? Or am I to be certified insane, or what?'

After some thought, Lennie replies, 'That's up to you.'

'Up to me? I don't understand.'

'There were not many choices open to us,' Lennie says. 'I tell you, if it were possible your uncle would have deported you at the dead of night without a soul knowing. He said as much. But countries cannot rid themselves of their undesirable citizens so easily. No, I tell you frankly his second choice was to have you thrown out of this house, to make it impossible for you to lead a decent normal life. He would have seen to it that you could never teach in school again, hound you, persecute you until you ended up a—a non-person, sinking lower and lower into the mud like a poor white. And he would have done it. Believe me.

'But I pleaded for you because—and I say this with all humility—I am an honest man and I can't deny that you are my son.' Several times he nods to himself as though reaffirming a doubtful fact. Then, snapping out of his confessional mood he says in a bright, optimistic way, 'I have here in my pocket a one-way ticket to London. Both your uncle and I will see to it that you are well taken care of financially.' He unbuttons his top pocket, removes the airline ticket and places it carefully on the desk. 'It is the best I could do under the circumstances. But at least you have a chance of a new life. Take it. Use it. You have seven days to make all your arrangements.'

The prisoner does not respond, but reads over and over again the letters B.O.A.C.

Lennie says as if in answer to an unasked question, 'No, you don't really have a choice. Stay here and you won't be able to exist, let alone live. Go, and at least you can start again. I grant you it would give me pleasure to feel I had done this for you. Yes, I admit it freely, I would feel I was paying off a debt.'

A gloomy silence descends, each man a victim of what the other is unable to say. Then, out of a need to absolve guilt, to banish self-reproach, Lennie says, 'Come on, cheer up, it's a wonderful chance for you. A new life. Think on the good side. London! You can grow your hair long, you can become part of a decadent society! Think, you can march on South Africa House every Sunday! And believe me you'll be well taken care of. Your uncle and I will be very generous. And by the way, this is just between us, you can take a little money out for me . . . I keep a little emergency fund in . . . everyone does it . . . Think of it, London! By the way, have you heard about van der Merwe in London? Wonderful this: some friends meet van der Merwe in London and they see he's wearing a Savile Row suit and driving around in a chauffeur-driven Rolls. So they say, "Hey, van der Merwe, you seem to be doing all right!" And he says, "Yes, I've got a wonderful job. At the Israeli Embassy. All I've got to do is come in twice a day and they pay me a fortune." "What's the job, then?" they ask. "All I've got to do," says van der Merwe, "is open their letters!" Good, hey? Yes . . . I have a son in Israel, Julian he's called . . . named after my late father . . . no, I don't really blame you . . . I had wonderful parents . . . no father was ever prouder of a son than my dad was of me . . . Well, I think I gave him cause . . . I made his last years very comfortable . . . they've a fine Jewish Old Aged Home in Cape Town, you know . . . I don't think I let him down . . . he wanted me to succeed . . .'

A sad, faraway look comes over his eyes and when he next speaks it is to utter his personal creed, for he feels within himself the compulsion to answer his son's silence as if it contains a dreadful, angry accusation. It is an apology; it is a well-rehearsed response; it is the litany of Leonard Levine, the litany of all those whose spirits are infected, of all those who have been swamped by a faith stronger than their own:

'This is our country, and this is how things are here. I do not agree with everything that is done but I live here and I abide by the law. That which I disapprove of, I prefer not to see, but if you cannot do that you must leave: that is the only path open to you and your kind. By living here, you condone.

'We have our lives to lead, ordinary mundane lives, with ordinary mundane wants and desires. We are not evil. We are the most generous people on God's earth. But we must be allowed to sort things out in our own fashion, in our own way.

'Believe me, I would like to see changes made but change can only be effected when two sides surrender the distance that separates them. Not a sacrifice by the one side or the other, but mutual surrender. And what chance is there of that? I tell you frankly, none.

'We would rather remain as we are, the world's leper colony, than endanger our stability and our way of life. You have only to look at what's happened in the rest of the continent: chaos, confusion, dictatorships, public executions, murder, rape, totalitarian governments, genocide. You know what I say? I say let the American Negroes emigrate and sort that lot out. Let them have their black African homelands and good luck to them. They will destroy each other before they have time to destroy us.

'My boy, there is not a sensible man in this country who does not want things to be different. But how, how? I used to think that it was possible to make changes, but I found out a long time ago that I'm not the stuff martyrs are made of. And one has to ask oneself, who is?' He comes close to the prisoner, wants in some way to embrace him but his hands continue to hang limply at his sides. 'Take my advice: go to London. You don't fit here. You are neither a Christian nor a Jew, neither Dutch nor English. You know what it's like to be someone apart. The vitality of our society depends on adherence to one group or another. Even the Bantu hate the Indians, and the Indians hate the Coloureds, and the Coloureds hate the Bantu. We live in separate pockets and you belong in none. That's not your fault. You did not ask to be born that way. So go, go to London. You'll have a comfortable life. Don't misunderstand me, comfort isn't bought cheaply, comfort of the body or comfort of the mind, it doesn't come cheap. But if I can give you some advice, it's this: don't despise comfort. It isn't a wicked thing in itself. I used to think that material things came second, but I tell you of my own experience that a full spiritual life is easier on a full stomach. One does not have to be a puritan to be pure. I don't say it's an admirable creed, but it's not wicked.'

The silence returns, and Lennie looks older now, as though still troubled by all that must remain unsaid. And unaccountably the prisoner feels a terrible, loathsome sympathy for this man who has allowed his aspirations to be swamped by his ambitions, who has detected a source of power and reached his hands out towards it. And Lennie, aware of his son's helpless affection, is suddenly savaged by hatred: hatred of his son, of himself, of all he has settled for, and hatred of what he has been forced to confess. 'You bloody fool!' he cries out. 'Why did you have to go and write that letter? How could you put down in black and white the words I love you? Look at the mess it's got us all into!'

The outburst is unexpected and violent, but does not draw a response from the prisoner, and hearing the older man speak the words causes the prisoner to withdraw deeper into himself. Any answer or explanation he may have is trapped within him.

'I apologise,' Lennie says, collecting himself. 'I didn't mean to shout like that,' and adds more quietly still, 'I don't have the right to ask of you favours, but for my sake, for my peace of mind use that ticket. God knows what'll happen to you if you don't.'

And without another word he is gone.

There are no guards any more; all signs of physical restraint have vanished; the prisoner has been informed officially that he is free. But for two days following his father's visit he does not even dare test the information for fear he has been tricked. And yet on his desk lies the airline ticket, valid five days hence and that, at least, appears to be genuine. But the offer of escape has no meaning to the prisoner, for he is aware that there is still something in him that is unresolved and that he has not yet faced, the answer to his father's question why? He cannot suppress a feeling of nausea.

On the third morning he wakes with a temperature: his tongue hurts, and his throat is dry and red. He discovers it is a comfort to believe that he is ill. The virus, or whatever it is, attacks him mercilessly: every bone aches and he is at times delirious, at others, painfully lucid. When he is not sleeping visions and recollections play havoc. At first, his mother dominates his thoughts. Anna, defiant and proud, coaxing him to manhood. But one memory in particular: on the sands at Muizenberg. 'Mummy, why is this called Christian Beach?' and her answer, baffling to the boy, 'Because your father doesn't come here.'

And Oupa Dawid, ever distant and disapproving, terrifying to a small boy. Jan Christian Smuts smelling of pine needles, visiting not Dawid but Granny Victoria ... 'Mummy, what's a donation?' and being photographed on the great man's knee ... and Uncle Jacobus taking him to rugby to watch the Universities of Stellenbosch and Cape Town fight it out, the Maties versus the Ikeys ... and Oupa Dawid shouting ... and Victoria retrieving the charred document from the glowing coals ... and Dawid unable to embrace his grandson even on his deathbed. A childhood without affection; adolescence and adulthood, too. An uneventful, lonely, unfeeling life.

Into his confused and fevered thoughts comes the face of the Coloured girl and secretly he knows a battle has begun. He twists and turns as though struggling to dismiss her from his mind, but she persists. He sees her naked, and remembers her unwillingness and his own insistence. His whole body is plagued by her, and even in sickness he feels a tension, remembers the excitement of unleashing upon her all the realisation of his fantasies, perversely making of her an object, yes, an animal, not a human being. And the hatred for him in her eyes; what else could she do, but hate? Both were being faithful to their inheritance.

He is shivering now, fighting for warmth, but he is approaching the crisis and knows it. The letter he remembers beginning 'Thou,' and the words, 'I love you.' He cries out. 'They were right, they were right!' Right to call it depraved. For the depravity lay not in the words but in the intention, in the lie it contained: his gaudy expressions of love, all lies, misused, meant only to entice her back so that he could once more command her. Believe they are animals and all else that follows is clothed in logic: herd them, abuse them, harry them, make of them beasts of burden, instruments of will.

Some time on the fourth day Oom Erik appears and sweetly nurses him, soaking a cloth in vinegar to lay across the prisoner's brow. A doctor is called and pills administered. Oom Erik says, 'Don't worry, you'll be well enough to travel. These things go away as quickly as they come.' And soon he is proved right: in the early hours of the morning the fever breaks. Shortly before dawn, ice-cold, the prisoner rises and goes into the library. He takes up pen and paper, and writes this letter to his father:

I want to inform you of a decision I have made. It is important to me that you know, though I do not fully understand why. When you were here, there were a thousand things, and one in particular, I should have said to you, but I had been too long alone, too long absent from daily human conflicts to find either the will or the courage.

I will not be using the ticket. I intend to stay and take my chances. I cannot accept the offer to escape. I have need to atone. Perhaps as a Jew you will understand that. I appreciate many of the things you said. I know that most of us here live out our lives unaware of the plight of others. In that I don't believe we are any more or any less inhuman than our fellow men. But there comes a time to cry halt, and my time has come.

You asked me why I wrote that letter and I could not answer. I should have told you the truth which was that I didn't mean a word of it; the letter had another intention which was neither loving nor compassionate. I too, you see, am subject to the faith made law, a product of precedent. I know how powerful that faith is, how in times past it has possessed the power to turn love into bestiality, caused men to devour human flesh and blood while others rejoiced. You have known it too in a court-room where a murderer was freed.

I, like you, am not the stuff martyrs are made of. And I do not for a moment believe that by remaining here I will make one jot of difference to anything, nor do I believe I will affect any other human being. But then perhaps martyrdom is always pointless, and comfort, as you told me, is not bought cheap. But I choose to remain for my own sake, an act, as I have said, of atonement. To alter the collective will, to bring about change, needs a faith stronger than Christ's. I will work for my own conversion.

Having made his decision and having written the letter, comes a certain relief that his ordeal is in part over, or in part begun. But Mpobe is ensnared, and knows it; nothing can free him. He knows it, looking out at the pearl-grey mountains, and at the trees, and at the vineyards, and at the rich brown earth now warmed by the fast-rising sun, he knows wherever he looks he will see the terrible obscene beauty of his prison.